SQUARE DANCE

SQUARE DANCE

Alan Hines

1817

HARPER & ROW, PUBLISHERS, New York

Cambridge, Philadelphia, San Francisco, London

Mexico City, São Paulo, Sydney

I would like to express my gratitude to
Leslie Palmer for her inestimable attention
to these people and places.

Grateful acknowledgment is made for permission to reprint:

"A New Life Begins for Janet Leigh." © 1956 Time Inc. Courtesy *Life* magazine.

"Blue Moon." Music by Richard Rodgers. Lyric by Lorenz Hart. © 1934 Metro-Goldwyn-Mayer Inc. © Renewed 1962 Metro-Goldwyn-Mayer Inc. Rights throughout the world controlled by Robbins Music, A Catalogue of CBS Songs, A Division of CBS Inc. All rights reserved. International copyright secured. Used by permission.

FIRST EDITION

Designer: Lydia Link

Library of Congress Cataloging in Publication Data

Hines, Alan.
    Square dance.

    I. Title.
PS3558.I526S66   1984   813'.54   83-48814
ISBN 0-06-015297-4

84 85 86 87 88 10 9 8 7 6 5 4 3 2 1

For
Clyde Lincoln Hines

TWILIGHT

🐓 *Fish bite best at dusk.*

Both headlights had been smashed out of the Chevrolet years before when Dillard had tried to park it himself one night in the car shed. Every afternoon he and Gemma drove back from the lake while there was still enough light to maneuver over the back roads. But this evening was different. "When they're biting like this," he said excitedly, swinging his line out over the water, "I can't leave 'em."

Dillard sometimes told himself, and Gemma too when she would listen, that the barge was the only place left where he felt at home, the last place he could find peace. Anchored in the middle of Twilight Lake, it was his territory. He'd built it himself out of steel drums, lumber, sheets of tin, and spit. He didn't need any of them there. Not Cora. Not Juanelle. And not Gemma, his granddaughter, squatting down at the other end of the barge now, riling his blood pressure. The girl didn't speak, but he could feel her trying to railroad him. She never let up.

Sitting back on her heels, Gemma watched the old man slump over the bamboo pole as he waited for something to happen, as he waited for another fish to gobble on the hook disguised with a grasshopper. She pressed her lips together and tried again: "Pop?"

He could be ornery; he could be cantankerous no matter how hard she tried. He was just like that. Had been forever maybe, cursing the chickens when they didn't lay, kicking doors

3

that stuck, throwing grimy pans in the trash when they were too hard to scrub clean, and not talking to her for days at a time. Living with him could be a trial and she didn't mind telling him so. "Well, you shouldn't try," he'd say. "You shouldn't even try."

She pushed up her glasses with the back of her hand. He didn't move. The muscles in his curved back tensed at the sound of her voice, but he wouldn't lift his head from the semi-praying position he fished in. Gemma shook the bucket of bass beside her. It held just enough water so that one of the fish could turn itself over sometimes. One eye stared up at her; it dared her to blink.

"Pop, we have to be going."

"Hush. You're making too much noise."

She clicked her tongue and slammed her fist against the slick tin deck, hearing it reverberate underneath like a drum. Dillard spun around, his eyes wide. He held the bamboo pole high in one hand as though he might strike her.

"I said to hush; you're scaring my fish."

Evening light began to turn the lake to a deep shade of green, then gray. The surface settled with a stillness, seeming solid enough for them to step out on from the barge and then back again without getting wet. Only a few other fishermen sat along the banks in the distance. But they soon left, or blended with the low line of trees separating sky and water, so that they might as well have been gone. Sometimes a breeze would pick up momentum and the barge would gently rock. Water lapping against the steel drums harmonized with crickets along the shore and the sound of occasional low-flying ducks. The night-time silence became clamorous. And later Gemma would recall this swell of quiet as she sat in the window, looking out upon the highway at the dusty shapes of cars distorted by blinking neon along the strip.

Dillard stared into the murky water, his straw hat still low over his eyes as though the sun continued to blaze across the landscape. They were down there, swimming around his baited

4

hook. At one time, his eyes had almost been sharp enough to see them glide to their doom.

"They said they'd take me this evening." The Hadleys were probably standing in the road by their car at that moment, wondering what had happened to her.

"Aint gonna hurt you to miss once. Once won't send you to hell."

She scooted her Bible across the deck. He almost expected her to curse. Though it probably scared the fish away, it tickled him to see her so mad.

"Just watch yourself, young lady. We aint leaving till I'm good and ready."

During the day, with the sun at a certain angle, he couldn't see her eyes behind those thick horn-rimmed glasses. She spooked him. Her straight dirty-blond hair was chopped off around the ears. She was at that awkward age, eleven, but she knew how to compensate for it with stern, thin-lipped expressions. Just like her mother. Sometimes Dillard was caught off guard when he looked back at her. He'd think it was Juanelle. Come home to pester him. He'd think: she's happening to me all over again.

The bobber floated on the smooth surface. He remembered how he'd held that child, that frowning baby, wondering just what he was supposed to do with it while his daughter got herself settled somewhere and found a job. He shook his head, muttering aloud: "Don't tell me that takes eleven years."

Suddenly he gasped as the line became taut and the bobber went down. Coming halfway out of his chair, he said: "I got another." Gemma sat behind him, her elbows planted against her thighs, her chin in her hands. "Gemma!" He cackled aloud, ripping the wiggling fish from the calm surface, pulling it high in the air and to the deck, where it flip-flopped wet markings on the tin like brush strokes. He rose in painful slow motion, his eyes fixed on the fish skidding sideways over the deck. "Girl!"

"I aint helping." She turned from him, peering down at the

bass in the bucket. An eye was trained on her; a mouth opened and closed. "Do it yourself."

"What I'd like to know is who the heck named you. You aint no jewel. You're a stone. Around my neck." He stooped over the fish, a hand at the small of his back. "I'm finding them Monroes one of these days."

"Well, I wish you would."

Her daddy's people must be out there somewhere, sad, grieving for their boy who had died for his country. If only they knew she existed, surely they'd want to take her in. Often when she looked at the old photo albums and saw those pictures of the tall, slim woman who was her mother, she wished there were photographs of him too. She studied photographs of soldiers in old *Life* magazines and wondered: do I look like him at all?

"They probably think I forgot," she said, rolling to her feet all at once. She went to the back of the barge and stood over the motor.

"What do you think you're doing?"

She wrapped the cord in her hand and pulled it hard, starting the motor on the first try. She tugged hand-over-hand on the rope until the bucket of cement they used as an anchor was on deck. The barge rose and fell as their eyes locked.

"It's almost dark, in case you haven't noticed," she said.

Dillard bent over the fish again and worked the hook from its mouth, snorting gleefully when he found part of the grasshopper. "Come put another grasshopper on this hook," he said, tossing the catch in the bucket, wiping his hands on his overalls.

"Just how are you expecting to get home?"

A strong wind came from the north across the water and the barge swayed and began to drift. He turned to look at her, steadying himself in his chair. Her mouth set, she watched him smugly because she knew she was about to get her way. He'd forgotten about the smashed-out headlights. The trees along the shore were blurred, and he wondered: is it really that late, or is it my eyes? He dropped the pole on the deck, glancing back at the bucket, and said: "You win."

As she steered the barge toward the rickety wooden pier, he sat flat on the deck, the bucket of fish between his legs. She cut the motor a few moments before they reached it, then jumped to the pier to tie the ropes. He wouldn't move.

"I'm leaving you if you don't get to the car right now," she said. At once she began to climb the overgrown bank. The Chevrolet, parked under the trees, was almost completely camouflaged by darkness. "Pop! I'm not just wolfin'."

"You did one sloppy job tying this rope," she heard from the darkness. A wind hit her head-on at the top of the bank. She hugged the Bible to her chest. Her teeth chattered for an instant, even though it was already June. "Can't 'spect the barge to be there tomorrow when you tie it off like that," he said, coming up the bank. The half-moon barely lit him, barely outlined his straw hat, his long-legged frame. The wind made weeping sounds through the treetops. Branches danced above them, and just as they got to the car, lightning flashed across the lake.

"See," she said, staring at him through thick lenses. "I think it's a tornado coming too."

"It aint no tornado." He followed just behind her, breathing heavily, his tackle in one hand and the bucket of fish in the other.

"Well, we'd a been struck by lightning if we'd stayed out there."

He mumbled as he slid his gear across the backseat. Gemma sat in front, waiting with both hands on the steering wheel. Thunder rumbled above the lake. She leaned forward to gaze upward through the windshield. Just then, the sky lit up again. And she could see him there, plain as day, stooped over as he moved around to the other side of the car.

"Those clouds are too far off," he said, sliding the bucket in next to her. He took a flashlight from underneath the seat.

"What are you doing with that?" she asked. The darkness

smelled like rain now. Sometimes the sky exploded with a light so vivid that she was able to see the water, the barge tied to the deck, and tall swaying grass on the banks.

"You gotta see to drive, don't you?" he said, turning the flashlight to his face and switching it on, off, then on again just as the lake lit up around them.

"That flashlight's no good for driving," she said, her hands still fixed on the steering wheel.

"Just wait and see." He'd sat her on an overturned wash-pan in the front seat of the car when she was seven and showed her how to drive. Somebody had to take him to the lake. Even then his sight was not much good past the windshield. Driving was Gemma's chore now, little enough considering he fed and clothed her 365 days a year.

"What is sown as an animal body, it is raised as a spiritual body," she said.

"What?" He stood outside, bending to look in at her.

Gemma stared into the bucket at the struggling fish. "We shall not all die, but we shall all be changed in a flash, in the twinkling of an eye, at the last trumpet call."

"Shut that business up," he said, standing upright, stomping once and holding his hat in place. "This aint the time for it."

"For the trumpet will sound, and the dead will rise immortal, and we shall be changed."

Thunder on the other side of the lake seemed to vibrate the ground underneath the Chevrolet. Dillard grasped the door. Here she was, railroading. He wasn't going to have it. Not now. Not when time was so precious.

She said: "What is sown in this earth as a perishable thing is raised up imperishable."

"Good God." She was the only one he knew, this Bible-toting grandchild of his, who could recite so many scriptures by heart. "I'm telling you for the last time, stop with that talk 'cause it don't impress me none."

"You fathers must not goad your children to resentment

but give 'em instruction, and the correction which belong to a Christian upbringing."

"I'll yank you outta there."

"That's in the letter to the Europeans, number six."

"Stop it; stop it. You don't got any idea what the hell you're talking about. Listen, I lived too long. I know all that stuff aint nothing but horsemanure."

She stared across at him soberly, one hand in the bucket. Wind swept around them and they could hear the barge creak as it batted against the dock.

"You aint nothing but a kid; you aint got all the answers."

"Get in so we can get going."

They stared at each other until he had to look away or else pull her out of there. He straightened himself once again. He'd sit on the hood, he told her, holding the flashlight. She would have to drive slowly. He straddled one fender and locked his feet underneath the grill, thinking: she knows it all, thinks she can tag a Bible verse onto everything and make it explainable. He had a feeling those Monroes lived in Dallas; at least that would be a good place to start looking. He'd heard Juanelle mention that name when she spoke of the baby's father. But could she or anybody be certain just who the rascal was? He'd look them up anyway; let them try to do something with the child.

Sitting on the fender, he blocked her view from the right side. He held the flashlight out before him and trained the dull beam of light on the dusty road. She started the car and it began to creep slowly along, caught sometimes by a sudden flash of light from the north and a crackle of sound nearby. Whenever the car hit an uneven place in the road, the flashlight jerked, and the old man would glare back at her over his shoulder like a crow.

"Just take it slow, aint in no rush. I want to get home in one piece."

She shook her head and pressed her lips together, straining

to see the road ahead. The fish made flapping noises at her side, and water splashed on her arm. "If I ram into a tree, it's your fault," she called into the windshield. "You know we shouldn't be out so late."

"Just keep your mind on your business, young lady," he called, instantly visible as though it were daylight. And then as quickly, all she could see was the weak spill from his flashlight.

They moved slowly over the dirt roads which led to Dillard's place. The Chevrolet, a 1940 model and the same age as Gemma, only left the road once, when she veered too far after a turn. Dillard was almost swept off the hood by a low-hanging branch. He leaned forward in time, then swiveled around and aimed the light through the windshield directly at her. She glared back into the light without blinking. Then he understood at once what she was doing, that she had turned off their regular back route. They were moving faster.

"What do you think you're doing?" he called, careful to grip the bumper with his feet and hold tightly to the flashlight. It was the only one they owned.

Faster. "Gemma Louise!" He bounced on the fender as though he were riding a bronc. His hat was lifted from his head before he could grab for it, and he saw it tumble into the darkness, then reappear in a flash of light.

And Gemma, gripping the wheel with both hands, lowered her head determinedly as she turned onto the highway. The paved road was smooth and she was able to accelerate. Ahead she could see the lights from Twilight, from the shabby dwellings on the fringe of town, and from farmhouses along the highway. The red light on top of the cotton gin flickered on and off, and she could see that Dillard had turned away from it, flattening himself on the hood. She stretched to look over his head at the road, at the broken white line running down the center of the flat, straight course which ran through the middle of the town, which was in fact the main street for four blocks before it became highway again, leading to Commerce, Fredonia, Jefferson, and other farm towns.

"Stop this car!" The old man screeched through the windshield, his face against the glass. She glanced at him once. His long, bony fingers gripped the windshield wipers. His face was weather-beaten, splotched. Straight white hair was plastered down on his forehead by the wind; he had bangs just like hers. "Stop right now, Gemma Louise!" She pretended not to hear while he screamed, pretended not to see him. Porch lights came on. She saw heads appear at screen doors. And nearer the outskirts of Twilight, Gemma glanced out her window at the town dump. Gigantic mounds of trash leapt upward from shadows as lightning illuminated them. The sight made her lose her breath. She faced forward again, thinking: it's like something come alive.

The main street was desolate. Stores were closed. In some, single bulbs gave off a ghostly light. As she turned off the street, she saw the Coca-Cola sign burning in Ferris Hardware. And then the church was in sight, just over the top of the old man's head, which he'd pressed face down into the hood. She could see all the way to the top of the steeple in one brief flash. The stained-glass window had lights dancing behind it. The street was lined with cars. In front, the Hadleys had parked their Studebaker. They'd probably waited for her; they'd probably been late themselves. Finally she turned in between two cars, stopping at the end of the long sidewalk that led to the front door. She sat back for an instant. They were singing inside.

Dillard's legs were tangled together; they felt like mush. He smacked his lips, lifted his head, and tried to swallow. He managed to roll from the hood as she opened her door and began to march up the sidewalk toward the white wooden-frame building. His fingers still gripped the flashlight, and he tossed it through the window before starting after her.

"Gemma Louise!"

Thunder shook the flat countryside. She took long strides, her Bible in one hand. He called her again, but she didn't turn. Cora had come to this church. Come every Sunday till she took off thirty years ago for Baton Rouge to visit her sister and never came back. And Dillard had come himself in those early days when they were first married, and when Juanelle was a baby.

"I'm tanning your hide."

"You'll have to wait till I'm done," she said, reaching the door, still not turning.

He bobbed down the sidewalk, his legs wobbly. She shook him free the first time he grabbed her. But when she opened the door, he had grabbed her arm with both hands, and she pulled him inside.

Yes, he thought, seeing the white pews, the white walls, the faces turning to see what was going on. This old place smells the same. Like disinfectant. They stood row after row, hymnals in hand, looking back at him and Gemma scuffling at the door. And some young man dressed in a preacher's robe stood up front with the choir. They sang "The Old Rugged Cross," yes, he even knew the name of that one. He glanced toward the back pew where he had sat ages ago with Cora, and later with her and Juanelle.

Gemma saw Bob and Doreen Hadley, their neighbors, and tried to wave. But Dillard had a grip on both her arms, trying to pull her back outside. The sky lit up once more, crackled, and then a heavy downpour pelted against the earth. The huge drops seemed to explode on impact.

Even though every voice was joined in the hymn, Dillard could barely hear them now because of the rain. He felt himself begin to tire, to breathe unsteadily. He was not aware at first that only one voice sang now, one angelic voice in the center of the white-robed choir. But something made him stop and squint up the center aisle, some memory that rushed over him. And there was Beecham, the old colored man who roamed the hills of garbage in the dump. "Well, that beats all," Dillard said aloud, staring at Beecham, at the oil-stained hat he still wore on his head and the neatly starched white robe. "If that don't beat all."

Beecham gazed down the center aisle along with the rest of the congregation, gazed loftily down at the old man in grass-stained overalls and muddy boots. Outside, the rain pelted down on cars, bouncing like hail. Beecham continued singing, and the others joined him on the refrain. His clear baritone soared over their heads, over the all-white congregation.

"I reckon this is what it's come to," Dillard said, his eyes still fixed on Beecham. "Niggers singing in church." She wiggled free from his grasp with a final tug that sent her glasses to the floor.

"He's one of God's children," she said, embarrassed because they were all looking. She stared up the aisle. Though everything was blurred without her glasses, she could see Beecham, her friend, standing in the center of the choir, his hymnal before him though he knew the words by heart. The bright lights made everything shimmer. She knew that the fuzzy figures must look the same to her grandfather.

"Aint he got his own church?" Dillard still gasped for breath. His exact age, Beecham was, close to eighty. They'd played together in dusty Twilight streets when they were boys. They'd hoed cotton, hunted, and fished. And then they were grown, men, separated by something that had been expected of them in maturity. Neither had questioned the end to that part of their lives. That was just how it was. Beecham lived in the shanties near the dump. He'd worked at the grocery, at the blacksmith's—taken odd jobs wherever he could find them. He'd worked at the hardware store until he was too old to hold down a job. Then he began to roam the hills of trash in the dump, looking for valuables, looking for anything he might make use of in his shack. Everyone said he had the voice of an angel, and they invited him to sing with the choir every Sunday and Wednesday night. Dillard shook his head, wondering: how can they allow this old nigger in their church?

"Do I gotta carry you outta here?"

"Let's sit," she whispered, looking down for her glasses.

But Dillard could hardly believe his eyes. Yes, he recalled, his mama had stood at the back screen door, hovering over him and the black boy while they ate oatmeal cookies. They squatted

13

in the dirt, drawing pictures. And his mama had said: "Give him another one, Homer. Share."

A blurred presence floated down the aisle toward them, and Gemma said: "Brother Tanner." It was not a question, not a plea for help, but just an acknowledgment, as though he were walking past their farm on a hot Sunday afternoon. By some supernatural force, she pulled the old man up the aisle to meet the preacher. Dillard's eyes became wild, like a spooked horse's, though he was unable to struggle. They passed people he saw in Twilight every week when he came in to deliver eggs and pick up groceries. Most of them he was able to place; he knew their parents. Hardly anyone he'd known before was left—nobody except that old man. Most of Twilight had been dead and buried for years as far as he was concerned.

"Gemma, hon, you need some help?" the preacher was asking, eyeing Dillard, putting a hand on the girl's head. Gemma closed her eyes in ecstasy as Dillard watched her in a kind of stupor. The choir began another verse of "The Old Rugged Cross." It covered the commotion in back. "I see you brought along your granddaddy."

The preacher put one hand on Dillard's shoulder, as if to direct him farther up the aisle. "There's a couple of seats in the front here," he said, meeting Dillard's eye.

Doreen Hadley seemed to glide toward them, her arms opened, a hymnal to her full bosom. She smelled like gardenias to Dillard. He stuck his hands into his back pockets, and looked down at his boots. His overalls felt clammy with sweat. Up front, that old coot was singing directly at him. And when he looked to the back pews, a chill went up his spine, as though he expected her to be sitting there, Cora, waiting for him. "Homer, come sit with us," Doreen Hadley said, indicating with her chin where they were. But Beecham looked down at him, at the way he was dressed. Dillard closed his eyes. His throat tightened and he felt those hands on his arms. And he could hear Cora's voice, sweet, young, singing the hymn into his ear. *On a hill far away . . . Stood an old rugged cross . . . The emblem of suffering and shame* . . . When he opened his eyes, he knew they were going to be able to see it in his look. All around, they watched him.

Gemma stepped forward, seeing the muscles in his face quiver. She said: "Pop, come on." She clutched the Bible to her chest, imitating Doreen's posture. She tried to smile.

He stared at her self-consciously, shaking his head. He was afraid to say anything. The sound of his voice would leave him powerless. The earth rumbled outside. He pulled away.

"I'm waiting in the car," he muttered, his voice cracking like a boy's. He turned from them, hearing the singing continue as he opened the door and slipped out. Even as he shut himself in the car, and rolled up the windows, he could still hear the voices. He lay back with one hand covering his eyes. The rain beat on the roof, just as it did on the tin roof at the house. He could hear them begin another hymn, somebody banging loudly on a piano. None of them knew him; nobody was left who knew him.

Now he breathed slower, thinking about how they'd stared at him as though he were Satan himself, trying to lead the girl astray. But they didn't know; they didn't know. Soon Beecham slipped out of the church and disappeared in the downpour, still wearing the white choir robe and oil-stained hat. Dillard waited more than an hour, thinking: they're all snooty. I'm lucky to be living where I do because they're all too damn snooty.

He woke himself snoring sometime later. The rain had stopped. They were coming from the church, chattering, looking up at the clear evening sky. They filed past the Chevrolet, some peering inside as though he were already lying in his coffin. He stared ahead, determined not to give any of them satisfaction by acknowledging them. Finally Gemma came out, flanked on either side by the Hadleys.

"Reckon they're gonna protect her," he muttered.

Gemma and Doreen stood on the sidewalk while Bob came to the car, opened his door, and told Dillard that he'd drive them home. They could pick up the Chevrolet tomorrow. Dillard stepped out, feeling a stiffness in his limbs. He got into the back seat of the Studebaker, the bucket of fish resting at his feet. He picked it up after a moment and held it in his lap. The fish were dead now; blank wide eyes stared at him glassily. He closed both his eyes and leaned his head against the door, tired, worn out, allowing himself to feel almost grateful that somebody was taking him home. He hugged the bucket to his middle, staring ahead at the three of them in front, staring at Gemma in the middle, thinking: people always take the side of a kid.

🐓 *Recipes are tried and proved.*

Gemma stood at the window in the kitchen and looked over the same fields and huge weathered barn that her mother and grandmother had looked at too. Four generations of women had stood where she did now, shucking corn, making bread, plucking chickens, canning vegetables, all the time looking out over the flat, black land that surrounded Dillard's house. The barn was locked now, filled with Bob Hadley's tractor and hay baler and harvesting machine. He leased most of Dillard's land for pasture and cotton. All that was left to Gemma and her grandfather was the henhouse—a long, low building to the left of the barn, and halfway between the barn and the house. It was hidden from the kitchen by pecan trees and a crape myrtle.

She cooked by the book. Those recipes she found in the cookbook bound together by women from the church had been handed down over generations. Shared secrets. She opened the book on the counter, and leaning over it, read: *½ cup sugar, 1 cup butter, 1 beaten egg.* She had never made this one, but he liked applesauce, could eat a can of it at one sitting. *½ cup dates, cut fine, 1 cup chopped seedless raisins.* He loved sweets, would put Karo syrup on everything if she let him. Gemma rested both elbows on the counter, then straightened up to look out the window at two blackbirds on the butane tank. They took several hops in single file, then flew away, circling to the tops of the pecan trees. *1½ cups flour.*

She lined each ingredient in order along the counter, then stooped to take a huge mixing bowl and the flour sifter from the shelves underneath. *1 teaspoon soda, 1 cup applesauce, ¼ teaspoon salt.* She could make a pound cake, angel food cake, and chocolate cake. She could make apple pie, and lemon pie with firm meringue. And she could make a banana pudding with vanilla wafers he said was better than his mama's. *2 teaspoons cinnamon, and ½ teaspoon each nutmeg and allspice.*

Carefully reading each ingredient once more, she touched every box or can or package with one finger, checking them off. Then she took the cookbook, walked around the kitchen table to the other side of the room, where her rocker was, and wedged herself into the seat. Her knees were higher than the seat now. Even though she was too big for it, she still liked to rock. She rested the book on her lap, and read: *Cream the butter and sugar. Add eggs, dates, and raisins. Mix the dry ingredients together and add to creamed mixture. Then work in applesauce. Bake in slow oven 325° about one hour.*

About one hour. She turned the rocker around so that she could light the oven, humming "The Yellow Rose of Texas." He was off somewhere. Finding an applesauce cake cooling for their dinner would be a big surprise when he came in. She rocked a few times, letting the oven preheat, holding the burned-out match between her fingers. The kitchen made her happy. It was sunny and warm. She knew he liked it because chickens covered the wallpaper, and he could sit at the table and tell her what he'd named each one of them when he was a boy. But for her it was something else, something she couldn't put into words.

When she got up, she brought the rocker halfway with her. That made her laugh out loud. Max trotted into the kitchen then, and rubbed against her legs while she mashed the butter in the mixing bowl, and added the sugar. Max was the only cat they'd ever had who liked to stay in the house. He hardly ever went outdoors, except when she or Dillard forced him to. He could watch her for hours, or disappear to some hiding place for a nap. "You helping, boy?"

Somewhere off behind the pecan trees, she could hear a hammering sound. The hens squawked as though they were being bludgeoned to death, and she could hear Dillard talking to them, mimicking them as they cried out. She remembered that he was repairing chicken wire along one of the coops, that's where he was that morning. She sang louder, mixing the ingredients together, turning the bowl with the palm of her hand.

Max purred and jumped to the top of the counter.

"You know better than that. This aint nothing for you."

She swatted him away, and he marched through the house with his tail pointing to the ceiling.

She stirred in the applesauce, then added eggs, dates, and raisins. The oven seemed hot enough. She poured the mixture into a greased pan, looked at the clock, then stuck the pan in. Sitting in her rocker once more, she sang la di da when she didn't remember the words, and flipped through her cookbook. It was something that made her feel they were with her, those women who had stood at the window, and those who'd contributed to the cookbook. Then she saw: *Mix the dry ingredients together and add to creamed mixture. Then work in applesauce.* Then work in applesauce.

Heat fogged her glasses and she pulled the pan from the oven even though it burned her hand. She looked down at the mixture. Max sat in the doorway. "This aint fit for nobody now," she said, spooning it into the trash, preparing to start again from scratch. "I'll get it right this time."

Hammering echoed like gunshots. Chickens screeched.

🐓 Resin-coated nails make tight, hard joints

Two roosters were one too many, but with fourteen hens, Dillard took no chances. He had customers who expected eggs at their door every Friday. He would have killed and eaten that feisty old rooster a long time ago, though the bird was probably all gristle and bone. He spit and jumped on Dillard sometimes when he came into the chicken yard, and he had to be chased around now and then when he got too mean. Some of those hens took a beating. So Dillard had gotten another one, younger, with vibrant-colored feathers across his chest, to keep him in check. They circled one another, marking off territory, and fanning out the feathers around their neck when the other stepped out of bounds. Dillard got a kick out of watching them strut, peck the ground, and keep their harems in line. Each morning they tried to outcrow the other. Competition never hurt anybody.

Cane backs and bottoms made the best rockers as far as he was concerned. He'd turned the old chair upside down behind the henhouse and supported it with an old stump he used as a chopping block. He kept his tools in the shed back there, the old henhouse. Saws and hammers hung from nails just inside the shed. Without looking, he could put his hand on any tool he needed. Dillard ran his hand along the runners he'd sawed, whittled, and sanded himself. After a while cane rockers start to fit a body. His had.

He could see them clucking and pecking in the chicken yard, foraging over the ground they'd razed free of vegetation. Those roosters circled their territory, squawking every time one of the hens ventured too far. "That's right, Handsome. Tell 'em."

They'd never had a proper henhouse before Dillard built the long, low building with a corrugated tin roof. There had just been the yard, fenced in, and the shed for night, the one he used now for tools. He'd built the henhouse years before, when he was young, about forty, and still single. And he had nailed up railings along each straw-filled shelf. He'd put in horizontal posts like stair steps along one wall for roosts. He'd cut a small opening at the bottom of the door so they could come and go whenever they wanted.

Every Friday, he'd carted eggs into Twilight in the buggy, selling them to families who didn't have their own chickens. As Dillard spread his feed every morning and checked the water in the trough, he'd stood over them and told them about the young girl he'd met in Twilight, Cora Dawson. She was visiting her mother's relatives. They would cluck over the feed, making gravelly sounds in their throats as it went down. Pretty red hair, he told them, and dimples when she smiled at him through the Mitchells' screen door. "Hidee," he'd said, taking off his hat, standing there with a sack of two dozen eggs. She came out to greet him, dressed fit to kill even though it was eleven o'clock in the morning. He looked down at her, a good twenty years younger than him, and felt light-headed. He would not feel anything similar again until he was close to seventy. He would shuffle around the porch after she took the eggs and paid him, talking about the weather, about how badly his alfalfa needed rain. That made her giggle. He looked down at his overalls and gray workshirt that hadn't been ironed exactly right since his mama breathed her last over the cistern ten years before. And he felt clumsy, like a lout. She rode in his buggy with him, rode around Twilight so all of them sitting on their porches could see that Homer Dillard had that Dawson girl from Crestline with him.

They could see him sitting proudly on the seat, holding the reins with one hand, glancing down sheepishly at the one who would be his wife before harvest. She loved the farm when she saw it, at least that's what she said. He wiped his hands on his trousers and carried her over the threshold just like she asked him to. She clasped her fingers behind his neck, gazing dreamily into his eyes, and she told him how happy she was, how happy she planned to be for the rest of her life.

Now he tended his hens. Some had been with him longer than Gemma, and he would call them by name every morning when he went along the path through the pecan trees to feed them. They clustered around him, scratching the dirt, still content that he was the one who came every morning.

"Aint you a sight, Becky," he said, cackling, standing at the fence with a hammer in his hand. He watched one of the hens crouched low under the new rooster, her wings outspread over the ground.

He put another nail in his mouth and returned to the chair. It was a rocker now; he'd made it for her. He wondered if she missed the chair, taken from its position on the back porch, where it had been for years. He couldn't remember the last time he'd seen anybody sit in it. They each had favorite chairs they liked to sit in, ones they went to automatically. She had one in the middle room, where she slept, and another in the kitchen. And he had his rocker on the front porch, and then the one in the kitchen, the same chair he'd sat in since his daddy died and he'd taken over the farm, working from sunup to sundown. His mama had told him: "You have to be the man now, Homer." And he sat at the kitchen table, naming chickens on the wall-paper, scared at first that what she expected was for him to move out of his room in the back and sleep in hers. He did take her room when her final breath was exhaled down into the cool, deep cistern and they buried her in the Twilight cemetery. Moved in that night, slept there later with Cora, slept there by himself while Juanelle grew up in the same room he'd grown up in. Then Gemma came. He moved back into his old room so the girl could have the larger room in the middle of the house. Maybe growing up in that tiny room hardly big enough for a bed and a dresser had made Juanelle so wild, wanting to run off before she'd even finished school, wanting to bring him all sorts of trouble he cared not to think about.

He positioned the last nail on the bottom of the runner, lining it up with the leg. Resin-coated nails make secure connections because a short time after the resin comes in contact with the wood, it begins to stick. He held the nail in place, feeling his lips stick slightly in the center where the nail had been before. And that evening there would be a new rocker in the corner of the kitchen, a new one where the old one had been since Juanelle was a girl. He'd made them both sit in it and face the wall when they lied, misbehaved, or got rowdy. Little good it had done with his daughter. With three short whacks, he drove the nail in. The chickens began to scream and flap their wings.

"*Bwaak* bwaak bwaak. Y'all aint dying," he called, shuffling to the fence so he could see them. Soon they were calm, forgetting him, pecking through the dirt for insects. The two roosters held court in opposite corners of the yard, stretching their necks to spy on each other. Dillard walked around to the gate and came into the yard. He stood in the middle, his hands resting in the bib of his overalls. "Bwaaaaak bwaaaak!" They made him grin. He took the hammer from the loop in his overalls and nailed down chicken wire along the fence. "Just take it easy there," he said when they fluttered excitedly. "Handsome, settle those girls down."

He fastened the gate and moved around to the shed, where the new rocker stood on its head. He took it off the stump, set it on level ground, and tried it out. It worked. "Bwaaaak!" He rocked back and forth, kicking up dust with his boots. He could see old Ulysses on the other side of the chicken wire, pacing back and forth, making grumbling noises as though he were talking to himself while he foraged. Keeping a steady motion, Dillard watched the old rooster. Through the pecan trees, he could hear the radio in the kitchen, blaring out the *Texas Gospel*

Hour with Brother Dub Mosley. Every morning. She bothered him with that singing and carrying on every morning of his life.

"Nobody to blame for it but me," he said to Ulysses, rocking, letting his feet leave the ground. "I got Doreen Hadley to take her to that church. She's gotta learn to get on with people her own age; that's what I was thinking. I aint gonna be here forever."

And when he'd brought her down the path between the trees to see his henhouse for the first time, Cora Dawson had clasped her hands together. She cooed at the chickens as though they were babies. But she'd never had much to do with them, never felt completely at ease about shoving an old hen aside to gather eggs. He tried to tell her that was just part of living on a farm. She never had before. She never adjusted to any of it, he figured now; that was her trouble.

He might have rocked himself to sleep if it hadn't been for Dub Mosley's voice blaring from the house. Sometimes Dillard wanted to take that radio out to Twilight Lake and dump it overboard from the barge. Getting up slowly, he went to the fence, leaned against a post, and turned soberly to look at his handiwork. "Well, Ulysses," he said, the rooster scratching in the earth just below him, "what you think about it?" Ulysses craned his neck and shook his red comb. The hens wandered nonchalantly around the yard. The rooster started after one, but it ran to the small opening of the henhouse and disappeared. He ambled back to the fence, grumbling, turning his head to peck at his back.

"You don't need 'em," Dillard said, looking down at him. "You don't need any of them."

♘ *Good business sense comes by instinct.*

They would begin before sunup every Friday, feeding the hens and gathering eggs. Sometimes customers along the route would give them empty cartons or folded paper sacks for the next week's delivery, and Gemma would help him divide the eggs and package them for the morning sale. Under her breath she'd count out thirteen eggs. A Dillard Dozen. He was sure this gimmick had kept him in business for as long as it had because "People always buy more if they think they're getting something for nothing." An egg by itself—even a farm-fresh egg— was not worth so much. It rose in value when it was part of a half dozen or dozen. And by adding an extra to make it thirteen, he made every egg that much more valuable. A third of his customers stayed with him, he figured, for that extra egg. After all, he was just as expensive as Woody's.

"Sounds mighty unlucky to me," Gemma said, counting to herself. "Everybody knows thirteen means bad luck."

"Not when it comes to getting something for free. It's the smartest idea I ever come up with." He reached into the bucket that they used to gather eggs, pulled one out, then stared at it a moment. "Now let's hurry. I want to get over to the barge this evening."

She folded the top of a sack and wrote *Hanson* across it in black ink. A Dillard dozen. Wasn't any kind of idea she'd ever use. Squeezing that extra egg into a carton was no easy task.

Usually they made the trip just after sunrise so Gemma would have time to get him home and then catch a ride back into town again before school started. But on this Friday, the first egg run of the summer, she drove him into Twilight about mid-morning. They loaded the backseat with cardboard boxes containing the orders, and she set the spiral notebook at her side.

Their first stop was next to the gas station, just across from the cotton gin. She waited while he carried sacks to three houses. On one of the porches, Katie Lawson, her fifth-grade teacher, stood with a gardening tool in her hand. She waved to Gemma and yelled: "Aint it gettin' real hot for so early in the summer!" Dillard left a sack at each house, nodded to Katie Lawson, and came back to the car with money in his fist. Gemma marked it in her notebook and put the coins in a cigar box on the floor.

"Records is important," she said, tapping the page of the notebook with her pencil. "That way you know how you're doing."

"I know how I'm doing; I'm doing just like I was when Mr. Wilson was President."

"That aint true." She went down the list, then started the car for their next drop-off. "We got two new customers this year alone that I can think of."

"And we had about that many die off, so it all evens out."

Gemma sat tall in the driver's seat, just in case Owen from the county sheriff's office might happen to drive by. She didn't think he would care anymore about her driving, especially after the time he'd stopped them and Dillard had rolled down his window, yelling: "Hardship case. I'm a hardship case. If this girl can't drive me, I can't get my eggs delivered and I'll starve."

"I don't believe it all evens out," she muttered, her hands gripping the steering wheel, her eyes fixed on the road. "No, sir. You just think it does 'cause you never took good records."

"That Miss Lawson teach you how to take good records?"

"Yes, sir. She did. We learned how to keep a bankbook."

"Well, then, as long as I got you I don't have no need for doing it myself."

They drove two blocks, then turned left on the street the church was on. Dillard could see it, the Twilight Baptist Church, standing like the Washington Monument, all white and clean. He shook his head, drumming his fingers on the dashboard.

"You take them their order," he said when they pulled up in front of the Tanners' house. He folded his arms and looked straight ahead.

"Eunice'll think something's wrong if you don't deliver 'em yourself."

"I brought eggs to her daddy and his family long before she ever went and married that Baptist preacher." Dillard pursed his lips. "I reckon they'll be quitting too. Be thinking I'm a troublemaker or something 'cause of that night."

Gemma looked as though she didn't know what he was talking about.

"That other night. When it rained." He glared at her. "Don't be sittin' there looking at me like that. You're the one what made a fool of me in that church."

He was going to be stubborn; he'd sit there all morning rather than take the Tanners their order. She got out, slammed the door, then took the eggs from the backseat.

"And take them sacks for the Coles and the Jacksons while you're at it," he spouted over his shoulder. "They was there that night."

"You're acting silly," she said.

"Don't tell me how I'm acting!" He watched her climb steep white-painted steps onto porch after porch. Each house was set back from the road, divided from it by a long front yard filled with oak and pecan trees, and flower-filled beds. Porches wrapped around the front of the homes, with a row of rockers pulled up to each railing. Dillard wondered what it was like, sitting up there under ceiling fans with tall glasses of lemonade, sitting there with a row of your own people on either side,

27

rocking, looking out over the townspeople who passed back and forth. He saw her standing on those neat white porches, standing there in her overalls and the shirt rolled up over her elbows while she waited for someone to come to the screen door. And then she'd push up her glasses as the screen opened and a hand ventured forth for the sack or carton of eggs. Will she be doing this with her own grandchild? he wondered, watching her. At the Coles' and then later at the Jacksons', he saw her take money from the hand behind the screen door, then put her foot out before the door could close.

"Now what? I hope she aint trying anything dumb."

Sunlight beat down through the windshield and his legs were scorching underneath his overalls. A dirt dobber flew inside the car, battering against the glass several times before it could find its way out. He watched her trot back toward the car, that bounce in each step.

"I hope you wasn't trying anything dumb," he said when she opened the door and got in.

"Like what?"

"Like I don't know, but I seen you putting your big ol' foot in those doors like some two-bit carny man."

"What's that?"

"Like some durn rascal trying to sell somebody an extra something they don't need."

She started the car and pulled away from the curb with such a jolt that Dillard's neck almost snapped. "If they didn't need it, they wouldn't order it."

"Oh, yes they would." He slapped his knee several times. "You'd set them up to do it whether they wanted to or not."

"That aint so."

"Yes, ma'am, it is. S'called railroading." She screeched on the brakes at the corner and wrote in the spiral notebook. "What's that you're writing now?"

"I'm keeping our records; somebody's got to." She checked the list, then took money from her pocket and put it into the cigar box. "Miss Cole will be wanting two dozen next week."

"The Coles aint ever had more than a dozen in all the years I been bringing them eggs," he said, turning to face her. She pressed her lips together and shoved up her glasses. "That's how customers are driven away. You can't be pushing off goods on them that they don't need."

"I didn't force her to do nothing." She pulled away from the corner, looking both ways. They seemed to be about the only car on the street. "Miss Cole was telling me that she had a lot of baking coming up 'cause her mama's people from Corsicana are visiting a week from Sunday. And I said, 'Well, then, Miss Cole, I reckon that means you'll be needing an extra dozen next week.' She looked like that never occurred to her, but that it sure made life easier."

"That makes me madder'n a wet hen for you to go doing that. Let them be the ones to come to you if they need something extra."

"Well, she ordered two dozen for next Friday, and if she wants anything less from then on, she can say so then."

"That's shady." Dillard smacked his lips and looked out his window as they passed the old Mitchell place, empty now, the gray roof collapsed in at one side from a tornado seasons ago. "I 'spect there's some Yankee blood somewhere in you for you to start thinking thataway."

She pulled up in front of the Stevens house, racing the motor before she turned it off. They could see Mrs. Stevens sitting on her front porch, stooped over in a cane-back chair. She nodded toward the Chevrolet, but didn't stop shelling peas.

"I'm taking this one up," Dillard said. "I aint gonna have you lose all my customers."

"Fine. Miss Cole thought you was mad at her 'cause you sat in the car. Didn't you see her peeking round the gardenia bush at you? I think she wants you for a boyfriend." Gemma looked up at him innocently, trying not to grin. She could see she'd gotten him flustered. When he slammed the door, he almost toppled over the curb.

He straightened himself and leaned down to speak to her

through his window. "I knowed Miss Cole too long, too many years to start thinking of her like that, I can tell you."

Gemma clapped her hands and laughed so loud as Dillard moved up the walk that Mrs. Stevens looked up again from the shelled peas which were beginning to gather in the pouch her skirt and apron made between her legs. Mrs. Stevens was one of those women who could snap beans or peas and carry on some other activity at the same time. The old man ambled up the walk, with snapdragons and petunias blooming on either side.

She had seen him stand like that in the doorway of the schoolhouse one day when she'd forgotten her lunch. Stood there waiting for something to happen. Gemma sat near the windows. She hadn't seen him at first, hadn't seen him till she heard snickers and there he was, Pop, standing in the doorway in his overalls and straw hat, her lunch sack in his hand. She wanted him to see her desk. He'd never been to the school before. He'd always said he wasn't her parent when they had parent night. But now he waited for her to come across the schoolroom, and he held out the paper sack for her to take before awkwardly backing away. Gemma stood at the door, looking after him. He moved down the center of the dirt road, and soon disappeared behind a cornfield. "That was my grandpop," she said, turning to Miss Lawson. The teacher smiled. She told them to take out their geography books. Back at her desk, Gemma watched the maps Miss Lawson pulled down, thinking: he never saw my desk; he never saw where I sit.

Dillard stood at the bottom of the Stevens porch in the same posture now, his hat in his hand. Gemma peered at him through the window on the passenger side. We aint ever gonna make no money if he does it like that, she thought. Mrs. Stevens looked down at him, her sunbonnet tilted back on her head, her mouth slack, and her face flushed from working in her yard all morning. Her fingers moved quickly down each pod. She didn't smile, didn't offer Dillard any expression. He looks like he'd done something wrong, Gemma thought. Like he's standing there waiting to be horsewhipped.

He moved timidly up the steps, taking each step one at a time as though it were Judgment Day. When he got to the top, he reached out to Mrs. Stevens. Her fingers stopped snapping long enough to accept the sack of eggs, then they continued. Gemma could see that she was saying something. And he was nodding, answering, trying to back down the steps. Would he leave without collecting? she wondered. At the last instant, as though she were trying to keep him from getting away, Mrs. Stevens took a purse from her apron and made him come back for forty cents. He bowed, ducking his head all the way down the steps, not turning his back on her till he was on level ground. Then he hurried down the walk, opened the car door, and fell inside, panting.

"You look like you think she's fixing to call you back and take the money from you," Gemma said, marking the notebook, then taking the change and depositing it in the cigar box.

His eyes narrowed. He looked at her soberly and said: "Just drive on to the Hansons'."

Gemma shook her head and started the car. "I can't understand how you been selling eggs all this time and you still act like you're doing something wrong by taking people's money. If I was them I'd buy at Woody's just not to have to see you squirm."

"I give 'em an egg extra. Woody don't do that."

"I don't care. You slink up there like you're doing something wrong. These people been buying eggs from you forever; their mamas bought their eggs from you."

"They talk about me."

"Miss Cole likes you; she thinks you're cute. She's always saying to me: 'Gemma, why do you keep that cute grandpa of yours out there in the Blackland all to yourself?' That's what she says."

"She does? Well, that makes me sick. She's the fattest old girl in town. I remember her getting stuck in one of the seats one time at the movie theater in Greenville. They had to call in the fire department, and they had to take the seat apart piece by piece to get her out."

Gemma stopped the Chevrolet in front of the Hansons'. She got out and took cartons from the back for both the Hansons and the Parkers. He didn't try to stop her. He watched as she walked around to the Hansons' back door, her chopped-off hair flopping as she bounced. He remembered himself when he was eleven, with that same dirty-blond hair, with that same bounce to his walk the other boys would kid him about when he had to go up to the front of the classroom to recite. They made faces while he had to think hard about the lines he was supposed to have memorized. And then he'd had to quit school because his daddy died and all at once he was in charge of running things around the farm. "You're the man now," his mother had said. He could still hear her say it, though now her voice echoed in his head as though it were coming from the bottom of the cistern. At first he was relieved; he'd never liked going to school anyway. The schoolhouse smelled like pine and apples. And later he would see those boys from school almost grown and he hardly knew them. He had too much work to do to be socializing, sitting around the drugstore, leaning against posts along the main street of Twilight. He knew they looked at him peculiarly. He could hear their voices when he'd walked a block past, jeering, calling after him, mimicking something he'd said too many years ago to remember. And they laughed out loud even later, when he was a man and they were men, and Henrietta Cole sat down next to him at the soda fountain in the drugstore. He'd never sat there again.

Gemma took long strides down the walk, her mouth set, looking at him. She got in the car, picked up the notebook, and said: "See there. All I did was say, 'Miz Hanson, we have you down for a dozen eggs, and we were just wondering if that was too many.' And she said, 'Why, no, hon. It aint.' So I said, 'Well, then, is it enough?'"

"Good Lord."

"I said: 'You maybe need some more?'"

"I give 'em all an extra egg. You're gonna wipe me out."

"Well, I'm talking 'bout an extra dozen. Or half dozen. She stood there thinking about it and said: 'Well, I could use a half dozen. I'm making pies for the church next week.' So, see. See what I'm talking about? We could be making more money on these eggs."

She leaned over to drop the coins in the cigar box. Dillard sat beside her with his shoulders slumped, his head down. When things could be better, when she tried to tell him how they could be making a profit, he just sat there. Acting like he never heard. She chewed her lip and started the car.

"And something else—you want to know something else?"

"You're gonna tell me anyway, aint you?"

"Miz Hanson told me that sometimes she runs out of eggs in the middle of the week and has to run down to Woody's for more. I think that's a crying shame."

Dillard studied his lap, following a stripe in his overalls with his thumbnail.

"I'll just bet you that more than half our customers have to do the same. Run to Woody's in the middle of the week."

"Good. Let 'em."

"Let 'em! We're supposed to be the ones supplying eggs. These folks should never run out, either. You aint satisfying them if they gotta go to Woody's just because you won't ask if they'll be needing extra eggs next time."

"What about Miz Parker?"

"I asked her too. She says she's just fine with what she's got."

"See."

"But I asked. More than she ever gets from you."

"They talk about us, and I don't like that."

Gemma drove down to the end of the street, then turned right. The houses that bordered Twilight were smaller, closer to the road.

"Nobody says a thing. Except maybe wonder why you shut yourself up out yonder."

"I reckon they're glad of it." He cleared his throat. "Heck, let's get these things delivered and finish with the errands. I want to get to the barge."

She scowled, exhaling loudly in a way that made him want to leap from the moving car. At the bend in the road which led to Greenville, they could see the old Perkins place, the barn huge, gray like a fortress, and the pasture filled with grazing sheep, leading up to the road. Gemma turned back toward the center of Twilight. Trees arched over the street, shading the Chevrolet from the sun. They passed the mayor's house, and next door to that, Carl Borland's, the funeral director. The homes in this section of Twilight were huge, two and three stories, built by early settlers who brought their own stained glass and their marble fireplaces with them. Behind tall double doors she could see dazzling chandeliers in some of the hallways. She drove slowly. A girl played on a second-story balcony of one of the houses.

"That's Dorothy Mullins; I never knew she lived over here."

"Her granddaddy built that house," Dillard said, his eyes on the road. "Built it twice. Once in '08, then all over again in '24 after we had that big tornado. I reckon it's too big to blow over now."

They stopped in front of the Ferris house, just before the main street of Twilight.

"Just keep the motor running," he said. "I'll take this up myself."

She could see him march up to the back door, see him wait until Mandy Ferris came to the screen and took the eggs. Back in the car, he pointed for her to turn onto the main street. They parked in front of Woody's.

"Just sit here," he said, reaching for the cigar box underneath his legs.

"While you're in there, ask Woody about his eggs," she said. "Maybe we could sell to him too."

"I'll do no such thing," he said, the cigar box under one arm as he slowly got out. "You just sit here. Sit here and keep records or something."

Stepping out, shuffling through the gravel and then onto the sidewalk in front of the grocery, he knew she was watching him. Knew she was squinting through those thick horn-rimmed glasses. Sell to Woody—the idea. Inside, he loaded his shopping cart with bread, milk, applesauce, and ice cream. He moved down the aisle muttering to himself, picking up toilet paper, paper towels, flour, sugar, and soap powder. That secretary from the church—he'd forgotten her name because she hadn't been in Twilight more than a few years—was at the front counter, blabbering to Woody. He could hardly concentrate on what he had come in for, hardly think from shelf to shelf whether or not he needed corn meal, bacon, butter. He tossed three packages of minute steaks into the basket, listening to that woman's long, slow drawl about congealed salad and how much she had to make for the church social. And Dillard shook his head, taking his time, staring at the display of Ritz crackers Woody had probably stacked himself. Anything not to have to check out at the counter behind that woman.

Telling him how to run his business, run his egg route that he'd done without mishap for longer than she could even imagine, longer than he could even remember sometimes. That was what he did. Did well. That durned kid had no right to tell him how to go about it. He'd be carting eggs into town every Friday long after she was gone too, long after those Monroes over in Dallas were given a chance to do something with her. He could see that spindly-legged woman at the counter, counting out boxes of Jell-O, asking Woody if he liked his with strawberries or bananas. Woody smiled, ringing up her purchases, smiled, not trying to sell that woman eighteen boxes of strawberries like somebody Dillard knew would try to do.

He picked up a sack of potatoes, one of rice, and poked his face down at the lettuce to see if it was wilted. Looking over the counter of fruits and vegetables, he called: "Woody, you got any prunes?"

Woody stuck his head around the shelves of Oxydol and Duz and said: "Only them in the boxes, Mr. Dillard."

Dillard turned to the counter behind him and took a box from the top shelf. A kid's gotta stay regular, he said to himself. And later he'd still grab for that box of prunes every Friday. His granddaughter's name would not pass his lips, he'd dare not think it, though he'd still be telling himself: a kid's gotta stay regular.

After that woman was gone, he wheeled his cart to the front and while Woody rang up all his purchases, Dillard dumped the cigar box of bills and coins on the counter, saying: "Hope this'll cover it." And as usual, he had some change left over, which he slipped into his pocket.

He came out with a sack of groceries in each arm.

"Help me with these things; they're heavier than a calf," he called from the sidewalk.

Gemma sat watching him try to look over the tops of the bulging sacks, sat in the car watching as he finally did and saw Beecham beside her. Dillard stepped off the sidewalk, almost falling into the front fender of the Chevrolet. She opened her door, then the back one so he could slide the sacks across the seat.

"What's this," he muttered, not looking up, placing the groceries one way, then putting them on the floor.

"I just asked Beecham to sit with me."

"How do, Homer," Beecham said, nodding, twisting a straw between his teeth.

"I saw him sitting over at the hardware store, sitting out yonder, and he came over to sit with me while you were in Woody's."

"Well, I'm back."

"Spend it all?" He saw that she'd gotten a straw from some-where and it was between her teeth too.

"Take that thing outta your mouth," he said, grabbing for the straw, stumbling as she turned her head. "You aint got any idea where it's been. Yes, ma'am. I spent it all, if that's any business of yours."

"Seen you last week, Homer," Beecham said, nodding to Dillard, holding the straw in place.

Dillard stooped low to stare in at the old man who was sitting in his place. Now aint this some stunt, he thought, almost muttering it aloud. Some stunt to get back at me, and I shoulda expected it. That nigger aint washed in a week, and not properly in no telling how long.

"Yep, I seen you taking eggs up to Miz Murphy's door," Beecham said, grinning. Most of his teeth in front were missing.

"Well, I didn't see you," Dillard said, thinking: he's really talking about that night at the church. Sure he is. Playing me for a fool. Gemma sat looking over the steering wheel at Woody's plate-glass window, cluttered with large sheets of butcher paper that had prices painted on them in red.

"You ask Woody 'bout the eggs?"

"I did not."

"You shoulda."

Dillard stood straight, slammed the back door, and went around to the passenger's side. He opened the door and waited for Beecham to step out. Old coot's nothing but skin and bones, he thought. Cora always said Beecham looked like he could squat on a dime.

"Yep. I seen you going up to Miz Murphy's door," Beecham said, slowly swinging his legs around so that his feet touched level ground. "I called out, but you didn't hear me."

He stood, his back still bent from getting out of the car. Dillard saw they were the same height; they'd always been the same height, first as boys, then as young men. And now they seemed to be shrinking at the same rate.

"Enjoyed settin' with you, Gemma," he said, facing the street, disoriented at first.

"I'll see you Sunday," she said, leaning forward to look up at him. "And bring your harmonica."

"Sure 'nough." He scratched his head and looked down at her. His gums were pink. "I'll have to hunt it up; aint played it in a long time."

Dillard stood with one arm on the door, looking down at the seat where Beecham had been, looking down as though he were waiting for the imprint in the vinyl to disappear. Beecham began his slow shuffle across the street to the hardware store. But he stopped midway and came back, holding to the back fender for support.

"Homer, you 'member them songs you 'n' me used to play together? We sure was good."

Dillard stared at him, past him, and said: "I can't recollect; no."

"Well, we sure was good." He started to come forward, to lean in to say something to Gemma. But Dillard got in quickly and closed the door.

"Let's go." He waved a hand for her to start the car. "My ice cream's melting."

Gemma turned to wave at Beecham. The old man stood in the gravel, his chest sunken, grinning like a jack-o'-lantern and waving as they drove away. Past the mill, past the gas station, they drove on open highway. She gripped the wheel with both hands, staring solemnly ahead.

"I want to get out to the barge soon's we put up them groceries," he said, folding his arms. He saw she still had the straw between her teeth. She hardly flinched when he pulled it out and threw it from his window. They passed the cemetery, and then the dump. Heat shimmered above the odd-sized foothills of trash. He said: "I don't want you messing with niggers. What are people gonna think to see you sitting in a parked car like that?"

"He's my friend."

"Well, I wouldn't go advertising."

"He plays dominoes with me."

"Where?"

"Down at the church. Sunday nights."

"That aint what you're going there for, young lady. I aint letting you go down there to play with niggers. You pick the strangest people to hang around with, I swear."

A dull warm breeze swept over the flat land, bringing with it faint wisps of stench from the dump. Dillard screwed up his nose. "Next thing, he'll have you out there roaming through garbage with him. Catching no telling what kind of diseases."

"He's one of God's children. Like you."

"Now don't start bringing that business into it. I'm telling you I lived too long for it. You can pick the ones you're gonna go through this life with, and it's plain common sense to see that some are better than others."

Gemma turned onto the farm road that zigzagged back to the Dillard place. "I didn't pick you," she said, her chin jutting forward, her eyes narrowed.

"Well, girlie, I didn't pick you, either."

Midafternoon shadows danced among the trees. Sometimes they waved across the water in the cove where she'd dropped their anchor. He sat with his back to her, sat hunched over the pole, waiting, getting angry because they'd been out for over an hour without catching anything. Gemma sat with her back to the box-encased motor. She looked across the water, wishing for clouds or wind, something to relieve them from the oppressive sun. If he'd let her, she could pull the barge in tighter to the cove. At least they'd get some shade now and then. But he was sure their luck would be where he told her to drop anchor first. It always was.

Her Bible cradled against her thighs, she tried to read, but the sun was too bright. She'd baited his hooks. She'd poured him a mason jar of iced tea. She'd sat completely still, not uttering a sound so the fish would bite.

Turning to one side, she was able to make enough shade with her body so that she could see the fine print on the page. Suddenly she said: "You never even told me you could play the harmonica."

He didn't answer. He kept his pose over the water.

"I'd a never known if it wasn't for Beecham. He's gonna teach me how to play."

"He aint teaching you nothing. Don't go—don't you know not to drink after other people, 'specially colored people? In them big stores over in Dallas, they even got two sets of water fountains. Playing the harmonica's even worse. All that slobbering."

"You still got a harmonica?" She ran her fingers down the print, stopping now and then to read.

"I don't know. I reckon. Somewheres. I aint seen it in a long time." He hovered. "Shh."

She pulled up her knees, scratching a bite on her ankle. He was stubborn; he wouldn't look for it, wouldn't show her how to play. Beecham told her that he'd known her granddaddy his entire life. Beecham's family had worked on the Dillard place, hoed their cotton, worked their fields.

"Come bait this dang hook," he said, calling over his shoulder. "I think a turtle keeps getting the grasshopper."

She did as he said, watching as he slung the line back into the water. She returned to her place at the other end, still thinking of Beecham, wondering how the old man could so easily have cast him away.

"I want you to listen to this," she said, beginning to read. *"Through wisdom is a house builded; and by understanding it is established. And by knowledge shall the chambers be filled with all precious and pleasant riches. Wisdom is too high for a fool: he openeth not his mouth in the gate."* She glanced up to see if he listened. But his position hadn't changed; he looked as though he might topple into the water, he waited so expectantly.

"If thou faint in the day of adversity, thy strength is small." She stopped reading and looked at him, pushing up her glasses. "See, what they're saying here is that—"

"What the heck is that?"

"It's in Proverbs."

"I'll give you a proverb: Kids is better seen and not heard.

Now what do you make of that one?" He turned halfway around to glare at her.

"Aint gonna hurt none for you to listen."

"And it aint gonna hurt you none to let me have some peace and quiet. The fish don't bite when you're reading out loud, even if it's that."

She closed the Bible, sniffled, and looked across the smooth surface of the lake. Three naked black boys splashed in shallow water far on the other side. Their bodies were dark shiny figures that dipped into the glistening surface, sometimes rising to a stance so that their thighs were encircled by the mirrored lake.

Through dinner, through scraping, washing, and drying the dishes, she would not speak to him. She hung the dish towel over the counter to dry, and was about to sit in her new rocker. But when Dillard sat at the kitchen table again, she moved into the middle room, the one he'd given her. He could hear her flipping pages in the dark.

"Gemma?"

He sat at the table, his half-filled coffee cup before him. Max rubbed at his foot, and sometimes Dillard would scratch the cat's head. He was calico-colored. Gemma had come home from school one day saying that all the different colors reminded her of the maps in her geography book. Dillard went across the back porch to his room, took a small box from the top of his closet, then returned to the kitchen table.

"Gemma, I'm speaking to you."

"What?" Her voice came from the darkened room.

"Come in here." He took his old harmonica from the case and set it on the table. She was just inside the door to her room. Her glasses caught a glint from the overhead light in the kitchen. She looked like a spook.

"This is it, what you asked me about."

She came into the room slowly, standing close to the table, staring down at it. "Go on, play it," he said, sipping his coffee. She looked at him hesitantly, then picked it up. Gently putting it to her lips, she blew quickly, then inhaled. The two sounds made her laugh.

"You aint gonna learn to play that thing if you're scared of it," he said. "Here. Give it to me."

He took the harmonica, wiped it across his sleeve, and held it close in the palm of his hand. He licked his lips, and closing his eyes, he brought it up. He slid up and down the instrument. "When you blow you get one sound, and when you suck in air you get another."

She nodded.

He wet his lips again, then began to play. One foot stamped the floor. Max circled around the table and sat by Gemma's side. "Now that song there was called 'Skip to My Lou,'" he said, shaking spit into the palm of his hand.

"I know."

Dillard wiped his hand on his overalls and nodded his head. "Now it takes a lot of practice to learn how to play this thing."

"What other songs do you know?"

"Let's see, I can play 'Red River Valley,' and 'Oh, Susanna,' and . . . Sometimes they'd ask me to play at their square dances."

"You?"

"Yes, me. When I'd go with your grandma. Long time ago."

Gemma thought for a moment, then pulled out her chair and sat next to him. "That where you and Beecham played?"

"They'd have dances every month back then, and your grandma loved to go. No niggers were ever allowed. That was all a long time before. Beecham don't know nothing 'bout square dancing."

Gemma held the instrument in both hands, turning it over, holding it up to the light to peer through the holes. All at once, Dillard stood up and said: "I got a idea." He clapped both his hands, shoved back his chair, and disappeared through the middle room, into the front of the house. She could hear him scrambling around in the dark. As she stood, he came back into the kitchen, hobbling with a quickness she wasn't accustomed to seeing.

"I'm gonna teach you how."

"To play the harmonica?"

"No, girl. To square dance." He pushed both their chairs under the table. "I got the old records under the Victrola in there. I'll show you how we did it."

Without saying a word, she watched him push back her rocker and shoo Max from the room. He told her to stand on his right, explaining that usually there were four couples who made a square, facing into the middle.

"Now they call it 'home' where your starting position is," he said. "And when you start out, you have to 'honor your partner.' That means I bow to you and you curtsy to me. Now try it."

Standing beside the table, he faced her and bowed low. She curtsied, and pushed up her glasses with the palm of her hand.

"Now they got what's called a 'caller' 'cause he calls out the different steps you gotta do. Whatever he says, you do. He keeps in time with the music."

"What if you don't know one of the steps?"

"I'm showing you right now. We'll start off with something easy. No sashaying or grapevine twists or nothing."

Hands on her hips, she stared down at her feet. "I don't know if I want to do this. You have to call 'em off slow."

"I will."

"And I don't have one of them big skirts, the kind that fan out when you twirl in 'em."

"You can still get the hang of it," he said, scratching his head, trying to recall some of those steps he'd learned in barns years back. With an almost dreamlike clarity, he could still visualize bales of hay stacked against the wall, the fiddler standing on an overturned washtub, and Cora. Cora. When he lay out to smoke or just listen to the music, she would continue to whirl through her pick of partners, and Dillard would watch her glide through the steps, thinking: next she will fly. Next she will circle left above the barn floor, smiling down, clapping her hands in time with the music. And as he saw her again after all that time, he all at once knew the steps too. "Do-si-do is when you pass each other by the right shoulders and come back by the left, back to back, without turning, to your original positions."

He showed her how, his arms folded before him. Almost by instinct, she pulled at the legs of her overalls as though they were a skirt.

"That's right. Now when they say 'promenade,' that means you stay on my right and we walk around, you know, counterclockwise. I hold your right hand in my right, and your left hand in my left."

"This is stupid," she said as they tried the step.

"Why, sure it seems silly now 'cause it aint connected, and we don't have the Victrola playing."

"It's still dumb."

"Just bear with me, and you'll see," he said. "I didn't tell you 'bout 'swing your partner.' That's a favorite step they always throw in somewheres."

"That where you get to sling me around off my feet?" she asked, her mouth rigid, her eyes soberly trained up to his face.

"I just might, if we get going good and the music is just right. I just might." He grabbed her hand, stooped to put an arm around her waist, then pivoted around clockwise, their right feet in place.

As he went into the darkened front room and rummaged through the records, something began to come over him. He cranked up the machine and heard the needle scratch until it found the groove. "This here's 'Billy Boy,'" he called through the house. She stood at the table, waiting for him, her hands self-consciously inside her overalls. The music had already started, but he took his place, then bowed to her. She remembered suddenly, laughed, and curtsied.

"I'll do the calling," he said. "Just follow what I do."

"Well, go on. The record's gonna be done with," she said, gazing through the room she slept in, to the front of the house.

Dillard thought for a moment, then he scurried back to begin the record again. And all those evenings, he'd stood there at the table himself, right where she stood, waiting for Cora to start the record, waiting for her to teach him to square dance. He had been frightened every time they had gone to one of the barn dances, even later when he'd mastered all the steps. His movements were rough, not nearly as good as those of the others, ones he'd had to sit with in that classroom years before. And he knew they could see his clumsiness, could see the unnaturalness of his movements. For all the dances they attended, he never experienced the same liberating freedom that he did in the kitchen when she taught him those first steps. He never felt himself about to leave the ground when he circled left or circled right, never felt a lightness in his stomach that raised him off the kitchen floor to become eye level with all those chickens on the wallpaper that he had named one by one.

"Just follow what I do in case I forgot to tell you something," he called, putting the needle back to the beginning. As it began again, he came into the kitchen, bouncing along with a jig step, keeping time by clapping his hands. He took his place beside her. "This first thing's called an introduction; that's when you square your sets."

Gemma nodded, biting her lip. "Go slow so I can get it," she said.

"I will. I will." He tapped his foot, then began:

> Square your sets with a smile on your face,
> Everybody dance, right in your place.

He did a jig step in place, staring across the table at the designs on the wallpaper. She followed him beats later, her bangs waving across her forehead.

> Honor your partners—and the

> Lady to your left—
> All join hands and circle left;
> Circle left all the way round.
> All the way round till you come home,
> You swing yours, leave mine alone.
> Everybody swing, and we'll
> Promenade round the ring.
> Promenade round the hall,
> Promenade the old corral.
> Promenade till you get home.

They circled the kitchen table and came back to their starting positions. She shoved her glasses up and grinned.

"Aint that something?"

"Nothing hard about that," she said, her hands in her back pockets.

"All you gotta do is follow me, and I'll show you the steps. It's all coming back to me now. It's been a long time."

"Well, I think you're real good at it," she said, suddenly curtsying to him. Dillard laughed out loud and bowed back.

Gemma ran to start the record again, then she took her place next to him. She watched his foot tap, then began to move her own, punctuating the beat with her shoulders.

"Ready?" Dillard looked down at her, then began his call:

> Oh, you all join hands and you circle to the left,
> Circle to the left, charming Billy,
> For she's a young thing and cannot leave her mother.
> First couple to the right.
> Circle four hands around.
> The other way back, charming Billy.
> Do-si-do the other gal.
> Swing the one who is your pal,
> For she's a young thing and cannot leave her mother.

Dillard stooped to grab her waist, and as he swung her

around the kitchen table past the stove, past the new rocker he'd made for her, they seemed to leave the ground. He swung her higher, laughing, hearing her giggle, as they began to orbit the table. The chickens on the wallpaper began to dance along the stripes in the design. The harmonica bounced in the center of the table every time he touched the floor.

Everybody swing, swing her high and swing her low,
Everybody swing, charming Billy.
Now when you get through, why you take her home,
For she's a young thing and cannot leave her mother.

And when she stood again next to him in the "home" position, breathing hard, her upper lip moist, he bowed low. Blood pumped in his ears. He could feel his chest tremble, and when he put a hand over his heart, she said: "Pop, you all right?"

He nodded and waved her away as he sat at the table. She stood planted in her "home" position, still rising on the balls of her feet, still bending her knees.

"Go switch off that Victrola," he said, his voice thick.

When she disappeared, he could hear the needle being lifted from the record with a sudden scratching. With two fingers, he rubbed at the center of his forehead, trying to dislodge whatever it was in there that made everything so stuffy. When he opened his eyes, the room still weaved and he felt light-headed.

"Gemma. Gemma, come in here."

"You all right, Pop?" She stood in the doorway, peering at him hesitantly. He saw that her hair was still tangled. "Pop?"

"Now that, what we did just now, that's called square dancing." He rested his cheek in the palm of his hand. "What you think 'bout that?"

"I reckon I like it okay." She sniffled and straightened her glasses. "Pop, you feeling all right?"

"I'm fine," he said, taking a deep breath. "I'm fine."

"You sound funny. You sound like you're talking under water."

Waving her away again with one hand, he said: "You're gonna know how to dance and them others will be jealous as all get-out when they see how you spin around the room." He wet his lips and cleared his throat. A thumping still rushed between his ears. "Remember it was me that taught you." He shut his eyes as though that might help him get his breath more quickly.

"I'll remember."

Moments later, he could hear her in the middle room as she slipped out of her overalls and into her nightshirt, hear her humming "Billy Boy." His breathing steadied finally, though his hands felt clammy, his throat dry, and his eyes teared as though a steady breeze were bathing his face. . . . *Oh, where have you been, charming Billy?* He could see her turn on the lamp beside her bed, then sit there with the opened Bible in her lap. *Dada da, and she cannot leave her mother.*

Maybe he felt strange because the room was so drafty. It seemed as though the kitchen had not been occupied for ages, as though the chickens had only danced in somebody's dreams in another life. Yet he knew Cora had danced him around that kitchen table on still summer evenings. It hadn't been that long ago. An oil lamp on the counter made their shadows swim around the room, made their figures fly across the window so that anyone passing along the lonely stretch of country road would think they were having a party. And she had taught him how, told him about every step. *Oh, where have you been . . . ?*

"Gemma." His voice cracked. He forced a cough to cover the sound. He leaned across in his chair until he could see her in the other room. Her humming died as she began to read the Bible to herself, her lips barely moving. And when he shut his eyes, a clear, sweet voice whispered: "That's it, that's right, Homer. Bow low, from the waist. Like a gentleman."

🐓 *If a wall comes between two people walking side by side, you can expect them to quarrel.*

Like every other morning, she had the house to herself. He never told her where he was going, though she could guess.

"I don't see what you do down there for hours," she'd say as he started down the path between the pecan trees. And he would tell her to mind her own business, to do what she was supposed to do or he'd give her plenty to occupy her time. "But they're only chickens. After you feed them and gather the eggs, why do you want to stick around?" He'd continue down the path without turning. Once the crape myrtle hid him from view, he'd yell: "I aint accountin' to you for everything I do, young lady. There's more to this business than you think." She knew how he stood in the chicken yard. She'd seen him when he thought he was alone, seen him talking to the chickens, scuffing his foot through the dust, answering his own questions.

She lined up the two washtubs on the screened-in porch and dragged the washing machine away from the wall. Most Mondays she had to be up before dawn, lugging washtubs out to the line and hurriedly hanging clothes before she had to catch the school bus. But today she could stretch the chore out till noon if she wanted. Summer Mondays were lazy.

Her favorite part was feeding the wet clothes into the long, tight wringer. They would wind out snakelike from the other side and fall in heaps into the washtubs. Both Gemma's and Dillard's garments looked the same when they were wrung dry, the life squeezed out of them. She had tried to roll her fingers through the wringer when she was a little girl, but it was too tight. She turned the crank slowly now, then faster, watching Dillard's long underwear roll into the tub like bark off a tree. In the distance, a tractor chugged over an unplowed field, and she looked up, expecting to see Doreen Hadley come across the yard in her sunbonnet and her gardening shoes. She'd told Gemma she would be around that morning to help weed the garden.

Gemma set one of the loaded washtubs on the cistern while she lugged the other out into the yard. The line had been stretched from the corner of the house to the nearest pecan tree. Dillard had fastened long cedar poles to it along the way so that when the line was full it wouldn't sag to the ground. The poles rocked and swayed as she draped garments on the line, a wooden clothespin in her mouth. She hung the clothes evenly, one pin overlapping the next garment. A pair of his overalls came after two of hers; two of his gray workshirts were like two of hers. Overhead an airplane passed, though she couldn't see it when she shaded her eyes. She stood back and squinted at the hanging clothes. The line was filled halfway down to the pecan trees. The clean white surface of towels and sheets reminded her of a solid wall. She ran her hand down one of the wet sheets, thinking how this new wall she'd built had chopped the world in two. On rainy days before she'd been old enough to start school, Dillard had let her drape the kitchen table with old blankets, and once she was inside her tent she was in a different world. Now that she was too old for that sort of thing, she was still able to make a new space from the old one that existed. The ugly side of the butane tank, the car shed, the open flat countryside which continued for acres without obstruction: they didn't exist anymore on her side of the gently waving screen of clothes. She glanced over the rosebushes which someone had planted long before she'd been there, and at the pecan trees. Their small garden of squash and beans and tomatoes was fenced off, but the ugly barbed wire was hidden by berry vines.

She stood for a moment, blinking, stroking the sheets. And the other side became obscured.

The back screen slammed and she carried the next washtub over to the line, weaving in and out between clothes, singing "Billy Boy" to herself. She took off her glasses and spit on the lenses before she wiped them on her shirttail. Her forehead was damp, and when she wiped her sleeve across it, her hair plastered back. She stooped to pick up a pair of Dillard's long underwear and underneath the waving towels saw a pair of feet. "I thought you'd be coming before I was done hanging out wash," she said, then lost her breath almost when she saw that the feet belonged to shapely legs. Doreen Hadley would never wear green pumps like those to weed in the garden. Gemma froze, Dillard's underwear in her hands. The feet turned hesitantly, then stepped toward her. And then the wall of sheets was opened by a hand with long fingers and a shiny black bracelet. At first Gemma only saw the face, fine-boned, long, and the mouth with bright red lips. The eyes were small, narrowed. The woman had a mass of red curls, which fell across the padded shoulders of her suit. Gemma had only seen velvet like that on the church altar.

"I was thinking you was my neighbor woman," she said, still stooped over the washtub, her hands cradling Dillard's underwear.

The woman moved forward so that her lanky figure was completely in view, draped on either side by the billowing white wall Gemma had constructed.

"Well, I thought you were a little boy," the woman said, and snorted a laugh through her nose. She stared down at Gemma, biting her lower lip, frowning slightly. Self-consciously, Gemma shook out the underwear and began to hang it on the line. The woman watched indifferently. She took a cigarette from her patent-leather handbag. When she lit it, she took a deep drag, blew smoke through her nostrils, and said: "I might have said something dumb, like call you 'boy' or 'son' or something, if you hadn't said something first. Anyone would take one look at you and think you were a boy."

Gemma stood with two clothespins in her hand, turning them, clicking them nervously together. She couldn't take her eyes from the woman, who stood now on this side of the sheets. The woman smoked; she fidgeted from one foot to the other. Gemma wondered how she managed to stand on such high heels.

"Anybody ever called you 'boy'?"

"No, ma'am." Gemma pushed up her horn-rimmed glasses at the nose and blinked.

"I'm surprised they haven't, with the way you're dressed. Course, once you start to fill out a little, they'll know what you are. Even in overalls."

"Aint nothing wrong with how I'm dressed. This is how I'm always dressed."

"Yes, I bet it is." The woman laughed and paced along the line of hanging clothes. She stood with her back to Gemma, facing the house, the screened-in back porch. "I know. And I probably dressed just like it, though I hope to hell I've forgotten all that."

"Aint no need to cuss."

The woman laughed again, throwing back her head and looking at Gemma. They stared at each other for a moment, then the woman rubbed the tight skin around her left eye with a little finger. "Couldn't get a love-starved GI to look twice if I dressed like that. Life's hard enough."

Gemma stood over the washtub, still half-filled with socks and underwear and undershirts. She stared down at the wrung-out clothes snaked in circles, thinking: if I was still in school, this wouldn't be happening now. I'd be in geography, or reading, or recess.

With one finger still massaging little circles beside her eye, the woman took another drag from her cigarette and stepped to the wall of sheets. She stuck her head through quickly, then came to the other side of the washtub. Gemma saw her take a deep breath, heard it come out in uneven spurts.

"Well," she said, smoke drifting from her nostrils, smiling slightly. "I reckon you're almost a woman, if you aren't already. Have you started yet?"

Gemma scooted her shoes through the dust. She turned from the woman and went to the edge of the pecan trees. On the other side of the barn she could see the long, low henhouse, could hear his chickens clucking and battering their wings against the roosts. Somewhere, either inside the henhouse or behind it, she knew Dillard was keeping them company, whispering to them, answering himself. "What is it you want, ma'am?"

"You don't know who I am. Course you don't."

Still facing the henhouse, wondering where he was just then, wondering if he would happen upon them suddenly and find the woman, Gemma said: "I know you." She turned to see the red mouth quiver. Smoke shot down from those nostrils. "I seen your picture in the photo album." She came back to the washtub and picked up another pair of Dillard's underwear. "You don't look like you did in those pictures, but I know you."

The woman's face flinched. She sighed and buried the cigarette in the dirt with the toe of her shoe. Then she moved to the pecan trees as though she were about to meet someone, someone she hadn't seen for a long time. "Where is he?"

"Yonder," Gemma mumbled, motioning with her head toward the henhouse.

The woman shook her head and came back to stand beside the hanging sheets as though the waving barricade offered more protection. "I suppose I don't look like those pictures anymore," she said, absently taking another cigarette from her purse. Fumbling with her lighter, she suddenly threw back her head and cackled. "My God, I hope I don't look like that anymore." She coughed when she exhaled. "I hope I've been doing something right all this time."

Gemma shook out the underwear, staring at her soberly. "I thought you had brown hair. In the pictures you look like you have brown hair."

"Honey, every woman you see looks like they got brown hair, unless they have sense enough to make themselves look special."

"But Pop told me. He said your hair was brown, just a little darker than mine."

"Shoot, maybe it was. I can't remember." She folded her arms and looked around the yard with a vague sense of disgust. "It was pretty close to that mousy shade of yours, if you want the truth. But that's a damn stupid thing to bring up. I knew coming here would make me remember stupid things like that, which don't have nothing to do with nothing, and what's the point."

"How did you get here? I didn't hear a car drive up."

"I parked in the road. That old bridge over the ditch looked like it would collapse if I drove over it. It was rotten when I was a kid. It must be crumbling by now."

"We drive over it every day."

The woman snorted and paced along the clothesline. "He be coming to the house soon?"

"Maybe. I don't know."

Gemma stood on the other side of the washtub, watching the woman sigh, watching her slouch just enough so that her lacy slip fell below the hem of her suit. The woman laughed and stood erect when she saw that Gemma was staring at her clothes. She put out a hand over the tub. Gemma hesitated, then took it.

"Gemma, honey, I'm your mama." The toes of her shoes clanked against the metal tub as she put both hands on the girl's shoulders. Her face twitched and Gemma thought the woman was about to cry. But she shook her head and said: "I never thought I'd get to see you again. Baby. I never thought the day would come when I'd get to be standing here with you. I can't tell you how long I've dreamed about this."

And though she had dreamed of this moment herself over countless days and nights, Gemma was unable to respond. She felt herself being pulled by the shoulders around the tub. Her cheek was crushed into the velvet and it was softer than she'd imagined, softer than anything she'd ever touched. As she was being kissed, she tried to remember how she had felt in those dreams, but she couldn't. The woman had a smell that reminded Gemma of the drugstore. She put her face close to Gemma's, and Gemma touched it. It wasn't the way she thought it would be. It was skin, made up. A little oily.

"Baby, I can't stay long. I can't stay at all." She held Gemma out before her and looked her up and down. "I got to be getting back to Fort Worth; that's where I'm living now. Fort Worth, honey. It's a big city, with lots of things going on. You'd love it."

"Pop says they got water fountains for white people and different ones for colored people."

The woman tossed back her head; her laugh was silent. "Did he now? As if he would know what they had in Fort Worth."

"He said it."

"It figures that's what he'd pick out." She shook her head. "He don't know, honey. He's never been anywhere—Fort Worth, Dallas, none of the big places like I have."

She chuckled to herself. Gemma backed away and stood looking down at the clothes still left to be hung, her hands deep in her pockets. Her mother opened her handbag for another cigarette, then stopped, clasped it shut, and put it under her arm.

"Anyway," she said, straightening herself, "I reckon I better get out yonder and tell him I'm here to get you. Sooner we get that over with, and put your things together, the sooner we can get out of here."

Gemma raised her head and looked at her for a moment, then said: "I aint going anywhere."

"Honey," her mother said, her hand to her throat, "I have come to take you with me. It's time you came to Fort Worth.

You're getting to be a young lady now, and I'll be damned if I'm letting you stay here. Now's the time when you need me."

Gemma walked to the edge of the trees. She paused for a moment, then disappeared through an opening in the sheets.

"Hey! Where you going?"

Her mother shoved clothes out of the way and followed. Gemma had started for the front of the house, taking long, definite strides. When she got to the front walk, she stopped and waited for her mother to catch up.

"Now, see there? That's not any way for a young lady to be walking. You look like a farmhand."

"That's what I am."

"Oh, no you're not. You're Juanelle King's daughter. Just because I haven't been able to take you till now don't mean you're gonna start out life as some hick."

"I done started my life," Gemma said, facing the road, staring at the dark green Plymouth parked along the ditch.

"I know that. That's not what I mean, though." Juanelle stood on the walk, just behind her. Gemma could hear her heels scrape across the stones. "I mean, I haven't been able to come for you yet because I've had to do a lot of things to make sure you'd have a good home. I had to be able to offer you something more than a room someplace."

"I got a home right here."

Juanelle came around to stand in front of her. Gemma saw a glistening line of sweat on her powdered temple. "I know you got a home here," her mother said, glancing over her shoulder at the car. "I was the one that brought you to it. I was doing my best to see you had a good roof over your head till I could do better. Well, I've done better." She put both hands on her hips and raised her chin. "And now you're coming with me."

"I told you. I aint going anywhere."

Juanelle exhaled disgustedly and shook her head. She paced before the girl, glancing up at the front of the house.

"He still have all those chickens?"

Gemma nodded.

"He used to drive me nuts the way he'd carry on over them. Took me a long time to realize he cared more about them than anyone else on this place."

"That aint so."

"Oh, yes it is, and you know it. He needs somebody to do his dirty work, and that's it. I know. Believe me. Did the same exact thing with my mama till she got fed up with it all and had sense enough to leave."

Gemma stuck her hands in her pockets, staring at the ground, wishing the woman would get into her car. And across fields of corn and wheat and cotton, she could hear highway traffic soar over asphalt. Sometimes she could see the top of a truck or bus move swiftly along as though it were driving through the fields.

"Honey, when I was fifteen—now I know you aint there yet, but you will be soon enough—when I was fifteen, I hurt so bad I thought I was gonna die in my sleep." Gemma looked up at her. "I was a grown-up woman treated like a tomboy. I aint saying it was his fault. He didn't know. How could he have known what it was like for me to have to work like a nigger on this place and do for him, when I wanted to see what the world was like? I don't want that happening to you."

"It aint."

"You don't know yet. Honey, you just don't know." Juanelle bit her lip. She started to say something, but swallowed several times and pressed the bridge of her nose with two fingers. "Is he all right? Is he doing okay?"

"I reckon," Gemma said, watching her mother. Juanelle had turned away, moving into the yard, where she leaned against the oak tree. "Sometimes his knees bother him when he sits too long, but I reckon we're doing fine."

When Juanelle turned again, Gemma saw that the makeup around her eyes had smeared. Neither of them said anything for a moment. Off across the fields, Gemma could hear Bob Hadley's tractor. She pushed up her glasses, her eyes trained in the direction of that sound, thinking: will he find her standing here with me?

"When I started, it scared the bejesus out of me," Juanelle said, shaking her head. "I didn't know what was happening to my body. There wasn't nobody here to tell me."

Gemma didn't say anything.

"I couldn't tell nobody 'cause I thought it was something that was wrong down there. God, I was scared. I bet I went through it four or five times before my teacher found out and she told me it was all right. She told me that what was happening was because I was a woman now and that it would happen every month from then on. But that didn't make it okay. I had to come back here every day, dressed like you are now, and I had to feed the chickens and go fishing with him. I had to work in the hot sun hoeing cotton and hauling hay, and he never knew any of it had happened to me. He never knew I wasn't some hired-out farmhand. Then when I left here, 'cause I had to, he made out like I wasn't even his daughter anymore. He took you. I knew he'd be good to you and give you everything you needed. But he acted like I wasn't me anymore."

She came toward Gemma and put a hand on her shoulder. "Hell with it." She wiped her nose with the back of her hand and looked at the clouds. "I want you to go inside now and get your things together. Looks like I'll have to buy you clothes, but then I planned on that."

Gemma rocked on her heels for a moment, thinking, feeling as though her head would burst. Without looking at her mother, she said: "I aint leaving here. I aint had anybody but him till now, and that's all I need."

"You're just as hardheaded as he is. You need your mother, honey."

"No, I don't. I just need him, Pop. And the good Lord."

Juanelle laughed, opening her mouth so that Gemma could see the fillings in her teeth. "Let's see how far that'll get you."

They watched each other without moving. Gemma could feel her eyes begin to tear, but she didn't look down. Finally she started walking toward the road, across the rough-planked bridge and over to the Plymouth. Juanelle followed, stopping suddenly when she saw Gemma open the car door.

"Just get in," Gemma said, eyeing her soberly.

Juanelle slouched on one leg and smiled. "Cut the crap. I'll leave you here if that's what you want. Believe me, it's no skin off my nose."

Gemma stood at the opened car door. She remained silent as the heat from inside hit her.

"Just like him—you know, you're just like him," Juanelle said, coming forward. She leaned an elbow on the hood of the car.

"Well, I don't want him finding you here."

Her mother laughed loudly and took her time lighting a cigarette. "If you want to rot out here, that's your business. Just don't say I never tried to bail you out. You'll see in a couple of years, when you start getting pretty. You'll see." She got in the car and closed the door. Gemma stood in the road, looking in at her. Juanelle took a piece of paper from her handbag and wrote something down, the cigarette dangling between her lips. She looked up at Gemma as she handed her the paper. "Send me a Christmas card."

Gemma watched as she started the car, then pulled away. The Plymouth stirred up a cloud of gray dust as it raced down the stretch of road and finally disappeared around the corner of a cornfield. Gemma stood in the middle of the road, directly across from the house. She opened the folded scrap of paper in her fist and read:

> Mrs. Frank King
> 7296 Jacksboro Hwy
> Fort Worth, Texas

And when she was leaning over the washtub once again, she heard him traipsing along the path between the pecan trees. Quickly she stuffed the slip of paper into her back pocket. Underneath the waving wall of clothes she could see his boots shuffle along the ground. Holding an undershirt in one hand, she waited quietly, hoping he would pass, hoping he would continue into the house without saying anything. But he stuck his head through the sheets and said: "I hear a car before?"

She shook her head and reached for a clothespin.

"I coulda swore I heard a car pull away."

"Nope," she said, her hands still shaking, her heart racing. He continued to watch her every move, watch as she pinned the shirt to the line and came back to the tub for another garment.

"It's taking you a mighty long time to hang them clothes," he said, spitting in the dirt, then rubbing it in with his foot.

"I'm almost done," she said, putting another clothespin in her mouth.

"Well, let's have our dinner so we can get out to the lake," he said, disappearing behind the white wall. She could hear him trudge up the back steps, grumbling because she'd taken so long with the clothes.

Gemma pinned their socks in pairs along the line. The clothes stretched all the way to the pecan trees now. He was on the porch, shoving the washing machine back in place, still mumbling under his breath. And she wanted to ask him: Pop, am I getting pretty yet? But she finished with the socks and then she walked up and down the line of clothes, gliding her fingers across rough wet textures, telling herself: you can make a wall, but it don't mean a thing.

🐓 *A whistling girl or a crowing hen . . . always comes to a bad end.*

Dillard held the bucket of fish with one hand and leaned his other arm on the sill of the opened window. He hardly noticed the countryside they passed along the highway, hardly realized they had pulled off onto the dusty shoulder across from the dump. A bad sign. Three perch were all he'd caught that day. After he'd twisted the hook from the third one's mouth, he'd stepped backward right over his pole without thinking.

"Dad blammit!" He'd stomped and whacked his thigh and would have tossed the bucket of perch into the lake if Gemma hadn't grabbed his arm.

"No need to cuss," she'd said, taking the bucket, placing it on the tin deck again. She'd carried it later to the car while he kicked through the grass.

"Stepping over a pole means you won't catch anything else all day; it's a bad sign."

"You could have stepped back over," she'd said, starting the car. "That would have erased it."

"You don't know nothin 'bout signs," he'd said, staring down into the bucket at the pitiful results of his day.

Now she sat with the car idling on the shoulder of the highway, staring across the field to the dump. Jack and Bubba Springer stood beside the dump truck. Three other pickups had parked recklessly nearby.

61

"Let's get into town if we're going," Dillard said, grinding his teeth. "This day's spoilt as it is."

A cherry pie was on the backseat of the Chevrolet, under a dish towel. She'd put it there before they went to the lake, and now, she'd told him, she had to drop it off at the church.

"Something's going on out yonder," she said, craning her neck out the window. Bob Hadley was there. So were Ray Ferris from the hardware store and Sid Hanson.

"Just people dumping trash," he said. "S'what I'm gonna do with this cherry pie if you don't get a move on."

Gemma jerked the clutch and turned down the winding black dirt road to the dump. Dillard knocked on the side of the bucket and slammed it down between them. Water sloshed over her lap. But she kept her eyes trained on the group of men standing around the Springers' dump truck.

"Something's the matter here," she said.

She stopped the car behind Ray Ferris's pickup and got out. Dillard sat completely still, thinking: I'm giving her one minute sixty seconds to get her tail back in this car before I drive it off myself. And she better not think I can't do it.

Bubba Springer stood on a rusted washtub, leaning forward from the waist as though he were about to dive into the middle of the drifts of garbage. Old tires, window frames, gutted mattresses, water-soaked cartons, and newspapers formed man-made hills around them. Gemma walked through coffee grounds; the stench of rotten meat was in the air.

"I think I can hear him down there," Bubba said. "Listen."

And Gemma stood beside the men, straining to hear what Bubba listened to. Jack Springer leaned against the front fender of the dump truck and all at once rammed his fist into the hood. It made them all jump.

"Now listen," Bubba said again, his head cocked to the side. "I know I heard something."

"Bubba, get down from there before you break your neck."

"What happened?" Gemma asked, looking to each of them.

"But, Daddy . . ."

"Bubba, there must be ten feet of garbage over him," Jack Springer said. "How do you expect to hear through all that mess? He'd have to have gills like a fish to breathe."

"Beecham never could do anything right," Bubba said, whimpering, pushing his chin downward so that layers of skin folded out.

"Nothing but sing like an angel," Bob Hadley said, his lips hardly moving. When he took off his hat, Gemma could see a wet band of perspiration around his head.

"Well," Jack Springer said, falling against the dump truck, "you don't hear him a-singing now."

Gemma thought she might gag on the smell. She turned away, still confused, and saw a line of cars and pickups turn off the highway in a slow procession toward the dump. "Are you gonna tell me what's going on here? Any of you? Where is Beecham?" Each of their faces seemed to harden. "Where is he?"

Bubba Springer stepped carefully off the washtub, pulled up his pants in back, and then pointed with a stubby finger at the mound of garbage.

"Jack sent Bubba running to my place soon's it happened," Bob was saying to her. Gemma stood frozen in place, her fingers pressed against her lips. "Maybe I ought to go fetch my tractor."

"No," Jack Springer said. "We got to do this by hand." The cars parked in a row-by-row formation. People began to run toward the dump truck. "A tractor would be too dangerous. It'd crush the daylights out of him—that is, if they aren't crushed out already."

Gemma moved slowly toward the mound of garbage, kicking a tin can.

"Gemma, hon, let's wait," Bob Hadley said, putting a hand on her shoulder. "Let's get organized."

"We got to get to him," she said. "We have to save him."

May Tompkins drove her Dodge through the people beginning to mill around the dump truck. She shoved through them, crying: "Y'all get to him yet? Is he alive?"

Jack Springer held back the secretary from the church and told her to stay calm; they'd do what they could.

Gemma walked around the outside of the mountain of trash, wondering: how could this happen? How could he let them bury him like this?

"I didn't see him standing there," Jack Springer was saying. "I might have; he's always out here. But I didn't see him till it was too late."

With his oil-stained hat down around his eyes, Beecham had roamed the hills of rubbish for years, singing hymns, rummaging through brittled cans, old clothes, and table scraps.

"We pushed the switch before we saw him," Bubba said. "He was standing down there in a valley with all that junk around him. He was holding an empty box of cornflakes up close to his face like he was trying to read the free offer on the back."

"Beecham doesn't know how to read," May Tompkins said, folding her arms, letting her glasses dangle by the cultured-pearl chain around her neck.

"The next think I know, a ton a garbage came out of nowhere, covering him like an avalanche."

"What do you mean by 'out of nowhere'?" May asked. "It came outta your truck, if I'm not mistaken."

"Now, now," Ray Ferris said. "Let's get going. We got to start digging."

"Poor ol' rascal probably never knew what hit him," Jack Springer said, shaking his head. "One minute he was standing down there in the valley, and the next minute the valley was gone. And so was Beecham."

Ray Ferris organized them in groups of five. May Tompkins walked away, saying: "I don't see how y'all can stand this place; it smells like a slop jar." They began methodically pulling away trash, passing wet sacks of garbage from hand to hand until it was finally deposited on another pile farther down.

"Now you're sure this is where he was buried," Ray Ferris said to the Springers.

"Why, sure," Jack Springer said. "I reckon it is. This is 'bout where I backed the truck up to."

And all this time, Dillard sat in the front seat of the Chevrolet, watching them, shaking his head at how Gemma was right there in the middle of it all, up to her knees in God knows what kind of filth. But he would not be the one to snatch her away, not in front of all these church people. Not again. A bad sign. He'd been sure that morning that one of the hens had crowed when he went down to feed them. And then he'd stepped over his pole. Bad luck. You had to take note of that kind of thing when you fished. A wind from the east or passing by a bare-footed woman could be just as bad. He could hear them now; there must have been over a dozen of them out there digging, saying something about Beecham, mumbling something which he couldn't quite hear. His palms began to sweat. He clasped a hand over his heart and whispered: "Bad luck, go away."

Just then two more cars of women from the church pulled up. Dust as thick as gravy hung in the air from all the traffic over the road to the dump. The women emerged from their cars, loaded down with baskets of food and lemonade. Gemma spotted Doreen Hadley standing over a box of foil-covered dishes she'd rested momentarily on the trunk of a car while she adjusted the back of her skirt. "Doreen! It's Beecham," she cried, running through the others toward the woman.

"I know, honey. Bob called us at church." Doreen Hadley opened her arms and held Gemma's head close to her bosom. The girl's glasses slid up on her forehead. "We'll do what we can. With the Lord's help."

Dillard shifted in his seat, slouching down, knowing at once what had happened. He stared across the hood of the Chevrolet at Gemma and Doreen and thought: she's forgot about me; she aint coming back to this car. I'll be dad-blamed if I'm getting out. He rubbed the stubble on his chin and said aloud: "That durned ol' nigger, that durned ol' stupid nigger."

The women spread cloths on the hoods of their cars and laid out the food. Eunice Tanner and Doreen took the tinfoil from the dishes of coleslaw and potato salad and baked beans. "Who brought this congealed salad?" Eunice asked.

"That's mine," May Tompkins said, striding up to Eunice. "I put in a lot of strawberries. Doesn't Brother Tanner like lots of strawberries?" Her wide-mouthed grin formed turned-up corners like those of her glasses.

"I reckon," Eunice said, swatting flies away from the fried chicken.

Doreen stood on the running board and announced that everyone could come eat whenever they wanted. Sid Hanson and Ray Ferris looked up for an instant from their kneeling positions. Dark, grimy mess was smeared to their elbows. May carried paper cups of lemonade to each of the diggers. Gemma shook her head, gazing across the piles of trash. She didn't want any. Midafternoon sun blazed down on them. The smell of food on the car hoods mixed with the odor from the dump, and together they seemed to bake under the sun.

Gemma worked by herself, pulling away layers of waste like a hound looking for a lost bone. The women around the cars had begun to sing "Bringing in the Sheaves." She pulled at an old bicycle pump and fell backward. Sitting down in the muck, she wiped her hands over her shirt and looked down the row of people busily excavating for Beecham. And she told herself: this is what's good about the church. Somebody'll always stand by you in an emergency. For an instant it made her forget the old man buried under ten feet of rubbish.

"Well, I reckon we'll have to have our church supper right here and now," May was saying. She shooed flies from the food and kept children from grabbing at the pies and cakes.

"I got a cherry pie in my car," Gemma called to her, straining her neck to see over a foothill of trash. And around the feast spread over the hood of Brother Tanner's car, the women sang: *We will come rejoicing, bringing in the sheaves.* Some of the men joined in, and their voices echoed above the dump. Gemma wondered if they could be heard in town.

Out from scrubby trees behind the dump, Jordan Loopis

and his baby sister wandered along the dirt path that led back to their place. They stood at a distance, watching the people from Twilight who swarmed over the garbage heap.

"Jordan, come help us," Gemma shouted. "They covered Beecham."

But the boy stood with one arm around his sister, his naked belly protruding over his pants. He whispered something into the girl's ear, watching the activity before him, his eyes huge.

Now aint that how it is, Dillard thought, sitting low in the front seat. Calling out to niggers and rutting around like a pig. She don't even know what she's doing out there. Don't matter long's them others are there doing it with her. And he could hear crickets begin to chirp their evening song in the fields and underneath the crumbling walls of refuse. He thought: *that's* him; that's Beecham singing.

He remembered six years ago when they'd set up the dump. It had meant only one thing: progress. Twilight formed a sanitation department as Greenville and Sulphur Springs had done, and Jack Springer had volunteered to be in charge of trash pickups once a week. For a time, everyone waited down by the road on Saturday mornings with their trash, just to see Jack and Bubba in action. The new dump was situated past the cemetery, right before the turnoff to Hadley's and Dillard's. Hadley raised a fuss at first. With the dump so close, he was afraid the cows would stop giving milk. But they hadn't seemed affected one way or the other.

The dump was the pride of Twilight. Better than any city park. In the beginning, Dillard had seen entire families drive out to it on a Sunday afternoon, just to look, or maybe have a picnic. Each week, they'd measure the garbage to see how much had accumulated since their last visit. Jack Springer had been set to burn it now and then, though he soon discovered that the town might take his job from him if he touched one scrap.

Garbage began to change the shape of the land. Flat stretches of Texas blackland began to form hills and valleys. Inside the dump, a person could stand in one spot and see nothing but waste in every direction. Sometimes they would rummage through the debris, just as Beecham did, and they'd come up with clothes, papers, and possessions they'd discarded months earlier. Finding their own garbage gave life a continuity that had never existed before in Twilight.

May Tompkins began a verse of "Throw Out the Lifeline" as she came up to the Chevrolet. She opened the back door and gasped.

"I didn't know anybody was in here," she said, leaning down to look at Dillard.

He glared over his shoulder at her.

"I'm May Tompkins, the church secretary." She held out her hand. "We sure do enjoy having Gemma there."

"Yeah?" he said, turning from her hand. "Well, why don't you keep her?"

She laughed and said: "My, my, Mr. Dillard," reaching for the pie. "I don't know how they can stand the smell here. You'd think the longer you were around it, the more you'd get used to it. But that just aint so."

Dillard stared her down.

"I'm getting Gemma's pie."

"I see that."

She closed the door, waving to him, soon joining in the hymn again. Dillard watched her traipse through tall grass toward Eunice Tanner's car. She turned midway and called: "Come get you a plate of food, Mr. Dillard. We got plenty here."

Roped in. Railroaded. May stood in the center of everyone, a chicken leg in one hand, and she called: "Y'all really think he's down there?" He muttered: "You got a voice that would sour fresh milk, woman."

"Course he is," Jack Springer said. "I saw him get covered; I ought to know. Just keep yourself quiet."

"Gemma Dillard," May called, "your granddaddy is settin' in that car there, and I bet he'll have a fit when he sees how black your hands are getting. I bet they stink to high heaven."

That's right, Dillard thought, I'm having a fit. But I'm having it where none of you can gawk at me this time. And when I get her home, I'm tanning her hide.

Gemma sat back on her knees, looking at her hands. They were greasy from scooping through the mess. She could see the top of Dillard's hat in the car. He leaned back as though he were asleep, and she thought: he won't care because it's Beecham down there.

May Tompkins stood over her, looking down into the oily mess of matted eggshells and orange peels. "I'd never been to a church where they had a colored person singing," she said, staring downward, hugging her arms. "All heck'd break loose most places. But Brother Tanner told me how y'all loved Beecham, how he'd sing around the hardware store as he swept up and how the congregation would go in to buy something just so they could hear him sing. I remember the first Sunday I was here and he sang 'Nearer My God to Thee' and it was all I could do to keep from clapping."

"Yes, ma'am," Gemma said, wiping a smudge from her glasses.

"People have gotten to expect that old rascal," May said, holding a Kleenex to her nose. "They know he'll be there every Sunday morning—just as regular as Jack Springer's Saturday trash runs."

Eunice Tanner stood on the running board and called her two sons. "I'm sorry, everybody," she said. "I got to get these boys home. I can't wait any longer—that is, if y'all are done with my food. If you do find him now, why I'm not so sure I want these younguns to see."

And by this time, the sun had almost lowered behind the cotton gin. Crickets sang in far hills of garbage, and over the barbed-wire fence in the cemetery. Some of the other women bounced down from the hoods of their cars and agreed with Eunice, saying, why sure, if that old colored man was found now, it wouldn't be a pretty sight for women and children. "Mercy me," May said, hugging herself, gazing across at the plowed fields on the other side of the highway. "I don't think he's in there at all." She walked around the edge of Sid Hanson's pickup and kicked at a crumpled can of Ajax.

Bob Hadley stood up over the mound of greasy muck he'd been working through and said: "Maybe he aint. Maybe he aint down there." He picked broken pecan shells from the palm of his hand. "We dug twelve feet down if we dug one, and he aint nowhere in sight."

"You calling me a liar, Hadley?" Jack Springer's round face burned. He slung a soaked cardboard box away from him and stumbled once when he tried to stand. "I happen to know he's down there."

"I aint calling anybody a liar," Bob Hadley said. "But where is he? Where is he? We been at this quite a spell. Six o'clock, and I'm heading home—Beecham or no Beecham. I got cows to milk."

On her knees, Gemma said: "Y'all can't talk about quitting. You can't leave him down there."

They both looked down at her, blank-faced, wiping their hands across their overalls. She waited for them to give her some assurance that they wouldn't abandon Beecham. But neither of them spoke. They stared at her until she began to dig again. She wouldn't stop; time was precious.

Dillard opened the car door and spit on the ground. "Me too, Mr. Bob Hadley," he muttered. "I'm heading home too."

The women busied themselves around the food, rewrapping, sorting out casserole dishes, loading backseats with leftovers. "Any y'all who didn't get to eat, stop by the church," Eunice Tanner called.

Blowing a kiss to her husband and Gemma, Doreen Hadley said: "I'll be there too if you need me, Bob. Y'all come on to the church; we'll still have our supper." She held her skirt to the back of her legs as she leaned into the car, counting dishes.

Gemma could see some of the Negroes who lived back in the woods where Beecham had his shack. They began to gather along the outskirts of the dump, not far from where Jordan Loopis stood with his sister. Gemma could see them staring across piles of trash at her, at Bob Hadley, Jack Springer, and all the other people who worked so busily over the garbage, and she thought: why do they just stand there?

"Nope, we can't save him now," May Tompkins said, sighing, jiggling her car keys in one hand. "Whatever any of you says, he can't be alive, even if he's down there."

Reverend Dixon, the preacher from the colored church, drove up with some of his congregation. Another car followed close behind. Gemma recognized a few of the women. They fished at Twilight Lake too, and some of them hoed Bob Hadley's cotton.

"We just heard what happened," Reverend Dixon said. "Y'all find Brother Beecham yet?"

He came close to where Gemma worked, and in fact she thought he seemed to be addressing only her. But Sid Hanson brushed one hand over the other and stood, saying: "Naw; it's like trying to find a needle in a haystack, Preacher."

Reverend Dixon nodded. His people who'd come with him huddled behind. Three of the women began to sing "In the Sweet Bye and Bye." Gemma wondered if the putrid smells bothered them. They waited expectantly in their group, watching Bob and Jack and the others as though the stench didn't exist. They waited right there just as the people on the outskirts did. If Beecham was to be found at all, the white people would be able to discover him better than they could.

As the women started their cars and pulled away, Bob Hadley got to his feet. He huffed loudly and put both hands on his hips.

"What's the matter?" Gemma asked from her kneeling position.

Bob Hadley looked at her for a moment, then shook his head. Nobody said anything as he started toward his pickup. "It'll be plumb dark before I round up them cows," he said, getting in, glaring across at Jack and Bubba Springer as though they had played a trick on him.

Sid Hanson and Ray Ferris stood by their trucks also, talking low, turning to look at the jagged mounds of garbage now and then. Jack Springer got up and brushed himself off. He walked over to them, Bubba close behind.

"Y'all can't leave him," Gemma said, her fingers squishing through the grime.

"It's gonna be dark soon," Ray Ferris said. And the others listened to each of his words as though they had been punctuated by some intrinsic truth. Bob Hadley started his pickup and pulled away.

"We can't leave Beecham out here," Gemma said.

Others from the town got into their cars and drove away, talking about the church picnic, about the baseball playoffs at the high school. The sun was low now. Gemma realized that they were all slowly leaving her alone in the valley of trash. The Negroes continued to sing their songs. Reverend Dixon whispered scriptures.

"We gonna stay out here and find nothing, then catch cold to boot," May Tompkins said, her arms wrapped around her. "I don't think there's a soul under that heap of trash." She thought for a moment, then strutted over to her Dodge and got in. "Not a soul."

She pulled away in an orange cloud of dust, momentarily eclipsing the sun on the horizon. Jack and Bubba Springer walked to their dump truck. Jack played with the keys.

"Maybe I *was* wrong," he mumbled, opening the door. "Bubba, d'you pick them tomatoes this morning?"

"I didn't get to 'em."

"I told you yesterday to get them picked; they been on the vine too long as it is."

Bubba Springer muttered something, hitched up his pants, and climbed into the truck beside his father. Jack Springer shook his head, then looked down at the others. "Maybe I was just so used to Beecham being out here that I only thought I saw him," he said. "He might be over in that shack of his right now, having his suppers."

Gemma stared in the direction of Beecham's shack along

with the men. Nobody said anything as Jack Springer started the dump truck.

"Any y'all coming to the church this evening?" he asked just before pulling away.

Ray Ferris nodded; he said he was. Sid didn't know for sure.

"Well, I got to go get cleaned up," Jack said. He laughed and spit into the garbage. "I'm gonna wring that old coot's neck next time I see him."

The dump truck bounced along the road, then turned onto smooth highway. "Okay, let's get to work," Gemma said. But Ray and Sid stood with their hands in their pockets, watching the truck until it disappeared toward Twilight.

"I think we all best get back to town," Sid said.

"Yep," Ray said. "Mandy'll be wanting to know why I'm not home getting ready for the 'do.'"

Gemma got up and walked around the edge of the trash, first one way, then the other. They seemed to be waiting for her to say something, waiting for her to dismiss them. But she was thinking: they'll leave me here; they'll leave me here alone to dig him out. She saw Sid rub at his eyes and glance nervously across at Ray. All at once, she knew there was nothing she could do to keep them. And with her eyes beginning to tear, she went to them.

"This aint no Christian way to be acting," she said.

"Aw, Gemma." Ray tousled her hair and touched her wet cheek. She pulled away.

"And if God cares so wonderful for flowers that are here today and gone tomorrow, won't he more surely care for you, O men of little faith?"

"Gemma, hon," Sid began, "Jack and Bubba made a mistake. Beecham can't be buried down there. We woulda found him by this time."

"None of us looked hard enough," she said, chewing her lip, glaring at them.

"Gemma, we had half the congregation out here digging," Ray said. "He just aint here."

She turned in place, then marched back to the mound of garbage. Sitting once more, she began to shuffle through debris, tossing it right and left. They watched her for some time, then started for their trucks. She didn't look up when she heard them drive away. Yanking at cartons and tin cans, she craned her neck forward, peering into the quickening shadows of trash.

"Gemma, it's getting dark now."

She heard his voice, but didn't turn, not even when she heard the familiar creak and slam of the Chevrolet door. Footsteps sounded close by, and then she heard him say: "They done ate the pie."

"That's what I made it for," she said, pushing up her glasses with the back of her hand.

Dillard stood at the edge of the mound, his hands in his pockets. He looked down at her, then across to the Negroes still gathered in their separate clusters.

"Well, young lady. It's getting dark."

"I know that."

He kicked at a broken badminton racket. "Just how do you expect us to drive home once it's dark?"

"I aint leaving Beecham here."

He sniffled and turned his back. When she looked up, he was framed by the last light of day.

"Them fish is starting to stink. I got to get 'em home; got to get my suppers ready. You been fooling around here long enough."

Gemma got to her feet then, brushing her hands on her pants, wiping a smudge from her face. Coming close to him, she said: "I want you to get down on your hands and knees and help me find Beecham right now. If you don't do it, nobody else will. They all left me here to do it on my own, and now you're gonna have to help."

"Get them niggers to do it."

"You're gonna come down here and help me," she re-

74

peated, trying to pull him downward by the shoulders. He slapped her away.

"What the heck do you think you're doing? Just who do you think you're talking to thataway?"

"They've gone and buried somebody you've known your whole life." She stood just under him, glaring up into his half-closed eyes. After a moment, he backed away. She started to move into him again, but he put out his hand.

"You smell."

She stomped in the muck and went around him to the pile of garbage.

"You smell like I don't know what. I'm getting in that car and I'm going home to eat my suppers. If you want to come with me, fine. If not, then to hell with you. Nobody else but you thinks Beecham got hisself buried. Did you think of that? You're acting like a fool."

With that, he stormed back to the Chevrolet and got in on the driver's side. Gemma heard the car start and peered over a stack of tin cans as he turned the car around and pulled away, swerving onto the highway. She attacked the trash with both fists.

A deep-throated humming filled the air. She could see some of the colored children begin to play leapfrog around their mothers. They hadn't moved from their group. On the edge of the dump, Jordan Loopis still stood watch with his sister and the others from back in the woods. "Go check Beecham's house," Gemma yelled to them. But neither of them moved; neither looked as though they heard what she said.

On the other side of the dump, along the fence that separated it from the cemetery, she could see dense trees. She got up and moved around to that side, touching the fence, feeling the barbs in the wire. In the cemetery on the other side, gray headstones hugged the ground. She could see names on some of them close by—FERRIS, LINDSAY, MULLINS, SPRINGER. The others, those farther away and already shaded deeply by the coming night, were not so easily read. But she knew whom those plots belonged to, which of the old Twilight families would rest finally under the well-kept cemetery grass. Granite slabs blurred together in the distance. Families, she thought. Twilight's best.

Making her way toward the other end of the dump, she stepped high over foothills of garbage. Old shoes and rusted pots and pans began to blend in with the terrain. The rich, deep voices were underscored by cricket chirping. And she thought: why do they stay too? Why are they here when the others have left him? She glanced over her shoulder at the darkening Twilight cemetery and almost stepped on Beecham's hat. She'd never seen it off his head. She picked it up and ran over the hills, stepping from one solid area to another, calling: "Reverend Dixon! I found him, his hat. I found Beecham's hat!"

Even as she ran into the midst of their huddle, out of breath, sweating and beginning to cry, they remained somber. Gemma thrust the hat into the preacher's hands. The man looked down at it, then spoke to two women behind him.

"Dena, let's be going now."

"But this means he's here," Gemma said. "He's been here all the time."

She gripped at his sleeve, but he remained rooted to the earth, his face stern.

"Dena, Miss Jackson, y'all get the kids rounded up and in the cars," he said. "We be goin' now."

As the others did what he said, Gemma put her arms around his middle. The preacher gasped, looking down at her. He unclasped her hands in back and pushed her away.

"He's down there," she said. "I'm telling you, I found his hat."

"Yes, miss. I know that be Beecham's hat." He followed his group to the cars and got into the car. "It be his time now. Brother Beecham be home. Aint nothing more for us to do."

"But we can't leave him here, even if he's dead."

Reverend Dixon started his car and glared at her through the opened window, his chin pointing toward the barbed-wire fence surrounding the Twilight cemetery. "Where you be putting him? Maybe he sang in y'all's church, but he won't be restin' over there."

"I know," she said, "but . . ."

"No, miss. Beecham be home."

Their cars left in a caravan. She was alone. She turned all at once to discover that Jordan Loopis and the others along the outside of the dump had disappeared into the darkened woods. She could barely see her own hands now as they grazed over wadded Kleenex and Coke bottles and soggy cartons. Crickets chirped all around her. They filled the air with a constant drone. Finally she sat down on flat ground, the sound becoming louder around her. She wiped the limp hat across her forehead. The crickets seemed to be closing her tightly into the valley of garbage. She held her hands over her ears, pressing hard. And she closed her eyes, breathing heavily, feeling her own heart almost burst from her chest, and thinking: this is them, they've come for him. The angels have come for him.

A glow began to fill the sky, passing across the horizon like a comet. She stood then to see that it was a car, moving steadily along the Twilight highway. As if drawn by the light, she began to run toward it. She folded the oil-stained hat into her back pocket and it rubbed up and down as she ran. The chirping sound rose around her, seemed to lift her feet from the jagged terrain. The car made a slow solo procession away from her, and she thought: will they leave me? Will they not bother to let me catch up?

The dump was dark. She looked back once, feeling sick, feeling a weight on her chest as though she'd been buried herself. From the turnoff onto the highway, the dump looked like a giant island rising from a flat, black sea, a giant granite island hugging the orange sky.

Sweeping the house after dark casts bad luck in the wind.

"Coffee?"

He could hear her on the porch. A board creaked. He finished putting the pot of coffee on the stove and stood in the doorway, staring through the dark recesses of her room, the front room, and toward the screened-in porch. "Put my gear away before you come in."

Not a sound came from the front of the house.

"I got coffee on, if you want some."

He stood framed in the door for a moment, then turned to finish cleaning the fish in the sink, thinking: let her stew. Let her stay out yonder and pout all damn night if that's what she wants. What did she expect me to do out there? I'm too old for this kind of treatment.

He sat at the table and took off his shoes, then put his feet next to the stove. His socks were damp. The sky, framed like a picture over the kitchen sink, was black. Now and then a june bug would batter against the screen. Dillard smacked his lips and bent forward to feel his long, bony toes through his socks. They were cold; they didn't seem to be a part of him. He wondered if that was where blood stopped flowing first, when the end was near.

"Hey, Gemma."

The front screen hadn't slammed. She was still out there, putting away his gear, taking her time, dawdling. She didn't appreciate what he'd done for her one iota. She'd never had to live anywhere that her wants and needs just weren't all laid out for her.

"Coffee's perkin'," he said, one foot rubbing against the other, then across the cat's head. It startled him when he turned and saw her standing in the doorway. She watched him get up and pour himself a cup. "I can't drink this whole pot here by myself."

"I'll fix my own coffee," she said, stepping back into her dark room. "After you gone to bed."

He leaned over the table, craning his neck, trying to peer into the room after her. He couldn't see what she was up to, though he knew. By the familiar harmony of bedsprings and page turning over page, he knew she was sitting in the dark with her glasses on. Reading.

"Gemma, get in here and start them taters cookin'." He scratched Max's ear with his big toe. The cat purred, then jumped onto his lap.

"Your ol' tomcat wants to eat, Gemma," he called. "You gonna let him starve?"

"Wouldn't matter none to you."

Her voice came from the black room, strong, deep as a grownup's. He wondered if she'd put away his fishing poles, if she'd straightened his tackle and left the front porch just as he liked it. She knew better than to leave the poles leaning against the house. "Did you do a good job out yonder?" She was quiet for a moment while he sipped his coffee and rubbed the back of Max's head. Then she appeared in the doorway again. She came forward and set a mason jar full of grasshoppers on the table.

"A few left over," he said, forcing a grin. "Didn't use too many today. Them don't look like no 'count. Might just as well throw 'em out. We can catch us a new batch before we go down yonder tomorrow."

"I aint going nowhere," she said. Her face was dark, smudged with greasy traces of garbage and veiled with a somberness that made him uneasy. "I aint doin' nothing else with you."

Max jumped down and lumbered over to where she stood in the door. He sniffed around her and jumped for her hands just as she tucked them into the top of her overalls. Dillard knew Max could smell those grasshoppers. A cat, he'd discovered, could sniff out about anything.

"Is everything put in order out there?" Along one end of the porch he'd stacked crates to make shelves for his fishing gear. He had hooks and lines and sinkers, and all sorts of fancy lures painted every color of the rainbow. And he knew where everything was. He could walk out onto the porch with his eyes closed and find whatever he wanted. It saved time, good fishing time.

"The wages of sin is death," she muttered, her eyes cloudy behind her glasses. She picked up the jar of grasshoppers and held it up to her face. Dillard thought they must all be dead. They'd been closed in the jar all day.

"I asked you a question. Did you get everything in order out yonder?"

She leaned forward and set the jar on the floor and buried her hands in her overalls again. Max crouched beside it, his nose at the glass.

"The soul that sinneth, it shall die," she said.

Now there was nothing he could do out there, he told himself, looking away from her, looking at the rows of chickens on the wallpaper. She should know that. Nothing anybody in Twilight could do.

"I want you to stop that talk, young lady. Just because it didn't go your way. You know, the sooner you learn you can't be bossing people to do things your way, the sooner you'll get along. Not everybody'll put up with it. Some people got just as much right to their way of life as you do."

Still watching him, she reached into her back pocket and pulled out Beecham's hat. She dangled it in front of her, limp, worn. Max sat up and sniffed the air.

"What the heck is that?"

"You know."

He rubbed his eyes with his fingers and leaned both elbows on the table.

"Where did it come from?"

"You know where. I found it when you and everybody else left. I found it when all y'all had gave up." She tossed the hat at him. It landed in the center of the table. "The wages of sin is death."

"Stop that talk," he said, his voice higher than usual. "Stop it right now, or I'll blister you good. I don't want to hear none of it."

He pushed his chair away from the table and got up, moving first to the stove, then around the room to the sink. He wrapped the cleaned fish in newspaper and put them into the freezer. Gemma stood behind him, motionless. "And get that thing off my kitchen table. No telling how dirty it is."

"I was the only one left out there. I just stumbled over it. Right there on the ground. It'd been there all along, but nobody else saw it."

"It looks like a piece of garbage, that's why. How the heck would anyone know?"

"We know."

He clenched his fists several times and stared out into the darkness.

"Aint anybody ever seen it off his head," Gemma said. "'Cept maybe you."

Dillard continued to face the darkness, though he could focus only as far as the rusted screen. Sometimes a bug attracted by the light in the kitchen would bounce off the screen and he would flinch. "Durned ol' stupid nigger."

"He's one of God's children."

"Well, he aint nothing now, so shut that up." He turned to glare at her. "I'm telling you, you're pushing me, girl. You're pushing me to just ship you off to Dallas. Let them Monroes worry over you." He came back to the table and sat with his head in his hands. They were quiet for a time; the only sound in the room was from Max's teeth clinking against the mason jar. "I told you to get that filthy hat off my table."

Gemma reached for it and then disappeared into her room. His head in his hands, Dillard could see the smudge Beecham's hat had made on the oilcloth. And when he closed his eyes, they were running. Down furrow after freshly plowed furrow, laughing, reaching out sometimes to knock the other off balance. "I be winning you, Homer." And he would gulp for air, trying not to laugh, trying to keep up with the long-legged colored boy who ran next to him. "I be winning you." "No, you aint." Then they were in the cornfield, and he could barely see the boy two rows away. But he could hear his peals of laughter, could hear the stalks being shoved this way and that over there, just as he was doing along his row. The furrows wound downward, lazily, and he knew they were about to the end, with sudden open spaces just ahead. He seemed to be propelled forward into free air, along the eroded terrain toward the pond. But the colored boy raced ahead, his mouth wide, shouting to the open sky as they made for the pond. Homer's feet hardly touched the ground. He watched the shining black limbs become bare, and almost tripped over the clothing in the path. "I be the winner, Homer!" And Homer stood on the bank, clumsily peeling down his overalls and kicking off his heavy shoes, laughing when he dove into the water with his socks still on. As he stood in water up to his neck, just managing to get the soaked wool socks from his feet, the boy came upon him from underneath and lifted him into the air. They screamed and shouted as Homer tossed the wet balls of wool onto the muddy bank, and then scuffled chest to chest, their arms holding each other in an awkward embrace. And then later, as they floated on their backs side by side, floated lazily so they could get their breaths, he thought: I'll be in trouble. If someone catches us lying like this, I'll be in trouble. And under the water, he encircled the shiny black torso and held the boy closely. When the boy shrieked and struggled away, he floated by himself, gently, gazing up at the cloudless sky.

Dillard sat up straight. He stretched out his legs and turned his feet each way. His socks were dry. He drank the rest of his coffee and looked into the bottom of his cup, at how the last of the brown liquid sank to the center. Finally Gemma came from her room. She sat across from him at the table.

"You think Beecham's dead?"

He got up without speaking and poured himself another cup of coffee.

"Because if you don't think he's dead, we have to go back out there."

"He's dead," Dillard said, his voice scratchy. "Dead as a doornail. Nobody could live under all that garbage."

They sat quietly, both watching Max paw the jar of grasshoppers. Dillard sighed, belched, and shook his head. He got up from the table slowly and said: "I thought we'd chicken-fry them steaks I picked up in town. Start up them taters so we can get supper done with."

He moved to the sink, then to the refrigerator.

"I aint eating."

She got up and went back to her room. Dillard laid the steaks on the counter.

"I'm settin' this table, Gemma." He took two plates from the cupboard. "I'm eatin' whether you do or not. You're gonna have to fix it yourself if you don't eat now."

He cut potatoes into large chunks, then put them into the frying pan. "What you doing in there?" he called, hearing her rustle around the room. "You're gonna ruin your eyes reading in the dark. I told you, they'll be worse than mine."

Max sat at his feet while he stabbed at the potatoes in the pan. Sometimes, the cat would return to the jar of grasshoppers just to make sure he hadn't missed some way of getting to them. Then he'd come back to Dillard's feet. Max liked his potatoes in big chunks too. Pudd had been the one that didn't like fried potatoes. They'd had to shoot him. Gemma'd only been four or five. They'd had to shoot Pudd because he'd gotten a festering sore between his eyes. It had never healed; it oozed constantly.

One morning before they'd taken off for Twilight Lake, they'd taken the cat out into a back field and shot him. Gemma stood behind, holding a shovel. Dillard had dug a hole next to where Pudd fell. Then they'd scooted the cat into the hole and covered him. He'd had to leave the child there; she refused to come to the barge that day. When he came home that night, she was still squatting in the field, standing watch over the tiny mound of dirt.

"What you reading, Gemma?"

He could hear her turning pages.

"Might do you good to sit here with me," she said. "I'll read to you."

He poked at the steaks with a fork, not turning around.

"Come here and sit."

"There wasn't a blame thing I coulda done," he said all at once, turning. She stood in the doorway. "You think I shoulda jumped in all that mess with the rest of you? You think that woulda saved him?"

"Sit." She glared at him through her thick glasses, her lips pressed firmly together, her Bible against her chest. "After death, the judgment."

He yanked the pan from the fire and turned off the stove. "Listen, missy. I got news for you. Some things is just meant to be. I don't care how willful you decide to be about it. I 'bout had it up to here, I can tell you that. I don't know who the heck you think you are. I sure to hell wish your mama was here. I'd give her a lickin' for dumping some snotnose on me like that."

"Nobody dumped me anywhere."

"The heck they didn't. I ought to know. I been the one having to put up with you for the past eleven years."

"Nobody dumped me; I'm here 'cause I want to be."

"Haw."

He stood at the table, staring down at her with both hands on his hips.

"I'm here to take care of you," she said, glaring back at him. "I could have gone if I'd wanted."

"That right?"

"Yes, it is. I could have."

"Then why the hell didn't you?"

"I wish I had. My mama was here just the other day to see how I was getting on, and I wish I'd gone with her."

Dillard watched her for a moment, then sat slowly at the table.

"She said I could come live with her in Fort Worth, but I said I was fine where I was."

"Fort Worth?"

"Yeah. She came for me."

Dillard didn't say anything, didn't take his eyes from her. Then: "If you're lying, I'll tan your hide."

"I aint. I know my own mama." She laid the Bible on the table. "I seen her picture enough to know who she is. She come right up while I was hanging out clothes and you was out in the chicken yard."

"When?" he asked, his voice constrained. "When was this?"

"Week ago or so."

"You're lying," he said, clenching his jaw. He beat his thigh with a fist and repeated: "You are standing there lying to me."

"No, I aint. I walked her to her shiny new car and told her you'd sure be sorry you missed her. But that we'd see her next time. Yes, I told her to come back and see us anytime."

Dillard sat, his fists into his groin. He glared down at the floor, his eyes wide. Something in his stomach rumbled.

"Pop?"

Though his vision was blurred, he could make out her form on the other side of the table, standing with her arms crossed, looking smug, looking like she knew it all. Dillard's head drooped against his chest. He rocked forward, his fists still against his lap.

"You okay, Pop?"

And he turned from her then, so she couldn't see the wetness around his failing eyes, turned and stared at the washing machine behind him on the darkened porch.

"When was it Juanelle was here?"

"I told you. A week or so ago. You was out with the chickens."

He nodded as though her answer was satisfactory, but he seemed to be waiting for something else. He felt a rushing in his ears suddenly that made him off balance.

"I told her we was just fine," Gemma said. "I told her I reckoned she made that long trip for nothing, 'cause you needed me here." Dillard kicked the cat away. "But I was wrong. I shoulda gone with her then and there. You don't need me here. You're so ornery, you don't need anybody."

"That's just what I been telling you for years."

"Well, I aint living here no more. I aint living with nobody who could do what you done out yonder at the dump. I'd rather live with my mama."

Dillard stood slowly, got his balance, then moved to the door. "If I can find Juanelle, I'll ship you off to her first thing tomorrow."

"Don't worry. I know where she is."

He turned to her then, blank-faced, his lip quivering. She sat at the table with her arms folded, her nose in the air. Though he couldn't help it, he knew he was about to whip her. In nothing flat. Before he turned to stomp out the back door, he said: "Get them grasshoppers outta here!" And when the back screen slammed, he could still see her narrow eyes behind those glasses, her thin-pressed lips, and that self-righteous expression that made him want to hunt down the razor strap.

Leaning against the butane tank, he could see her silhouette in the doorway. She stood with both hands on her hips, her neck stretched forward. That was just the way Juanelle stood. Both of them had inherited a sluggish sort of slouch from some-where—surely not from his side of the family. Gemma called him a few times, but he sat very still so she couldn't see where he was. He didn't expect she could see him in the darkness, but then he remembered how she was able to read that Bible in her room without turning on a light. Dillard folded his arms, watching her, hearing her voice lilt through the stillness, hearing how it had already begun to change, to take on a richer, adult tone. And he thought: she was such a sweet little girl. She'd have been better off sitting out here with me till she was grown rather than get mixed up with that church. "I ruined her," he whispered aloud. "I let her be swayed."

As though she had either spotted him or been repelled by the sound of his voice, Gemma returned to the kitchen. She stood over the kitchen sink. He could see a reflection from her glasses now and then, though he couldn't tell what she was doing. Light from inside spread over the yard in a wide shaft. He leaned against the butane tank, wondering just how long she'd let him sit out there before she came to fetch him. Max sauntered across the yard, through the field of light, toward him. Dillard leaned over, picked up the cat, and placed him gently on the tank beside him. They waited together.

Suddenly organ music came from the kitchen, and Dillard remembered: this was Saturday evening. If she had gone to the church social as she'd planned, he would have had a Saturday night free from listening to Oral Roberts. Every week, she listened and laid her hands on the Zenith radio to find her "point of contact" with the Lord. That's what Brother Oral said to do. His voice came clearly from the house as though he were sitting in Dillard's kitchen, talking to Gemma while she held to the radio for dear life. And as usual, Dillard shook his head and muttered. He had no business with any child.

Max stiffened. A horny toad moved through tall grass on the other side of the tank, and the cat leapt from his perch beside Dillard. He watched the cat chase out to Bob Hadley's tractor parked in the lot, and then back. Max circled the tank several times, then sat at Dillard's feet.

"Make your mind up," Dillard said to him. "I aint gonna be bending down every two seconds to put you up here if you're just gonna hop down again."

He watched Max for a few moments, that soaring voice from the radio swelling through the air around him, and then finally he picked up the cat again. Max crouched on the smooth surface, peering into the tall grass. Dillard tapped him on the head, and the cat sat up quickly.

"See there," he said, his eyes locked with the cat's. "You have sense enough to see that I mean what I say."

And all at once, a breeze stirred, rocking the cedar poles holding up the clothesline. He could hear the poles groan and creak, and he thought of sitting in the old Ford with the motor running. Across from the Rialto in Twilight, the theater now long vacant and boarded up, he sat with the motor running because she told him she'd be out at eight o'clock. And Dillard would see mothers and fathers come for their children, come stand under the solid ceiling of tiny white bulbs until the movie let out. Brightly colored movie posters were encased in glass, and Thelma Goins sat in the ticket booth, talking to some of those parents, telling about the film she'd only been able to see in bits and pieces. Dillard had rolled down his window and tried to hear what she was saying. Juanelle always told him to wait in the car. Some of the other parents came in, or waited at the door. But she didn't need that. He could wait in the car, across the street, she said. And he would spot the same parents week after week, parents of Juanelle's friends, as they gathered under the dazzling marquee. Soon their children would be on the sidewalk, shouting with their friends, making their fathers come look at a certain photograph next to the poster under glass. Dillard gripped the steering wheel, the motor running, and he would wait until they had all gone, until Thelma Goins had sold tickets for the last show and closed down her booth. And then Juanelle would traipse across the street, pushing scraggly hair from her face. As she got into the car, he'd say: "I thought you wasn't coming; all those others left." She'd sigh in the dark next to him as they drove out of town, and say: "I wanted to see the beginning again," or "I was in the bathroom."

And now the cedar poles made moaning noises in the

night, just as the shutters did across the locked-up doors of the Rialto. It was dark now, vacant, the tiny white lights all removed and their sockets rusted, the display cases for the posters all broken, and the same yellowed shade still drawn closed over Thelma Goins's ticket window, the way she'd pulled it ten years ago. Juanelle never wanted him to fetch her from the movies; he knew that. And later, when she was older, when those boys would come by for her and she would leave without telling him anything, he would wait across the darkened street from the theater again, wait till she came out with two or three of them, smoking. They would all be drinking out of the same Coke bottle, and with the lights out, with his motor cut, he would watch as a couple of them got into the back seat with her. He would think: I'm still waiting for her. It would make him sad and angry at the same time. He'd drive home afterward, feeling empty, wondering if it would make any difference to her if she knew.

The house was quiet. Her program was over, and the radio was turned off. Maybe now she'll come get me, he thought. Not a sound came from the kitchen.

"Hardheaded," he said to Max, shaking his head. "Either you and me can sit out here all night, or we can go in and get our suppers over with."

Max followed him to the door.

"Gemma."

He pulled at the handle, then kicked the screen.

"Gemma, come unlock this here door and let me in."

Cora. Cora had been the same. She'd taken the mattress from their bed and dragged it down the road. She said she wouldn't sleep with him till he washed the cow smell from his hands. They smelled like udders, she said, and he wasn't about to touch her till he washed his hands. He let her sleep outside two nights before he called her in. She dragged the mattress back inside, but slept with Juanelle in the back room. It was only a week later that she headed for Baton Rouge to visit her sister. Visit her sister, he thought now to himself. Some joke.

Dillard walked to the front of the house. The screen was latched there too. He could see inside the screened-in porch enough to tell that she hadn't done what he'd told her to do. Max was at his heels.

"Gemma!" His tackle was all over the porch, just as he'd left it. "Gemma Louise! Open this door or I'll tan your hide."

The cat whimpered. Poor thing, Dillard thought. You must be starved too.

"Gemma! You aint even my relations, you know that? You aint even kin to me!"

He sat on the steps and hugged his arms around him. The night air was damp and he didn't have on his shoes. Did she know that? He'd catch his death because she'd locked him out of his own house without shoes.

"Are you gonna open this door?"

He got up and banged on the screen. Nothing, she'd done nothing that he told her to do. "I can beat in this door, and then you'll get a lickin'. The lickin' of your life."

Max sat at the bottom of the steps with his tail curled around his feet. Juanelle'd be the one to get the licking, he said to himself, if she ever dared show her face again and not take that child. Leaving him with that squalling baby. What did they all take him for?

He walked across the yard in his socks, past the Chevrolet to the car shed. As high-and-mighty as she was, Gemma would go to bed and leave him outside all night. He knew she would. He grabbed an armload of old Greenville papers and carried them to the front steps. Then he went back for the can of gasoline. Wadding up sheet after sheet of the newspaper, he thought: leave me out here all night and feel justified about doing it. He made a pile of newspaper next to the front steps. It lit with just a few splashes of gasoline. He had himself a bonfire.

"I can sit out here all night, Gemma. I can sit here, and it aint gonna matter none to me. But I can tell you, if I do, if you don't open this door right now, I'll mail you right to your mama as soon as the sun comes up. I aint got time for this."

The house was quiet. Somewhere inside, a light went out.

"I can burn you outta there. How'd you like that? I don't know you're any relation to me nohow."

And all at once he remembered the old colored man buried under a ton of garbage out in the Twilight dump. He stared at black floating cinders as they rose from the fire. He thought of his daughter, still making trouble behind his back. Just then a weariness ached through him. He could do it; he could burn her out. Why not burn her out? She'd beat him down, just like she'd been trying to do all along. They'd all beat him down. He could slop gasoline over the porch, through the meshed screen. He could soak his tackle, could douse the entire porch until the can was empty, then toss a match to it. What would it matter? Wouldn't think twice. Then she'd open up; she'd open up fast.

Breathing heavily, he dropped the can at his feet. It was empty. Max had retreated underneath the Chevrolet. Sickly fumes came from the front of the house. He could see the liquid glisten on the porch, gleam like sweat on a black man. All his fishing gear took on an iridescent glow. He could do it. The house would explode into flames as soon as he struck a match. And he didn't care.

"Come back in the house."

He turned quickly, jerking backward when he saw her. She stood just behind him, wearing her nightshirt. The matchbook crumpled in his hands. Gulping for air, he watched her. She looked like a spook.

"How'd you get out here?"

"Come on in." She started back around the house, saying: "I'll fix them steaks."

As if drawn by some invisible leash, he followed the white waving nightshirt as it trailed across the yard, through the field of light coming from the kitchen window, and up the back steps. His hands smelled of gasoline. He stopped at the cistern to wash them, looking down into the dark, cool earth. And somewhere in that void he could hear someone whispering: *You're the man now, Homer. You have to be the man.*

Standing in the doorway to the kitchen, he waited for her to say something. He couldn't see her eyes through those glasses.

"Thought you'd gone to sleep," he muttered, not moving.

She stood over the counter, dipping the steaks in flour and egg.

"I liked to catch my death out there," he said. "I didn't have no shoes on. You want me to catch my death?"

"You aren't catching nothing," she said, her back to him. Max came to the door, and Dillard let him in before he sat at the table.

"I 'bout did."

She went to the refrigerator for milk, then poured it in the pan. A little at a time, she added flour to make the gravy. Max sat in one of the kitchen chairs across from Dillard, his chin on the table. He kept his eyes on the old man as he drank his coffee.

"You got no right locking me outta my own house. I don't care what you think about me. I aint done nothing. I give you that room in there. I kept you all these years."

"I'll get me a job when I'm at my mama's. I'll send money to pay you back."

"I aint asking for no reward. Just not to be locked outta my own home in the dead of night." He pushed the cup aside and folded his hands on the table. "'Sides, you can't pay me back all that time. Time don't mean nothing to you yet. You aint old enough."

She used a fork to stir the gravy. Over her shoulder, she asked: "You drinking iced tea or coffee?"

Coffee, he told her, but a fresh cup. His was cold. She brought their plates to the table, then poured him another cup, and one for herself. She sat down without looking at him and began to eat.

"You fixed them steaks real nice," he said.

She chewed each mouthful, looking past him, looking down sometimes at Max in the chair next to hers.

"You reckon Beecham knew we was all out there digging, trying to save him?" she asked suddenly.

Dillard put down his knife and held his coffee cup close to his face. "I 'spect he didn't. I 'spect he didn't know nothing for too long. 'Cept that garbage was coming in at him from every direction. He probably didn't know y'all was there."

"I was hoping he knew," she said, staring off into space. At once he was able to see her eyes through those thick glasses. They were red. There was something stubborn in her look, as though she didn't believe him. But there was also something sad, defeated, something that he would never be able to soothe as long as he lived. It wasn't in his power to, and seeing how helpless he was instantly shattered something in his soul.

Dillard cleared his throat, wanting to say something, wanting somehow to make the right gesture. But he noticed the mason jar of grasshoppers, and said: "I told you to get them things off the table."

He reached for the jar. At the same time, Max swatted at his hand and the grasshoppers crashed to the floor. Jagged pieces of glass and dead grasshoppers splashed across the floor around the table. Max perched on the edge of his seat, ready to pounce. Dillard felt his throat tighten, and he sprang for the cat so he wouldn't jump.

"Gemma, put him in my room and shut the door," he said, frightened, feeling a rush of excitement travel through the cat. Once Gemma had the cat in her arms, he sat back in his chair.

"I'll get the broom," she said thickly. He could hear her close the door to his room. His hands shook over the plate.

"No! Come back to the table. Them grasshoppers'll have to wait till we're done with our suppers."

He watched her wade through the broken glass, watched her shoes trample over the small dead creatures. When she was seated again, she said: "You'll cut your feet when you get up."

"No, I won't."

She stabbed at a fried potato with her fork and said, still looking at her plate: "I decided. I'm going to my mama's."

"No, I decided. And that's right, you are."

They didn't say anything for a moment. Suddenly she brought a hand to her mouth.

"I forgot to say the blessing."

Dillard put down his fork and let his hands go limp in his lap. As she mumbled off the prayer, the same prayer she insisted upon chanting every mealtime, he thought he could smell nauseating fumes as they came through the house. After supper, he'd have to hose down the porch. He'd have to sweep up all those dead grasshoppers and glass, getting down on his hands and knees to make sure he got it all. Max might get some in a paw if he wasn't careful. Yes, he'd be glad to ship her off. Be done with it all. And brother, he muttered with her "Amen," he'd shed no tears.

🐓 *Never look back after starting a trip.*

Katie Lawson had taught them about timetables in fifth grade. They had planned imaginary trips in social studies, using the bus schedules Miss Lawson had given each of them. Gemma had folded and refolded the sample from Lone Star Lines so many times that the creases had had to be taped. And she had memorized the arrival and departure times, that minute of the day when a bus would pull down the main street of Twilight and stop in front of Ferris Hardware for passengers. At 12:04 every afternoon, a bus came in from Dallas, headed for Wichita Falls. She knew that one pulled through for Waco at 6:30. Sometimes on their Friday morning egg runs, she would sit in front of Woody's, waiting while Dillard was inside, and she would see a bus pull through with HOUSTON or LUBBOCK across the top and she would know that it was 10:45 or 11:30. She'd know without looking.

Fully dressed in overalls and her best white shirt, she got down on her hands and knees and reached for the shoe box underneath her bed. The timetables were inside. Though it was almost too dark to read it, she ran a fingernail across the line that said FORT WORTH and knew from memory that the time was 7:05. She put the schedule into her pocket, then reached into the shoe box for her color postcards. They almost filled the box. On her knees, she spread them across her bed. It was still made, hadn't been slept in all night. She sorted through all the cards—

95

the Alamo, the Grand Canyon, the Washington Monument—
and decided which ones she'd take. Miss Lawson had given
them to her. She'd given everyone in the class a selected few,
but she'd given Gemma the shoe box full of cards when school
was out for the summer. A kind of "going-away present," the
teacher told her, smiling, because Gemma was so interested.
They were all pictures of places the teacher had visited at one
time or another, places she helped them plan imaginary trips to.
And now Gemma smiled, just as she had when Miss Lawson
handed her the shoe box. She might be visiting some of those
places soon herself.

She squinted at them, fanning them across her bed. She
selected ones of the stockyards in Fort Worth, of the Will Rogers
Coliseum, of bluebonnets on a hill below the county courthouse,
of old cowboys sitting on wooden porches along the main street
of the city. She'd see these for herself. And she took others too, of
San Antonio, of the marketplace in Matamoros, just over the
border, and of the state fair in Dallas. She might even see those
one day. She gathered the other postcards, put them back into
the shoe box, and shoved it underneath the bed. The night
before, she had cut two photographs of her mother from the
photo album and put them in the back of her Bible. She checked
again to see they were there, along with the slip of paper that said
Mrs. Frank King, with the Fort Worth address. The scrap of paper
smelled sweet. She put the postcards and her Bible into the small
cardboard suitcase she'd taken from underneath his bed while he
was outside the night before, muttering to himself, clucking like
one of his chickens while he hosed down the porch.

After she finished packing, she lay down again on her bed,
fully clothed, her horn-rimmed glasses in place. Too early to
leave. The bus would not pull through Twilight for several
hours. She watched the ceiling as flowerlike water markings
became sharper in the early light. Then she sat on the edge of
her bed, thinking: at 7:05, the bus to Fort Worth, arriving at 9:00.
I'll be there for dinner.

She opened the suitcase once more to make sure she hadn't

forgotten anything. Standing in the middle of her room, the suitcase in her hand, she suddenly remembered Beecham's hat. It felt damp when she took it from underneath her pillow and tucked it into the suitcase.

Floorboards creaked under her in the kitchen, and the light just before dawn seemed to make the chickens on the wallpaper dance around the room. She stood at his door, opening it slightly, just enough to see him lying on his back in the center of the bed. He slept with the sheet clutched at his stomach. She watched his chest, waited to see the white long underwear rise and fall several times. His mouth was open, slack, and sometimes hoarse sounds came out with his breath, hoarse scratching sounds as though he were talking to someone in his dreams. And then he smacked his lips together and jerked his head to one side, so that she could see his face fully. His fists brought the sheet up under his chin, and she thought: a kid, he aint nothing more than a kid.

She slipped past the screen without a sound, and stepped into the yard. Stars still filled the morning sky. Glancing back at the house only briefly, she headed down the path between the pecan trees, hidden now by the crape myrtle and morning darkness. A few of the hens rutted around the chicken yard. They made gravelly sounds in their throats when she came inside and walked across the beaten dusty ground.

"Hush," she whispered, her finger to her lips.

And when she opened the door of the henhouse, the others inside sat on their roosts or in their nests, awake, watching her. The two roosters ran past her into the yard, spitting, clawing the earth.

"My bus leaves at 7:05," she whispered, beginning to rummage through the hay in each of the nests. "I won't be here to get your eggs no more."

They began to cluck and flap their wings. Some hit the ground with a thud to get out of her way as she moved down the row, bits of hay twirling through the air, dust stirring. She felt each nest methodically, searching under straw and feathers.

On all sides of her now, chickens were moving, craning their necks, stretching, strutting out of her way. Finally at the last nest, she found it. She wiped a hand over the top of the cigar box and blew across it. A hen screeched and toppled from a nest above her to the ground as she opened the box and took out the coins and wadded-up bills.

"I knew they was here," she whispered, watching the hen scurry for the door. She dropped the cigar box and counted the money. Three hens watched her from their nests across the henhouse. She whistled. "I didn't think it would be so much."

Outside, one of the roosters, Handsome or Ulysses, began to crow. Gemma quickly shoved the money into her pocket. She stared back at the hens and said: "This money is just as much mine as his." They clucked. She left the henhouse quickly, picked up her suitcase, and closed the gate to the yard behind her. As she moved through the pecan trees, she heard the rooster crow again, and then the sound was answered and matched by one of the hens. The crowing made her stop in her tracks. She stared back toward the chicken yard, and almost immediately the back screen slammed.

"I'm coming," Dillard called. She could hear his boots thud over the ground, just behind the crape myrtle. "Just hold your horses."

In a flash Gemma ran through the pecan trees, making a wide circle around the house. She could still hear his footsteps, plodding steadily toward the chicken yard, but she dared not look back. She knew she was making too much noise. Finally the road was in sight. She crossed it, ran across one of Bob Hadley's plowed fields toward the highway, and flagged down a pickup going into Twilight.

And a short time later, when she was sitting high above the road in a Lone Star bus with her suitcase in the luggage rack, she heard a siren. The other passengers on the bus were asleep. Two soldiers who sat across the aisle from her were smoking and showing each other photographs. The siren was someplace far behind them on the flat stretch of highway. And then it was just behind the bus, passing it, moving swiftly ahead so that she had to crane her neck and press against the glass to see the red and white ambulance with flashing lights before it disappeared down the straight road ahead of them into the horizon. Gemma sat back and closed her eyes; her stomach ached. She stood uneasily and tried to get her suitcase down from the rack. One of the soldiers helped her, then continued his conversation with his friend. The bus rushed past a sign that told how many miles they were from somewhere, but she couldn't see. She sat back in the soft leather seat, studying each postcard again and again. At McKinney—that was on the schedule, she'd seen that place on the schedule—one of the soldiers put his wallet back into his jacket, reached for his duffel bag, and tipped his cap to her as he got off.

The bus started again, swinging around onto open highway like a sailing ship. The Alamo, the Grand Canyon, the Washington Monument. The Alamo . . .

FORT WORTH

If your thumb joint itches, expect an unwelcome visitor.

Outside the gas station, a man in blue overalls and a cap stared as she got out of the pickup and set her suitcase on the pavement. She saw the address over the door and checked the slip of paper. This was it: 7296 Jacksboro Highway. And then as she nodded to the man in the pickup and it pulled away, rattling loudly until its clatter meshed with other traffic noises, she picked up her suitcase and trudged over to the pumps. The man went about his business, aware of her, but not looking now. He filled the Pontiac, took some money from the woman in the front seat, and saluted as she drove off into the traffic. Just like that soldier, Gemma thought. Just like that soldier on the bus. Just like those soldiers in the magazines.

This part of the highway was densely populated with low, flat buildings. Gas stations, diners, beauty parlors, shops that sold auto parts. The strip of pavement was congested with cars, trucks, and huge diesels, bearing down the long, straight road in either direction. The flow was constant. Horns blared here, then farther down the line of traffic. Engines churned discordantly as they slowed. And on both sides of the road, an amber cloud of dust whirled over gravel. It changed the color of the sky along the horizon for as far as she could see. It made her mouth feel dry, made it taste like grit.

Gemma dragged her suitcase across the pavement, stepping on the long black hose by accident and ringing the bell. The man looked up at her once.

"What can I do for you today?"

She came to the door of the gas station, where he stood framed, the money still in his hand. He took a red cloth from his back pocket and wiped his forehead. Grime smeared with his sweat. He was tall, taller than Dillard or any other man she'd known before. His eyes were on her now, big, blue, and watery, as though they perspired too in the July heat. His hair was sandy-colored, almost like hers. It was cut close, shaved up over the ears. When he smiled, his teeth were crooked.

"I come to see Mrs. Frank King," Gemma said, putting down the suitcase, giving him the slip of paper.

The man took it from her, read it, and turned it over as though he expected something else to be written on the back. He looked at Gemma again, his look changing slightly, his mouth closed and covering the big crooked teeth.

"I was give this address for Mrs. Frank King."

"Yep. This is the right place," he said, returning the slip of paper. He looked at her for a moment, then walked around the side of the building and into the double-doored garage. He slid underneath a car which had been jacked up in front and began tinkering with something. Gemma followed. She stood at his feet, looking down as his long-fingered hand came from underneath and moved like a spider till it found a wrench.

"Is Mrs. Frank King here?"

At first he didn't say anything, then: "She's here."

"She live in a gas station?"

Gemma could hear something clank underneath the car. Outside, the traffic churned. Someone shouted in Spanish, then two horns blared.

"Juanelle lives upstairs. We got a place upstairs." He coughed and dropped the wrench at his side. "I'm Frank King."

Gemma squatted and looked beneath the car. His eyes were on her. She reached out a hand, and said: "Well, my name's

Gemma Dillard, and my mama told me her name was Mrs. Frank King."

He wiped a hand on the rag and shook hers. "Juanelle expecting you?"

Gemma bit her lip. "I reckon she aint. She just give me this slip of paper and told me to get in touch with her if I ever needed something."

His eyes still trained intensely on her, he said: "You need something, Gemma Dillard?"

Gemma steadied herself by touching the pavement. She turned to stare out at the glaring movement of automobiles. She had never seen so many different kinds all together, one right after the other, as though they were all either coming from or going to the same place.

"I reckon I need a place to live," Gemma said.

Frank looked at her, then his eyes darted down to his side. He groped till he found the wrench again.

"How'd you get here?" he asked, resuming his work.

"Bus."

"But how'd you get *here*? The bus station is downtown a ways."

Gemma knelt beside the car and wiped her forearm across her face. "A man at the station seen me standing there with my suitcase. He asked where I was going. He said he was coming out this way and I could ride with him. He had a brand-new pickup."

"I seen it."

"Well, that's how I got here."

Neither of them said anything for a few moments. Sometimes the clank of his wrench made her flinch. All at once, Frank pushed himself out from underneath the car. She almost fell backward getting to her feet. He went to a workbench in the back of the garage and lit a Camel.

"You know, you shouldn't be getting in just any ol' car with strangers," he said, turning to face her. She didn't say anything.

"That's mighty dangerous." He picked tobacco from the tip of his tongue with two fingers.

"I won't be doing it no more," she said, her hands clasped before her.

"Good."

He turned to the table for the tool he needed. Gemma didn't move. He came back to the car and was about to slide underneath.

"Nice to meet you, Gemma."

"Nice meeting you too."

They grinned at each other.

"Go on round the side of the garage and up the steps. Juanelle should be up. She's goin' into work shortly, I think."

She'd left her suitcase by the door. Dragging it across the pavement, passing the opened garage once more, she saw Frank King sitting up beside the car. He waved, the cigarette at the side of his mouth.

"Glad you come." His teeth made his smile lopsided. "Now get on up there and surprise your mama."

Gemma carried the suitcase with two hands, hurrying around the corner, climbing the old wooden stairs toward the opened screen door. The back of Frank King's gas station looked over a vacant weeded lot with bits of debris scattered here and there, caught by tall grass. A woman stood beside a trailer, hanging out clothes, grabbing clothespins from a pocket in her apron. From where she was, Gemma thought maybe that was her mother. She stood on the landing, staring across at the woman. Then all at once, she heard a noise from inside the screen door, and then: "Frank, you got any cigarettes?"

The sun was so bright that when she stood at the screen, she couldn't see inside, not even when she shaded both hands around her face.

"Frank?"

Juanelle turned just as Gemma opened the screen. She sat at a small dinette table, her back to the door. She put down the box of kitchen matches she'd been using to try to light the cigarette butt between her lips. She pulled the ragged blue terry cloth robe snugly around her. Gemma opened the door with her foot and carried in her suitcase.

"I thought you were Frank."

Gemma stood there, finally shaking her head, waiting for her mother to do something. But the woman turned to the table again, brushed strands of red hair away from her face, and sipped her coffee. Gemma took several steps into the room until she was beside her. Without her face made up as it had been that day before, Juanelle looked pale. Dark circles hung beneath her eyes.

"Well," Juanelle said, still not looking at her, struggling with the cigarette butt and finally throwing it down. "What brings you to Cowtown?"

"I come to live with you," Gemma said. After a moment, she pulled out a chair and sat next to Juanelle.

"Thought you didn't need me."

Gemma didn't say anything. Her mother flipped the box of kitchen matches over and over, staring down at the table. "This place is like an oven, I swear. Every window up to the hilt and I'm 'bout to fry." Suddenly she pushed herself away from the table. Gemma could see her breasts inside the robe before she wrapped it tightly around her. She watched her mother traipse into the other room, what looked like a bedroom. Juanelle leaned against the window and yelled: "Frank, you got any cigarettes up here?"

Gemma could hear the man below them call back, but his words were flattened by the roar of a diesel. Fumes came through the apartment, and Juanelle coughed as she rummaged in the other room for Frank's cigarettes. She stood in the doorway then, blowing smoke through her nose.

"So you had enough of him?"

Gemma didn't say anything.

"I thought you and he was real tight. Like an old married couple."

"You come for me before."

"And you gave me the old heave-ho." She watched Gemma, a half-smile on her lips broadening till she had to cough. "Told me to get the hell out. Almost chased me off with a shotgun."

Gemma stared at her soberly.

"Now here you are. Out of the blue."

"I just decided I wanted to come live with you now, like what you said. I'm getting older . . ."

She broke off her words and felt as though she might cry if the woman in the doorway didn't stop looking at her. She examined the flower-patterned oilcloth on the table. Juanelle came back to the table and drank the rest of her coffee.

"I know, kid," she said. "I bailed outta there in the middle of the night too." They stared at each other. Finally Juanelle came around the table and squeezed Gemma's shoulder. "Hey, I gotta shake a leg." She hurried into the other room and tossed the robe on the bed. Pulling a slip over her head, she said: "I have to go into work today, kiddo. Even if it is Sunday. Sorry I can't fix you breakfast or nothing. Aggie's got me working the deadheads today. Some rush job."

"Where you work?"

"'Cross the highway. Aggie's House of Curl. We do wigs too. Just started 'em. With this weather, business has been so good that they've stacked up."

Gemma could see her stepping into a skirt, then leaning into a dresser mirror as she put on makeup.

"Hey, kiddo, there's some enchiladas left over if you're hungry. There in the Frigidaire."

"I aint."

"Well, if you are. You can heat 'em up, can't you?"

Gemma nodded, but Juanelle didn't take her eyes from the mirror, where she brushed on long swirls of mascara. Gemma got up from the table and walked to the bedroom door. Empty bottles in several sizes were on the floor next to the unmade bed.

"Get caught up on those wigs and I'll be back to see what we're gonna do with you."

"I can stay, can't I?"

Juanelle looked at her abruptly, only one eye done.

"I met Frank down there, and he said he was glad to have me here."

"Yeah." She resumed her makeup chore. "This place isn't big enough for two, much less three. And this heat is driving me crazy. I keep that fan on in front of the window and all it does is rotate the hot air." She pressed her red lips together, then blotted them with a Kleenex. "Hey, how'd you get here anyway?"

Gemma told her, all the time watching as she put on a frilly white off-the-shoulder blouse. "Like this? Frank got it for me in Mexico."

Gemma felt her cheek being pinched as Juanelle passed through to the other room for matches.

"Say, there's some old guy who drives a brand-new pickup who keeps coming in here for gas," she said. "He comes in all the time, even when he don't need that much. He'll get outta the pickup, hike up his trousers, you know how they do. And he'll mosey on around to the office where I sit sometimes 'cause it's so damn hot up here. He tries to look down my blouse, all the time watching Frank out there wiping his windshield or something. Tries to start up all kinds of small talk, smiling, winking like a kid. Dumb hick. Cute, but too slow with the moves. The kind you can play games with, run circles around, and they're just too slow to notice. Say—that guy who picked you up, did he have a big mustache?"

"No. He had red hair and freckles."

"Freckles!" Juanelle laughed and put her cup in the sink. "Well, this guy that's been coming here has a thick ol' mustache. Just a dumb hick cowboy. You'll see a lot of 'em here."

Juanelle stood at the table, tying a yellow scarf around her neck. Her eyes kept a close watch on Gemma as she made the knot.

"You still dress like a hick yourself."

Gemma stared at the floor.

"Well, we can fix all that, I reckon." Juanelle came to put one arm around the girl. She squeezed Gemma and pressed her head against her so that the girl's glasses slid sideways over her face. "Better having you here than with that old man. We'll make do. Least you know how to take care of yourself."

She went across the room to a broken-down sofa which was covered with a shawl. "I should be done with them wigs before too long," she said, holding one arm of the sofa as she stepped into her heels. They clicked across the floor. At the door, she turned and said: "You wouldn't mind washing up them dishes, would you?" Then she smiled, opening the screen. "Eat them enchiladas if you want."

Gemma went to the door, watching her mother move down the last of the wooden steps. At the bottom, Juanelle turned to look up; her face was rigid. Her fingernails scratched across the thumb joint of her other hand as though she were trying to scrape her skin down to the bone. "Feels like I got poison ivy," she said, smiling sickly at Gemma. Then she hurried away. And across the vacant lot Gemma heard fiddle music, scratching notes and rhythms that soared through the dense summer air, dipping sometimes into the low, convulsive fanfare from the highway.

🜲 *Long-legged spiders mean good luck.*

Across the traffic-blurred highway, she could see Frank King standing beside one of the gas pumps. He counted bills as a car pulled away into the moving line of dusty vans and automobiles, then put them into his back pocket.

"Get that broom," Gwen said.

Standing at the opened door, Gemma saw him tip his hat, though the car was already a block down the strip. She saw his wide-mouthed grin flash at nothing as he hesitated. He wiped his hands on the seat of his overalls and stood there a few moments, as though he waited for another customer to pull into the station.

"When you're done, Mrs. Weeks wants a manicure," Juanelle said. And Gemma leaned against the doorframe, watching the heat rise from the pavement. Sunlight glared off Mrs. Weeks's or Miss Harley's car parked in front of Aggie's House of Curl. There were dark brown spots in the gravel in front of the shop, where grease had dripped from other cars. She could see him in the shade of the garage now, leaning over into the front of a car, looking like Jonah. The high slanting hood looked as though it might clamp down and swallow him.

"That broom is by the candy machine back yonder," Gwen said, pushing up her harlequin glasses with her wrist. "Or by the Coke machine."

"Seems like I just had a cut," Miss Harley, the woman in Gwen's chair, was saying.

"Nope, it was back in the spring," Gwen said, brushing her ponytail behind her.

And back at the opened door, Gemma stood with the broom, making halfhearted sweeps across the floor. Somewhere over the surflike rush of traffic, she could hear fiddle music. She imagined that it rose with the waving heat from the asphalt on the highway. She slid the broom back and forth in rhythm.

"Sweep over by the chairs," Gwen said, her fingers cold on Gemma's arm.

"You aint doing no good back there, kiddo," Juanelle said, pointing a long, thin comb at her. "Hair's piling up over here." Gwen wiped her hands on her smock and went back to her customer.

"Seems like my hair grows so fast," Miss Harley said.

"Well, I read an article in a magazine last week when I was waiting to be combed out that said the more you cut your hair, the more it grows," Mrs. Weeks said, watching Juanelle comb her wet hair in the mirror.

"I think it's got something to do with the time of year too," Miss Harley said, wiggling her nose as though stray hair made it itch.

"Could be," Mrs. Weeks said. "Does hair grow faster in the summer, Juanelle?"

Juanelle parted the woman's hair one way, then another, chuckling. "Shoot, I don't know. Mine's not grown a quarter inch all year.

"That's because the color you use," Gwen said, rummaging through one of the drawers for the long-nosed hair clips.

"Now cut that out," Juanelle said, looking at her in the mirror. "You know that aint true. You'll have these women afraid to tint their hair."

"I reckon I don't mind if it don't grow," Miss Harley said. "I'll still keep using that rinse. Better than gray hair showing through before it should."

"Amen," Juanelle said.

Holding the broom like a staff, Gemma stood between the

two women working busily over their customers. Cutting, setting, rolling. Permanents. So much seemed to go into being a beautician—more than she'd ever be able to learn, though Juanelle assured her she'd be good at it. She held the broom in one hand and surveyed herself in the mirror, over the shelf of waving solutions, combs, scissors, and plastic boxes of curlers that came in so many shapes. She hardly recognized herself— that dress with the puffed-out sleeves and full petticoat and the big sash that was tied in a bow in back. Her hair was a mass of tight little curls. It looked shorter than it actually was; it made her ears show. She hated the way they stuck out. She adjusted her horn-rimmed glasses and tongued her lips the way she'd seen her mother do.

"What is it, kiddo?" Juanelle dipped her comb in a solution on the counter and took a drag from her cigarette. "You want to get some new glasses? Like Gwen's?"

Gwen laughed. Gemma could see the rhinestones at each tip of her glasses sparkle as she fastened the scissorlike clips to the pocket of her smock.

"We'll have to get you some glasses like hers; get you two pair if you want. Just as soon's Frank's land starts paying."

"They got them in blue, green, and white," Gwen said, beginning to roll Miss Harley's hair.

Gemma swept the hair around both chairs into one pile. "My glasses are fine."

"Well, you need you some fancy ones," Gwen said. "The boys aint gonna look at you if you're wearing big ol' glasses like that."

As Gemma swept the broom over the linoleum, something moved. Gwen saw it, and lunged forward to stomp on the long-legged spider.

"Why'd you do that?" Gemma wrinkled her nose so that her glasses moved up. She stared at the other girl, who wasn't much taller.

"I don't want no spider running loose in here."

"Heavens, no," Miss Harley said, shuddering.

"Well, that's one of God's children; it was a living thing."

"It aint living here," Gwen said, bending down to pick it up with a tissue. Her black stretch pants stopped the bulge around her middle.

"Well, they come out this time of year," Mrs. Weeks said. "Around my place, the scorpions are awful. Like they own the place. When my babies were little I used to have to watch 'em like a hawk. Stinging scorpions. Black widow spiders."

"I aint living nowhere where there are spiders, once Frank's deal starts paying off," Juanelle said. "I don't care where I gotta go. I'll leave Texas."

"Mercy," Miss Harley said.

"I mean it," Juanelle said, putting out her cigarette. "Anyplace. We won't have to put up with any of that."

"You aint leaving, Juanelle," Gwen said. Two long-curved clips waved in her mouth as she spoke.

"Oh, yeah? Why the hell would I want to stay in this hole if I didn't have to?" she said, her voice raspy, then: "Sorry, Aggie," she called to the back of the shop. But the woman behind the partition didn't answer. "You gotta be plumb nuts to think I'd live over a gas station once Frank's deal comes off. It's one thing to pump it, hon, like he's over there doing now, and another to take it out of the ground. Ground you own."

"I always think it's bad luck to talk about things like that before they happen," Miss Harley said, pursing her lips, staring into the mirror.

"I don't believe in that crap," Juanelle said, fumbling in her pocket for the scissors. "I watched too many a pot, and they'll always boil if the heat's up."

"You wouldn't leave, would you, Juanelle?" Gwen asked, moving away from Miss Harley. She watched her friend work, taking the last two pieces of candy corn from a cellophane bag, then wadding it up. "I'll die."

"I don't know where I'd find another hairdresser like you, Juanelle," Mrs. Weeks said, sighing, closing a magazine in her lap.

114

"You'll find one," Juanelle said flatly, the butt end of a cigarette hanging from her lips for an instant before she pressed it into the ashtray.

"Well," Gwen said, using two bobby pins crisscrossed on the flat curls she rolled at Miss Harley's ears. "You're mighty lucky. You're always lucky, though." She put a hand on her hip and said to Miss Harley: "Down at The Spur they fall all over themselves to sit next to Juanelle. It'd give me a complex if I didn't know better. Juanelle was born with a silver spoon in her mouth."

"I was," Juanelle said, concentrating on the large, even rows of curls she made on Mrs. Weeks's head, and whistling. "Sometimes I think I was."

"My cousin, Thelma, who lives down in Waco, she knows a lady whose husband found oil on their property, this was maybe twenty years ago. And they made a right smart sum out of it." Miss Harley nodded her head.

"How much?" Juanelle asked. "Were they millionaires?"

"Well, enough to rip down their house, just tear everything down right to the ground and build 'em a mansion with a swimming pool."

"Now that's what I'm talking about." Juanelle lit another cigarette.

"But they didn't have to go off; they didn't have to leave Texas."

"Well, they coulda," Juanelle said, slouching. Gemma could see the black straps of her brassiere under her pink smock. "You don't think I'm gonna bulldoze down Frank's gas station and build a five-bedroom home, do you? It'd still be the Jacksboro Highway, honey."

"I just don't see why people make good and leave home," Miss Harley said, shaking her head.

Juanelle blew smoke from her nostrils and rattled the long comb in the waving solution before combing it through Mrs. Weeks's hair. "Mrs. Weeks, you still want those spit curls over your ears?"

"Yeah, just like last time."

Juanelle bobby-pinned a curl over one of Mrs. Weeks's ears, then said: "Gemma, when did you get those glasses?"

"I don't know. When I was starting school."

Juanelle stepped around Mrs. Weeks and took off the girl's horn-rimmed glasses with both hands. In the mirror, Gemma could see a fuzzy image of curls and puffed-out sleeves. "There, that's better. You look much better without them."

"What a pretty face," Miss Harley said.

"Can you see without them?" Juanelle asked, standing over her.

"Not really. Everything's blurry."

"That's just because your eyes aren't focused yet. They aren't used to not having these ugly old glasses to use like crutches."

Gemma blinked. She looked around the shop, at the bright sunlight coming through the window and opened door. A hazy movement of chrome and color passed along the highway.

"You can see just fine," Juanelle said.

"I can't read too good if I don't have them."

"Then wear them when you read," Juanelle said. "But you don't have to any other time." She held up a fist. "How many fingers am I holding up?" Gemma grinned. "Now see?"

"It's amazing what these doctors have us do," Mrs. Weeks said, feeling the rolled curls on top of her head. "I read this article about a man someplace up North who was told by some doctor that he was allergic to all kinds of fabric. *All* kinds, mind you. And this fellow just ran around stark naked all the time for a year before his neighbors finally had a fit and called the police. Can you imagine that?"

"What town did you say he was at?" Gwen asked, laughing.

"You better watch out, Mrs. Weeks," Juanelle said. "You'll have Gwen peeping into windows from here to I don't know where."

Juanelle took the broom from Gemma.

"Go back yonder and find the dustpan. Then come give Mrs. Weeks a manicure while she's under the dryer."

"Yes, ma'am." Back by the Coke machine, she could hear the women laugh about something. She found the dustpan wedged behind Coke cartons. Behind her, Aggie sat at a worktable, hidden from the rest of the shop by a partition. A cigarette burned in the ashtray. A half-empty Dr. Pepper bottle was on the table. Aggie sat with a faceless Styrofoam head between her legs. She primped the cascade of curls pinned to the top of it.

"How you doing? You finding everything okay?"

Gemma nodded.

"You're a good girl." Aggie's teeth were badly stained. Gemma thought she smiled like she did so people could see how bad they looked. The woman adjusted her weight on the stool and scratched her short, matted hair. "We'll have you working here before too long. Have you working here with your mama just as soon as we can persuade some man to take Gwen off our hands."

Gwen called: "Heck Aggie. Sooner the better." She straightened the seam of her stretch pants, then leaned forward to pick up a bobby pin from the floor. When she stood up again, she swept her blond ponytail behind her. "I had me somebody all picked out Saturday night, Aggie."

Gemma saw Aggie's body tremble. Then the woman got down off the stool and came from behind the partition. She was Gwen's height, hardly taller than Gemma herself.

"This fellow's name is Doyle. Just moved here from Corsicana."

"That right?" Aggie stood at the back of the shop, the faceless head of curls in one hand.

"Yep. He's J.B. Atkin's brother. He just moved here the other day and he's working for J.B. at the store. I seen him at The Spur."

"J.B. selling that many used auto parts that he can afford to take someone in?"

"Don't know." Gwen took the rubber band from her

ponytail and ran her fingers through her hair, combing it, glancing back at Aggie. "He's as tall as Frank. Right, Juanelle?"

"Almost."

"And big shoulders. I think he's twenty-five."

Fingers spread on both hands, Juanelle opened a net and brought it down carefully over Mrs. Weeks's head. "Shoot. That big ol' hick was slobbering all over Gwen. He was pressing against me, then he was pressing 'gainst her. She let him look down her blouse and make adjustments with his finger till he could see what he wanted."

"That right, Gwen?" Aggie's voice was cool.

Gwen tied her hair back into a ponytail. "Ah, Aggie, it don't mean nothing. We was just havin' a little fun like we always do, but it don't mean nothin'."

Juanelle led Mrs. Weeks back to the dryer. Gemma followed, returning the broom and dustpan. Aggie held the head upright, pacing back and forth, straightening magazines beside the divan. Gemma sat on a stool at Mrs. Weeks's feet and began her manicure.

"Shoot," Aggie said abruptly. "There's Rory."

She and Gwen watched a young man hop from foot to foot as he waited to cross the highway.

"He's a long-legged thing," Gwen said, checking her lipstick in the mirror.

"Yep," Aggie said, watching till he'd gotten across safely.

Gemma saw the thin young man walk toward the door of the shop. Opening the screen, he stepped inside, still hopping from foot to foot. Miss Harley stared at him in the mirror. Gwen smiled, winked, and said: "You sure fiddle some pretty tunes on that thing. I listen all the time."

He grinned. Aggie walked to the back, her house slippers sliding across the linoleum. "Gwen, don't be botherin' that boy."

"I'm not, Ag."

Aggie turned at the partition and said: "Rory, just wait right there for five minutes and I'll have your mama's hair done."

He giggled and ducked his head. Then he walked quickly to where Miss Harley sat and leaned forward to gently touch one of the pink curlers on her head.

"What on earth is he doing?" Miss Harley almost leapt from the chair.

"Rory, now you can't bother one of my customers," Gwen said. She led him to the divan and sat beside him. He bobbed his head. Gwen picked up a magazine and put it in his hands. "Now read this till Aggie's done with Dolores's hair."

"Poor thing probably can't even read," Miss Harley said, cautiously looking at him in the mirror.

Rory held the magazine in his lap, turning the pages and running a finger down the lines of print.

Juanelle stood before him with her hands on her hips. "What you reading, Rory?"

"Magazine."

"Yeah? Well, what does it say?"

"It say how to make chicken casserole." Gemma thought his voice sounded sweet. She filed one of Mrs. Weeks's nails just as Gwen had shown her, but she couldn't help watching him.

"Well, how does it say you make a chicken casserole?" Juanelle glanced back at the others with a wide grin.

"Well, it say you take a can of mushroom soup. And then you take you chicken and you wash him . . ."

"Do you use soap?"

He thought for a moment, then said: "If he's real dirty, it say use soap. And you use a pack of noodles . . ."

"You could use some noodles," Juanelle said, turning her back, lighting a cigarette. She went back to check the heat from Mrs. Weeks's dryer. "Aint he something?"

"He's something," Gwen said.

"Now don't be egging him on," Aggie said, finishing the wig.

"Me?" Juanelle put her hand to her chest and raised her eyebrows. "Rory, am I egging you on?"

Rory laughed, shifting his eyes. "I think you do. I think you do in the casserole. I aint read down that far. But I'm making it for my mama's supper tonight."

"You?" Juanelle asked, after throwing back her head and cackling. "Hey, if you're such a good cook, why don't you go work with your mama at the drive-in?"

"Juanelle," Aggie warned.

"I might," he said. "I might be working there."

He got up from the vinyl-covered divan and came back toward the dryers. "I might make something at the drive-in next week."

"And just what might that be?" Juanelle asked, leaning against the wall.

"I might make my casserole and mash potatoes with gravy and I might make peach cobbler with vanilla ice cream." He stopped when he saw Gemma.

"Rory, this here's my daughter," Juanelle said. "Her name is Gemma."

"How do," he said, holding out his other hand for her to shake. "I'm making a casserole."

Gemma took his hand. It felt warm. His eyes were light blue, like a child's. She looked up into them and said: "I just moved here. I live 'cross the highway."

"I live 'cross the highway too," he said. "I live in a trailer house with Dolores."

"Here's your mama's hair," Aggie said, coming up behind them. "Now take it right home and don't stop nowhere along the way."

Rory backed to the door, grinning. He had to put down the wig case to open the screen. But then he came back inside and walked to the back of the shop, where Gemma was finishing Mrs. Weeks's manicure.

"Mighty nice meeting you," he said, ducking his head. His sandy-colored hair was curly on top. "I'm coming home with my mama's hair. Ever' time she needs it washed, she takes it off and sends it over to Miss Aggie's." His grin broadened. Gemma could see his gums.

After he'd finally gone, Juanelle checked Mrs. Weeks's hair and told her she needed another fifteen minutes.

"Them empty Coke bottles can be stacked out back," Aggie said to Gemma. "Stack 'em in the cartons against the side of the building so they'll be out yonder when the Coke man comes tomorrow."

The alley was dusty, paved with brick, and had boarded-up windows down either side. Where a drainpipe came off Aggie's roof, a small tree had started to grow. Sounds from the Jacksboro Highway were muffled, disconnected with this heavily shadowed path. Trash cans lined the cracked walls. The curls on her head felt stiff. A calico cat sat on top of one of the trash cans, busily scratching himself. "That means a sandstorm is coming," she said aloud. And looking both ways, she thought she could almost see it. The sky changed colors just above the highway. The heat left a metallic taste in her mouth. Inside, Juanelle cackled. Gemma moved closer to the building, into the shade. The empty wooden Coca-Cola cartons had been tossed haphazardly in a pile. She began placing them upright and filling them with bottles, dry now, hazed over with a film of grime and cigarette smoke. Some had lipstick around the rim.

"Aint nothing wrong-looking with him," she could hear someone say; it was Gwen. Their shadows moved about inside. Mrs. Weeks had returned to Juanelle's chair, where Gemma's mother was combing, brushing, and spraying her hair. Miss Harley was under one of the dryers. "What did you say?" she called, uncovering one ear.

"I said he aint that bad-looking," Gwen repeated. "For a pea brain."

Gemma lined up bottle after bottle—Coca-Cola, Dr. Pepper, Orange Crush, R.C.

"Well, I read in an article where they're able to tell now

much sooner if you're gonna have a retarded baby," Mrs. Weeks was saying.

"They wasn't anything wrong with Rory when he was born," Juanelle said. "Dolores told me he was all right till he was 'bout six, then he just sorta started going backwards. She had him in all sorts of schools."

"That's a shame, a good-looking boy," Miss Harley said.

"Dolores don't let him outside much. Afraid he'll get in the highway and get hit," Juanelle said.

"Well, he gets mighty good care," Aggie was saying. "Put him in a home somewheres like some people think oughta be done, and they'd let him die."

"I don't know but what that wouldn't be a blessing," Juanelle said.

"Juanelle!"

"Well, I don't, Aggie. Shoot." She strangled with a fit of coughing. "Aint much he's good for. Can't live all that long anyway, I'd reckon."

Gemma could see Gwen's silhouette framed at the front window, the ponytail wagging, the wide hips swaying.

"I seen him sitting back a your house, back there in the shade of that old trailer, with his hands down his pants," Gwen said. "I wonder what he does for it."

"What the heck are you talking about?" Aggie called. "He's got the mind of a five-year-old."

"But his body is a nice grown-up twenty-five, I'd say." Gwen moved away from the window, somewhere inside the shop, so that she was out of Gemma's view. "Looks mighty fit to me."

"Fit as a fiddle," Juanelle said flatly, then broke into a laugh with the others.

"I reckon he never thinks about those things," Mrs. Weeks said. "I mean, I bet his mind aint developed enough, you know, to put two and two together."

"Shoot. I never seen a man yet where his mind had anything to do with it," Juanelle said. "If he was sitting back yonder

122

with his hand down his pants, it wasn't 'cause he thought out with logic what to do."

"Heavens," Miss Harley said loudly, her head under the dryer. "Someone like that could almost be dangerous."

Behind the screen, Aggie's bulky frame moved around the partition. "Now you girls cut that out. Aint nothing the least bit dangerous 'bout Rory. I known that kid since he was a baby. And there's nothing dangerous 'bout him."

"Bless his heart," Miss Harley said.

"I reckon most those rednecks down at The Spur don't got much more of a mind than Rory," Gwen said. "They just know how to act in public. Wouldn't surprise me none to see one of them off in a corner playing with himself."

Juanelle laughed. With her face close to the screen, Gemma could see her mother standing over Mrs. Weeks, combing, spraying the newly formed curls.

"I still wonder what he does for it," Gwen was saying. "If he's ever been with anyone. He aint no kid."

"He's twenty-four, Aggie said."

"Well, he aint been with me," Juanelle said. "Least not that I remember."

"My Lord in heaven I hope not," Miss Harley called out.

Gemma sat on a piece of cardboard so she wouldn't get her dress dirty. She arranged the rows of bottles in the cartons. Inside the shop, Mrs. Weeks was paying. Gemma heard the woman call goodbye, but didn't answer. She shifted the cardboard along the ground so they wouldn't be able to see her. His eyes were sky blue, just like Jesus' in that picture in her Bible. Aggie was leaving too, telling them to lock up when they finished for the day. And then Miss Harley was sitting in Gwen's chair again. Eyes just like Jesus'.

"He probably gets lonely," Gwen said.

"He's got that fiddle," Juanelle said, her voice muffled. "Aggie got it for him, I remember, and he taught himself to play."

"That's something there," Miss Harley said. "That's something if he can teach himself to play the fiddle. I don't reckon I could do that."

"Well," Gwen said, "I'd sure as heck give him the time of day."

"Gwen!"

"I would, Miss Harley. It'd sure beat having to put up with hearing that big-man cowboy crap."

"Amen, sister," Juanelle said.

"I bet he'd be real sweet." Gemma could hear Gwen ringing up the cash register. "Don't you reckon, Juanelle?"

"Yeah," her mother said. "Probably would. I'd have to be feeling mighty good, though. I guess I been too spoiled. I wouldn't know how to act with someone real sweet."

"You girls are outta my league," Miss Harley said. Gemma could hear car keys rattle.

"I'm afraid old Gwen and me are in a league by ourselves," Juanelle said, standing up and stretching. "It comes from spending all our time making women beautiful, making 'em desirous creatures."

"Heavens," Miss Harley said.

The front screen creaked and closed and Gemma could hear Miss Harley's car start.

"Come on in here." Juanelle stood at the back door. "You'll get that dress filthy."

She came back into the shop as Gwen was leaving and sat on a stool watching as her mother took the last appointment for the day. Juanelle washed the new customer's hair, continuing the same conversation she'd had all day with other women about kids and men and recipes. Her mother never glanced back at her. And she wondered then: does she know I'm sitting here? Does she know I'm here?

Later, when the woman had paid, and she and Juanelle were the only ones left in the shop, Gemma said: "That guy, Rory, he sure had pretty eyes."

Startled, Juanelle looked up from the sink, where she was washing out combs.

"I guess he does."

Her mother seemed pleased that she'd noticed. "I thought he was real nice."

"Nice enough." Juanelle put the combs into a tall glass container.

"I reckon Gwen thought his eyes were pretty too."

Juanelle laughed, drying her hands. "I don't think it was his eyes she was gawking at."

Gemma sat in her mother's chair, looking at her hazy image in the mirror. She saw her glasses sitting on the counter where Juanelle had left them. Watching her mother, she ran a finger over her lower lip.

"I like the hairdo you gave me real good," she said.

"It's better'n that stringy mess you had before." Juanelle turned off the fluorescent lights overhead. Late afternoon light streamed in the front window. Traffic from the highway made constant waves of shadow across the floor.

"Does it make me a desirous woman?"

Juanelle cackled. Lighting a cigarette, she came over and put both arms around Gemma from behind the chair. "You just about are, kiddo. You just about are." Then she stood in front of the mirror and put on fresh lipstick. Gemma watched every movement. From the corner of her eye, Juanelle noticed her eagerness, and said: "Here you go." She handed her the gold-plated tube. Gemma put some on, smacked her lips, and looked in the mirror.

"I got too much on," she said, wiping some off with her finger.

"I'll teach you," her mother said. "It takes practice."

Gemma opened her mouth, then puckered her lips, never taking her eyes from her own blurred reflection in the mirror. Juanelle was putting all the money from the cash register into an envelope.

"Is my last name Monroe?"

Juanelle glanced at her, then took the envelope of money and disappeared behind the partition.

"Why you asking that?"

"'Cause that's what Pop told me. He said my daddy's name was Monroe."

"He don't know nothing." Juanelle stood in the middle of the room, a hand on her hip. "I don't know why he'd go and tell you a thing like that."

"Well, that's what he said. But I go by Dillard."

"Don't listen to him," she said, blowing smoke through her nose, distracted. She took off her smock and hung it on a hanger. "He's an old fool. Besides, it don't matter what your last name is, not for a woman. That changes when you marry."

"Like yours did. With Frank."

"You could say that." She stood with her hands on her hips for a moment, in her straight black skirt and black brassiere. "He still eat with his face down to the plate? He used to burn me up doing that."

Gemma didn't say anything.

"Well, I 'spect he does. You do yourself sometimes." She took her blouse from the hanger and put it on, buttoning slowly. "Then he'd belch when he was done and wipe the back of his hand across his mouth. Like a farmhand."

"You got any pictures of my daddy?" Gemma sat very still in the chair, watching her mother in the mirror.

"Are you kidding?" Juanelle started to laugh, then said flatly: "No; no, I don't."

Gemma chewed her lip. "Well, I know he was in the war."

"I don't remember."

"I used to look at those pictures in *Life* and wonder if one of them soldiers was him. I saved some of 'em. I dreamed about him too, for a long time, even when Pop told me he'd been killed over there fighting."

"That old buzzard told you that?" She stopped buttoning for a moment, staring at the floor.

"Pop told me he died fighting for our country. He said if my daddy wasn't in the war, we might be speaking German now.

Alice Farley says Germans spit when they talk. Her daddy was over yonder, but he came back."

Juanelle slowly tucked in her blouse. She came to the mirror to tie the scarf around her neck. "The old man track chicken shit through the house? That used to irk me. He'd a brought them inside to sleep if we'd let him."

"We got a lot of regular customers now. Every Friday."

Juanelle laughed, taking off her earrings and rubbing her earlobes one at a time before clipping them back on. "Big businessman."

"Were you and my daddy together for a long spell before he was called away?" She stared at her mother, waiting.

"I told you before, I don't remember," Juanelle snapped. Then she stared at herself in the mirror, rubbing at the tiny lines across her forehead and around her eyes. "It's been a long time."

"Well, Pop told me I got the Monroe forehead. Do I?"

Juanelle turned to her, not saying anything for a long time, just staring at the girl sitting up in the chair. "I reckon you do," she said, sighing. "Sure." She opened her handbag, took out a tissue, and blew her nose. Then she hooked her handbag over her arm. "He never cared about anything but those damned chickens."

Gemma stood in the gravel out front while her mother locked the door. Whirls of dust blew across the roofs and hoods of cars along the highway. The sign over Frank's gas station suddenly lit up.

"It's a dust storm coming," Gemma said.

"Yeah? Well, that's just great. We'll have to sit home with the windows closed tonight and fry."

They waded through creeping afternoon traffic, touching hoods and fenders on either side. Wind made the traffic light sway. Juanelle held the back of her dress to her legs. She told Gemma to do the same. Frank was sitting inside the station, his feet propped up on the desk. When he saw them, he grinned lopsidedly and waved. Gemma's eyes began to water.

"I sure do like Frank," she said to her mother.

"Yeah," her mother said, glancing sideways down the line of traffic, her mouth set firmly. "He's a sweetheart, all right."

🐓 *Bathe on Friday, and sins are forgiven.*

He could just stretch his legs out in the long metal tub. Water covered the lower half of his body, almost to the middle of his chest. Dillard sat back, resting his arms on the rounded rim. From where he sat, in the middle of the screened-in porch, he could see across the flat, black land. Almost forever. In the summers, they never bothered to maneuver the long metal bathtub into the kitchen. Bathing was simpler on the porch, near the cistern. And he could lie back in the water and gaze up at the sky.

He swatted the cake of soap, smiling, thinking: now aint they right—this soap floats, sure enough. He gazed down at his body underneath the murky surface. Patches of suds floated on top like clouds, covering a knee, part of his leg. He brushed some of the foam away. He watched himself for a moment, fascinated, tilting his pelvis. Like floating through midair, he thought. It don't look real. He grabbed the bar of soap and slid it between his legs. The soap was smooth, hard, and it wedged itself down there when he brought his hand out of the water. Dillard waited until the surface became calm again. Then he opened his thighs slightly and chuckled aloud when the white cake shot upward, bobbing just below his chin. It floats.

And then while his eyes were still trained on the shimmering pale thighs and stomach, he felt a hollowness in his belly. He leaned his head back against the cold metal rim and closed his eyes. His body almost rose to the surface. Long before, in that space of time which startled him, troubled him now and then because he realized it was always with him, he could feel the boy next to him as they floated on their backs. The black face squinted into the sun, then turned to him, grinning. *I be the winner, Homer.* He'd lift his head from the water enough to see their figures bobbing just under the surface—his stark, and the other so dark that it seemed to blend with the depths below. Their arms fanned outward, treading. Sometimes a foot would kick a hole in the stillness of the afternoon, kerplunk. It fascinated him, gliding together side by side, whenever the gloomy surface next to his paleness would be broken with gleaming black flesh—a thigh, the flat, glowing belly, genitals. It made the black boy laugh loudly, then sink into more blackness and come up under him suddenly in surprise.

Well, I 'spect he aint laughing now, Dillard thought, staring up at a dirt dobber nest in the corner of the porch. Not if what Bob Hadley says is true, how they got him strung up in all sorts of contraptions in the hospital. He aint laughing, but he's alive. He's alive. Only that morning, Hadley had told him that the word was good. Some of the old rascal's bones had been broken when everything plummeted down upon him, sandwiching him into the trash. But in time, they thought, he would mend.

"Wouldn't a been possible if you hadn't dragged me out yonder the next morning," Hadley said. "He wouldn't a had a prayer."

"I reckon," Dillard said, stepping to the side. "Well."

And he wondered if what they'd said was true, that somehow pockets of air had kept the unconscious old man alive until they reached him.

"But how'd you know he was there?"

"I just did," Dillard said, his jaw set, his narrowed eyes staring past Hadley. "I just knew."

And Dillard had walked away before Bob Hadley could say another word, walked down the dirt road all the way to his house without looking back. *I just knew it.* He'd breathed heavily, traipsing up the back steps, going inside, carefully closing the door behind him as though someone were following.

And then, just as now, he was alone in the house. Just him, motionless. Listening to his own breathing, his own heart. Sometimes the house would creak, or a branch would scrape against a window. And nobody heard it but him.

That Friday on his egg run, his customers didn't say anything, but they knew. He could tell they all knew. Mrs. Stevens kept smiling as she rummaged through her purse for change. Others tried to talk; they'd never done that before. He had to tell them that if he didn't get moving, he'd never finish all his deliveries. It didn't matter. None of it mattered. He was alive. He held his head upright, thinking: they'll forget it in good time and let me be. It won't be nothing.

Clouds of soap churned against his chest. He let them take their own course for a moment, then swept them aside with his arm. He was so pale and dried up down there, he kept thinking, like that part of his body had never seen the light of day. And then he could hear the black boy's rich laughter. He brought his face down so that the tip of his chin got wet, staring down at himself, thinking: it don't look real.

🐓 *If your socks slip down, somebody's thinking about you.*

Gemma would dress and have her breakfast most mornings before they stirred. She would have the sofa made up and her cereal bowl washed by the time Frank dashed from their room for the bathroom in his boxer shorts, grinning sheepishly, scratching the stubble on his chin. In those first days she'd awakened in the rooms over the gas station, she'd waited for them to get up. At the dinette table, or sitting on the sofa, she'd listened for the slightest noise to come from their room before she would begin to move about. Traffic noises would accelerate as the sun came up; Frank would have to open the station soon. But later, as days and weeks began to pass, she didn't feel as though she had to wait. She would wander through the apartment, or sit on the back steps. After a while, she began to venture across the vacant lot each morning, finally sitting in an uncluttered spot, where she had her daily devotional. She'd read her Bible before doors began to slam in the rooms over the gas station, and her mother's voice called her name or Frank's. She awakened at the same hour as she always had. But these early hours were different now. They were hers.

Jumping down the steps two at a time, she stopped suddenly at the bottom and held her breath. She hoped she wasn't making too much noise. If she was, she knew Juanelle would certainly tell her. The sun wasn't up, not quite. The morning air was damp. She fumbled in the pocket of the pinafore her mother had gotten for her and pulled out her glasses. When she put them on, the lot, the fence, and the trailer in the distance were much sharper. Even the traffic sounds seemed more defined. As she started off through the tall grass, a butterfly darted around her head, and she giggled, thinking: that means I'm getting married soon. She skipped through the weeds, turning sometimes, humming to herself. She found the spot she came to every morning. She'd picked up scraps of newspapers, beer bottles, and crumpled wrappers. And now the grass was flattened from her regular visits. When she lay down, the tall weeds blocked out the low buildings around her, and it made her think of Twilight. Home. She pulled off her shoes, then her socks. They kept slipping down around her ankles. Her toes dug into the grass; it felt cool. The morning sky was pink now, but she could still see the moon and a few stars. A breeze caused the grass around her to wave and flutter like long caressing fingers dipping down into her line of vision.

She rested the opened Bible on her stomach for a while, before finally beginning to read: *"Who then is Paul, and who is Apollos, but ministers by whom ye believed, even as the Lord gave to every man? I have planted, Apollos watered; but God gave the increase. So then neither is he that planteth any thing, neither he that watereth; but God that giveth the increase. Now he that planteth and he that watereth are one: and every man shall receive his own reward according to his own labour. For we are labourers together with God: ye are God's husbandry, ye are God's building."* And she held the Bible upright on her stomach, reading, hearing the grasses rustle like waves against a man-made wall of engines and groaning brakes.

"Stickers get in my feet when I go barefooted."

She brought the Bible down flat on her chest and saw him standing over her, a tall, curly-headed silhouette in the early light. She didn't move for a few moments. And then she closed the Bible and put it on the ground beside her.

"I got a sticker patch on the other side of my and Dolores's trailer house and when I step in that they go in my feet and I can't walk till somebody come pull 'em out."

He squatted down beside her then, and she could see his face, those childlike blue eyes. She didn't move.

"And the other day I forgot 'em and I run out the door and step in that sticker patch and 'bout eighteen go in my foot, 'tween my toes. They was in deep. 'N' I have to sit down and pull 'em out, 'cause my Dolores she at work. I sit down right in 'em and I have to be there till it was dark and she come home from her work." He scratched his leg. "They still be itchin' me."

Gemma sat up slowly. She turned pages, searching, then finally reading aloud: "*And straightway Jesus constrained his disciples to get into a ship, and to go before him unto the other side, while he sent the multitudes away. And when he had sent the multitudes away, he went up into a mountain apart to pray: and when the evening was come, he was there alone. But the ship was now in the midst of the sea, tossed with waves: for the wind was contrary. And in the fourth watch of the night Jesus went unto them, walking on the sea. And when the disciples saw him walking on the sea, they were troubled, saying, It is a spirit; and they cried out for fear. But straightway Jesus spake unto them, saying, Be of good cheer; it is I; be not afraid.*"

She paused, looking up into his eyes. He had edged over into her beaten-down clearing.

"I like that story." He grinned and nodded. "You read me a good story."

"It aint done," she said, then continued: "*And Peter answered him and said, Lord, if it be thou, bid me come unto thee on the water. And he said, Come. And when Peter was come down out of the ship, he walked on the water, to go to Jesus.* Are you listening to this?"

Rory nodded.

"Well," she said, looking down at the page, then again at him as she closed the book, "the story goes that this disciple Peter walks over the water, right on top of it, to Jesus. But then all of a sudden, he saw the winds a-whooping up like a tornado and them big waves and he got all scared and that's when he started to sink." Rory listened closely. "Started going right down, right into the sea there, and he screamed out real loud, 'Jesus, save me!' And right then and there, Jesus reached out a hand to him and yanked him up. He said, 'What you getting scared for, Peter?' And Peter sorta ducked his head, still glad that Jesus had aholt of him. Jesus says, 'You got no faith!' Then they get back in the boat and right then and there the wind died down to nothing. All those disciples fell down on their hands and knees and said, 'Jesus, you are the son of God.'" She folded her hands in her lap. "And now that's the end of the story."

Rory clapped both hands together, nodding his head.

"You ever hear that one before?"

He thought for a moment, then grinned.

"Well, that's one of the stories in the Bible. 'Bout Jesus."

"I like him."

"Course you do, Rory. He's your Savior. Your Lord and Savior. You just gotta have faith."

"I know." Rory sat down flat on the ground beside her, still grinning. Sometimes he would chew. "I like that one 'bout bears eating their cereal. You like that one? Tell me that one."

"I don't think I ever heard that one," she said, wiggling her toes under the grass.

"Sure you have," he said. "It's 'bout three bears and they eat cereal. A mama, a daddy, and a baby bear."

"I don't know that one," she said again. "It aint in my Bible, or I'd know it."

"Yeah, it is. Miss Aggie read me that one ever' time."

They sat quietly for a moment. He rocked. The sky was filled with gray low-hanging clouds that swept over the gas station, over the increasingly steady buzz of noise from the highway.

Chewing, he said suddenly: "'N' they huff 'n' they puff 'n' they blow they house down."

"What are you chewing on?"

He looked at her blankly, then spit out a button when she held a hand under his mouth. "Good way for you to choke."

"I know."

"Rory," she said, shifting so that she faced him directly, "did you know that the Lord loves you?"

He shook his head, his eyes still on her fist where the button was hidden.

"Well, I'm gonna tell you 'bout it right now," she said. "Did your mother never take you to church?"

He looked at her for a moment, then said: "That where they say them stories?"

"Sometimes. That and other stuff."

"Yes, Miss Aggie take me there one time, but I don't like it. They make me do ever'thing. They make me draw pictures; they make me draw letters—'n' they make me sit by myself. Dolores she say I don't have to go no more if I don't want to, 'n' reading aint nothin'. 'Cause I don't like it; I don't like it. You hear my fiddle?"

"Yes," she said, quietly watching him. "You play real good."

He laughed and brought a hand to his mouth. "Well, you tell them stories real good." He reached forward and patted her on the back.

She folded her arms and looked him in the eye. "Rory, now you can't ask him to save you till you believe in Him. Do you?"

He nodded.

"How can you believe in Him if you aint ever heard nothin' 'bout Him?"

"I don't know; I think I have. At that school place they was telling us a story before we take our nap. Everybody bring a towel from they home and they take them a nap on it. My towel was bran' new. One a Miss Aggie's."

She shook her head and sighed. "Listen now, right here in Romans, listen what it says." She flipped through the Bible till she found what she was looking for. "Now they're talking here 'bout the same thing. How can you have faith in the Word if you aint ever heard it? And how can you hear if they aint somebody to spread it? *How beautiful are the feet of them that preach the gospel of peace, and bring glad tiding of good things!* Then it says that faith is coming by message and that the message comes from the Word of Christ. But maybe they didn't hear the message, but it says here: *But I say, Have they not heard? Yes verily, their sound went into all the earth, and their words unto the ends of the world.* Isaiah says here: *I was found of them that sought me not; I was made manifest unto them that asked not after me. But to Israel he saith, All day long I have stretched forth my hands unto a disobedient and gainsaying people.*" She closed the book in her lap. "That's just like you, Rory."

He ducked his head and grinned. "I know."

"And faith comes from listening to the Good News, the Good News about Jesus Christ, your Lord and Savior."

Somewhere in the tall grass, birds cavorted about their nests. A door slammed above the gas station. Gemma could hear Frank's voice, then Juanelle's.

"That's my mama; she's up now."

"My Dolores is up too; she up to the drive-in, working."

Her arms clasped around her knees, she sat with him beside her, listening as a radio was turned on, and then the sound of running water. When she glanced at him, he smiled weakly.

"I best be going in there before she wonders where I am," Gemma said.

He held both ankles and rocked forward. "Ever' time my mama go to the drive-in, my Dolores, well, she walking down the road there 'n' I see you."

"I didn't know that," Gemma said, looking down. Her face began to burn.

"That's 'cause you layin' down readin' your book," he said, looking at her intently. "Ever' morning."

"I didn't know that."

"Yep. They say that I can't do it, so I have to leave that school place, but I was readin'. Some. I still make out words, but my Dolores say I don't. I know 'Dr. Pepper,' 'Chevrolet,' and 'TV set.' How's that?"

"Good. That's good."

"I aint be reading like you. I aint ever be reading like you."
He grinned at her, then bobbed his head. "That was a pretty
good story you was tellin', readin' to me before. You're a good
reader."

"Thanks, Rory. You remember my name?"

He grinned. She saw his ears go red. "Gemma."

They sat side by side, cross-legged on the ground. Overhead the clouds had opened to a clear sky, except over the
highway, where the air was dense. Gemma picked a blade of
grass and held it close like a flower. Then she folded her hands
around it and tried to make a whistle. Nothing came out. "My
Pop makes it so loud the dogs bark," she said, smiling, then all
at once folding her hands self-consciously over her lap.

"Can I get that thing, that button you got? You take my
button."

She reached into the pocket of her pinafore and found the
dark button. "Now don't put this in your mouth," she said.
"You might swallow it or something."

He took it from her and rolled it from hand to hand, looking
up at her suddenly. Across the vacant lot, she could hear their
voices from the upstairs window. They rode through the air on
the hum from the highway, and she closed her eyes, thinking:
just like crickets chirping at the lake. When she looked at him
again, he was watching her closely. It made her feel funny. She
took off her glasses and put them into her pocket.

"I only gotta wear these things for readin'."

He nodded, ducking his head with a grin. "I never got
any," he said. "Can I see 'em?"

She hesitated, then took them from her pinafore. He held
them out in front of his face, then put them on. They made his
eyes larger. He picked up her Bible and began turning pages,
running his finger up and down the lines of print.

"I got to get me some too," he said.

"They probably don't fit your eyes. The doctor give 'em to
me."

"No, they fit 'em all right." He turned pages, silently moving his lips as though he were reading. "Looky here, Gemma," he said, pointing to the print, his magnified blue eyes taking her in. "I can see this readin' good. Looky here. Aint this sayin' 'lorden saver' right here?"

She turned from him, her face flushed, and without looking, said: "Yes, it does. That's real good, Rory."

"I know."

"But I don't think them glasses is good for you. The doctor give 'em to fit my eyes, nobody else's. Everybody has different eyesight."

"I know," he said, moving his lips as he traced the page of print. "'N' you got the goodest eyesight I ever seen."

"Thank you," she whispered, looking down into her lap. Across the lot, she could hear Juanelle in the kitchen, banging cabinet doors, coughing. Someplace in those rooms, Frank whistled along with the radio, adding trills and flourishes to the ends of his phrases. Gemma wiped her hands on her dress. She folded her arms, not daring to look up.

"I'm assin' my Dolores to get me some of these things," he said, closing the Bible, grinning at her. "I'm assin' her when she come home from the drive-in, 'n' then you 'n' me can read with each other." He carefully took off Gemma's horn-rimmed glasses and folded them. She accepted them without raising her eyes and put them back into her pinafore. "At that school place they don't got nothing like that. I wisht they had a got 'em when I was there."

He stared off into space, lost, the left side of his face twitching slightly from some garbled memory. And without a thought, without a moment's hesitation because of the leaden feeling in her chest, she took his hand. They sat together, hands locked, both staring over the top of the tall grass toward the low, flat buildings that lined the highway. Juanelle called for Frank to get his coffee.

"Who taught you to play the fiddle?" she asked, her voice raspy. For just an instant, something in the sound reminded her of her mother.

"Nobody teached me; I learned it myself," he said. He opened his fingers, then closed them tightly around her hand. "'N' my Dolores she say I got me a ear 'cause I play songs right off the radio."

"You mean you can listen to songs, then just play them?"

"Yep. Somebody play them something 'n' I can play it right back."

When she felt his thumb graze over her fingers, she dared to look at their hands. And then she looked at his face, at the muscles in his jaw working. All at once, she said: "Rory, I told you not to put that nasty thing in your mouth."

He looked at her timidly, his mouth clamped.

"Now give me that thing," she said, breaking her hand from his and holding it out. He shook his head. "Give it to me! You'll choke on it and die and I don't want that."

He shook his head again, then looked at her for a moment before he spit it into her hand. The small black button glistened in her palm like a jewel. She made a fist over it and shook her head back and forth at him. "You're a bad boy."

"I know." He grinned.

Suddenly she was on her feet, the button in her fist. She took a few steps backward, laughing at him, laughing out loud at how he almost toppled over when he stood. And then she was running through the lot, looking over her shoulder to make sure he was following.

"Give it back to me," he called, his laughter deep, rich.

But she ran across the neglected ground covered with broken cinder blocks, tires, yellowed newspaper, and tin cans. She headed for the far fence, looking back every few yards, then down at the ground under her bare feet. As she moved faster, she knew he was gaining on her, could hear his breath come out in short, ecstatic pants. She touched the fence post as though it were a base, then veered along the line of barbed wire. He was just behind, reaching, his fingers grabbing. And she raced harder, her feet thudding through the grass, over naked ground, all the time knowing that he would catch her soon.

Even though she could hear him call out through her own out-of-breath elation, she dashed for the far side of the ramshackle trailer house. Contact with the ground jarred her cries. She ran around the rust-stained aluminum trailer, and stopped almost at once. When she fell forward, she felt the same needlelike stabs in her hands she felt in her feet. She was able to stand again. Raising a foot at a time, she could see the tiny grass burrs embedded in her skin. She pulled them from her hands one at a time, flinching, wiping at pinheads of blood which specked her palms.

"I told you 'bout this sticker patch," he said, breathing heavily, leaning forward as he held to one side of the trailer.

Gemma didn't say anything. She rubbed at her hands.

"Other day when my Dolores was at the drive-in, I come out here and they stick in me all over. Right through my pants."

She tried to walk; pain shot up through her feet. She looked at him helplessly as he got his breath back. When he started for her, she put out a hand.

"No, I can do it. It aint nothing." She took another step, feeling tears come to her eyes as the burrs ground themselves deeper into her flesh. Remembering suddenly, she looked at the ground. The blur of tough vines were matted close to the earth. She knelt when she thought she saw the button, but had to feel through the grass until she found it. "There aint none over there by you, is there?"

He shook his head, starting forward several times to help. Each time she put out a hand to stop him as she waded through the patch, walking on the sides of her feet, her arms spread for balance.

"My Dolores come home when it was dark and she have to get me out," he said.

She moved forward a step at a time, concentrating on the blurred ground below. Finally she was before him, and he put out his arms to catch her as she fell against the side of the trailer.

"See," she said, her throat tight. "See."

She lay against the rusted side, panting, squinching her

141

eyes each time he pulled a burr from her feet. He sat before her, pulling them off, throwing them back into the patch. Gemma watched him triumphantly, letting him rub the soles of her feet when they were gone. He looked at her now and then, his brow narrowed.

"Mine are still be itchin' me," he said, massaging her feet.

Gemma felt herself go limp, her head falling back into brittle grass. All at once she saw a hazy figure on the other side of the lot, standing at the top of the steps.

"That's my mama," she managed to say, sitting up abruptly. She pulled her feet from him. They tingled. She could see her mother standing motionless, then fumbling through her purse. Gemma got to her feet and walked slowly away, turning to him suddenly, then continuing to the clearing where she'd left her shoes. He stood by the trailer, watching her. She glanced back once as she got into her shoes and socks. And then she walked toward her mother, burying the button deeper in the pocket of her pinafore.

Juanelle turned her head toward the screen door and called: "Frank, you got a customer down there."

🐓 *A girl will be kissed if she hears a bird sing after dark.*

Crouched over the dinette table with cigarettes and a fresh pot of coffee, Aggie and Frank studied the papers. Gemma watched them murmur and laugh sometimes as they flipped through page after page.

"I don't get some of this legal stuff, Aggie," Frank said.

"You aint supposed to get it," she said, using the sharp end of her pencil to scratch under her wig. "That's what I got my guys down at the D.A.'s office for. They'll tell me if this aint on the up-and-up."

"Well, I hope so," Frank said, looking at her meekly. He poured them both cups of coffee. "I just want to understand what this is saying here, since I own it."

"Honey, you own it," she said, sitting back, stretching her arms over her head. Gemma could see her back bulge between her slacks and her brassiere. "You own you a piece and I own me a piece, and just as soon as those boys at the oil company get out yonder and do their tests, we'll own a heck of a lot more."

"I don't know," he said, his eyes glazing over.

"I'm getting me a swimming pool and filling it with ice cubes," Juanelle said, fanning herself with a magazine. She sat across the room on the sofa, opposite Gemma, and smoothed down the black slip over her thighs. "Ag, just get 'em to do those tests, will you? I can't stand this heat."

Gemma sat in her mother's kimono, her hair still wet from

her bath. Self-consciously, she'd put on her glasses to read her Bible. Through the dark front bedroom she could see headlights sometimes, and neon flashes in red and amber. Out the back windows, crickets chirped in the dark.

"I'm going over to Dallas to get me a chargaplate at Neiman's." Juanelle leaned her head against the wall, stroking one hand down her long neck. "And then I'm going somewhere."

"*We're* going somewhere, sugar," Frank said, grinning at her from across the room.

"All right, where we going?" Juanelle asked coyly.

"Wherever you want."

"New York?"

"If that's what you want."

"Hollywood?"

He nodded and laughed. "They'll end up putting you in pictures."

"Probably," Juanelle said, looking back at her magazine. "Humphrey Bogart or one of those guys'll probably want to use me in one of their movies." She stretched, both arms flailing to her sides so that Gemma could see a page full of movie stars in her hand. "What are you reading?" she asked Gemma.

"'Bout when Jesus fed all them people with just seven loaves and a couple small fish."

Juanelle looked at her, the dim light from the lamp on the end table making the woman's skin look mottled. "Shoot."

"You ever read that story?"

"Course I have, kiddo. You know you 'n' me came from the same place. Hard to get away from there without having that shoved down your throat." She took a long drag from her cigarette, her eyes on Frank and Aggie. She watched them closely, smiling to herself, sometimes fanning her face with the magazine. "You ever see *The Ten Commandments*? It's an old one."

Gemma shook her head.

"Well, if you ever get a chance to see it . . . I read somewhere in one of these magazines that they want to make it again, but bigger and better this time."

"Maybe they'll put you in it, Juanelle," Frank said, his lop-sided grin spreading through cigarette smoke.

"Why not," she said flatly. "Why the heck not."

Gemma held the Bible close to her face, reading, her lips moving, almost saying the words aloud.

"Now that we got the deeds filed with the county out there, aint nothing more to do but wait," Aggie said, crossing one leg over the other and turning slightly to Juanelle.

"I *can't* wait, Aggie," Juanelle said.

"Well, you'll just have to," Aggie said. "I been waiting ten years, and if I can wait that long you can wait a couple months."

"Shoot."

"My brother dropped dead two days after he found out they was oil on this property. Dropped dead and left no will. It took me this long to get Margie to see." Aggie tapped a cigarette on the table before she lit it. "Wanted to keep hold of the land just 'cause R.D. loved it so much."

"Shoot, she probably wanted that oil for herself."

"She didn't know," Aggie said, nodding her head at both Juanelle and Frank. "I thought that was it for a long time, but she didn't know. R.D. never told her, for one reason or another. He was that way 'bout certain things. I was out there visiting at the time they made those tests. He just never told her. She was only being obstinate and hardheaded. And it took a mighty long time for her to decide to sell out and get a smaller place in town."

"Mighty nice of you to think about me, Aggie," Frank said.

"Heck, partner, there's plenty of land there for both of us," she said, reaching across to slap his shoulder. "Two hundred and thirty acres' worth. And Margie's got her a nice little duplex in Tyler, something she can manage in her old age. I figger we all come out happy."

"If you ask me," Juanelle said, suddenly standing and turn-ing the fan which pointed at her from the window to "high," "she's a damn fool to give up all that oil. If them tests were ten years ago, I figger that oil's been collecting down underground

145

all this time, and shoot, no telling what it's worth." She fell back heavily into the sofa cushions. "And I'm gonna have me something nice to manage in my old age."

Aggie chuckled and turned back to Frank. Gemma could see him point to various spots on the legal-size page before him and nod eagerly.

"Poor ol' Frank," Juanelle said, her voice pitched so just Gemma could hear below the fan's loud motor. "He's finally gonna be something. He aint never known how before."

And Gemma sat with her Bible facedown in her lap, watching her mother lounge beside her. Juanelle brought a cigarette lazily to her lips, puffed a few times, then flicked the ashes in the standing ashtray next to the sofa. For the first time she could remember, Gemma could see her ears. Juanelle had just scrubbed her face, massaging the tiny lines around her eyes and along her forehead, and she had pinned back her hair for that. The roots were brown. Gemma looked at her mother's ears, absently feeling her own earlobes, thinking: they're big, just like his.

"Well, I'd sure be teed off if I was Margie and found out I'd thrown away a fortune," Juanelle called above the din of the fan.

Aggie turned her head, each hair on the curled champagne-colored wig she wore moving in place so that her head seemed independent of her body. "She aint gonna know. Them boys from Austin will be up shortly to do the test. I was on the phone with 'em today. They'll give the results to me. Me and Frank, now that we're the owners. She aint gonna know." Her head rotated back again with the same ease.

Juanelle clapped her hands together. "We're gonna be rich!" She trembled all over. "Kiddo, I'm gonna fix you a bubble bath. You ever had one?"

"I don't know."

"You don't know? Well, you'll be taking plenty from now on." She leaned forward momentarily to put out her cigarette. "You 'n' me will sit in the bubble bath all morning if we want."

"We will?"

Juanelle leaned across and patted her knee. "We'll get ourselves facials and mud baths, and then go shopping."

Gemma watched Juanelle's eyes flash toward the ceiling as she rested her head against the wall. It made her knees shake when she saw her mother so excited. She studied the woman's face and wondered what she was thinking, wondered if she was picturing the two of them in a gigantic bathtub filled with bubbles. And then Juanelle belched, holding her chest and whistling at the same time. Gemma caught a scent of the chili they'd had for supper.

"Hey," her mother said all at once, "you want to go to finishing school?"

Gemma blinked several times. She said she didn't know what that was.

"That's where they teach you to walk with a book on your head, and how to sit right, and how to know which fork to pick up. They also teach you how to be a model and sometimes they'll put you in magazine ads. I wish I'd had that chance." She looked absently across the room at Frank, her head slightly tilted. "I'd a been in Neiman's catalog right now, I bet."

The dull constant hum of the fan had blocked out most of the highway noises. It began to make Gemma drowsy. She wondered when they'd let her make up the sofa and go to sleep. It must have been after ten. She could not remember if she and Dillard had ever stayed up so late. Her hair was almost dry. Suddenly Juanelle reached across the sofa and felt it.

"Shoot. I don't feel up to rolling another head today," she said, squeezing the girl's hair. "What you say we just wet it in the morning and I'll roll it quick then. That oughta give you enough curl."

Gemma shrugged, mumbling that she didn't care.

"Your hair is just like mine, falls straight as a board in this weather."

Juanelle flipped through the magazine, stopping now and then to show Gemma some movie star's dress. Gemma didn't know who many of these women were, but she guessed they must be important. Her mother was so impressed by them. She turned her Bible over and tried to read, but the words stood still on the page; she was too sleepy to make them flow.

"You tickle me to death the way you read that thing," Juanelle said. Gemma looked up. "I bet you read that cover to cover more times than I read *Gone With the Wind*. I know you have—I never got through that once."

Gemma watched her closely, wanting to ask if Juanelle would like her to read aloud, but not daring. Her mother closed the magazine and rested it in her lap.

"What you get outta that?"

"Stories. 'Bout Jesus and how he wants us to live."

Juanelle cackled low in her throat and said: "Why, that's 'bout just what I get outta here." She patted the magazine. "I figger those big ol' movie stars and Jesus Christ got a lot in common."

"That aint true," Gemma said, holding the Bible against her kimono, her back rigid. "None them ever loved the Lord. None them ever died for your sins."

"Whew," Juanelle said, amused, lighting another cigarette. "Not my sins, kiddo. I 'spect they're too busy answering for their own."

"After death, the judgment," Gemma said, her face dark. "We all gotta answer."

"I reckon you're right."

"Then why do you worship 'em like graven images?"

Juanelle gazed at her curiously, then laughed, saying: "Frank, Aggie, listen to this . . ." Then more quietly, when she saw tears well behind Gemma's thick glasses: "You take that stuff pretty seriously, don't you?" She reached over and brushed hair from the girl's forehead.

Gemma didn't answer. She saw Aggie and Frank look up from their papers momentarily. She could feel the cushions move as her mother inched closer.

"That's all right if you wanna believe in that stuff," Juanelle said softly, leaning forward and resting her elbows on her knees. "I found out you go through life believing a whole mess of things before it's all over. I reckon I felt kinda like you one time, long time ago, though I wouldn't admit it to a living soul now." She smiled at Gemma, her face close to the girl's. "Shoot, when I was a kid—and heck, I can't remember what it was that happened—but one summer I started spending lots of time by myself out there in the middle of nowhere. That's after my mama had left. And I was thinking 'bout nature, and all that kind of stuff, and why the heck I was there. I couldn't come up with no answers. I 'bout forgot all this." She leaned back and dragged the ashtray to her with one foot. Then even more softly, her lips close to the girl's cheek: "I never studied the Bible or nothing, but I'd gone to Sunday school when I was little, gone with Mama. I started going again for almost a year and I was saved and everything. The whole routine. I'd stand up there pretty as you please, singing those songs at the top of my voice every Sunday, and I'd listen to the preacher. Take in every word like I knew what he was talking about. My God, it made me feel so full inside. Made me feel all different.

"Then this guy started coming to church. We'd sit together in the back, all us kids. He started coming and I liked him a lot. Pretty soon we was sitting together, him and me, and some-times at Wednesday prayer meeting or evening service, he'd bend toward me and give me a kiss. Heck, I thought some-body'd see, but they never did. We was always in the back, over to the side. All my girlfriends knew 'bout it, and they thought it was real fine I was in love. They'd let us alone, even sit in front of us so nobody'd see what was going on. He had the prettiest green eyes and yellow hair. I like to melt when he looked at me. Soon he'd be sitting with one arm round me there in the dark church, and he'd slide another hand up my dress during the prayer. That 'bout made me fall to pieces. Fall to pieces. I wasn't scared of getting caught. I just didn't know what I was feeling, but I knew he liked it too. Liked it so much he wasn't able to stand up for the invitational." Her voice became even more of a whisper. Her breath grazed Gemma's neck. "Pretty soon, we'd skip that evening service altogether and we'd sit out in the parking lot in his pickup. Shoot, I wasn't much older than you and I didn't know what was going on. I had an idea, but not really. I just knew it felt good, and I didn't want him to quit, either. It was like singing hymns; it made me feel all full inside."

Her voice trailed off. Wild strands of her hair tickled Gemma's nose. She could hear her mother breathing. On the spur of the moment, Gemma asked: "Was he my father?"

Juanelle looked into her eyes, shaking her head. "I never knew what became of that boy. He just stopped coming."

They were both quiet for a while, and then Juanelle patted her knee briskly, looking across the room toward the others. "I got something I best talk to you about."

"Hey, what y'all whispering about over there?" Frank asked.

"Nothing. Girl talk," Juanelle said flatly. Her eyes wandered over the ceiling, then she moved in closely to the girl again. "You know, the first time I saw Frank King, I was pumping gas over on the north side of Dallas," she said, her voice lowered again. "He was a mechanic, come in to see 'bout some parts he needed for somebody's car. Well, I saw him and something hit me right here, right in the gut. I just figgered out what that was. He reminded me of that boy in the pickup. He don't look nothing like him, maybe just round the eyes. But something reminded me."

She turned to Gemma and laughed, then hugged the girl to her. Gemma could feel her mother's hand, cold, firm, as it slipped inside the kimono, rubbing across her chest. "I know you aint already, but one day soon you're gonna be a woman. You're already showing signs."

Gemma pulled away, wrapping the garment around her, glancing across at Frank. He and Aggie were engrossed in their contracts. Gemma held the Bible against her chest, not moving, knowing her mother had something to tell her, knowing it was something important. That urgency alone made her eyes water. She blinked, waiting.

"Sometimes when a man and a woman get together," Juanelle began, studying the ceiling for a moment, searching for the right words, "sometimes they make a baby in the woman."

"I know that," Gemma said, her eyes darting to Frank, her voice barely above a whisper.

"You do?" Juanelle laughed. "Well, well. You ever seen a boy naked?"

Gemma nodded.

"Where did you see that?"

Gemma watched her carefully, then said: "At the lake. They was swimming and they didn't have anything on."

Juanelle nodded, lighting another cigarette. "All right. That's a start. Now I reckon you noticed what was different 'bout them, how they were put together down there 'tween their legs."

"I know; I know all about that."

"Well, when a man and a woman are havin' sex, or makin' love, whatever you wanna call it, they're joined together . . . the man's . . ."

"Juanelle, what are you two talking about over there?" Frank asked.

"I told you: nothing. Just mother-to-daughter talk." She moved her face into Gemma's. "Anyway, the man's . . ."

"I know," Gemma said quietly. "I know all about that already."

"Now how the heck do you know that?"

"Doreen told me," Gemma said, looking down.

"That old busybody," Juanelle said, sitting upright. "Who does she think she is?" She sat with her arms folded, her face rigid, and she stared across the room into the kitchen area for a time without saying anything.

"She just explained it to me in case I was wondering about

any of that stuff. She said they wasn't nobody else to. Pop couldn't."

"That's for sure," Juanelle said. "And were you? Wondering?"

Gemma didn't know what to say. She said: "Yes."

Juanelle smiled; she exhaled as though she were relieved. "Well," she said. "I reckon that's all right." She stroked the girl's head. "Doreen Hadley probably mixed in some church stuff 'bout marrying, and it don't always work out that way. Most times it don't. You understand what I'm talking about?"

"I think so."

."You gotta know that they aint nothing wrong with it. Shoot. Only thing that's wrong is if you think it is." She pointed to her head. "Just 'cause that happens don't mean a baby is coming, not by a long shot. You can't have that hanging over your head all the time or you'll hate yourself. They's ways of making sure it don't happen, too."

Gemma listened carefully.

"Gwen always makes 'em pull out at the right moment, but that's no good. Heck, that aint fun for anyone. Only makes 'em grumpy. Best thing is for you to make sure they're wearing something, you know, one of those things they get in the men's room at gas stations. Most gas stations got 'em. Frank's got one downstairs. Make sure they're wearing one of them and you won't get pregnant."

"I got one what, Juanelle?" Frank asked, sitting up, staring over at them.

"Just never you mind," she said.

"Now I want to know what you're telling that girl I got," he said, pointing a pencil at her.

Juanelle waved him away and whispered to Gemma: "It's one thing to know how to have babies, and another to know how to not have them and enjoy yourself without being scared all the time."

"Were you scared?"

"Shoot." Juanelle sniffled. "I didn't know nothing, nothing 'cept that I sure liked boys. I sure liked being with 'em."

Gemma sat with the Bible closed in her lap. Aggie was explaining something to Frank. Neither of them was aware of what the girl and her mother were talking about, but Frank's brow knitted from the snatches of conversation he'd heard. She watched her mother bend forward with deliberation and press out the cigarette in the ashtray.

"You wish you'd a not done that with my father," Gemma asked suddenly, "not had me?"

Juanelle turned her head sharply, her face tense. She continued pressing the cigarette butt around the sides of the ashtray. Suddenly her expression eased. She took Gemma in her arms and held her closely. Gemma could smell rose water about her throat. Chili and rose water.

"I aint sorry for nothing," Juanelle whispered. Gemma could feel how the words vibrated in her throat. "I aint sorry for it, kiddo. I'm glad you came along. It just aint been easy, these past few years especially. I've been moving here and there; I've had more jobs and addresses than I can remember."

"You never came to see me."

"I never did 'cause I knew you were all right. I knew you'd be taken care of. I wasn't in a place to." Her mother's voice was choked. "I came as soon as I could, as soon as I thought I could manage it. I knew you'd be needing me about now."

Gemma let her mother rock her for a while. She didn't think she'd ever pull away, even when Juanelle was racked with a fit of coughing.

"You just don't know what it's been like for me."

"I figgered you didn't want me."

"That wasn't it. You just don't know. Someday you'll understand, when you're a mother; you'll know then."

"I was just wondering if you was glad I come," she said. "Here."

Juanelle held her at arms' length, shaking her head. She

kissed the girl's forehead and said: "Course I am; that's what I went back to Twilight for."

"I was just wondering."

And then somebody was rapping on the door and it opened before anyone could call out. Gwen stood inside the kitchen, bathed in dim-watted light. Her hair was pulled back tightly in a French twist. She slouched to one side, her straight black skirt taut against one thigh. One hand rested on her hip while the other patted the collar of her blouse.

"They're animals down yonder," she said, smiling at the others. "'Bout eat me alive."

"What you talking 'bout, Gwen?" Juanelle said, getting up, almost pulling Gemma with her.

"Ol' J.B. and his brother. Don Doyle."

"Shoot," Juanelle said, waving a hand at her. "I thought you was talking 'bout something exciting."

"Exciting! They 'bout tore up The Spur just now over me."

"Come on."

"Over *me*, I'm telling you." Gwen threw back her head, laughing, one hand smoothing the curve of her French twist. Her glasses caught the overhead light. She came forward and rested her hands on the back of one of the dinette chairs.

"What you going down there and teasing those boys for?" Aggie asked, shifting in her seat. "You aint nothing but a tease." She pursed her lips and lit a cigarette, looking perturbed. Gwen moved around to her and pinched her cheek, which didn't help. Aggie slapped Gwen's hand away.

"Ah, come on, Ags. Come on."

"Get on outta here," Aggie mumbled, stewing, her chin buried down in her blouse.

"I was just having fun with 'em."

Aggie didn't say anything for a moment, then: "I think you have too much fun."

Gwen backed away, a smile still on her face.

"I don't like it," Aggie mumbled quietly. "You know that." She looked up at Gwen, her jaw set firmly. "You know that."

"I know," Gwen said, returning the look. They stared at each other for a long, uncomfortable moment. The only sound that could be heard in the room was the electric fan in the window. And just then, while the rest of them watched, the girl's spirit seemed to deflate. She *was* a girl, all at once looking too young behind hard-edged makeup, too young, masquerading in wishbook garb, to be out on her own. She shifted her weight as though she were on trial, as though she might begin to sob in front of them all and plead for leniency. Gemma could feel a tension pass between the others, one she didn't quite understand. It embarrassed her.

"Well," Juanelle said, breaking the spell, "tell me what happened." Now that her mother had moved away, Gemma tucked her feet under her on the sofa. The Bible lay closed at her side. Her mother's and Gwen's shadows danced over the walls of the room.

"Oh, it wasn't nothing, not really," Gwen said uneasily, stealing a glance at the two figures hovered over the dinette table. "Started out as a joke, but things got outta hand and before I knew what was going on there, they was fists flying and glass breaking and J.B. was saying he was gonna beat his brother to a pulp. But that pretty young thing, he was just standing there with his big ol' shoulders and twinkling eyes, smiling like I don't know what. That made J.B. madder."

"Shoot!" Juanelle squealed, slapping her hands together. Gemma saw her eye Aggie. "I sure wish I'd been there."

"Girl, you'd a died." Gwen shook her head, blowing smoke through her nose. "You'd a died."

"What was that, Aggie?" Juanelle asked, turning to the dinette table. "You say something?"

Aggie tightened her fist around the pencil and looked up at them from the papers.

"I'm glad you wasn't there, Juanelle," Frank said.

"Oh, shoot," she said, waving him away, annoyed. She took Gwen by the arm and led her to the sofa. Gemma had to shift to give them room. The two women faced each other, talking through the din of the fan. "Now tell me how it started."

"Well, it . . . if you'd been there, it never would of happened."

"No! Oh, shoot."

"Yes, ma'am, I'm telling you. The whole thing started 'cause J.B. wanted to sit by me at the bar and so did Don. Course, I wanted Don there and I s'pose he knew it too. Lordy! Well, ol' J.B. was feeling pretty good and he says that since I was the only good-looking woman at the bar he was gonna sit by me. He says, 'That Juanelle, she don't wanna come down and have a good time with me, so I'll have to sit with you, Gwen, honey.' And I says, 'J.B., are you insultin' me? That's sure what it sounds like.' You know, I was just kidding. Heck. And that boy with me, Don, he gets all riled up and starts a fight with his brother. Glass was flying."

"Oh, I wish I'd gone down there tonight," Juanelle said. Gemma could see the excitement on her face.

"Now, hon," Frank said, his words coming out in a slow drawl. "You know I don't like you spending your evening down there."

"Stop it, Frank," Juanelle snapped. "Gwen and I go down there to unwind. Aint nothin' wrong with that. You aint showed me anything better here, 'cept going to sleep right after dinner."

"I get tired; I put in a full day."

"Well, I don't lay around in no hammock. I gotta unwind. Till you can come up with something better, Gwen and me will do what we want." She lit her cigarette, then Gwen's, her face flaring in the light from the match. "Right, Gwen?"

"I reckon, Juanelle."

"Right, Aggie? Frank?"

The two sat across the room at the dinette table, both bowed over the papers before them. Neither of them looked at the women on the sofa.

It took a few moments for Juanelle to control her anger

when she turned back to Gwen. Gemma got up, pulling the kimono snugly around her. She went to the window, standing to one side so that she wouldn't block the fan from her mother, and she stared into the darkness.

"Miss Gwen's gonna get herself in trouble one of these days," Aggie said, loud enough for the women to hear across the room. "I sure hope she has somebody to get her out of it."

"Ag . . ." Gwen began, but Juanelle put out her hand.

"Won't you be there to get her out, Ag?" Juanelle asked.

The woman at the dinette sat up straight, her back rigid. She still didn't turn. After a moment, Frank said something and they continued their careful deliberation over the papers before them. Frank grinned once, his fist shaking excitedly in midair as though he were about to throw dice. Across the expanse of hazy city darkness a fiddle began to play. Gemma pressed her cheek against the screen, listening intently for each note to rise and fall and eventually rise again over the hum of the fan beside her. The two women relaxed finally and sprawled across the sofa, busily working over Gwen's story. At the table, Frank stretched both arms over his head, his fingers spread, and he said: "Juanelle, honey. We're gonna be rich. We're gonna make a killing."

As she listened to the fiddler scratch out his melody, Gemma saw her mother's gaze shift suddenly from Gwen to the man at the table. Juanelle's eyes flared with urgency, with a passion and turbulence that frightened the girl. Gemma closed her eyes and haltingly hummed "Turkey in the Straw" to herself, slightly out of tempo, with the erratic nocturne floating across the weed-covered lot.

𝕐 *Make a joyful noise.*

Behind freshly painted white doors, a piano struck the opening chords, languishing at the end of the refrain while hymnals were pulled from their racks. Cushions on the pews made rasping noises as people stood.

> *Come home . . . come home . . .*
> *Ye who are weary, come home . . .*
> *Earnestly, tenderly, Jesus is calling . . .*
> *Calling, O sinner, come home!*

And outside, the sun beat down on the hoods and windshields of their automobiles. Heat shimmered from the asphalt on the parking lot, almost diffusing the glare of chrome from bumpers and rearview mirrors. The piano chords quickened with spitfire succession. Music from the opened windows seemed to hang suspended over the parking lot in the stillness of the midday temperature. Between Casa Loma Courts, its hutlike cottages lined in a tight row along a dusty graveled drive, and Smitty's Knife and Saw Sharpeners, there seemed to be a special sphere, a magnetic field, with Bethel Bible Church at the hub. Traffic along the Jacksboro Highway streamed noiselessly by, the regular cadences absorbed in the reverberation from the redbrick building with a squat lighthouse-type steeple at its peak.

And now inside they were standing, row after row, in their best summer clothes. The piano filled the church with a sharp flourishing melody. It might have echoed, had the ceiling been higher. The pianist, her chin thrust forward, leaned into the opened hymnal resting in front of her face. She hit each chord with zeal, and the sound of pedals being pressed to the floor groaned through each phrase with a whisper. The men in the congregation were in shirtsleeves, their suit coats draped over the backs of the pews. They stood red-faced, ties still in place. Some looked straight ahead at the altar; some gazed at their hymnals or, absently, toward the opened windows, where sunlight was framed by still, stagnant draperies. Wet, sweeping circles under the arms marked white shirt after white shirt, giving the air a sweet, sickening scent of roll-on.

The women pressed handkerchiefs to their necks. Across the church, the shift of their flower-trimmed hats gave the illusion of a spring field just awakening. Some fanned themselves with church bulletins.

The preacher began the hymn, waving one hand out from the pulpit. He tilted his head toward the choir and choir director as if to give them the correct pitch. The sleeve of his robe billowed as though he possessed a gentle cooling breeze all to himself. He began the hymn much more quickly than it should have been sung, his gaze serious, his eyes moist, and his voice still quivering from the feverish message he'd delivered. Into the verse, his pace slowed, and for a moment most of the congregation raced ahead into the next phrase.

> *Tho' we have sinned, he has mercy and pardon.*
> *Pardon for you and for me.*

He paused to smile down upon them until they were singing together once more.

"*Lift* your voices in praise," he shouted through the chorus. "Lift them up and praise the Lord!"

He stood in front of the pulpit now, singing over their heads, not looking at the hymnal he held opened in his left hand. His mouth quivered as he plunged into: *Why should we tarry when Jesus is pleading*, leading them into the next verse. To one side, the woman at the piano swayed, her hands lifting high from the keys, fingers spread, then pouncing down again in attack. She sat in profile to the congregation, turning sometimes to sing to them, and sometimes to the white-robed choir lined in two rows on her other side. *Come home . . . come home . . .*

The preacher rested one hand on the pulpit, singing into the faces in the front row. His hand slipped out of sight, and the large golden cross mounted on the back wall over the choir slowly began to grow brighter. Around the church, people began to sniffle. Opened palms were brought up to wipe cheeks. *Coming for you and for me.* He stepped down, one gold-carpeted step at a time, until he was standing on their level, just behind the altar.

"Let this be the time," he said in a rich voice when the hymn was finished. "Let this be the time *you* come. You come and accept the Lord Jesus Christ as your personal Savior. *This* is the day. Now. Don't put it off, my friends. Don't say to yourselves, maybe next time, next week. *Now* is the time He wants you to come and declare yourselves. You know it in your hearts." The piano continued softly. Purse clasps opened and closed. Some blew their noses. "He don't want you to wait. He's asking you now. Be glad! Rejoice if He's touched your heart today."

And across the church, people began to shift from one foot to the other. From where they sat on the aisle in the middle, Gemma could see women crying, men covering their faces with their hands. Juanelle stood next to her, on the aisle. Gemma looked up at her, feeling her own eyes fill. Her mother stared straight ahead at the preacher, at the softly singing choir, at the golden-lit cross glowing over the congregation. Holding the opened hymnal to her chest, she seemed completely unaware that Gemma was beside her. They wore their seersucker mother/daughter dresses, and Juanelle had added a red wide-brimmed straw hat she said she hadn't had occasion to wear for years.

"Come home!" the preacher beckoned, his arms raised. "Jesus is calling, come home."

And around the church, Gemma could hear hymnals being slid back into the racks, and people shifting, stepping aside so that their neighbors could walk down the aisle toward the front. A man passed them, his ears sunburned. Then two girls. They lumbered up the center aisle toward the preacher, who welcomed them with opened arms. He put his arms around each of them and spoke into their ears. The choir continued to sing. The three people up front knelt at the altar. Gemma could see the man's shoulders quiver. Both girls were sobbing, their arms around each other.

"*If* He has touched you today, please come," the preacher cried. "You know it if He has. You may not want to come up, because you're afraid. But He's watching over you. He'll keep you."

Then the piano changed chords. The choir director stood at the pulpit, gazing down at them through wire-rimmed spectacles. He let the music build halfway through the refrain and then he said: "Turn to number 54. 'Throw Out the Lifeline.'" The preacher leaned over those at the altar one at a time, his hand gripping theirs above their heads. The choir director raised one hand to lead the hymn.

Though she wasn't wearing her glasses, Gemma found the page almost at once. She didn't need to look at the words: she knew them by heart. *Throw out the lifeline across the dark wave . . . There is a brother whom someone should save.* Juanelle still clutched the book to her chest, and when Gemma tried to pull it away so that she could find the new hymn for her, the woman's arms grew rigid. *Somebody's brother! oh, who then will dare . . . To throw out the lifeline, his peril to share?* Gemma was startled at first. She pulled her mother's sleeve, but Juanelle did not look down. Her eyes were still trained forward as though the brightly lit cross had transfixed her. Early that morning, her mother had agreed to come with her three miles down the highway, walking on the shoulder, moving against the traffic. Juanelle's lips had pressed into a smirk at the dinette table, and she had put out her cigarette, saying: "Why the heck not?" When Gemma asked her. And now the girl was confused. Her mother stood beside her as though she'd been struck dumb. It was as though a thread from the past had suddenly tickled her memory. She blinked. Then she looked down at the hymnal, singing along with the chorus.

Throw out the lifeline! Throw out the lifeline!
Someone is drifting away. Someone is sinking today.

The preacher was standing again, moving to one side behind the altar. He swept one arm toward the heavens and said: "Lord, Lord, these children have come to be saved. They have come to accept Jesus Christ as their personal Savior. Let Your light shine upon them."

Suddenly, Gemma sensed a shudder run through her mother's body. She looked up to see Juanelle staring ahead into the man's back before them, her gaze leaden, her brow pinched. When she touched her mother's arm, Juanelle's eyes darted to her. She opened her mouth to say something to the girl, then swallowed. *Throw out the lifeline to danger-fraught men . . . Sinking in anguish where you've never been.* Gemma put one hand on her shoulder, as if to guide her. Juanelle shook her head repeatedly. *Winds of temptation and billows of woe . . . Will soon hurl them out where the dark waters flow.* And then they were looking at one another. Gemma could feel her tremble, could see her eyes close and then reopen with a glaze of tears.

"Mother," she whispered, tears stinging her eyes when she said it. *Throw out the lifeline! Throw out the lifeline!*

"No!" Juanelle said, startled, her eyes wide. And then Gemma was walking up the aisle with her, row after row of people on either side watching their procession to the altar, where the preacher waited. They walked side by side, quickly, her mother not turning to the glances around her. The choir and piano sounded around them. Through her hazy vision, Gemma could see the congregation face forward, and her breath quickened. The preacher had reached to envelop Juanelle with a robed arm. And she was bowing low, her head on a level with the preacher's. He spoke into her ear, comforting, holding a hand out for Gemma to join them. And her mother was nodding, nodding. Gemma came forward into the muffle of their warm bodies. Her mother was on her knees now, her folded hands against the bridge of her nose. Before the last verse, the preacher had them all stand at the altar and face the congregation.

"This brother and these sisters have come forward today to join God's kingdom. In the true spirit of Christianity, come forward yourselves after the service and meet them, shake their hands, let them know how glad you are to have them in our fold." He signaled the piano player. *Soon will the season of rescue be o'er . . . Soon will they drift to eternity's shore.*

As the service ended, they came down the aisle. They shook the hands of those standing at the altar, and then the preacher's, before leaving by the side door. The choir still sang. Gemma stood next to her mother, taking hand after hand, listening to names, saying: "Gemma. Gemma Dillard." Juanelle barely spoke above a whisper. She stood, smiling, tears in her eyes. *Someone is drifting away . . . Someone is sinking today.* Gemma watched her, tears still stinging her cheeks. She felt like singing; she felt then as though her heart might burst with joy.

A-men.

🐓 *Sneeze on Wednesday, and get a good letter.*

Gemma left her mother at the cosmetics counter, haggling
with the salesgirl. "It aint my shade," Juanelle said. "I don't like
it."

"We don't take makeup back," the girl told her, her drawl
slow, her eyelids drooping. "Mr. Hill don't let us take nothin'
back like this that somebody mighta used. It aint sanitary."

"Shoot. Aint nothin' dirty 'bout me, young lady," Juanelle
said, clicking her fingernails on the glass-top counter. "Can't
you see that?"

"That's just what he says."

"Where is this Mr. Hill?"

Gemma wandered through the aisles of toothpaste and
shampoo and soap. She stopped for a moment in front of the
school supplies, then again at the rack of postcards. She found
one of a cowgirl riding in the Fat Stock Show parade, to send to
Miss Lawson.

"Mr. Hill is making deliveries now," the girl was saying.
"He'll be right back."

"I can wait. That's silly; I aint hardly used it."

The salesgirl was putting away boxes of perfume on a back
counter. Gemma turned the rack, searching the cards to make
sure this was the best one for Miss Lawson. And then she saw
another one, on the bottom rack. It made her laugh out loud,
and Juanelle glanced at her. "What is it?"

"Nothing." Gemma shook her head, looking at the card closely. It was of a long line of chickens strutting down the center white stripe of a highway. She started for the counter with both cards, thinking: he'll get a kick outta this. But as the girl began to ring up the cards, Gemma stopped her. She looked at the card for a moment, then put it back in the bottom rack.

"I'll just be taking this one, I reckon."

"Mr. Hill won't take back that lipstick," the girl said to Juanelle as she put Gemma's postcard into a paper bag. "That's our policy on makeup."

"Shoot." Juanelle fumed for a moment, staring at the display of lipsticks, row after row of various shades. She lit a cigarette, then said: "Well, I aint waiting. And I'll be buying my makeup somewheres else from now on."

The girl shrugged and turned back to the perfume boxes. Juanelle motioned for Gemma to follow her out to the car, where Frank waited. Gemma could see him resting one hand on the steering wheel as he stared across the parking lot at the highway. As they left, she glanced back at the postcards, at the card of chickens strutting down a road. She had put it back in the rack upside down, and for a moment they looked as though they were being hurled through the air, that maybe the world had turned upside down and they were being blown into oblivion.

Just as they began to pull away, Juanelle tossed the lipstick from the car. It clattered against the plate-glass door.

% *Count sheep.*

Lying on his back in the cramped room, Dillard stared up into darkness. The house was empty now. He might have moved into the middle room. He might have at least slept there. But it didn't seem right. He'd decided long ago that the back room would be his, even though it was hardly large enough for a bed. He'd slept there for more nights than he could readily remember, and now there didn't seem to be much sense in changing.

It was hot. It was the middle of summer. Though his window was raised and he kept the door opened, the air never stirred. He lay in a sweat, the long underwear buttoned to his throat. When he closed his eyes to still more darkness, he tried counting sheep, tried to see them on the inside of his eyelids as they jumped over a small fence. At times, they would stop short at this fence and refuse to go over; they dawdled. They would rub against the rough wood, sometimes going around the easy way, sometimes turning back. He lost count.

Most nights now he had the same dream: he was already dead. All there was for him was a discarded florist box which long-stemmed roses had come in. In his dream, he was lying in the box, nestled in green tissue paper. The box was set on two overturned washtubs on the porch. He would have to remain there forever, until the house decayed and crumbled into the earth. Nobody was left to bury him properly. Nobody was left to take care of things as they should be taken care of. Mice came to nibble at his eyes. He couldn't fend them off. He couldn't see past the tissue paper, or call for help. His pleas would be useless. He knew that. Nobody was left.

The room was just as dark when he opened his eyes. Soon the sky would change colors and birds would begin their morning chants. Handsome or Ulysses would crow. He could get up then, dress, and go about his business as he did every day. Some weeks he never spoke to another soul until his Friday egg run.

One morning shortly after Gemma left, Doreen Hadley had come down the road to check on him. He had seen her from the kitchen window, moving through the yard in heavy hoeing boots, her flimsy skirt flying, her sunbonnet cocked back on her head. And he had crept quickly through the house as though it were his mama out there, looking for him to finish his chores. He stood behind the closed door of his room, listening, waiting until her knocks and calls stopped. When he was sure she was gone, he came out. Came out carefully, quietly, in case she was still there. From the living room window he spied her walking back down the road to her place. And he thought: she knows I'm left alone. Again.

He turned to his side. He'd put the small school picture he'd found of Gemma in an old frame and set it on the table next to his bed. He reached over and moved the pocket watch so that he could see her completely, the small stoop-shouldered little girl looking out through thick glasses, her dirty-blond hair straight over her forehead, her lips set into a thin crease of sourness. He'd found the photograph when he'd searched through her room for the money. Little thief. She'd taken it all; she'd emptied the cigar box. And now he'd have to start from scratch. He had never seen the photograph before, had never even known it had been taken. When he found it in the bottom drawer of her dresser under some school papers, he had to sit on her bed awhile. He stared at it for a long time, thinking: can't be nothing but a Dillard.

He tried to slow his breathing. That worked sometimes when he was trying to sleep. How long would it be before it stopped altogether? And then his dream, his long, restless confinement in the florist box, would begin for real. Dallas. Fort Worth. It might take some doing to find Juanelle and Gemma, take time, energy, and money he didn't have now. He sighed, almost admitting aloud to himself: it's too late. Too late to mend any of it, even if I knew how.

The sheep were stubborn. They knew he wouldn't be sleeping that night. They knew he never liked sheep anyhow. He'd be better off counting chickens. He lay back, waiting for the shadows, waiting for the signals that would let him start the day. Getting up reassured him that he hadn't passed over yet, though in the past days and weeks he wondered sometimes if he'd be able to tell when that moment came.

On the table next to his bed, the pocket watch kept ticking.

🐓 *Cold hands mean she's in love.*

About the time Frank King went down to open the station every morning, Gemma would hear fiddle music coming across the vacant field. She would run to the screen to see Rory playing in the opened trailer door. And she would think: soon, Rory. I'll be there soon.

Some time before, she would have seen his mother saunter down the dirt path toward the highway, headed for The Lone Star. Dolores always wore her waitress uniform and apron on the street, and Gemma thought she looked like a movie star from one of her mother's magazines, walking across the back lot of a studio.

"This heat aint healthy for a young girl," Juanelle would say, stooping to see herself in the mirror as she combed her hair. "Don't you feel like you're gonna pass out?"

Gemma would sit on her mother's bed, watching her dress, watching her put on makeup and comb her hair. "No," she'd say. "It don't bother me none."

"Well, I sure as heck hate it. Aint right to have to work in it. I hate sweating buckets while I'm trying to make some woman beautiful."

And once, when Gemma told her, "Heat's just part of God's world," Juanelle had smirked, and snorted smoke through her nose: "Then it's a hell of a world."

After Juanelle finished dressing, she'd leave Gemma a list

of chores. Aggie didn't need the girl in the shop every day. And Frank didn't need her downstairs. She could hand him tools, or make change, but he didn't really need her.

"Well, I aint never been one for housework," Juanelle said, moving from room to room, trying to think of things to keep the girl busy. She usually came up with the same tasks every day—washing the breakfast dishes and the ones from the night before, dusting, sweeping. "Heck, just tidy up," Juanelle would say. "You can do that, can't you?"

"Yes, ma'am."

The chores never took long. Alone in the rooms over the gas station, she began to read through her mother's movie magazines. In her closet Juanelle had two boxes of magazines she'd collected since before the war. Gemma saw that all those movie stars lived in big mansions and drove fancy cars. But they did have problems. How can they look so beautiful all the time and be so miserable, she'd wonder. Sometimes when she was the only one in the house, she'd go into her mother's room and close the door. Looking through the closet, she'd find a blouse or a skirt or a dress that she thought might make her look glamorous too, and she'd try it on. And she'd admire herself in the mirror, even though the image never appeared quite complete until she took off her glasses. She'd stand close to the glass and stare at herself until her eyes would water and she could say: "I do—I do look something like Elizabeth Taylor." Whenever she used Juanelle's makeup, she was careful to replace the powder and rouge and lipstick exactly as she'd found it. Her mother never seemed to notice that it had been used.

And sometimes as she leaned into her mother's mirror, made up, holding one of Juanelle's strapless dresses in place by squeezing her arms to her body, she would hear it again: fiddle music. She'd hurry to hang up the clothes and wash her face so that she could run across the lot. He always waited, never stopped his rambling tune until she was standing before him, breathing hard, smiling, wiping falling curls from her forehead, and hesitantly touching her newly scrubbed cheeks.

"You're lookin' mighty nice today," he'd say, the fiddle still resting on his shoulder. And she'd blush and stammer and reach out to tickle him under the chin.

They'd sit in the door to the trailer sometimes, or go inside. She made him coffee. They pretended it was their trailer and that they were traveling around the country. Gemma would straighten up for him—dust, sweep, wash dishes. He would sit at the table, pretending to read the paper though he was absorbed in every move she made.

On this morning, Gemma told him she would make him an applesauce cake. She stood in the narrow passageway that was the trailer's kitchen, and surveyed the contents of the cupboards, her hands on her hips.

"I make this cake real good," she said, reaching to take down a box of raisins.

"I know."

"How do you know?"

He sat at the table, a newspaper in his lap. He reached over with it to swat at a fly buzzing against the window.

"I sure liked the one you made the other day."

"That wasn't applesauce; that one was chocolate."

"I know."

"Don't you know the difference between applesauce and chocolate?" she asked.

He didn't say anything, but grinned when he saw her smile.

"I hope I can remember how to do it without my recipe. I only made it once for Pop. But it was real good."

"I might take it to The Lone Star and sell it where my Dolores . . ." He hesitated, fingers to his lips, then he began again. "I might sell it down there at The Lone Star with my other things. It'll be good business." He grinned and drummed his fingers on the table. "Where are the kids?"

"Shhhhh!" She put a finger to her lips. "They're sleeping in yonder. Don't make much noise, 'cause they need their nap. I swear, I was up with 'em most of the night."

"Oh," he said, his voice low. "I won't." He reached across and opened the café curtains all the way, letting in a stream of light. "Where did you say we was today?"

"Mexico." She put a mixing bowl on the counter.

"Oh." He rested the fiddle in his lap. "I just saw a Mexican."

"Did you?" She lined up the ingredients on the narrow counter. Sugar, eggs, butter, a can of applesauce. Flour, she needed flour. "Rory, where's your mama keep the flour?"

He looked at her, puzzled.

"You know, flour, that white stuff you gotta use for baking and making chicken-fried steaks."

He raised his shoulders, grinned, and rubbed the sandy-colored curls on top of his head. Gemma began opening cabinets and drawers until she found it. "I swear, you men," she said. "Helpless sometimes."

"I know," he said, testing his coffee with his tongue. "I just saw me another."

"Another what?" She tied on an apron she found hanging from a doorknob.

"'Nother Mexican. Just walking round out there like he don't know where he's headed."

"I told you, we're in Mexico today. You see a lot of Mexicans over there." She began to mix the ingredients together, humming something to herself. Rory brought his fiddle to his chin, but she held a finger to her lips.

"I forgot. The kids. Where did you say they are?"

"There in the bedroom," she whispered, wiping a hand on the apron. "They need to get their nap out or they'll be cranky all evening."

"I know." He laughed, rolling his eyes and taking a deep breath. He put the fiddle down in the chair next to him and watched her, his hands locked behind his head. "Where you got them napping?"

"There." She pointed to the closed door on the other side of the kitchen.

"You got 'em in our room?" he asked, grinning.

"I couldn't put them out here in their bed," she said, "not while I was working. This way we can talk before you have to go to work."

He nodded, raising his eyes toward the folded-up bunk he usually slept on, over the café curtains. Gemma held the bowl against one hip and stirred in the applesauce with a wooden spoon. She could feel his eyes on her, though she didn't look at him. All at once, she set the bowl on the counter and brought her hand to her mouth. "I plumb forgot to preheat my oven," she said, smiling at him. She turned and set the dial at 325°. "Best I remember, this needs to cook slow."

She dried her hands on a dish towel and came to the table, glancing back once at the bowl on the counter. "I just wasn't thinking," she said.

Rory had been leaning back in his chair. Now he brought all four legs down flat on the floor and put an arm around her waist. It took her breath away, but she stood there, frozen, letting him move his fingers in and out of the apron sash.

"You cook real good," he said. She stared down at the floor, at his enormous feet, which seemed to be tapping out an inaudible rhythm. "I think you fix me good things."

"Thanks," she said, feeling her face flush.

"I told my Dolores that you 'n' me was gettin' married sometime."

Gemma pulled away, flustered, working over the bowl once more though the ingredients were already mixed.

"I told her," he said, his voice quiet, his hands hanging between his legs, "'cause you're so smart. You know how to do everything."

"No, I don't." She cut off a slice of butter and began greasing the pan.

"Yes, you do, Gemma. 'N' I told her."

Gemma covered the bottom and sides with a thin coat of butter, then sprinkled flour in the pan, shaking it around until the deeply burned metallic pan had a dull gray coating. "And what did your mama say?"

"Well, she say that is fine by her. She say that I need me somebody good like that. 'N' I say: 'I know.'" He took a sip of coffee, then drained the cup in one gulp. "I sure do like you, Gemma."

She washed her hands, saying: "Now cut that out, Rory. That aint no way for you to be talking." All the time, she stared through the café curtains over the sink, stared at the heat-burned field behind the trailer, at black billowing smoke pouring from factories in the distance. She could hear him rocking in his chair, hear him tap his fingers on the table. She stared out the window, wishing for once that she'd brought her glasses with her.

"Besides," she said, her voice even, but sounding strangely grown-up to her, "I aint gonna be able to get my license for another couple years yet. Aggie says she'll help me. She says she'll help me all she can, then I can work with her."

"Aggie done told me."

"She did?"

"Yep. But you don't need no help, that's what she say. You're smart 'nough right now to get your license."

"Is that what she said?"

"No." He laughed. "That what I done told her." He grinned and she could see the corners of his eyes crinkle. "My Dolores she told me my daddy was ten years older'n her." The sun caught his eyes. And Gemma could see him suddenly, this grown man she'd played house with every day for weeks. When he stood, his head almost hit the ceiling of the trailer. He opened the door, stood in the doorway and stared out for a moment, before turning back to her.

"I reckon that oven is ready," she said, pouring the mixture into the pan, then carefully putting it into the oven. "It takes 'bout an hour."

They stared at each other for a few moments before he brought a hand over his face, wiping away a sudden twitch.

"I got to be getting ready for my work," he said, sitting back in his chair, looking across the trailer at the window. The sun was so bright now that it made the dust-coated windows appear almost impenetrable. She pulled out a chair and sat next to him.

"We been busy all week there," he said, looking at her, his face sad, almost sullen. "I don't know where they all come from, I swear. I been out there waitin' on tables and going out to the drive-in. Least it makes the day go fast." He sighed, and rested his chin in his hands.

"I got to take the kids to the store to buy their school supplies," she said, her hands in her lap. "I reckon they'll be starting up next week. I'd like 'em to have some new school clothes too."

He nodded, sucking in his bottom lip. "Well, I'm going to my drive-in now," he said, getting up.

"Okay, have a good day at work." She stood too. "I'll have you a applesauce cake when you get home."

"Okay." He stood with his neck stretched forward so that his head wouldn't hit the ceiling. Abruptly, he leaned down to kiss her cheek. And then he left. Standing in the kitchen, she could hear him moving around behind the trailer, kicking through leaves, talking to himself. She stood at the window, trying to catch a glimpse of him, when suddenly he came back inside.

"Well, how was work?" She stood there, still in her apron, her hands on her hips. "You get off early today?"

"I'll be getting off this time every day from now on," he said, staring across at her. "New hours."

He didn't move from the door, but kept watching her.

"Well, that's good," she said finally. "About your hours." She smiled, then began to set the table, putting out plates, knives, forks, and spoons.

"What we having for dinner?" He sat in his seat once again, his arms folded against his chest.

"Well, we're having pork chops and bake beans and mash potatoes."

"That's all my favorite."

"I know it is," she said. "And applesauce cake for dessert."

He nodded, satisfied. Gemma stood beside the oven, waiting, not knowing just what to do then. She could still feel his gaze on her. She peeked inside the oven once. "It's coming along all right." Out of the corner of her eye she saw him begin to rock back and forth in his chair.

"You say today this is Mexico?"

"That's right. We had to drive all night, practically. I was up with the kids; they didn't travel well, none of 'em did. And we got lost, had to detour one time and that threw us all off. 'Bout ended up in Canada." She looked at him suddenly. He still stared, and began playing with the strings of his fiddle.

"Today at the drive-in," he said all at once, "they was these two Mexicans who came in and they wanted to order something. 'N' I say: 'What you want to eat?' 'N' they tell me, but I can't unnerstand 'em too good. But I write it down on my pad 'n' the cook she fix what I write down. Well, they get they dinner and they say: 'This aint what we tell you we want.' I tell 'em that it is, and I show 'em my pad what I wrote on. 'N' they say: 'That aint what we told you.' 'N' I tell 'em it is; it sure is. We 'bout had a fight."

"Did they eat it?"

"Course they did, 'cause I make it good for them. Chicken casserole with mash potatoes. 'N' I tell 'em next time I give 'em a bag of potato chips on the house. They liked that."

"Well, that was sure nice of you."

"I know. It make good business, that what my Dolores always say."

They sat at the table and pretended to eat. He made chewing noises and nodded, rocking back and forth. "This sure is good," he said. "Aint the kids eating?"

"They're taking a siesta." She used her knife and fork, pretending to cut something on her plate. He looked puzzled.

"My Dolores say folks'll come back every time if you give 'em something free, like a bag of potato chips."

"I reckon that's pretty smart thinking," Gemma said. She brought her fork to her mouth and pretended to chew. She could see the muscles in his jaw contract as he chewed. His eyes sparkled, darting to her as he nodded his head and pretended to swallow.

"Was it, Gemma?" He looked pleased with himself.

"Shoot, yeah," she said, touching her paper napkin to each corner of her mouth. "Real smart."

He laughed deep in his throat, nodding, looking down at the empty plate. "Where you say the kids are taking to see?"

"I said they're taking a siesta," she said, stacking his plate on top of hers to clear the table. "Did you have enough?"

He exhaled loudly and rubbed his belly. Gemma put the dishes in the kitchen sink, then opened the oven and said: "I 'spect it's done." She put the cake on the counter and touched the top with her fingers. "Gotta let it cool a bit before we can have our dessert." She felt him staring at her, perplexed, his head tilted to one side.

"What did you say they're taking?"

"A siesta," she said. "That's what they call a nap in Mexico."

"Oh. I know." He relaxed in his chair, drumming on his thighs.

"Miss Lawson told us that every day they take a siesta down here, everybody does. They close down everything— schools, banks, grocery stores—and they all go home and take a nap in the afternoon, when it's so hot. Then later they all go back to school and work."

"I don't like to take naps."

"That don't matter. Everybody does it in Mexico. They do it to get outta the sun."

"Oh." He nodded, staring down at the Formica on the table. Suddenly he looked up at her. "You sure are smart, Gemma."

"It's just what Miss Lawson told us in school." She stood at the counter, patting the top of the cake. "Aint nothing."

Rory folded his arms and rocked forward, his eyes down. When he looked at her again, she saw that something was wrong. "I gotta let this cake cool," she said again, seeing his milky blue eyes brim with tears, starting toward him finally, stopping, then going to his side. She put one hand on his shoulder. He was trembling.

"I wisht they'd told me that when I was at that school place," he said. He put his head against her chest. It made her tingle, and she thought: he can hear my heart thumping ninety-to-nothin'. "They was just making me draw them letters, making me draw them pictures. I had to sit by myself all the time till Miss Aggie come and take me outta there."

Gemma hugged his face close to her. She could feel his tears on her breast through her dress. She rested her chin on the top of his head, then touched his curls with her fingertips. They were soft.

"Siesta," he whispered. "Now I can unnerstand that. I bet next time you 'n' me read something, I bet I know that word. Why didn't they tell me that when I was at that school place?"

"I don't know, Rory."

And then one of his arms was around her and she could feel those fluffy curls shift until his face was against her own and their lips were touching. Her face smarted from his beard. It was blond, invisible. But his lips were warm, not at all as she had always imagined. She didn't move. She tried to remember what those women in her mother's magazines looked like when they kissed their leading men, but her thoughts were confused. All at once, he was standing, banging his head against the metal ceiling. It sounded as though they were on the inside of a drum. Rooted to one place beside the table, she watched as he reached across and unlatched the bunk. He let it down slowly, then stepped on a chair and swung up onto it. He put both arms out to help her.

"We better take our siesta too," he said, his voice low. He stretched out on the bunk. Gemma lay down beside him; their arms barely touched. They both stared at the rust-corroded ceiling hardly two feet away. Several times he reached over to stroke her shoulder. And then he turned to his side at the same time she did. Her back rested snugly against his stomach and he draped one arm around her. She could hardly catch her breath. The arm pulled her into his body. Every time he took a breath, she could feel it. She could feel his voice vibrate between her shoulder blades when he spoke softly: "We're taking a siesta." Soon she could hear him breathe steadily, heavily, exhaling cumbrously through his lips. Gemma clasped both hands between her legs, thumbjoints pressing into herself so that she felt that close warm sensation. It was how she slept every night, the position she woke up in. Though it was a posture she took from habit, it felt different now. She pressed hard, fitting her body closely against his sleeping form. The smell of applesauce filled the trailer; it made her dizzy. His breath pinpointed itself on the nape of her neck. It seemed to blaze down through her body to where her thumbs were pressing. It made her shudder. And she thought: I'm gonna get sick. If I don't get down from here, I'm gonna get sick. But she didn't move, couldn't move. The feeling made her drowsy.

"Rory," she said, turning her head toward the ceiling. "It's sweltering in here."

She could hear him smack his lips, turn over, and scratch his shoulder.

"I think our siesta time is done," she said.

He tried to sit, and thumped his head against the ceiling. It made her laugh. He turned to her, grinning. And then he was over her, talking, saying something she couldn't understand at first. She stared up into his eyes. A line of sweat traveled across her body, down to her armpit.

"I reckon I mean it, Gemma. I sure do like you and I want us to get married."

She smiled at him, then saw that he was serious. She reached to touch his cheek.

"I want us to get married. . . ." His voice trailed off. He stared across the trailer and she could see that he was trying to say the right thing. Something swelled inside her chest and she pulled his face down to her shoulder.

"All right, Rory," she said. She closed her eyes. "All right, you and me'll get married and I'll take care of you." She could feel him tremble, feel it ripple down the length of his body. Then he laughed.

They lay together for a while, neither speaking, neither daring to move away from the other. Her clothes stuck to her body. She got up and rolled from the bunk finally, stepping down on a chair. He looked down from the nest, smiling, and said: "Our siesta is done, I reckon."

"I reckon it is," she said. She took a deep breath. The apples and cinnamon in the air made her head spin.

"Better get the kids up," he said.

"Reckon so," she said, not taking her eyes from him. "If I don't, they'll be up all night." She turned then and went to the kitchen. "This cake's ready."

Without moving, he watched her slice two pieces. "You sure do fix me good things, Gemma."

She looked up at him then, sprawled over the bunk. He let one arm drop over the side, and he waved it back and forth as though he were treading water. She smiled. And then she opened the cupboard, looking for two small plates that matched.

♈ *Marry in white, you'll do all right.*

"I 'spect this aint the worse thing that coulda happened," Juanelle said, biting her lip and staring past Gwen, past the plate-glass window of Aggie's House of Curl, toward the highway. Her fingers scratched inside her smock. "Why, I 'spect she mighta gotten herself tangled up sooner or later with one of them boys down at The Spur, one of them good-for-nothing rednecks who'd leave her with five kids by the time she's old enough to vote."

Gwen sat in her seat, waiting for the next customer to come in from the midday heat. She leafed through a *Good Housekeeping* without looking at the pages, licking her thumb sometimes. Once she closed the magazine and stared at herself head-on in the mirror, not blinking, her eyelids heavy. Juanelle leaned over the empty chair next to hers, brushing off the seat.

"Heck, Juanelle," Gwen said, keeping her voice lowered. "I don't know but what I'd just as soon have me one of them than be stuck with a dummy." She shifted in her seat, bringing one thigh over the other. "That poor girl's gonna have to spend the rest of her days leading him around by the hand."

"I know it," Juanelle said, shaking her head, looking down at the floor and kicking aside a fuzzy ball of hair and dust. "But maybe not; maybe not. I just don't know."

And from the rear of the shop, where Gemma sat painting her fingernails bright red, she could see her mother's back rise and fall. She finished her left hand and held it out. The color made her hand look bigger, she decided, like a grownup's. The two women continued to speak in hushed voices, sometimes glancing at her. Now and then their conversation would slip by the gigantic upright fan facing into the shop, and Gemma would catch words, phrases.

"Aint nothing wrong with Rory, you know."

"Naw," Gwen said. "Just to look at him, you wouldn't guess that he didn't have nothing going on upstairs."

"Now I talked to Dolores last night at the drive-in," Juanelle said, "and she thinks they'll be just fine. I reckon she ought to know, if anybody. I can't imagine she'd agree to it if there was any danger."

"Any danger?"

"I don't mean that. Heck, you know what I'm talking about. His mother is saying it's okay. He's okay to marry."

Gwen leaned forward for her Dr. Pepper. "Course she says that. It takes all the responsibility off her now to have that sweet child take over. I don't know, Juanelle. I just don't know 'bout this."

"I wisht to hell you'd stop saying that. They're gonna be all right. He's a good kid. And Dolores is having them live there in the trailer with her. That's all straightened out. It's gonna take some of the pressure off her."

"I don't see how it's gonna do that. Only pressure she's got is working ten shifts a week."

"Well, now she won't have to if she doesn't want to. Gemma'll be working soon. And Rory. I think she's gonna try to get him on at The Lone Star. Washing dishes or something."

"Oh, brother. Remind me to bring my own silverware when I eat out over there."

Juanelle stood at the screen door, looking out into the bright August glare. Moving reflections of chrome and glass were so brilliant that Gemma wondered how they didn't blind her. After a time, the woman turned to Gwen.

"Everything's gonna be all right. Now I done made my mind up that it is."

"Takes a load off you," Gwen said.

"You kidding me?" Juanelle laughed, moving next to her. "I aint got no load here. I just want to do the right thing by her. For eleven years I wasn't there to do nothing, but now that I am, I want it to be the right thing." She took a swig of Gwen's Dr. Pepper. "'Sides, once Frank's deal comes through, I can afford to give her anything. Send her to one of them big girl schools like the debutantes go to. Or anything. I just want her to do what's gonna make her happy."

"And you think this is it?"

"Why not? She's old enough. Lots a girls got married back home by the time they was twelve."

"I'm not saying that," Gwen said, taking the bottle from Juanelle and wedging it into the corner of the chair next to her. "I'm asking if you think it's the right thing. I mean . . . this kid's not all there. What if their babies turn out that way?"

Juanelle moved around to the counter, took a cigarette from her purse, and lit it. "Shoot, Gwen, now don't go saying things like that. Dolores says he's all right, he's all right physically."

"Well, I can see that for myself." Gwen chuckled. Then suddenly she opened the magazine and stared at the page. "And if you want the truth, well, I don't think she's old enough. Things are different here than out in the country. I mean, Juanelle, girls here don't have to get married so soon. They don't have to."

Juanelle leaned against the counter, her back to the mirror. Holding the cigarette to her lips, she looked at Gwen and said: "And then some girls never do."

Gwen seemed to sink into the chair as she flipped one page after another without looking. Gemma blew on her fingernails; she waved them in the air as she watched the two women. And she thought: you can't even get them to look at you down at The Spur, Gwen, and you're almost twenty.

"My cousin Linda," Gwen mumbled into the magazine, "she's two years older'n me. She's got a good typing job over in Dallas. She never married."

Gemma smiled to herself, putting her hands palm to palm, holding them close to her chest. Her fingernails glowed. Just like her mother's.

Every day now was filled with preparations. The hours, which had crept slowly by in the weeks before, were suddenly charged with plans for the future. There was a dress to buy. There were clothes to pick out. She wanted new dishes and an electric mixer she'd seen in the Sears catalog. She wanted a new nightgown. Underwear.

Rory couldn't understand why their daily routine had come to a halt.

"I thought we was getting married," he said.

"We are, hon. But I got a lot of stuff to do."

"But if we was getting married, I thought we'd be spending time together. You don't come play with me like you used to."

"I got to get ready, you know. There's a lot of things a woman's got to tend to."

"I liked it better when we was just playing together," he said, pouting on the other side of her screen door.

"Rory! Don't be talking like that. We're gonna have a long time to play together once I get everything set."

"I know," he said, moving away, trudging down the steps.

At first her mother had agreed to a church wedding, though she didn't know which church they could have it in.

"Bethel Bible, that one you 'n' me went to," Gemma said.

Juanelle wrinkled her nose and said: "I aint going back in there. It smells like a hospital. I don't want you getting married in a church that smells like a hospital."

"I didn't notice."

"That's cause you wasn't smelling that day or something. Besides, I don't think you oughta mix in that religion crap with marriage. I seen it spoil too many." She thought for a minute, then shook her head.

"I figgered you'd want me to get married there," Gemma said. "You said you 'n' me'd go back there sometime."

Juanelle laughed through her nose and put up her hand. "Count me out, kiddo. I shouldn't a lied to you. It's crummy for a mother to lie to her own kid. Once was enough."

"You liked it, I thought."

"Yeah, so much I came home and threw up."

Gemma didn't say anything.

"I think you'd be better off getting married in the courthouse, by a judge. That way you'll know it's legal. Any old preacher can say some words, and heck, how do you know he's got the power to make it legal? Some of these preachers aint nothing but crooks. A nice courthouse wedding would be the best. Nothing fancy; just legal."

"That what you and Frank had when you got married?"

Juanelle looked at her blankly and said: "Yeah." She sniffled and reached for a cigarette. "Yeah, we kept it simple."

Some mornings, Gemma would lie back in the bathtub and listen to Frank downstairs, waiting on his customers. She would hear him try to make jokes with the men and small talk with the women. It always made her giggle: "Men."

And always, over the blur of traffic noises, she would hear fiddle music. She would look up from whatever she was doing—the magazine she was cutting recipes from, the cookies she was baking, the wildflowers she was arranging for the dinette table—and she would smile, shaking her head.

"Someday I want me a real big table you can seat eight at for dinner," she told her mother one night as they sat at the harshly lit table in the kitchen.

"Shoot." Juanelle leaned back in her chair, looking upward into the bare bulb. Her eyes glistened as she tilted her head to the side. "Me'n Frank'll have us a big one. We'll have us one that goes the whole length of the dining room, with a big ol' glass light fixture hanging over it." She folded her arms over the top of her pink slip and smiled dreamily.

Gemma smoothed the kimono around her and leaned back

too, her fingers laced behind her head. "Oh, me'n Rory aint gonna have a big light fixture. I mean, we might, but most times we'll use candlesticks to eat by."

"We will too," her mother said. "We'll just have that light up there if we want to use it." She looked at the girl, nodding. "I don't know if I want to have eight people at dinner, though. Course you can't always help it. Those that got things have to share, and I'm sure we'll be having to share plenty with a bunch of them that'll be hanging around."

"I'm having Pop come stay with us," Gemma said, staring at the bulb overhead.

Juanelle looked at her through a haze of smoke. "Sounds to me like a good way to spoil a good time. He aint 'bout to move."

"He can still come eat with me and Rory and the kids sometimes," she said.

"Well, I know he aint gonna be at my place," Juanelle said soberly, then abruptly laughed. "I always heard long-lost relatives come outta the woodwork when you come into money. I could just picture him coming to my house sitting there under a big shining glass light fixture all dressed up in a tuxedo and wearing that straw hat."

She brought her chair down flat on the floor and reached across to slap Gemma's arm. Laughing along with her, Gemma got up to pour them each a glass of iced tea.

"Heck," Juanelle said, coughing a laugh, bringing the glass to her lips. "I aint never gonna cook another meal unless I just decide I want to. And knowing me, I aint ever gonna be wanting to again."

"I will." Gemma sighed.

"First thing I'm gonna do is get me a girl to come in to do all that," her mother said. "Fact, I might just get me one soon's the money starts coming in, and not wait till we get our place built."

"You want a Mexican?" Gemma hiccuped and brought a hand to her mouth.

"Shoot, it don't matter none to me—Mexican, nigger, Yankee." She chuckled. "Just so she can keep it all clean and do the cooking. And if she can't, I'll just have to get me two."

Gemma swallowed and ran the tassel of her mother's kimono up and down her arm. "I got an idea. Why don't you just get Gwen to do it?"

"What? What are you talking about? That's the silliest thing I ever heard."

"No, it's not."

"But she's got a job."

"I know, but when I start there, she'll . . . I don't know."

"Don't you and her get along? You get along."

Gemma looked down at the Formica, thinking for a moment. "She keeps bothering me 'bout Rory."

Juanelle laughed. "She's just jealous. She'll get over that quick as she finds her somebody."

"She makes fun of me."

"I told you, it aint nothing. I reckon it just makes her feel over the hill." She rolled her eyes to the ceiling. "Why would she want to be a maid—heck, she'd bust a gut if I asked her that. Besides, you ever seen the way she keeps house?" Gemma hiccuped when she shook her head. "Well, go on over yonder sometime and that'd change your mind about that."

Gemma sat for a moment, thinking, then she said: "I'm getting up every day and doing everything myself—all the cooking, dusting, everything. I'll make Rory a sack lunch—" She hiccuped again.

"You been telling lies?" Juanelle asked, laughing. Gemma shook her head. "Then why are you hiccuping?"

Gemma shrugged.

"Take a sip of tea." It didn't help. They sat quietly, waiting for the next hiccup. When it came, her mother pointed a finger and said, "You been telling lies. I can get rid of 'em for you." She sprang across the top of the dinette table and shouted: *"Boo!"* Gemma sat still, her eyes lowered, her concentration focused inward. *"Boo!"* Finally her eyes lifted to the woman above her. Beads of perspiration covered her mother's upper lip, and she shoved back matted red hair that had fallen onto her forehead. Gemma could see her bony ribs underneath the slip. "There. See what I told you?"

They were gone. Gemma sat waiting for the next one, but it never came. Juanelle hovered over the table, grinning, swaying just enough so that the girl could see her nipples. "Cured."

In the afternoons, Aggie took her under her wing.

"Aint nothing to it," she told the girl, ushering her into the back room of the shop for haircutting lessons. She sat Gemma on a stool. "All you gotta remember is that every head is different and what works on one won't work on another, though some these women come in and don't understand why they can't do their hair just like Grace Kelly's."

"But what happens if you make a mistake?" Gemma asked, watching the stockily built woman take a wooden form and pin a wig to it. "What do you do then?"

Aggie pointed the long comb at her and said: "What you do is never let the customer know. One thing 'bout hair, it'll always grow. Might take longer for some than for others, but it'll always grow. What you do is, you make it right. You'll be just fine. I don't think it'll take you no time to learn."

"I sure hope it don't, Aggie," she said, watching the woman comb out the wig and take the scissors and begin to snip.

"The thing is—now remember this—you gotta make those old gals think they're glamorous. Flatter 'em. Tell 'em how much younger they look. That aint too hard. That's what most of 'em want to hear anyway."

"Yeah, I seen that already," Gemma said. "But you can't just tell any of 'em that and 'spect 'em to believe it."

"No, you gotta know what you're doing; you gotta know. Course, some these girls come in and you do the best you can and they'll never be satisfied. Never. You gotta coax 'em along."

Gemma nodded, her eyes fixed upon the faceless wooden head planted between Aggie's thighs.

"You won't have no trouble," Aggie said. "I get you a job working here after school this fall, and then soon's you and Rory marry, I'll get you into beauty school."

"I was thinking I'd have to wait till I was older."

"Hey, don't worry." She leaned forward and winked. "I'll get you in. I got connections downtown."

Gemma nodded. She took one of the heads on the workbench, put it between her legs, then pinned on a wig.

And later she sat in the beauty shop, hemming two of her mother's old black skirts. "Sewing things," Juanelle had hooted. "Are you pulling my leg? I aint never threaded a needle and I don't intend to try."

Gemma sat on the divan, the skirt over her lap, and she watched Gwen hover against the mirror as she put on her makeup.

"I'm meeting someone at The Spur this evening," she said. Gemma could see her eyes dart to the side, looking back at her. "We was there all night last night, practically all night."

"I thought you was looking tired," the girl said.

"He wanted me to go back to his room."

Gemma continued to stitch along the hem, pulling the needle through the fabric, raising her arm high in the air with the thread. As she went along, she took pins from the skirt and stuck them into the cushion fastened around her wrist.

"He was saying he aint never seen eyes like mine. He was saying they was like some kind of jewel, I forgot what he called it now. It was his birthstone, he said."

"You wear your glasses?"

"Course I did. I wore 'em till he fogged 'em up, and then I took 'em off."

Gemma turned the skirt, then held out the part she'd just finished.

"You'll probably put that thing on and it'll be lopsided," Gwen said, her eyes in the mirror on Gemma.

"I measured."

Gwen pressed her lips together, then opened them slightly. "You taking home ec in school this year?"

"They don't give that till the eighth grade."

"Well, you got a ways to go then, don't you." She pulled away from the mirror, inspected her efforts, and arched her back.

"No," Gemma said, putting the skirt down. "Aggie's checking into me taking some kind of test; I forget what you call it. And anyway, I can get out early."

"That'll be pretty early, won't it?"

"Yep." She returned to the skirt. "So I reckon the only home ec I'll get will be for real."

Gwen ran a finger over an eyebrow. "This guy, his name's Mike, he asked me if I wanted to spend next weekend with him at the lake. He's got property out there, I think he said. I believe I just might go." She puckered her lips. Then she watched herself, thinking, her mouth slightly parted. "I made the cutest ruffle to go around my bed and dressing table when I was in home ec." She turned to Gemma. "Can you use a machine?"

Gemma set her jaw, finishing the skirt without answering.

And then one evening Juanelle came home and stopped cold at the front door.

"What the heck?"

Gemma stood in the middle of the room, a hammer in her hand. She squatted down to close a box of tacks.

"What you been up to?"

"I covered the couch."

Juanelle cautiously approached the sofa across the room. Green-striped fabric had been stretched over the back and arms. Gemma hurried past to smooth out a wrinkle.

"I found that piece of material out back of Aggie's and it was big enough to cover the couch with, so I done it."

Juanelle moved up and down the length of the sofa.

"I still gotta do the cushions." Her mother still didn't say anything. She reached over and touched the back, running her fingers along the place where white stuffing had begun to seep through.

"Well, shoot."

"Don't it look better?"

Juanelle turned to her and shook her head. "Course it looks better. Heck, you could go into business. This thing wasn't worth a plug nickel."

"They got some things over there at the trailer that need covering. I was practicing."

And some evenings while Aggie went over her books, Gemma would sit on the stool behind her. Aggie would tell her about her first shop in East Texas. "It was my brother, R.D., who set me up in that, got me my start. It always helps to have somebody to give you a start."

"Shoot, Aggie," Gemma said, slouching on one leg, her hand on her hip. "I know that."

"I paid him off in no time," Aggie said, looking up from the ledger, looking up at the blank wall, at something Gemma couldn't see. She shook her head. "I'd a never done it if it hadn't been for R.D., bless him."

Gemma sat back on the stool. They were quiet for a moment. She could hear Aggie's pen begin to scratch again on the page. "I just don't want to make any mistakes. I don't want to start fixing hair till I'm sure I won't make any mistakes."

"Honey, you're gonna make mistakes."

"No, I'm not." Gemma shook her head. "I know I won't. If I gotta stay in that beauty school for six years, I'm gonna make sure I can do it the right way."

Aggie turned in her chair. "Go and spend sixteen years there at school and you'll still do something wrong when you start out. I'm telling you. That's the way it's supposed to be. You can't do everything right in the beginning. It takes practice. You'll see. Everything's thataway. Even getting married."

"You're being so good to me, Aggie. Helping me get my start." Gemma moved next to her and put a hand on the

191

woman's shoulder. Aggie looked at the hand, then into Gemma's eyes.

"It aint nothing."

"I 'preciate it."

"You're a fine young lady and I want you to do good. And Rory, well, he's like—like my own. I want y'all to be all right."

Gemma hugged her. She felt Aggie tense her shoulders before she patted her on the back.

"Don't worry. You'll do fine. Just remember, it all takes practice."

On the stool again, Gemma watched her scribble figures, use the adding machine, then scribble some more.

And then one morning amid these plans and preparations, something was wrong.

She lay on the sofa, staring at the stripes in the new fabric. She'd been awake for a long time, but for some reason she didn't feel like getting up. She heard her mother rouse in the other room and go into the bathroom. And then the cramps in her stomach sharpened. The ache had been dull; it had stirred her from a dream. It was dull again. She could hear water running, then Juanelle began to sing. Gemma sat up and swung her legs around to the floor. Then she felt it; it confused her. The water in the other room was turned off. She could hear the towel holder rattle against tile. She was about to pull down her nightshirt and stand when she saw the droplet of blood on her underwear. She tugged the nightshirt down quickly, then raised it cautiously once more to peer at the bead of redness on white.

"You okay, kiddo?" Juanelle stood outside the bathroom door, watching her. She came to the sofa and knelt in front of the girl. Gemma was embarrassed. "Well, kid, this means you're a woman."

Gemma stared at her.

"What's the matter? You told me you know all about this."

"I do, but . . ." She lowered her nightshirt, afraid to move.

"This is it," Juanelle said, standing. "Come on in here."

Gemma hesitated, but then she heard Frank moving around in the bedroom. "Come on, it aint gonna hurt you none to get up."

And she found that she was able to stand; she could walk. She followed her mother into the bathroom, thinking: everything's the same, but I'm different now.

"Just take it easy today," Juanelle told her as she was getting dressed. "Come on over in the afternoon if you want."

"Can I come with you now?" Gemma said.

"Heck, that's up to you," Juanelle said, slipping the dress over her head.

"I'd rather come sit with you now."

She looked at her image in Juanelle's dresser mirror. She didn't seem any different. Sitting at the dinette table, she put on her socks one at a time, her movements cautious. All at once she got up and went to the corner where she'd stowed the cardboard suitcase she'd brought with her from Twilight. She opened the clasps and reached inside for Beecham's hat. It was still there. She pulled it out; instantly the smell brought tears to her eyes.

"I'd run round naked if they'd let me," Juanelle was saying. She stood in the doorway to her bedroom, zipping her skirt, then turning it so that the zipper was in back. "This heat takes it out of me."

Gemma slid the hat back into the suitcase and stood in the corner with her hands behind her back. She wondered if her mother would mind if she wore her glasses that day.

Practice, she remembered. It all takes practice.

Home-cooked dinners bring families together.

Through the half-window behind the counter, Gemma could see Rory in the back, his hands on his hips. His T-shirt was soaked down the front, and his apron had been tied high around his ribs. He stooped every few minutes to wave.

"Give me a nickel, Frank," Juanelle said, looking out at the row of cars parked under the canopy in front of The Lone Star, then focusing on her own reflection in the plate glass.

"I don't think I got one," Frank said. He drummed his fingers on the table.

"Ah, come on."

"We're getting it fixed in here," Rory called across the room. Dolores was sliding a piece of lemon meringue pie onto a plate. She leaned toward the window and said: "Hush up! You know you aint supposed to be hollering 'cross the restrunt."

Juanelle glanced back at them, over the top of the red Naugahyde booth. Then she rested her eyes on Frank, momentarily staring at his profile till he noticed. She took a drag from her cigarette.

"Well, I guess they *are* fixing it. Nice to get a weather report, though." She lazily flipped the jukebox cards on the wall of their booth. She craned her neck past Frank and called: "Dolores, you can go ahead and bring our iced tea."

Behind the cash register, Dolores nodded, a check between her teeth while she took money from a customer. She put the check on a spindle, said: "Thank you now, y'all come back," and wiped her hands on her apron. "I'll get your tea here directly," she called, her voice nasal. She brushed her cheek against the corsage of yellow roses she wore on her uniform.

"What song you wanna hear?" Juanelle asked Gemma. "You wanna hear something? Frank, she wants to hear something."

"I don't care."

Gemma tucked her feet underneath the booth, glancing up once at Frank. He reached down into his pocket. Juanelle took the nickel from him and put it into the slot. Kay Starr's voice came over the speakers.

"Ohhh, wheel of fortune, don't pass me by," Juanelle sang with the record. "I played that one for you, Frankie. You spinnin' my wheel of fortune?"

Frank King blushed. His Adam's apple rippled upward. "I already spinned it, Juanelle," he said, grinning.

"Well, shoot. Did it land on my number?" She nudged him.

"Course it did." He picked up his glass of tea as soon as Dolores put it on the table. "Soon's Aggie gets back here from Tyler, we'll know just what the number is."

"Hot dog!" Juanelle blew smoke over Gemma's head and let out a whoop. "Spinning, spinning, spinning . . ."

"I reckon she'll be back here Monday or Tuesday next week, and then it's only a matter of time," Frank said, slinging one arm around the back of the booth, around Juanelle. She cuddled against him. "You smell good tonight, Juanelle."

"See, kiddo," Juanelle said. "Cuddle up next to 'em, bat your eyes, put on a dab of perfume, and they'll give you anything."

"Juanelle . . ." Frank turned away from her.

"You give me a nickel, didn't you?"

"Yeah, but . . ."

"See?" Her eyes were wide as she nodded to Gemma, then Dolores.

"I don't know if that'll work on Rory," Dolores said, her

arms folded. She smiled, glancing down at Gemma, touching the girl's shoulder. Dolores had thin, red-painted lips that crinkled into tiny vertical lines when she pressed them together.

"Heck, yes, it'll work," Juanelle said, slapping past Frank at the waitress's arm. "He's a man, aint he? I seen it work on all kinds of men."

Dolores sighed and tilted her head to one side. She thought for a moment, then shook her head. Her eyes met Gemma's, and the girl looked down at her iced tea glass, embarrassed, unsure what to say. And then Dolores put her order pad on their table and leaned down to pat the girl's cheek. "I just love you to death, darling." She hurried back behind the counter, sliding a cup of coffee in front of someone. The man shifted on the stool, and said: "What you got good this evening?" Dolores leaned across the counter and whispered into his ear.

"It's coming right out in a minute," Rory called, his face even with the service shelf, which held stacks of dirty dishes.

"You getting one eager boy there," Juanelle said, laughing. "He's gonna wear you out."

"Stop, Juanelle," Frank said, clearing his throat and sitting up straight.

"Stop what?"

"Talking thataway. It aint no way to be talking in front of her."

Juanelle looked at him for a moment, then at Gemma. She shrugged and lit another cigarette. "I aint talking any way. She knows. She knows what she's in for. Don't you worry about that."

Dolores put three identical plates in front of them—chicken-fried steaks, green beans, and mashed potatoes with gravy.

"Darnit, y'all, I forgot to bring the salad. Y'all be wanting salad?" Dolores stood at the table, her hands on her hips.

"I don't want any," Frank said, picking up his knife and fork. Gemma shook her head.

"Juanelle, hon?"

Without looking up, Juanelle said: "I don't care. Bring some on if you want."

"Well, I don't mind bringing it, but you already got your plates."

"Sure, bring it; bring it," Juanelle said, her mouth full. "If I don't eat it, he will." She chewed, looking out the plate-glass window.

"How is it?" Rory called, his head coming through the window.

"Don't they got enough dishes back there for him to wash?" Juanelle's eyes flashed around at him, then down at the Formica table.

"Sometimes he's got sixteen tubfuls to wash a night," Gemma said.

"Then he must be standing back there letting 'em stack up," Juanelle said. "He's gonna get fired. If his mama don't watch out after him, they'll come in here and see him sticking his fool head through there like a rooster and they'll chop it off."

They ate in silence. Dolores came to the table and set down a plastic bowl of coleslaw with orange-colored dressing. Juanelle waved it toward Frank, saying: "Take it."

"Sometimes they make him scrub all the pots and pans till they're spotless, and it takes him two hours."

"Now, I don't doubt that," Juanelle said. She brought the tip of her knife to her mouth and licked the gravy. "Course, he'll still be raring to go when he gets home, just wait 'n' see."

"Juanelle."

"I aint saying there's anything wrong with it. Lord! That's the idea. I'm just telling her that's what she can expect." She smiled broadly, brought a hand to her mouth, saying, "'Scuse me," when she belched, and pushed back her plate. She lit a cigarette. "I can't eat no more."

Frank looked across at Gemma. "How's your steak?"

"Good. No gristle."

He nodded, chewing, eyeing Juanelle's half-touched plate. Gemma saw her mother's hand slide over into his lap.

"You be a good boy and you can have mine when you get done with yours."

He shifted in his seat, swallowing. His face turned crimson. "Stop that, now," he said, pushing her hand away.

Juanelle shrugged. Her eyes settled on Gemma, watching the girl for a long time. "You gotta make 'em think sometimes that if they're good boys, they can have the food on your plate. They like that."

"Okay," Gemma said.

Frank stared over the girl's head. Gemma held her tea glass to her face as long as she could. She could hear her mother sucking her teeth.

"Hey, I feel like going dancing tonight," Juanelle said, stretching both arms over her head. "And it aint even Friday."

Frank blew his nose into the paper napkin, then put it under the rim of his plate.

"Course, I can't get Frankie to go with me anymore. He don't like it at The Spur."

"You know I got to get up at five-thirty."

"Shoot, that never stopped you when we met. You were out partying all night and working all day and you never looked better."

"That was only for a couple weeks."

"Yep, and when I moved in, the party was over." Juanelle switched his empty plate with hers. "I don't want nothing else."

Frank looked down, then away toward the counter. "I aint hungry anymore."

"Gemma, you want it?" Juanelle started to move it across the booth, but Gemma shook her head.

"I hate to see good food go to waste," Juanelle said. "All them people out there starving. Maybe Rory'll eat it."

"They give him a hamburger every night," Gemma said. "Free."

"Well, I hope he knows enough to scrape this plate before he goes to wash it." She took a bobby pin from her hair and repositioned it. Looking suddenly at Gemma's stony expression, she said: "I'm just kidding! Don't take it so serious."

They sat across from Gemma, smoking, lost in their thoughts. She kicked her feet under the table, wadding her napkin around in her lap.

"Things is gonna start moving," Juanelle said dreamily. "Only a matter of time—right, Frank?"

He nodded without looking at her.

"Yes, sir. Only a matter of time and I'll start writing checks like it was going out of style." She giggled, bringing her face low to the table.

"We gotta wait and see what happens," Frank said.

"I'd love to see it. Be out there in the flesh and see it. I'd take off my clothes and just wallow in it when it comes gushing outta the ground. Get black as a fieldhand."

Frank laughed and shook his head.

"What, sugar? Will you go out yonder and strip down naked and wallow with me?"

He grinned, his eyes watering. Juanelle shifted restlessly in the booth, one arm propped on the ledge. She stared at her reflection again.

"Give me a nickel."

"I don't have another one."

She clicked her fingernails against the glass. "I didn't 'spect you did." She began to whistle. "Are we ready?"

"I wanted a piece of that lemon meringue pie," he said. "And I bet Gemma does too."

Gemma didn't say anything.

"Well, let me out. I'm going home. Or over to Gwen's. Maybe she'll put on a skirt and we can go dancing. It's too hot in here."

She scooted across the Naugahyde when Frank got up. They watched her leave without looking back or saying another word. Dolores stacked their dishes on one arm.

"That be all here?"

Frank told her to bring two slices of pie and a glass of milk. When he'd taken his first bite, he said: "Your mama's kinda antsy tonight. I reckon it's waiting to hear what Aggie's got ta say when she comes back from Tyler. She's got those guys making tests, you know."

"Everything will be okay."

He grinned. "Course it will. I think your mama just wants to know how rich she's gonna be." He chewed a mouthful of meringue slowly. Gemma wanted to reach over and wipe the smear of lemon from his chin. "I reckon by Christmas everything'll be hopping. I'll get you anything you want."

"I don't want nothing." She made furrows in the golden swirls of meringue.

"Sure, you'll want something. You and Rory. Maybe I'll get y'all a car. A convertible. I'm getting us one, a big white convertible that drives like a dream."

Gemma didn't say anything. She continued eating the pie. Across the table, she could see one of his hands beside the plate. His fingernails were black, and the skin around his fingertips had been scratched and nicked.

"You was in the army, wasn't you?"

He nodded.

"Well, my daddy was too. In the war. I always knew he got killed over there fighting. But I was hoping anyway that maybe he didn't and you was him."

He looked away, drinking some of his milk, tonguing the white mark at the corner of his mouth.

"When I first come here, I figgered you were my daddy." She looked up into his face, thinking: he's turning red—like I was offering him the rest of my pie.

"You think that?"

She nodded.

"I wish I was your daddy. But I aint."

His eyes were fixed upon her now. He wasn't blushing.

"Well, did you ever know him?"

Frank shook his head, his lopsided grin half-faded. She

sighed. Outside, the sun was down. The lights came on underneath the canopy. She could see Dolores set a tray at a car window, then reach into her apron for a couple of straws.

"Listen," he said. "When this deal comes through, I'm gonna buy you whatever you want. I mean it, Gemma. Anything." He reached across the table and touched the curls over her forehead. She could smell axle grease from his hands.

And then she heard a high-pitched squeal from the back room, and through the half-window she could see Rory take off his apron and sling it down. His torso was framed by the door. She saw him yank up the T-shirt, drenched now, and pull it off. Dolores came into the drive-in, looking through at him, saying, "That boy's gotta change his shirt twice a night, the way he slings water. Gemma, hon, I have to do a whole load of nothing but T-shirts twice a week."

Dolores disappeared into the back. She patted his bare stomach with a dish towel, and Gemma could see her hand Rory a dry white T-shirt. He put it on and tied another apron around his waist.

"What about a mink coat? I could get you one of those. Or maybe you'll want a swimming pool. That's what your mama's got her heart set on."

"No," she said, staring up at him, liking the way his hair curled on the top of his head, wanting to know if it was as soft as it looked. "I can't think of nothing. Not now, anyway."

"Well, you give it some thought."

And in front of her on the Formica she could almost see the picture: a row of men in helmets, rifles slung over their shoulders, their faces sooty. They stared into the camera from *Life* with the same solemn, lonely looks. Like they knew one of their own little girls back home would study the photograph in years to come and think: he would have come back if he could.

🐓 *Dead snakes hung over a fence bring rain.*

In the dry, crusty August heat, Dillard had taken to napping after dinnertime, when the afternoon sun was so hot that he couldn't bear to be out on the lake. He found he was able to sleep better on the shore of Twilight Lake, or leaning against the butane tank in the yard, or even curled up in the lot with the chickens, than he could in his own bed at night. Sleep came easiest when it caught him off guard.

Thunder woke him. He'd been lying against a tree near the lake, sleeping, dreaming. He remembered now. Cora. He peered upward through fanning pecan leaves. Moments before—it could only be moments; he hadn't dozed that long—the sky had been clear. Now swirls of green and gray floated just above the lake, churning thickly like the contents of the slop bucket on his back porch. He brought one foot up under him, almost standing, but then slid down against the tree when a flash of lightning blazed across the lake.

He could smell it in the air. Rain. And then he thought: it's a tornado coming up. Picking up steam. He yawned, the back of his hand to his mouth. Naw, too early yet for that.

Weeks before, when he'd found himself in town once around noon, he'd sauntered up to the side of the drugstore where Yancy and the other old men sat every day—Yancy, the fattest boy in his class at school, still so fat that he took two spaces on the bench. They sat day after day on the long planked bench and whittled, leaning their backs against the paint-chipped wall with the huge, rusty Coca-Cola sign that was big as a full moon just over their heads.

For the first time ever, he stood there in front of them, waiting, watching them whittle shreds of wood down into piles of shavings at their feet. On his Friday egg runs he had always passed the drugstore looking the other way, never daring to look in their direction. He'd known each of them forever. And now he stood waiting, listening to Yancy tell Red Crowley something insignificant about Crowley's cotton crop. Later Dillard couldn't remember what it had been, only that it had been so slight, so mundane, that it had surprised him. He waited till they glanced up at him, first Yancy, then Crowley and the others. Without waiting for them to say a word, he sat on the end of the bench and took out his pocket knife. Yancy paused, then nodded. He gave Dillard a stick to work on. Dillard stared down at it, thinking: I'm sitting here on a roost just like one of them chickens. He worked the stick down shorter and shorter. They talked now about knots and gristles in their feet, how they had to soak them every night. And Dillard sat beside them whittling, silent, unwilling to talk about his own feet with any of them. When he'd finished his stick, Yancy motioned down at the bench where he'd laid several others. But Dillard shook his head and got up. He heard them begin to complain about their knees as he moved away into the main street of Twilight, in the direction of home. He imagined them working up their bodies, slowly, torturing up every ailment they had for each other's benefit until the sun was low and it was time to go home. And he headed down the highway, kicking gravel on the shoulder, thinking: I did it; I sat down there on their bench and shaved down a stick and it was nothing. Now it's done.

He lay back against the tree now, content to be by himself. Something wrenched in his stomach, rumbled in his innards. He remembered; she was back. She was back home. He spread his legs out in front of him on the ground. Someplace in his tackle box, he'd packed a mason jar of iced tea. He fumbled for it now, clearing his throat as he unscrewed the lid. He was the only one around the shore of the lake. Another roll of thunder bellowed from the opposite shore, and he strained to see it, see something of the tremendous sound which made the hair on the back of his neck stand up.

Cora. She was back. Now that he was awake, he sat cradling the mason jar in his lap, thinking, wondering what had made him dream something like that. It had been so long since she'd appeared in his dreams. Neither of them spoke, but he could remember wanting to touch her, the small round-backed woman with white hair who moved through his house. He followed her from room to room. Sometimes she'd say: "What's this?" and he'd tell her: "That's Gemma's radio," or "That's the quilt we got a few years back." He wanted to touch her but he was afraid, even in his dream, that if he did, she'd disappear.

And then she *was* gone. He ran from room to room, calling her, pleading, finally going into the yard to see if maybe she'd wandered outside to see what changes had been made since she'd been gone. But she wasn't there, either. Of course not, she wouldn't be, he thought out rationally in his sleep. She never liked the farm anyway, never liked the chores that went along with it. She wasn't anywhere to be found. And he'd begun to whimper like a kid, until he was awakened by thunder. Raindrops began to ricochet off the lake. He could feel some that trickled through the pecan leaves. He stared across the water, hardly blinking.

He sat under the tree even though he knew it might be dangerous, and watched the rain. The sky flashed around him, and he shivered. Someone had draped two dead rattlers over the barbed-wire fence on the lane that led back toward the house. He stared at it, blinking. She had looked about the same, after all those years, only a little more worn. His heart still raced from it. The downpour gained momentum and he turned from the two dead snakes, thinking to himself: that's what done it, them rattlers. I reckon there's a charm for just 'bout anything.

Saturday haircuts look neat all week.

Gemma lay on the sofa, worn out, hardly able to keep her eyes open. She could hear Juanelle singing to herself in the bedroom. Shadows fanned over the linoleum from the vanity lights on her dresser. Gemma closed her eyes and was almost asleep when her mother came into the room singing: *"Blue moon, you knew just what I was there for . . . you heard me saying a prayer for . . . Someone I really could care for."*

"Well?" Juanelle stood at the dinette table and pulled on the light. Then she whirled around in her straight black skirt and posed, one hand poised in midair, the other stroking down the front of her tight emerald green wraparound blouse. She had pinned up her hair on top into a jumble of red curls. "How do I look?"

"Real pretty," Gemma said. She sat up on her elbows, her movie magazine falling to the floor. She rubbed one eye, turning to lie on her side.

"I better." Juanelle reached behind her to grab a cigarette from the pack on the table. "It takes longer to pull everything together than it used to."

Gemma stared at her, blinking. She'd spent the day washing the floors. And now her mother moved around in her black pumps as though she were on a fancy ballroom floor.

"Frank going?" she asked. Juanelle lit her cigarette and went back into the bedroom for her handbag. She opened it, took inventory, then slipped it under her arm.

"Frank's working. Doing books." She blew smoke upward, then down through her nose. "He's a stick-in-the-mud. Nobody at The Spur jumps for joy when they see him come in anyhow. He can sip on one beer all night long, and that aint no fun. It's just us girls tonight."

She stood under the light, smoking her cigarette, staring hard at the paint-peeled walls.

"Shoot," she said. "I hope that ol' boy from Weatherford don't come in and I bet he does, 'cause it's Saturday."

"Why don't you want him coming in?"

Juanelle chuckled to herself, checking the clock on the kitchen wall. She patted the back of her hair and said; "'Cause he'll be buying me drinks all night, trying to get me drunk. Gwen'll have a fit. She'll sit there quiet and stone sober and hold it against me, 'cause she'll want to be dancing round the jukebox with him."

"Just tell him not to buy you anything," Gemma said, sitting up. She pulled up her skirt enough to look at her knees. They were red from kneeling all day.

"Honey, I aint telling nobody not to buy me nothin'." Her mother's eyes widened. "I'm not all dolled up just to sit at a bar and talk to some old rednecks I have to look at every night of the week." She lowered her head, smiling, bending down to straighten the seam in her stocking. "Besides, he's handsome as they come."

"Handsome?" Gemma smiled, thinking of Dillard's new rooster.

"Yeah, kiddo. Handsome." She put out her cigarette and frowned at Gemma. "Eyes blue enough to melt your heart."

"Yeah?"

"Yeah. But don't be getting any ideas, 'cause he's got an eye for me."

"I'm not getting any ideas," Gemma said. "But what about Gwen? Won't she get mad?"

Juanelle narrowed her brow for a moment. "Sometimes those things just can't be helped."

And then from outside, down the flight of stairs in the gravel drive, a high-pitched, twangy voice called Juanelle's name.

"There she is now, poor girl," Juanelle said, chuckling, rushing forward to give Gemma a peck on the cheek. She stood over the sofa, touching her hair, glancing at her fingernails. "Now," she said, thinking, starting to say something several times, "now don't stay up late."

Gemma smiled at her mother as she hurried out the screen door. She could hear the black, shiny pumps click down the wooden steps. And then her mother's voice meshed with Gwen's and both of them died away after a while, traffic noises from the highway burying their giggles. Gemma sighed. She could hear Frank's radio blaring from inside the gas station. Her eyes became heavy and her head fell back against the sofa.

A scratching noise woke her. She sat up, saying: "Max. Pop, I'll let Max in." But she could see that it was Rory at the door, standing there in a white T-shirt and jeans, peering through the screen at her.

She went to the door to let him in. He stood in the kitchen, shifting from foot to foot. "I just dozed off," she said, yawning. She smoothed her skirt.

"I come by to take you out," he said. "I'm home from work."

"Already?"

"It's ten-thirty. I got all the dishes washed."

She pulled out a chair and sat at the table, resting her head in the crook of her arm.

"I come by to take you out," he said again, grinning, scratching his head. He pulled up his T-shirt and wiped his mouth. "We're going out. My Dolores done went out too."

"Rory, I'm pooped."

He came over and put a hand on her shoulder, patting her. He bent down to kiss the top of her head.

"I washed all these floors today."

"They're pretty."

"They were so dirty I had to go over 'em twice."

He came around and sat next to her. He pulled her toward him, holding her head on his shoulder.

"I know. Sometimes I wash my dishes twice. I wash 'em up once and then my Dolores come and tell me to wash 'em up again." He stroked her head; she could hear his heart beat in his chest.

"I don't think I feel like doing anything tonight," she said.

"Oh, come on; come on." He patted his toes excitedly against the floor.

"Rory."

"Just for a little while." She sat up and turned to look at him. "Please."

After a moment, she said, "Just for a while. Maybe for a walk. I'm bushed."

"I know."

She told him to wait while she got ready. In her mother's room, she stood staring at herself in the mirror. Then she used some of her mother's makeup—rouge, lipstick. She curled her lashes. "I'll be in there in a minute."

"That's fine," he called.

She searched through her mother's jewelry box for something else—a bracelet, a necklace, something that would be the right finishing touch. Finally she chose one of her mother's scarves. She tied the knot to one side, then looked at herself in the mirror. "I'll be right out."

She heard the screen open and slam. He was gone. She came back into the room, standing by the dinette table, and stared at the door. Outside, the night was pitch black. She could hear a train in the distance, then horns blare on the highway. A breeze came from somewhere, just enough to make the light bulb overhead stir. She watched her shadow weave across the floor. Resting one hand on the back of a chair, she listened for his footsteps on the stairs. But all she could hear was Frank's radio sputter as he turned the dial, and the highway, and her own breathing. She stared absently across the dingy kitchen at the wall. Sometimes a car light turning from the highway would brighten the yellowed surface, making dry cracks on the wall appear like lines on a road map. Caught in her own momentary flight, a standing dream, she thought: he named 'em all; every chicken on that wall. And suddenly, she became bone-weary again. All she wanted was sleep. She was about to slip into one of the chairs, when she heard his voice call her downstairs.

"Gemma, let's go!" At the screen, she could see him standing at the bottom of the stairs. The announcer's voice on Frank's radio was saying something about General Eisenhower, and then a Burma Shave ad filled the air. She opened the door and stood on the top landing.

"Where did you go?"

"At my trailer house," he said, stepping up one step. He held the fiddle out in front of him. "I got this so I could play something for you."

She held the rail, coming down. *If your peach keeps out of reach . . . Better practice what we preach. Burma Shave.* He held out a hand to her.

"You sure do look pretty tonight."

She smiled, trying not to yawn. He was so tall that she could barely see his face in the dark as he led her around the side of the gas station.

"I'm gonna have to get back soon," she said. "I got to get a good night's rest."

"I know. Me too."

They walked through the gravel, between cars parked in the drive, cars Frank was supposed to work on. All at once he stopped and put a hand on her shoulder. Her cheek brushed against it; it smelled like Old Spice.

"Miss Aggie's car," he said, pointing across the highway. He dragged her to the road and she could see it too. Aggie's big Pontiac was parked in front of the beauty parlor.

"I reckon she got back from East Texas," Gemma said.

Rory started across the highway, then looked both ways.

They crossed together through a lull in traffic. She could feel heat rise from the asphalt as though it had been collecting all day. Rory ran ahead of her into the shop. She could see him disappear, then come to meet her again at the door.

"She didn't come."

He stood with his nose against the screen, watching her traipse through gravel toward the shop.

"She's here," Gemma said. "The door's unlocked. Maybe she's over with Frank, or at The Spur."

"Oh," he said, his hands flapping against his thighs. "I guess she is."

They stood together in the center of the shop, neither of them speaking, as though they were waiting for Aggie to emerge from the back room. Rory began to wander around the shop, touching the dryers, opening drawers, turning on faucets.

"When you coming to work here?"

"Soon." Gemma yawned, coming forward. She could see herself in the mirror. The scarf billowed over her chest like a bib, and with a single gesture she swept one end over her shoulder. "Aggie's been teaching me all about it."

"I know; my Dolores told me already." He ran a long comb through his hair. Gemma watched him for a moment, then took the comb from him.

"Let me show you how," she said, pulling his arm toward the chair. "I been watching them comb plenty of people out."

Rory sat in the chair, watching as she began to comb his hair. He hardly took his eyes from his image in the mirror. He grinned when she wet the comb and combed his hair down into a curl on his forehead.

Gemma rested her hand on his shoulder and looked at him in the mirror. "Why don't you let me give you a haircut," she said, her eyes dancing. He grinned and made a noise in his throat.

"I just had one last Saturday."

"I can give you a trim," she said, coming forward to search through the drawers for scissors. "It'll be good practice."

He let her tie a towel around his shoulders. She had to stand on an overturned Coke carton to see the top of his head. "Ever' time they give me a Tootsie Roll pop or some Dubble Bubble when I'm done."

"Well, I will too," she said, climbing on top of the carton. "Even though I'm just giving you a trim."

He watched as she combed his hair up on top and began snipping a little at a time. "Now we don't have a razor," she said, "so I can't do too much on the sides."

"That's okay," he said.

"We'll just trim it and give it some shape."

She worked slowly, cutting each combed-out strand of hair just as she'd seen her mother and Gwen do it. Rory folded his hands in his lap and watched.

"From now on, I'll be giving you all your haircuts," she said, thinking: aint nothing too hard about this. It's just common sense. Whenever he began to fidget, she patted his shoulder.

"What side you wanna part your hair on?" she asked, combing it over both ways. A curl on the back of his head wouldn't lie down either way, so she snipped it off at the scalp.

"My mama's been talking to me 'bout taking care of you," he said.

"What did she say?" she asked, setting her mouth, turning the scissors in and out as she cut. She saw his ears turn red first, then the rest of his face in the mirror.

"Well, she was just saying things 'bout man and wife, and I told her not to tell me 'cause I already knew. You 'n' me, we already knew 'bout that stuff."

"What you mean?"

"You know. That stuff. I told her we was already acting thataway with each other."

"Rory, what is she gonna think?" Gemma rested the scissors on his shoulder.

"It's okay. I told her we know 'bout love things you do. I told her I love you."

Gemma pressed his shoulder. "Well, I love you too." She brushed her lips across his head.

He was quiet for a moment, his eyes down. Suddenly he told her: "I said we take naps together."

"Why did you tell her that?" She stepped down from the carton and came around to face him.

"'Cause we do sometimes. And she said that was good."

Gemma looked at him, smiling when he did. He brought his arms forward to reach for her. She put her hand to her mouth. "I forgot something."

"What?"

"I forgot to give you a wash."

"I know."

"Well, I'm sure it aint too late. I don't think it matters if you do it before or after." She took him by the hand and led him to the sink. He lay back in the chair and let her wet his hair, then lather it with shampoo. She kneaded her fingers through his scalp. When she rinsed his hair, and put a towel around it, he said: "Maybe you better do that again."

She laughed, helping him up. "That's plenty. It's clean enough. Now come over here."

She led him to one of the dryers, sat him down, put the hood in place, and turned it on. Leaning down to look at him, she said: "You want a magazine to read?"

He shook his head, smiling at her. And she thought: he has eyes blue enough to make my heart melt.

From time to time, she'd stick her hand inside the plastic hood and feel how much more time he needed. It didn't take long for his hair to dry. She lifted the hood and stepped back, watching speechlessly as he got up and went to the mirror. He stood close, looking at himself in the glass, looking at the jagged ends of hair that stood out from his head at odd, stiff angles. Several spots had been cut away so that his scalp showed. He turned one way, then another.

"Am I getting my gum now?"

She came up behind him and put her arms around his

waist. "You're my first haircut," she said. He turned and looked down at her. "I didn't think I could do it, but I did."

"I'd rather get a Tootsie Roll pop if y'all got those, but I don't care." He looked down at the top of her head, his own looking gnarled and chewed up.

Gemma backed away a few steps and studied him. "Now it aint perfect, but it's gonna look okay, I think."

"I know." He grinned, his hands in his pockets. She went to the drawer at her mother's station and took out a piece of gum for him. He popped it into his mouth and began chewing at once, grinning.

"No, wait," she said, turning him into the mirror. He stood there looking at himself, chewing harder. "Now aint that a beauty of a haircut!" He nodded. "Why, I aint seen nothing so good-looking in a long time."

"I know." He chewed.

"Shoot," she said, thinking about what Aggie had told her. "I don't know but what that makes you look ten years younger. And all them women will be swooning over you at the drive-in. I better not let you go to work by yourself. They'll eat you alive."

He laughed low in his throat.

She turned him around so that he was facing her. "We're gonna be real happy," she said, gazing up into his eyes, feeling her chest rise with a sudden intake of air. He tried to say something, but almost choked on his gum. Moving to the sofa, he picked up his fiddle and played a few notes. Then he began a song she'd heard on the radio. She put her arms out to her sides and twirled around, laughing.

"I aint tired anymore." She laughed. Suddenly she stopped, facing him, her hands clinched in excitement. "I got a good idea. I'm gonna teach you how to square dance."

He nodded and put down his fiddle. Stooping, he took her in his arms and spun her around, his mouth open in laughter, the pink wad of bubble gum visible in the darkness of his mouth.

"No, now listen," she said, pulling away. "I'm gonna show you how to do this and it's real fun."

"I know."

"How do you know? You ever done it?"

"One time I did. Last year."

"Where? Where did you square dance last year?" She folded her arms.

"Well, I forgot, but I know how 'cause I did it."

She backed away, running her fingers down the front of her dress, then fussing with the scarf at her neck.

"Now then, if you've done it before, then how do you start?" she asked, one hand on her hip.

"Well, you take you place and you wait for the music," he said. "And you get set ready and go when the music comes on. You go."

"Yeah," she said, pushing back the chairs. He stood in place, watching her clear an area in the middle of the shop. "But *where* is it you start from? What do they call it?" She turned to face him, waiting for an answer.

"Well," he began, looking down at the linoleum, rocking back on his heels. "They turn on the music and you start dancin' on the floor." He grinned suddenly, chewing vigorously.

"Course you dance on the floor, silly. But they got a name for where you start. It's called 'home.'"

"Home."

"Yes, and when you start out, you gotta do this thing called 'honor your partner.' That means you bow to me and I have to curtsy to you." She held out her skirt and dipped, then went to him and showed him how to bow from the waist.

"Like this?" he asked, stooping forward several times, one arm at his back and the other across his middle.

"That's it; you have it. That's called 'honor your partner.'"

"Honor your partner."

"Now let's try it," she said, taking her place beside him. "What position are we in now?"

"We're in Aggie's beauty shop."

"Home; we're in home."

"Home. Honor your partner."

"Now let's try it."

She turned to him and curtsied, and a beat later he bowed, saying: "I'm honoring you now."

She pivoted him around so that he faced her.

"That's good," she said, clapping her hands together. He grinned. "Now I'm gonna start you off real easy, no hard stuff right away, till you get the hang of it." He listened attentively. "They got someone called a 'caller,' and he calls out the steps everybody has to do. Usually you have four couples all facing in, standing in a square."

"This is called home."

"Right. Now the main ones are something called 'do-si-do.'" She folded her arms and danced around him, first one way and then the other. Rory tried to follow her with his eyes, all the time chewing, laughing. "Now let's try it." It took several times for them not to collide into each other head-on.

"Now the other thing I want to teach you is called 'promenade,' and that just means to walk. I take your arm and we go round the circle till we get back to our home position."

He nodded, a frown beginning to crease his brow.

"Then you have to know 'swing your partner.' Put your arms around my waist and we swing around."

"I got a lot to remember."

"It's easy; you'll see." She grabbed his hands and pulled them around her waist. They began to twirl until he was laughing.

"I think you're real good at it," she said. She straightened her scarf. "Now we don't have no music, but I'll do the calling." She saw that he looked puzzled. "I'll be the caller—remember, like I told you before."

"I know."

"I'll try to go slow, so you get the steps. Just follow me."

Standing in place, she began to bounce in a jig step. Rory looked down at her feet. Then he began to hop too, jumping in so that he would be in rhythm with her, though he was just slightly behind. When Gemma started clapping her hands, he pounded his own together, fingers spread, his palms connecting with thuds.

Gemma nodded her head in time to the beat in her head, beginning: "Everybody stand and dance right in your place."

"Like we're doin' now," he sang out, still clapping, blinking with each connection of his hands.

"Rory, that's part of the calling. I call things out like that and then we have to do 'em."

"Everybody stand and dance in your place," she began again. "Now honor your partners, and the lady on your left," she called, curtsying. He bowed, facing forward, then remembering and swinging around toward her.

> Everybody hold hands and circle to the left.
> Circle to the left around six times,
> Then circle to the right six times.
> Keep on goin' till you get home.

He continued to spin around and she had to pull him in to her side.

"Now everybody do-si-do, then promenade back home."

He fell into her. She squealed and held the side of her face. He brought up both hands, fluttering them around her. Then he stepped back.

"I went the wrong way," he said. She could see his eyes begin to tear.

"It's all right," she said. His elbow had jabbed into her cheek. She worked her jaw a few times, then straightened up, regaining her composure. "Now let's do it again," she said, smoothing the front of her dress.

He stepped back, his lower lip curled out. He stared at the floor.

"Rory," she said. "Come on. I'm in home position."

He stood completely frozen; she saw his eyes blink a few times. "Rory."

He wouldn't respond. She took his hand. He looked at her then.

"My Dolores told me the other day not to hit you. 'N' I did."

"It's okay; you didn't mean it."

"I told her, I said I wouldn't ever do nothing like that when you 'n' me was married 'cause we love each other, and I done it anyway."

"You didn't mean it," she said in almost a whisper. Outside, a horn blared down the highway and for a moment they both turned toward the screen door, looking out into the darkness as though they were watching the sound.

"I did 'home'; I did 'honor my partner.'"

"Yes," she said.

He shrugged, turning his back to her and falling onto the divan. He sat there for a few moments before his hands reached across for his fiddle.

"Play something for me, Rory."

He brought the fiddle to his chin and traced the bow up and down the strings several times. Gemma stood with her hands clasped before her. He began to play a tune, one she'd heard him repeat over and over during the summer. She held out her skirt and bowed low to him. And then, as his music began to flourish and glide over the melody, she started to dance. He sat with the fiddle tucked into his chin, his legs open, and his knees jutting into the air because the divan was so low. She bowed twice more, then holding her arms out before her, she spun around. She put both hands against the small of her back and began to weave across the linoleum. Standing with her knees slightly bent, and one hand out to the side, she dipped with the music, slowly, in a kind of courtly dance, and then she twirled around the room as he finished the song, ending just in front of him with his last chord.

"You play that prettier than anything I ever heard," she said.

Slowly, he brought the fiddle to his lap. She came toward

him and brushed the erratic shoots of hair on his head, but none of them lay down. She knelt on the floor, between his legs, and rested her chin on his thigh. One hand hung across his knee. She felt his hand on her back, patting her gently, then stopping suddenly when he saw it too: the figure staring at them from the plate-glass window. Two hands were pressing against the glass as though trying to burst through. Gemma gave a faint cry when she recognized the features, the dirty-blond hair wrapped around into a French twist, the harlequin glasses askew, and the red-painted lips mouthing silent words at them. They sat rigidly in place, listening to the silent words, wincing when the tongue and huge lips pressed against the window. And then the form disappeared into the shadows, leaving only a wet smudge on the glass that glistened in midair every time headlights passed along the highway.

🐓 *When evil thoughts and evil desires cloud your eye, beware—you are in spiritual darkness.*

Touching bottom, she sprang upward again toward the surface, surprised by the power in her lungs. The mass of oil drums lashed together blotted out the sun, making a dark impression on the bottom of the lake. And she swam upward. Her eyes opened into glaring sun. It could not have been more than twenty feet up to the open space, to air, but it seemed much farther. Even under water, she could hear him calling. She broke through, water spouting from her mouth. And as she slid back down into the warm murkiness, she could hear him say: "Be careful of that hook! You'll get caught on that hook!" She could see him scurry frantically over the deck above her. Far to the left of the barge, she could see the red and white bobber floating on the surface of the water, the hook weighted below. She stretched out on her back and kicked toward it. He jumped up and down, reaching out for her, his look horrified. She splashed along next to the bobber, letting her nakedness break the surface sometimes, and she thought: am I getting pretty, Pop? Am I getting pretty?

But then something crashed against the wall and she sat up, sweating, gulping for air. It had thudded against her mother's bedroom wall. She could see a light come from underneath their door.

"Now look." Her mother's words slurred.

"Clean it up."

"I aint doin' nothin'. Stop tellin' me what to do, goddammit. You can't tell me what to do anymore."

Gemma sat up, listening. They were moving around in there. She could hear floorboards creak, and furniture scrape against the floor.

"Clean it up; I told you to clean it up." It was Frank's voice, hard, barely recognizable in its thickness. Something about the roughness of his words scared her. She swung her feet to the floor, pressing them against the linoleum for support. Her nightgown was soaked down the front; her chest was chilled from her own sweat. And before she could grasp for it, she could feel it slipping away, her dream, slipping into another dimension.

A shadow broke the thin line underneath their door and she heard glass break.

"Drink from that, why don't you," he said. "Slice up that mouth of yours."

"I'll be slicing something awright, Frankie. I'll be slicing something."

And Gemma stood then, wanting to turn on a light, but not daring to. She stood next to the sofa, afraid to move. Frank was mumbling something now she couldn't quite understand. Then her mother laughed.

"I mighta known it," Juanelle said. "I mighta known you'd blow it, Frankie. You don't got the smarts to pull something that simple off. Now why didn't I know that?"

"I'm warning you."

"Why couldn't I figure that out right away? I'll tell you why. Cause I thought maybe this was it, thought maybe you were making something of yourself this time around. But shoot . . ."

She could hear them pacing, walking up and down behind the closed door. And as though their movements primed her, she began walking too. She walked back and forth in front of the sofa, in the dark, each step tightening the knots in her stomach.

"I didn't know," he said. There was something pitiful about his voice, whining and pitiful. "Heck, Aggie didn't know either."

"Now that's a crock if I ever heard one," she spewed at him.

"No, it aint. It aint. How could Aggie a known something like that would happen?"

"Are you nuts? How can you sit there with your goddam mouth hanging open and say that? Course she knew. She knew there was a chance there wouldn't be anything down there. Then she bamboozled you into paying all the money." Juanelle's voice broke with a sob. "I bet she only paid a fraction of what you did. That's it! Got you to pay all that money out, got you to take all the risk and put her name on the deed too. She aint out nothin."

"Juanelle, you don't know how it is."

"She said there was oil down there. It was collecting all these years. It was collecting."

"You don't understand," he said. "This is business that's between Aggie and me."

"Business, my ass. What do you know about business?"

They were quiet for a minute. Finally he said: "She paid too. She did pay."

"Shoot, I'd quit her damn place, but I can't now. I'll be there till shit. . . . I'm up to my ears in that place now. I aint never getting out. I aint never getting out." Gemma could hear her choke with a fit of coughing. "Where could it have gone? That oil. Where could it have gone?"

Gemma stopped pacing. She could hear Frank explain something to her mother, his words slurred together. Now and then Juanelle would stop him, but his voice would rise above hers.

"You let her ruin us!" Her words made Gemma shudder. She could feel her heart pounding. She could feel her forehead break into a sweat. "You let her sucker us into paying more, I knew it. I knew you did."

"You don't know nothing 'bout business."

"To hell with your business. I'd a never done what you done if I'd a known about it."

"It was part of our deal," he said. "She found the property.

It was part of the deal. When the wells started producing, I'd have . . ."

"But they aint ever gonna produce! They aint ever gonna pay. And we're stuck with a worthless piece of property out in god-knows-where." Her mother was crying; Gemma could hear her voice crack. The sound made the girl's stomach wrench and she could feel her own tears begin to swell. "It's not even ours . . . not completely. It's part hers too."

"We got the land, Juanelle." He sniffled. "That's something."

"Shoot." Juanelle was sobbing. Gemma could hear Frank's voice trying to soothe her. She went to their door, standing with one cheek against the frame. Their words were garbled. Gemma felt her breath quicken. She almost opened the door; she wanted to. She sounds wounded, she thought. She sounds like she's fixin' to die.

And then she could hear her mother begin to move around again, thrashing madly through furniture, clothing, and trinkets on her dresser. Something hit the floor, and Frank, annoyed, said: "Pick that thing up."

"I don't care," her mother said flatly.

"Pick it up. You'll step on it and get it dirty."

"What do you care? You'll wear it anyhow."

Gemma sat back on the sofa. She'd never be able to fall asleep now. She listened for a moment, but couldn't hear anything. Maybe they were asleep. Asleep while she sat there in the dark, alone, her hands shaking. But then something else hit the wall, harder this time. The door rattled and the light bulb began to stir over the dinette table. Gemma gripped the front of her nightgown in one hand.

"Go to hell; go to hell," her mother screamed. The noise seared through Gemma's middle.

"Come to bed, Juanelle. There aint nothin' you can do."

"Stupid! You sonofabitch! I know there aint nothing I can do. I know it. I know there aint nothing I can ever do. You ruined me; you ruined ever'thing. You said we was getting outta here. You said we was getting that big place and a pool and a convertible. And now we aint gonna get nothing. I hate you for it."

"Lay down here. I'll smack you."

"Goddam, I hate you. I don't know why I ever stayed in this hole so long. You aren't worth it. Any man I could find out there on the road would be better'n you."

"That right? Find one then."

"Don't think I haven't. You think I haven't? Frankie, I haven't stayed with you 'cause you're a great lovin' man."

Gemma heard a smack, then Juanelle gasp. Stop it, she thought. Stop it. Then something thudded against the floor inside and she could hear them arguing.

"Where you going this time a night?" he muttered.

"It doesn't matter; I'm going."

"Put that thing away. I'll wallop you again."

Stop it. Stop it.

And then she was on her feet, losing balance at first and falling against the edge of the sofa. She grasped the sheet, pulled herself up, and grabbed her Bible. Opening their door in a rush, she swept into the room, the Bible held high over her head. Panting, the curls around her face plastered down with perspiration, she swayed in front of them.

"If anyone defiles and spoils God's home, God will destroy him. For God's home is holy and clean, and *you are that home.*"

And fixed before her, entranced by her stormy entrance, Juanelle stared at her with glassy, drunken eyes. She hovered over the end of the bed like a hunchback. She dropped the black skirt in her hand on top of the other clothes piled haphazardly on the opened suitcase. Frank lay back on the bed, his head propped against the wall. He was naked, except for light blue boxer shorts. The way he'd rested his legs, knees to the ceiling, gave Gemma an instant view of the darkness inside his shorts. She breathed more quickly, angry with herself for seeing that part of him, angry that he didn't shift his legs to stop her. The room was littered with empty cigarette wrappers and half-filled bottles. Gemma saw a broken jelly glass on the floor. Both Frank and her mother stared at her, their eyelids drooping, their postures weaving forward, or to the side, then rallying abruptly.

"He said: 'Watch out! Don't let my sudden coming catch you unawares; don't let me find you living in careless ease, carousing and drinking, and occupied with the problems of this life, like all the rest of the world.'"

She brought the Bible down in front of her chest, panting, averting her eyes from Frank. He'd folded his arms over his bare chest, smiling at her. It made her uneasy.

"Watch out!"

"What is she babbling 'bout there?" he asked, his tongue thick in his mouth. Gemma could see where he'd dropped his clothes over the floor. She could see her mother's things strewn across the bed, on the floor, and across the dresser. Some of her blouses had been halfway pulled off hangers in the closet.

"She's babblin' 'bout that Good Book," Juanelle said, standing up straight now. She was in her slip. Gemma could see where her makeup had been smeared, the imprint of a hand on her cheek. "Babblin' 'bout the Good Book. Shoot." She cackled. Frank was quiet on the bed.

"I'm just tellin' you what it says," Gemma said, her voice breathy. She rested her eyes on the disarray of clothing her mother had wadded into the suitcase. "It's how He wants us to live."

Juanelle looked at Frank, one hand hooked to the back of her neck, a hip slung to one side. "If that's not just what we need now," she muttered flatly.

"A man who loves pleasure becomes poor; wine and luxury are not the way to riches!"

"Brother," Juanelle exhaled, turning her head away to the window, where the night was colored with a haze of neon and red brake lights. "I reckon that says it all. No wonder I'm poor, and gonna be poor till I'm dead and gone. Heck, I can't never expect nothin' outta life, to hear you tell it."

Gemma watched her, her mouth clenched.

"I love pleasure. I love wine." She turned to Frank. "And I love draggin' me a big ol' oily-smellin' guy into the can down at

The Spur. . . ." She threw back her head with a laugh. "Axle grease, I reckon I better say, not *oil* oil. I love standing there with our butts wedged in the stall and him hikin' my skirt up and me fiddling with his belt buckle."

Frank was off the bed in a leap, his hands outstretched for her throat. Juanelle did not move. She stood over her suitcase, continuing to speak as he locked his grip around her throat. Gemma rushed forward, ramming herself between them, using the Bible to pry him away from her mother. Juanelle staggered as he released her. He fell onto the bed, sitting on the edge with his head buried in his hands.

"I aint ever gonna be rich," Juanelle said matter-of-factly, just as though nothing had happened. Gemma had backed into the suitcase. From her nest of Juanelle's clothes, she could hear Frank breathing heavily behind her, could see the trembling of that narrow trail of hair which plunged beneath the waistband of his shorts. Juanelle took a step into the center of the room, rotating her neck, smiling at nothing.

"Bitch." Frank sounded as though he might cry. "I shoulda left you where I found you."

"Left me?"

"Yeah, left you at that filling station over in Dallas. That's where you belong."

"Well, aint that just where I am?"

Gemma heard him snort as he fell against a pillow. She was afraid to turn to him then, afraid she might see his body instead of his face. Afraid she wouldn't be able to look away.

Juanelle smiled, turning her back on them. She walked to the opened window and stared out into the night. Her black slip eclipsed the swells of light that played across the blinds. Gemma lay among her clothes, thinking: they smell like her.

"You left me," Juanelle muttered flatly. "You left me."

"Woe to you who get up early in the morning to go on long drinking bouts that last till late at night—woe to you drunken bums. You furnish lovely music—"

"Calling your mother a bum now?" Juanelle snapped,

225

swinging around. Gemma cradled the Bible in her arm, watching her defiantly. "Are you calling me that?"

"I'm just saying what's in the Bible."

"I don't believe this," Juanelle said.

Behind Gemma, Frank made rustling noises with the sheet. He sprawled across the bed, taking a sip of something in a bottle, screwing the top back on and setting it on the floor. "We got the land, Juanelle," he mumbled. "Aint that something?"

"I don't believe this," Juanelle cried at them. The veins along her neck bulged; her forehead turned crimson. "I don't believe the two of you." She took a step forward, stopped with her arms stiff and her fists clenched, and reeled slightly to one side. Her eyes trailed over to the mirror above her dresser, and for a moment she seemed to be preoccupied with her own image. Her lips moved as though she were about to say something to the stooped lanky figure looking back at her.

Gemma sat up, the Bible in her lap. "Let me read to y'all."

Her mother slowly turned her eyes to the bed. "Can't you get it in your head? How many times do I have to let you people know? Goddammit, I look a mess. I look like shit. I look like I been run over by a truck."

"Let me read this here," Gemma said, opening the Bible, flipping pages.

"And I aint ever gonna look any better," Juanelle said, closing her eyes, massaging her temples. "Nobody'll look twice this time next year if I have to go on living like this, I swear."

"Why then should we, mere humans as we are, murmur and complain when punished for our sins? Let us examine ourselves instead, and repent and turn again to the Lord."

Gemma started to turn a page, but her mother was on top of her, tearing the book from her hands.

"Stop. I aint takin' it. Stop!" Juanelle held the Bible high over her head. She looked down at the girl with blazing eyes. Her breath smelled sour.

"It's the Lord's word."

"It's nothing!" Juanelle screamed, darting to the window as

though she might toss the Bible out over the highway. Gemma stood on reflex, and when she did her mother came at her.

"When are you gonna stop this crap, stop this trying to lead people around by a noose?"

"I aint leading." Gemma cowered under her.

"The hell you aint," Juanelle shouted at her point-blank. It made Gemma blink. "You're just like him, like the old man."

"I aint leading."

Juanelle tossed the Bible at her. It buckled open, the pages creasing facedown on the heap of clothes.

"Nobody cares 'bout this shit," she said, her lips pressed firm. She stared at some point on the wall above the bed. "You can't go blabbing it like a fool. 'Cause it makes you *look* like a fool, you know that? You know that?"

Frank smacked his lips and rolled over, burying his face into a pillow.

"You aint doing that here, not anymore. I aint living with it."

Gemma picked up the Bible, straightening the pages. She held it to her chest, looking up soberly into her mother's face. "My conscience is clear," she said, her voice dark, "but even that isn't final proof. It is the Lord himself who must examine me and decide."

Her mother plunged forward and grabbed her by the nightshirt. "Do I gotta beat it outta you?"

"Juanelle." Frank's voice came from the pillow, muffled. "Come on to bed, Juanelle."

Gemma stared into her mother's eyes, her mouth rigid. Juanelle gripped her daughter's shoulders tightly. All at once, her eyes narrowed. Just as she was about to speak, a fit of coughing made her convulse. She clutched her chest and held the girl with one hand until she had to put her fist against her mouth.

"Won't you ever learn?" she asked, getting her breath. "You aint nothing special. You aint one to be telling me, *me*, how to live."

Her expression dark, Gemma said: "After death, the judgment."

Juanelle laughed, backing away. She moved to the window and sat against the ledge. "You're going back. I'm sending you back to Twilight."

"No, you're not," Gemma said, taking a step forward. "I'm getting married to Rory."

"You just think you are," her mother said flatly. "I let you do that, and you'll be hanging around my neck. Shoot. You'll both be hanging around my neck." She went to the dresser for a cigarette. Lighting it, she leaned on the wall, folding her arms, pressing her shoulder blades against the faded wallpaper. "No, kiddo. You're going back. That is, if Frankie here can scrape enough together for a bus ticket."

"Juanelle, come over here, honey. Come on over here."

She looked at him for a moment as though she were trying to place him, as though she were trying to understand what he was saying. Her eyes had almost drooped shut. Then she bolted upright and took a drag from her cigarette. "I shoulda sent you back the morning you came. You aint nothing but a pain in my rear."

Gemma stood in the middle of the room, gazing down at the floorboards. "Maybe Rory and me'll just get married right away."

"You just think different. You aint getting married without my consent." She slapped her chest. "And I aint giving it. All I'm giving you is a bus ticket, kiddo."

"I aint going back there."

"Well, you aint staying here. I can't afford you now. I can't afford anything." Her brow creased and her face began to contort. Gemma thought she was about to cry. "I want you outta here. I want you outta here. Shoot. Both of you."

"If my daddy was here, you wouldn't say that," Gemma said.

"Now, why are you saying that?"

"'Cause it's true. If he was here, alive, you wouldn't be saying that."

Juanelle stood with one arm against her waist, the other elbow resting against her wrist. She held the cigarette out before her, staring across the room into blank space. "Listen," she said suddenly. "You aint ever had a daddy. You aint ever had one, alive or dead. Shoot, do you understand me?"

Gemma didn't say anything.

"Your daddy could be any one of a half dozen I remember. Maybe more. I don't remember that much—just that you came along right in the middle of it all, and I was having a good time but had to quit 'cause I blew up fat and ugly with a baby. He aint neither dead or alive. I can't even remember a face."

Gemma stared at the woman, trying to keep the tears from distorting her vision.

"You're going back."

"I aint. I don't belong there."

Juanelle pressed the cigarette out in an ashtray on her dresser. She looked across at the girl, her face blank. "You don't belong anywhere, kiddo. You're just like me. You don't belong anywhere."

And backing away, backing through their door and across the linoleum in the front room, Gemma began to run. The screen door slammed behind her, rasping in the night air like a noise under water. She clomped down the wooden steps, her eyes stinging, her bare feet finally sinking into gravel on the ground. She ran around the station, the Bible against her chest. She could see shadows sweep across the ceiling upstairs. Their voices rose above the nighttime swish of traffic. Her mother's flat twang riveted into the man on the bed. And she thought: I aint going back there. I aint going back.

Though the night was still and the air so heavy that it seemed to make the power lines sag along the highway, she could feel a coolness brush over her face. It was sweat. She rubbed her eyes and squinted across the highway. Lights were on in Aggie's place. She looked both ways, even though the only traffic along the strip was a pickup idling at the stoplight and a few cars in the distance, their headlights beaming toward Fort Worth. Aggie would help; she could talk to Aggie. She knew the woman wouldn't let her mother send her away. Just drink, she said to herself, crossing the highway. Drink and carousing that causes her to act thataway. She won't be like that in the morning.

She trotted across the gravel in front of Aggie's House of Curl. Her heart was beating faster. The front door was closed, but she could hear the radio playing quietly in the back room. Maybe Aggie was working late, catching up from when she was away. Gemma couldn't believe that Aggie would cheat Frank. Not Aggie. She was going to help her, get her into school, give her a job at the shop. It was her mother. Juanelle expected too much. She had probably misunderstood everything from the beginning.

When she peered into the shop, she could see that the lights were coming from the back room, just as she'd expected. She opened the screen and then the door. As she came into the shop, rustling noises stopped abruptly to one side, near the divan. She stood inside the door, all at once aware that someone was in the shadows. One of the floorboards creaked from her own step. It sent a chill down her back. There were rags in a heap before her—no, clothes. They were clothes, she saw, squinting. She leaned toward them to get a closer look. And as she did so, she saw the two figures on the sofa. They had already seen her come in, already heard the floor creak. They were frozen in place, though their bodies still caused the joints of the divan to squeak.

She knew that face, that one glaring over at her with a slack jaw and smeared makeup and loosened hair. She knew the other face too, the one she saw simultaneously, lying down on the sofa. Gwen sat in a straddling position, her huge breasts and stomach sagging against his chest. The lower part of her body seemed to grind him into the upholstery. Gemma saw both their faces, watching her, waiting. She was unable to focus until she saw his botched-up haircut, shoots of stray hair standing out next to bald spots.

Rory made a gurgling sound somewhere deep in his throat as he tried to sit. Gwen shoved him back, pinning him down with her hands against his shoulders. She began to laugh, riding him, her flanks making sucking noises when she pulled them away from his body.

Gemma made fists around the Bible in front of her. She could see that he was trying to get up, but the woman wouldn't let him. His shoes were still on, and his trousers had been stretched down around his ankles. Gwen pursed her lips, letting a thin strand of spit connect her mouth to his thin chest. She released him with one hand to sweep back strands of blond hair which had become unpinned from her French twist. Then she clutched him again, shifting her body, lifting one thigh and lowering the other so that Gemma could see where they were joined, see how each time she rose above him they were still joined.

Gemma could barely breathe, could barely see them, though she knew she was moving closer, knew she was beginning to charge with a momentum that sparked from the pit of her stomach. Rory was trying to sit again, strangling noises still bubbling in his throat. He was halfway sitting when Gemma made contact, ramming the book against the bouncing woman's shoulder. The two bodies, still joined, tilted to one side like a sinking battleship. And the force of Gemma's blow was still bombarding against them, almost in slow motion, slamming them against the wall.

Gemma heard a crack, then a chalklike crumbling of Sheetrock. She backed away, to see the glistening body protrude from the wall where the top of the head had already disappeared. Gemma dropped the Bible, but as though she were still under water, it didn't make a sound. Gwen's body hung huge and lifeless from the wallboard. Rory's eyes were fixed with Gemma's. They were bulging, horrified. But his pelvis twitched against the wrecked body above him, which looked more headless with his every thrust.

Close scissors if you find them open, or expect trouble with someone you love.

Pipes rattled in the walls. Dust settled. Wrenches, fan belts, and jumper cables seemed to stir and settle along the pegboard, and a stack of hubcaps swayed of its own accord against the glass garage doors. Oil dripped from the innards of a car's cavity high on the hydraulic lift, into a metal bucket on the concrete floor. The sound was like the inside of a cave; Gemma weaved it into her sleep. Water was running. Something cold was pressed against her face. She breathed in dampness. She didn't pull away, not even when she opened her eyes enough to see it wasn't a cave anymore, but Frank's garage, where she'd fallen asleep on top of the worktable. Electrical wiring, headlamps, Camels, and a pair of opened scissors had made crazy jagged imprints along her arm and cheek. And she was about to close the scissors—she knew the saying—when the coolness pressed against her forehead again.

"Come on, get up. Get up," the voice said, pleaded almost. It was her mother. And then she saw Juanelle standing over her, wiping a wet cloth nervously over the girl's eyes. She remembered. Running. Their bodies still suspended in the empty space in front of her. Running. Plunging through the air, her bare feet slapping pavement, then smarting in gravel. She had been running, blinded, using her hands to guide her around the station, halfway up the wooden stairs, then back again to the garage. She had buried herself deeply within, inside the dankness of the garage, letting the smell and darkness blanket her momentarily before she fell into unconsciousness.

"Get up, kiddo. I'm not playing with you, either."

Gemma didn't say anything, only felt along the ridges across her skin made by Frank's tools.

"You're in a lot of trouble."

Gemma sat. It was still dark outside, though she could see the red flashing light shining grotesquely over fenders and other car parts Frank had hung from the top of the garage.

"You better wake up, 'cause they're gonna be in here asking you questions."

Gemma looked at her mother blankly. She was different now, different from the last time she'd seen her. Juanelle moved around nervously, pushing back hair that fell across her face, letting the blue terry cloth robe fall open.

"What time is it?" Gemma asked, watching her. It was difficult for her to imagine that this was the same woman from the night before. Juanelle seemed concerned.

"Hell, I don't know what time it is," Juanelle said flatly, one hand against her chest. "It don't matter what time it is. You're in trouble, or will be once they get wind of things. They're still over there, the cops, the ambulance."

"Why am I in trouble?" Gemma asked, sitting up now, hanging her feet over the side of the table. She shoved a crowbar to the back. "It was them that was doin' something, not me."

"Come on," Juanelle said, standing in front of her, her hands on her hips. "You better sit right here and tell me exactly what went on over yonder, and you better tell it to me right too, or they're gonna cart you off and you'll end up in some place that you wouldn't wanna think about."

"It was them that was doin' something."

"Yeah? Well, I 'spect they wasn't readin' Bible verses to each other." Juanelle's breath hit her face; Gemma turned away, frowning, her blood pounding as though she'd been dropped suddenly into icy water.

"They're over there now, the cops, snooping around, asking Aggie questions. Shoot, that boy he can't say anything."

"Rory?"

"Can't do nothin' but lie there." Juanelle glanced over her shoulder toward the front of the station. Flashing red light gave her an erratic radiance.

"I killed her."

Juanelle snapped her head around, glared at the girl and shifted from foot to foot. "It was me who spotted that damn Bible on the floor when Aggie called me over. I never seen her like that. When I answered the pay phone down in the station, she was crying, carrying on. I figured it was about Frank and the land deal, and then I finally got it that she was talking about Rory and Gwen."

"I killed her; it was me that done it."

"Oh, come on, you didn't kill nobody. Least not tonight." She walked away, her fingers spread and caught in a tangle of hair. "So I went over there a while ago—I told Aggie not to call the cops till I got there, but she was scared, him bleeding, Gwen, well, Gwen out of it. The sirens was blaring soon's I was in the door. I spotted it, that Bible, and I knew you'd been there. It was laying open on the floor, looking like it had been leafed through, only by the looks of them, I could tell it hadn't. I got it in the back room before anyone saw. Shoot, Aggie was pulling her hair out over yonder. She was crazy."

"I killed her," Gemma said again, her voice even. "I did it; I did it."

"She aint dead," Juanelle shouted, her eyes red, bulging. "She may have a headache for the next five years, but she aint dead. They got her in the ambulance just now, and him in another. If they start talking, the cops are gonna come after you. The way Aggie's carrying on, she's liable to press charges."

"I don't care," Gemma said, hugging her arms around her.

"Course you care," her mother said, holding her by the shoulders. "You better tell me just what the heck happened over yonder. I walk in and 'bout got sick—first seeing her hang outta the wall, that big rump, then him."

"She aint dead?"

Her mother frowned at her, folding her arms, not answering.

"She went through it, her head went through the wall and I figgered she was dead. She was hanging there so limp."

"Like shoddy plumbing," her mother snorted. "Then him, laying there, bleeding, looking up at me 'n' Aggie but not seeing either of us. I reckon he was in shock."

"Bleeding?" She sat up, sliding to the edge of the bench. "I don't remember him bleeding when I left."

"I hope your memory is as good for this as it is for them verses. Pair of my hair-cutting scissors laying there on the floor next to your Bible. It looked like he'd butchered his hair first, or someone had—those scissors was laying open next to your Bible. And then—"

"I did it; I give him the haircut."

"Shoot."

"He liked it real good," Gemma said. Her mother turned her back to her.

"They're gonna be over here." She put a hand to her mouth. "I gotta get you outta here. I gotta take you somewheres."

Gemma sat quietly, finally saying: "I don't care. I'll tell 'em what happened."

"Tell 'em you gave him a haircut, then tried to cut off his thing!"

Gemma stared at her mother, her mouth open. Juanelle dug a fist into her chest, worrying the terry cloth robe.

"I shoulda known this business with Rory and you was a bad idea. I shoulda known you wouldn't be ready."

"I am ready."

"I gotta find you somewhere to hide."

235

She came forward to pull the girl from the bench. Gemma stiffened.

"I aint hiding."

Juanelle looked into her face. Gemma could see tiny lines furrow around her eyes. The skin on her forehead crinkled. And Gemma thought: he did it 'cause of me.

"You tried to mutilate him," Juanelle said, turning to the door suddenly as though she thought somebody was watching. Gemma jumped down from the bench, tugging the nightshirt in back.

"I didn't do nothing to hurt Rory. You said he was bleeding. Is he bad?"

Juanelle looked down at her absently, one palm rubbing against her head. Gemma started for the garage doors, but her mother caught her. "You can't go out there. They'll take you; they'll find out. I have to put you somewhere."

"I asked you, is he bad?" She broke from Juanelle's grasp.

"He aint bad." She stared at Gemma. "Only a little blood."

"He tried to hurt hisself 'cause he loves me."

"Shoot. No man is gonna do something like that because he loves a woman," Juanelle said, walking in front of her, covering her view of the ambulances and police cars across the highway.

"No, he did it because he loves me, 'cause he was doing that with Gwen. I know it."

Juanelle frowned, looking down at her.

"I walked in there and saw 'em on the divan," Gemma said, trying to peer past her mother. "And they was, you know, they was together." Across the way, she could see Aggie standing outside her shop. She was talking to two policemen. The three of them stood washed by a band of white glaring light from the headlights of an ambulance. Their faces shone in red flashes.

"What happened?" Juanelle said, touching her shoulder. "What happened then?"

"Well, it was all so fast. I don't remember. 'Cept that they were together, like I was saying. And Rory was trying to get up but she wouldn't let him. Then I sorta ran at 'em."

"Shoot."

"I ran at 'em and the next thing I know, she's hanging from the wall. And they're still together."

"Shoot." Juanelle turned to face the street. She gripped both hands against her chest. "What am I gonna do?" Her shoulders had started to tremble.

Gemma came forward to stand next to her mother. "I gotta go over there. If he's hurt. I gotta go see him."

Juanelle moved against the glass door, pressing her forehead against a pane. "Only a little blood. He's mostly in shock, I'd guess you'd say."

"I gotta go," Gemma said.

"I don't want them to take you." Her mother was looking down at her now, her brow pinched, her eyes watery.

"They aint gonna take me," Gemma said soberly.

"Don't tell 'em nothing," her mother said, opening the door for her, standing back so that the early morning chill swept against the girl. "Gemma."

Gemma moved into the early light, slowly at first, then more quickly. She didn't look back at her mother, but ran across the asphalt to the gravel skirting the highway.

"Gemma!" Juanelle called. And when Gemma turned, she could see her mother framed in the garage door, a hazy backdrop of car parts behind her. She leaned against the metal frame, her robe sweeping the ground. Gemma watched for a moment, then raised her hand in a wave.

Across the highway, she could see that one of the ambulances was just pulling away. She hurried over to Aggie and the policemen.

"Rory," she said to the woman. "Was that him they took?"

Aggie couldn't answer. She shook her head and motioned toward the other ambulance. Gemma could see that she'd been crying. Her eyes were puffy and she kept rubbing an arm across her face. Gemma moved slowly to the ambulance, to the opened door in back, where she could see the foot of the stretcher. A medic worked over the figure under a sheet.

"Rory," she said, her arms hanging weakly at her sides. The man inside the ambulance looked up at her and smiled, saying: "Hi, I'm Fred Gary." And she thought: that aint right. I don't wanna know who you are.

The officers had moved around the ambulance with Aggie. One of them supported her. She stood next to Gemma, peering inside. Rory didn't move.

"He's like my boy," she was saying. "Like my own boy. I 'bout raised him, specially after my brother passed on." One of the policemen looked down at Gemma.

"Did y'all get Dolores?" Gemma asked.

"She aint at the restaurant," Aggie said. "And she aint at the trailer, neither."

"Somebody oughta find her," Gemma said.

One of the policemen said they were looking. "Anyway, she'll be back at The Lone Star in 'bout an hour," Aggie said. "That's when they open. I can go over then."

"Rory?" She climbed into the back of the ambulance, almost touching him, but afraid to. She moved up in a stooped-over position.

The attendant grinned at her. "He'll be just fine."

She stared at his face, at his sweating forehead and glassy eyes. His hair was matted in uneven clumps.

"Rory, it's me. Do you know me?"

He turned his eyes to her then and stared. "Sure. I know you, Gemma." He reached for her hand.

And outside, Aggie was saying: "I shoulda rode with her to the hospital. I hate I had to let her go alone. She's all by herself. She's my girl, just like Rory here. Just like Rory. I love 'em both. I love 'em."

The policemen were trying to leave. They'd put away their reports now and listened with distant politeness.

"His mama was working for me out in East Texas, out there in Tyler. And I feel like they're my own. When R.D. died, and I moved out here, well, they came with me." Gemma could see her standing at the foot of the stretcher, her face framed by

Rory's hooded feet. "She was only a young thing when she come to me, when R.D. met her."

Gemma pressed his hand against her chest. "Are you gonna be all right?"

He nodded, not taking his eyes from her. One of the policemen stepped up into the ambulance. Rory darted his eyes down toward him.

"He's just gotta ride with us," the attendant said.

"I was worried 'bout you," Gemma said, gripping his hand.

"I know," he said, still watching the policeman.

"I tried to do everything I could," Aggie said, looking in at them. "It hadn't been much, I know. I tried to take care of him." The policeman outside took her arm.

"We better be getting this young fellow to the hospital," the other policeman said, kneeling next to Gemma. "He needs to get his rest."

"Gemma," Rory said, pulling her hand to his lips. She leaned over him, wiping moisture from his face. "I want you to come with me."

Gemma looked at the officer. She knew she couldn't.

"I can come visit you tomorrow," she whispered.

"They won't let you, I bet."

"Sure they will. I can come tomorrow. And when you come home, I'm taking care of you. I'll fix you anything you want."

He almost smiled. But she could tell he was frightened. He held her hand so tightly that her fingers ached. "Sometimes people they think I don't know something and I really do," he said.

"What are you talking about?"

"Like now," he said, swallowing. "I know, Gemma. I know."

"What do you know?"

He tried to sit, but the ambulance attendant held him down.

"Gemma," he whispered. She rested her head on his shoulder, still holding to his hand. The policeman looked at his watch. "People sometimes they don't listen to me."

"I listen to you, Rory."

"I mean, they think, well, they think they . . . sometimes I know things they think I don't know. And they just figure I'm . . . But I know things."

She looked at him; he smiled feebly. And all at once, tears burned her cheeks. They sat holding hands. Aggie had moved out of sight, though Gemma could hear her voice near the shop door, and then the officer's. The attendant touched her shoulder, but she held fast to Rory's hand, thinking: I aint letting go; I aint letting go.

"I'll ride back here," the officer next to Gemma said.

Outside, Aggie began to sob. "I did what Brother woulda wanted, but it wasn't enough. It wasn't enough."

The grown man on the stretcher beside Gemma turned his face to the window. The morning outside had become pearl gray. He began to cry.

🐓 *A white button in your path means you'll have a good trip.*

When she opened the screen, her mother looked up from the table as though she was about to say somebody's name—not Gemma's, but somebody else's who was no longer there. Her lips moved, but they were too dry to finish the sound. Gemma could hear it, though. Somehow she knew. And it seemed that for her mother, his absence had already settled into her bones. Frank King would only come back in her dreams, when his presence would be so real, just below the waking surface, that in days and weeks to come she would stir from uneasy slumber to say the name aloud. Say it so that her own voice would spring her into a wakefulness that embarrassed her, even though she was alone.

Gemma let the door close gently. She took a step toward her mother. Juanelle was still dressed in her robe though it was already late afternoon, evening almost. The girl turned from her, not because of the way she looked—the deep creases under her eyes, her matted hair, and the smell of bourbon about her—but because she could hear the name Juanelle had almost called out.

"Get it done?"

"Yep. It's done." Gemma looked down at her shoes. "Painted. Patched. It's done."

"Anybody stop and wanna know what was going on?"

"No. Just Miss Lyles."

Juanelle stared at her, her gaze bearing down as though the girl were somehow different. Maybe even somebody else. She reached across the Formica top and pulled a cigarette from the pack.

"What did she want?"

"She was asking if the shop was closed tomorrow. She was just driving by and saw us working. Thought maybe Aggie was redoing the shop or something."

Juanelle lit her cigarette and still watched the girl, waiting, her head cocked to one side.

"She said she had her an appointment for nine. Tomorrow morning."

"Ever' Monday. For as long as I been here. For the rest of my life."

"She thought maybe Aggie wouldn't be open, but Aggie told her the appointment was still good."

Juanelle laughed through her nose and lifted a hand to her forehead, covering her eyes. Gemma could see her other hand shake as she brought the cigarette to her mouth.

"You won't even be able to tell there was a hole there," Gemma said, coming closer. "Aggie says maybe later she'll get a picture to hang over it. Maybe a painting of mountains."

Juanelle seemed aware that Gemma had moved past her, into the room and over to the sofa, but she didn't make a sound.

"Wasn't nothing to it," Gemma said.

"To what?"

"Patching." She saw that the sofa still hadn't been made from the night before. The sheets were wound together in a mass of white knots. Somebody had placed her Bible facedown on the crumpled pillow.

"Then I can stand there at my chair and look in the mirror and see some pretty scenery—snow-capped mountains, places," Juanelle said.

"I reckon." Gemma faced her mother's back. She wondered why Juanelle sat in the shadows, why she didn't pull on the

242

overhead light. And then she remembered: the name. "You want me to fix us something to eat?"

"I sure hope it's a pretty painting," Juanelle said, her voice biting. She gazed at the screen door. The light outside had turned dusky. She rested an elbow on the table, letting a long ash fall into her lap. She looked down, absently rubbing it into the terry cloth.

"I can make chili dogs if you want something to eat," Gemma said, stepping toward her, standing so close to the hunched-over figure that she could have touched her.

Juanelle threw a look over her shoulder. "I aint eating tonight."

"I aint hungry either," Gemma said. "You want me to fix you some iced tea?"

"I don't want nothing," Juanelle said. "I just want to sit here. I may sit here forever."

Gemma took the chair next to her. Juanelle hardly seemed to notice. She let the cigarette fall into an ashtray overflowing with butts and shredded Kleenex. Gemma watched her fumble nervously with the collar of her robe.

"Rory's gonna be all right."

Her mother turned, slowly bringing her into focus. "Aggie at the hospital with Gwen?"

Gemma nodded, her fingers laced together and pressed between her thighs.

"And? What about her?"

Gemma sat still for a moment, remembering wet lips pressed against the plate-glass window. "Aggie's bringing her over to her place this evening. I reckon she's all right. I think she's staying with Aggie till she's feeling good enough to come to work."

"That could be a month. Aggie'll keep her laying up in bed as long as she can."

"Aggie says she'll be okay. The doctors thought she might have a concussion at first, but she doesn't."

Juanelle stared at her. Her fingers busily explored the ash-tray.

"I came back over this afternoon to tell you. You were asleep in there, I reckon."

"I wasn't asleep."

"Well, I came back and the door was closed." She slumped in the chair, tired all at once. "Aggie says she's resting real peaceful."

"Shoot. I bet she is. I just bet she is. This couldn't a worked out better for Aggie."

"You mean getting her wall fixed?"

"Yeah. Nothing." She wrapped the robe tightly around her and shifted in her chair. "Aggie ask you any questions?"

Gemma shook her head.

"You tell her anything?"

"No. I didn't. Like you said."

"No reason to start trouble for yourself. Or start it for any-body. Better if things just work out how they have to."

"Aggie seems all right. She wasn't carrying on like last night. She says maybe later this evening she'll carry me over to see Rory; she'll tell 'em at the hospital I'm already sixteen."

Juanelle reached for another cigarette, but the pack was empty. She crumpled it in her fist. "They aint ever letting him outta there."

"Aggie says they have to keep him in for a while to make sure there aint any infection."

"I don't know why she's filling you with that crap."

"It aint; it's the truth. She says they always do that."

"Crap." Her mother stared at her. "Kiddo, it's time you faced up to something. He aint getting out. And not 'cause he nicked himself with some dull ol' scissors, either."

"Aggie says it's called observation. . . ."

"Will you just forget what Aggie says! She says a lot and you're in for a lot of heartache if you start believing it all." She swallowed, crossing one leg over the other, losing her hands in

244

the folds of her robe. "Hell, I'm surprised they didn't try to pin him with rape. If it wasn't for Aggie, they probably woulda."

"It wasn't that. I know it wasn't that."

"Yeah, you know it. But I'll bet you a plug nickel she don't. She was probably too drunk to remember much of anything. When she left The Spur, she was reeling." She laughed. "I can see her doing something like that, saying it was him forcing her. But Aggie wouldn't let her do it."

"There wasn't no force."

Her mother laughed. "Probably the best tumble she's had in a while."

Gemma stared at the flecks on the tabletop.

"There aint nothing wrong with Rory," she said solemnly.

"Now aint that sweet of you." Juanelle stood, shakily gaining her balance before shuffling to the bedroom to get cigarettes. Reappearing in the doorway, empty-handed, she stared at the girl and said: "I used to say the same thing 'bout Frank."

"I mean it; there aint nothing wrong with him."

"Not now there aint. They'll make sure of that. They'll protect him." She stared at the floor, chuckling to herself.

"He don't need protecting. Aggie won't let Gwen hurt him 'cause of this."

"I don't mean 'protecting' like that, kiddo. I mean . . . He's better off. Shoot. I wish I had somebody to protect me."

"It's not fair."

Juanelle came back to the table. She started to sit, but moved to the screen door instead. Gemma followed her with her eyes, thinking: she's looking for him.

"That's right. It aint fair. But it had to happen sooner or later. I know what you think about Rory. But the truth is, he oughta been put somewhere long time ago. Some school or something where he could learn a trade. Make brooms or whatever those people do."

"They put him in a school once. He told me."

"Yeah, that was Aggie. Doin' good. Takin' over. Those kids

'bout swallowed him up." She stared down at the girl, her mouth set. "What he needs is a special school. Someplace for people like him."

"You mean a hospital."

"No, I mean someplace special. Shoot, I don't know what you call 'em." Juanelle looked away, then back without changing her expression. "If he stays like he is now, he won't be no 'count to anybody."

"He would be to me."

"Yeah. Sure. Till you passed him up in age, and that wouldn't be too long." She sat at the table again, wearily easing herself into the chair. "This will be better off for him; he'll be happier in the end. I don't know why I went along with the two of you getting together."

"Aggie's taking me to see him this evening," Gemma said. "She says I can get in."

Juanelle leaned forward across the table, her face close to the girl's. "Haven't you been listening to a word I said? You aren't going there. They won't let you in, and even if they would, I wouldn't let you. Rory's not in any shape to marry— you or anybody. That's over between you and him, so just forget it."

"No, it's not. We got it all planned."

Juanelle stared at her until the girl had to look down. Gemma could still feel her mother's presence, her face, almost against hers—not because of the shadow on the Formica but because of the stale warmth emitted by her body. And suddenly the girl began to cry. She closed her eyes and put her cheek against the cold surface of the table. A hand pressed against her back, patted, then was gone.

"I know, kiddo. But it's for the best."

Gemma sat limply over the table, sobbing aloud, continuing to cry long after the tears had ceased to come. Her mother sat next to her, legs crossed, arms in her lap, patiently waiting for her to stop. Gemma turned her face on the tabletop so that she could see her. Juanelle was staring at some point over the kitchen sink, above the window. Her absorption in the spot quieted Gemma. She sat up, shifting in her seat. Juanelle looked over at her slowly.

"I'm sending you back to Twilight," she said flatly. Her expression was rigid. "First thing in the morning. You're going back."

"I aint going back. I told you that before," Gemma said. "I can't live there anymore."

"Well, you can't live here, either."

"I'll just get on a bus then and go somewhere. You won't have to worry about me."

Juanelle exhaled through her nose and shook her head.

"You're getting on a bus, kiddo, and you're going to Twilight. I already decided. Tomorrow."

For a moment, Gemma didn't say anything. She ran a hand over both cheeks, then down the front of her dress. She set her mouth stubbornly and took command of that point over the sink her mother had trained her eyes on before.

"You can sit there and pout, I don't care," her mother said. "But you gotta go." She turned slightly to the girl. "You gotta go back there. He'll take you; I know he will."

"He won't."

"Sure he will. I know the two of you got on. You had to. I see his—see his expressions on your face. His voice comes outta your mouth sometimes."

"That aint true."

"It is. I'm telling you. Maybe you can't see it, but it's there." She drummed her fingernails on her thigh. "Shoot. He aint so bad."

"Yeah? Then why'd you leave?"

Juanelle looked down into her lap, creasing the folds of her robe with her thumb. "That was different. That was different." She seemed to slump further in the chair and her brow narrowed. "The two of you shared something, while him and me, well, we're just . . ." Her eyes seemed huge; they were moist, fixed on Gemma. "He'll love you, Gemma."

247

"And you won't."

Though a muscle at the side of her face twitched, she did not move. "That aint true. I love you; you're my baby. I just can't . . ." She dropped her head forward, catching her face with a shaky hand. She rubbed her forehead and eyes, then straightened, breathing deeply. "I can't keep you here, can't you understand that? I can't do it. I tried to; I tried to be a mother and do all that for you, but I just wasn't any good at it. I couldn't pull it off."

Gemma didn't say anything.

"And now, well, Frank aint here right now."

"Where is he?"

The eyes were on her again.

"He's gone," Juanelle said, smiling thinly.

"For good?"

Juanelle narrowed her eyes and shook her head. "Naw. Heck, he 'bout can't tie his own damn shoes himself." She cleared her throat and lowered her eyes. "I 'spect he'll be back in a day or so. He's just gotta get it outta his system. I reckon I was kinda rough on him about the land deal."

"He has to come back. Who'll run the station?"

"Any fool can pump gas." Juanelle smiled. "I did it myself for a long time. That's how I met him." She got up all at once and grabbed her purse on top of the refrigerator. She began rummaging through the contents until she found a half-empty pack of cigarettes. She lit one and came back to the table. Sitting, inhaling the smoke deeply into her lungs, holding it, then slowly letting it out, she said: "I just can't do it. I should have known that. I reckon that's why I never came to get you before."

Gemma got up from the table and moved over beside the sofa. She hugged the Bible close to her.

"I'll get you a bus ticket in the morning. I think the sooner the better for you."

Gemma sat on the sheets, slamming the Bible against her legs. Then she flung it to the floor. "I don't want you buying me any bus ticket. I'll get my own."

"You don't have any money."

"Then I'll get it. I'll hitchhike back yonder, I don't care. I don't want your ticket."

"Gemma, honey."

"Don't be calling me that," she cried, her voice catching in her throat. "You can't be calling me that. I can get back on my own. I don't need you; I never needed you."

Juanelle's back was to her. She could see her mother's head rise and fall, start to turn, then stop. "Please don't be saying that," she said, her voice quiet. "Please don't."

"Well, I mean it." Gemma dug her fists angrily through the swirl of sheets.

"'Cause that makes me feel bad. It makes me feel real bad now." She turned in her chair, resting her arm on the back. "I just can't do it. You know I tried; you know I did. Don't you?"

And then something made Gemma swallow, and she thought her throat might never open again. She could not bear the sight of the woman across the room from her, hovered over the back of the chair, disheveled, barely able to sit on her own. She felt her muscles involuntarily constrict when Juanelle said: "Let me buy you a ticket." She wanted to say the name: Mother. But she leaned back into the sofa, whispering: "Okay."

Juanelle turned back to the table, silent, a dome of cigarette smoke enclosing her. They sat with the lights out. After a while, Gemma lay on top of the sheets, one hand sweeping across the floor. Her mother hardly moved, and sometime later, when it was completely dark and neon flashes came through the other room, spilling harsh yellow light over the woman, Gemma spoke. She had been dozing off and on, gradually aware each time she stirred how night was taking over. In a matter of hours she would be sitting on a bus, headed back to Twilight. And she would stretch forward in the seat to get a good last look at the gas station, The Lone Star, the stockyards. She would lie back and watch the landscape shift gradually from auto repair shops and barbecue stands to houses along the highway spaced farther and farther apart, until they were riding through fields and open country. And she would wonder: will I go back there; will I go back there too?

"Why don't you go on in to bed?"

Juanelle didn't say anything. She sat at the table, in the dark. Smoking.

"I reckon I'll go if that's what you want."

"It is. I can't do nothing else."

Gemma could barely make her out in the dark, and then one of those flashes would catch her, slumped over in the chair, a glass to her lips.

"You reckon they'll let me write Rory?"

"Course. Dolores will. They won't care any."

"I hope so," she said. "I hope he remembers me."

And the room was dark momentarily. She hoped that when the flash came again, maybe her mother wouldn't be there. But it caught Juanelle in the same position, an amber silhouette, one hand combing through her hair again and again.

"Why don't you go on in to bed?" the girl repeated. She watched the woman. Something was struck down in her now each time the neon glare faded across the figure. She wanted to say the name.

"I just wanna sit here," Juanelle said in the dark. "I may just sit here forever."

PROMENADE HOME

🐓 *If a woman drops a fork, a man is on the way.*

She walked down the Commerce highway toward the farm, dragging the cardboard suitcase behind her. She shoved up her glasses, and stopped for a pickup to pass before she crossed the road. The land was burned out. Dead. On both sides, the scorched flat ground led to black furrows which had baked under the sun for too many weeks. The furrows led to scraggly end plants of cotton. Into the fields, though, the cotton grew thick, rich, as though it was nurtured solely by existing in the midst of other plants.

She shaded her eyes. Across a field of alfalfa she could see the Hadley place. It was on a smooth bed of landscape, surrounded by a few mesquites and several pecan trees. It looked like an oasis. And still farther along the dirt road that she could see clearly now, as though she were standing on a high plain of earth, she could see the Dillard place.

The sun was almost on the horizon. It glared over the land like a huge brush fire in the distance, and it made the dried-out fields and low line of trees along the barbed-wire fences seem as though they'd been set ablaze. And as she turned from the highway, staying to the dirt road that zigzagged back to their place, she could see the old shack, long abandoned. Once Beecham had lived there with his family, when they'd worked the Dillard place. The gray boards had rotted and its tin roof shimmered from direct sun. It sagged against a tree, one last rest before it would finally sink into the earth.

253

The bus had dropped her in front of the hardware store. Like every Sunday she could remember, the main street of Twilight was deserted, though she could see a row of cars parked down in front of the church as she began walking toward home. "I've been down in Fort Worth," she'd told a heavyset black woman who sat next to her on the bus. "Spending the summer with some of my people." "Now aint that something," the woman said, grinning. She held a baby in her lap. "Mighty long trip for you to be takin' on your own." She'd let Gemma hold the baby all the way from McKinney to Greenville. "I don't reckon I be lettin' my baby ever take a trip like that." "Oh, you shoulda seen 'em, giving that poor bus driver instructions 'bout me. On both ends—my folks down there in Fort Worth, and my Pop in Twilight." "I jus' don't know," the woman said, shaking her head. Gemma rocked the baby, singing softly, thinking: it thinks I'm its mama.

Her footsteps crunched through gravel as she walked down the center of the road. Muddy patches in tire ruts had dried and cracked. She moved quickly, afraid that one of the Hadleys might spot her as she passed by their house. Before, in town, she could have waited for a ride. Sooner or later someone would have come along who could have driven her out to Dillard's. But she wanted to get there by herself, especially on this last leg of the journey. Anything else didn't seem right.

And there it was! She came around the big pecan trees in the front and saw it, the house. She crossed the wooden-planked bridge over the culvert and stood in the yard. The Chevrolet was parked at an angle in front of the car shed, just as it was when she'd left. Grass had overtaken the walk to the front steps. She stood on the broad, flat stones, looking on either side, thinking: he just let this flower bed go to pot.

Just as she was about to move around the side of the house, she stopped suddenly. Nestled in the grass before her was a white button. She leaned over to pick it up, relieved suddenly, taking it for a good sign. She thought: I did have a good trip, and then aloud: "So far."

When she opened the back screen, she caught the smell of the place instantly; it made her dizzy.

"Hello?"

Boards creaked someplace in the house. Sunlight came through the window in his room. She tiptoed across the porch and peered inside. Before her eyes could adjust to the direct light, she was startled; he was in the bed. And then she saw that it was only the covers, wound together in a lump.

"I bet he aint made this bed since I been gone."

She finally set down her suitcase in the kitchen door. Her kitchen; it almost made her cry. And there they were, the chickens, dancing around the wallpaper. Her rocker next to the stove. But dirty dishes covered the table, left over from breakfast, or some other meal. Flies took off from a bowl of black-eyed peas he'd left there uncovered. She swatted at them, taking the dishes to the sink. "Filth," she muttered. "Filth." The sink was already piled with dishes; so was the counter. And in one corner, crouched low, was Max, poised over a crusted bowl of mashed potatoes. Gemma flung him to the floor. The calendar on the wall over the stove still said JUNE.

Her room seemed to be the only one he hadn't destroyed. She lifted her suitcase to the bed, muttering under her breath. Max watched her from the doorway, rubbing his head against the molding.

"This place is a pigsty."

She walked through each of the rooms again, talking to herself, kicking Max when he got in the way. She decided to start with the dishes. That alone would take all night. She rolled up her sleeves and turned on the water. Ice cold. She flicked her hand under the stream, waiting for it to get warm.

"This place'll take me a week to get back in shape," she said. "Shoot."

She blew out her breath, short on patience, and dried her hand on her overalls. She marched back to his room and began making his bed. The smell made her turn up her nose.

"Musta been sleeping with his fish," she said, ripping the

sheets from the bed. And then she saw it: her school picture, looking lost in the frame he'd stuck it in. She sat slowly on the bed, holding it in both hands. She stared at herself for a long time, listening to the water run in the kitchen, thinking: this aint me no more, this aint me.

Now the water ran hot. She pulled back her hand and adjusted the stream. Food had hardened in bowls. Gravy had changed the shape of plates. She took everything out of the sink, put in the stopper, and then began her task, all the while muttering to herself and to Max. She shoved up her glasses with the back of her hand, getting suds on her nose. She scraped at a fork so hard with Brillo that it flew across the room. That's when she saw him. He sauntered down the road, carrying his pole and fishing tackle. Quickly she dried her hands and marched through the house, stomping out to the screened-in porch.

It took a few moments for him to come into view. She waited, her face dark, her mouth set. "Just you wait. You."

She flung open the screen and started down the steps.

And Dillard, his mind somewhere else, on the three measly fish he'd caught that afternoon, was trying to move easy. It was his knees; they'd locked out there on the barge. He'd sat too long in one position, even though he knew better, and now they were stiff as a board. Just aint worth it, he thought. Fighting to get out there, fighting to get the barge going, then wrestling them grasshoppers on the hook and finally getting 'em into the water so I can get some scrawny no-'count fish like these. Then my dang knees go out. It just aint worth it. He was stooped over low, looking down at them as he moved, lifting them high as he walked over the bridge. "One thing I got left to enjoy and I can't get out there to do it."

And then he heard something; it was the screen. He thought: a prowler; somebody's in my house. He looked up, startled, realizing that yes, someone was there. He couldn't make the person out at first, but then he recognized her, heading toward him, her head lowered as though she were about to charge. Instantly forgetting the soreness in his knees, he dropped the tackle and started for her.

"This house looks like a pigsty if I ever seen one," she said, taking long strides up to him. They met halfway down the walk. "Aint you done nothing while I was gone?"

Dillard reeled with anger. He almost fell over, but managed to steady himself. "Where the heck did you come from?"

"You got dishes piled up in there to the ceiling. It's gonna take me all night to get 'em cleaned up."

"No, it aint."

"I may have to throw some of 'em away." She pressed her lips together and folded her arms. "I'm surprised *you* didn't do that; you done it before."

"What do you think you're doing here?" He looked down at her, opening his mouth, grinding his teeth together.

"I looked in them cabinets and you aint got one clean glass left. How do you 'spect me to fix us something for supper?"

"I don't. You aint fixing anything." He stretched his neck, looking down at her. "What in tarnation happened to your hair?"

"I curled it," she said. "Ever' week I had it done."

"Hmmph."

"My mama did it for me. At the shop where she works."

"I thought she was working at a gas station," Dillard said. "Fixing cars or something. She do that to cars?"

"She works at a beauty shop," Gemma said, flapping her arms to her sides. "She's got a good job there."

He smacked his lips and turned away. Taking several steps down the walk, he turned abruptly. "Well, I don't like it."

"I do. It looks good on me," she shouted, coming after him. "It suits the shape of my face!"

"Hmmph. *She* tell you that?"

"Everybody told me that!"

"Now you watch it, young lady. I don't know what the heck you think you're doing here, but I aint having it, that tone of voice." He wagged a finger at her, then moved his hand over his mouth, rubbing it back and forth as he looked down at the ground.

"You mighta least cleaned up some. It's a mess in there."

He stared at her, hard, not saying a word, not daring to let her get him riled anymore. They didn't take their eyes from each other for moments. Then he turned away, picked up his tackle, and moved past her without another glance.

Gemma watched every step he took.

"I thought I told you I didn't want you here no more," he said at the top step, turning to look at her. "I aint got time for this kind of foolishness." He stared down the walk at her with huge panicked eyes. "What are you doing here?"

"I come back," Gemma said, standing in place, not blinking.

"Back?" He forced a laugh. "Back? What happened over yonder—she not let you get your way all the time?"

Standing down there, that girl, just waiting for him to pat her on the back and say, "Good to have you back, Gemma girl," made him furious. Waiting to be invited in, and he wasn't about to have it.

"I can't abide it, young lady." He shook his head. "I oughta tan your hide is what I oughta do. Tan your hide, then ship you back to where you come from. Taking my money like that."

"I didn't take nothing."

"Liar."

"I didn't take nothing that wasn't mine too."

"Is that right? Yours! Well, now." He nodded his head, grinning, weaving back and forth. Then he spit on the ground. "You are just like her. Come back here and right off start trying to railroad me." He stepped inside and set down his pole and tackle. The screen slammed behind him. "Coming back here," he said, straightening slowly, looking out at her from behind the screen. "Robbing me, then showing up like it's nothin'. You know how long it took me to get all that money? Course you don't. You aint old enough to know the value of a buck."

"I am too."

"Well, if you was, you wouldn't a done what you did." He took off his hat and wiped his arm across his forehead.

"It was mine too."

"Don't you say that again," he said, his jaws clamped. "I aint listening to you talk thataway."

"I helped."

"But I kept you here. I give you a place to sleep, put clothes on your back and give you a home. You was helpin' out, but that don't mean I owe you for it."

She didn't say anything.

"I almost called the sheriff," he said, squinting at her. The sun was all but gone now. And where she stood, in the shadows of a pecan tree, made it difficult for him to see her. "I coulda done that, you know. Anybody else woulda."

"Well," she said, taking a step toward him, "I still got most of it. I didn't spend hardly nothing."

"Aint that something," he said, his spit catching on the screen. "I been scrimping all summer long, getting by week to week on what my hens'd produce. Because of you. Had to get Hadley to carry me in to town on Fridays when I was feeling too poorly to walk. I aint having this. I aint having you stealing my money, going off for a high time, then coming back here 'specting me to take you in. Where do you get thinking like that?" He pulled off his hat and tossed it down on top of his tackle. "I know where you get it; I know dang well where you get it from."

"I wasn't gonna take it all," she said, her voice low. She clasped her hands behind her back and looked at the ground.

"But you did!" he shouted. He could see her down the walk, looking pitiful. Still aint nothing but trouble, he thought. He latched the screen. "Well, I aint taking you in. Just get on."

"I got it all there in my suitcase. In there on my bed."

"Just get on," he said again, waving her away with his hand. He backed from the screen and she could barely see him when he said: "You shoulda bought you a round-trip ticket, wherever you was." And then he was gone.

She ran to the screen and pulled at it. "Pop. Let me in there. I got it; it's on my bed in the suitcase." She could hear him stumble through the house, talking to himself, slamming into furniture.

"And don't bother comin' round thisaway, either," he shouted. "'Cause I locked the back too."

"Shoot." She kicked at the screen. "Pop, open this door." She yanked at the screen, then rattled it against the frame. "Your ol' money is in yonder. Now let me in. If you don't open this door . . ."

"What?" His voice was at the screen suddenly, level with her own. "If I don't open this door, what?" His mouth sagged at both ends. He frightened her, waiting for an answer.

"Nothing. Don't open it." Her face was dark. She backed down the steps. "I wisht I'd a spent it all."

He kicked the doorframe as she turned away.

"You stole from your own Pop. Like a thief."

She could hear him stomp away, rattling through the house, his voice rising now and then as he argued out loud. Gemma stood at the bottom of the steps, listening for a time. "Pop." He was back in the kitchen, or in his room. *"Pop!"* Even if he did hear her, he wouldn't answer. She sat on the steps, resting her hands on her knees, looking out into the oblong shadows over the front yard. In the house behind her, doors opened and closed. Water was running. She could hear floorboards give in the back of the house, where he tramped from room to room. Dillard mumbled to himself, and sometimes she could hear his voice rasp against the sound of dishes clattering together.

Gemma rested her head in her hands. Whenever she shut her eyes for a moment, they ached. Had she slept the night before? She couldn't remember. She couldn't remember the night before that. And Rory, seeing him stretched out in the back of that ambulance. Aggie. It seemed as though it had happened too long ago to remember except by sudden inaudible pictures that would flash through her head. She stared out toward the road, at the field of cotton across from the house. She leaned against the steps and closed her eyes. A glass shattered on the floor in the kitchen. She could hear him cuss.

Dillard only had to bring up the back of his hand and Max fled the kitchen. He stooped down to sweep the pieces into a dustpan. "'Spectin' to come back here," he grumbled. He reached out to steady himself on the counter. "I shoulda moved out yonder to the barge when I had the chance." He finished sweeping the floor, then walked quietly through the house. Lifting the shade over the front door, he peered out at her sitting down there, her hands around her knees, her back to him. And then, as if she knew he was watching, she turned her head slowly and stared at the window. Dillard slapped the shade back into place, shaking his head, slapping his flank. She sat there like a spook. He'd whip her within an inch of her life; that's what he'd oughta done the minute he'd seen that it was her heading down the front steps toward him. Strutting down those steps like she owned the place, like he'd taken something that belonged to her. He went back to the kitchen, rubbing his eyes. Everything was so blurry that he had to sit in her rocker for a moment before doing anything else. She could just sit out there and stew. Sit out there all night or till she had the good sense to leave. He looked down into his lap, rocking a bit, feeling a weight press against his chest, and he thought: I was done with all that; I was done with her a long time ago.

Gemma could hear night insects around her now. A breeze swept through the top of the pecan trees. She sat with her back wedged against one of the steps, gazing up for the first stars. The sky looked different here. She could see it extend in a full arc, down to the horizon, complete. She knew that he was back again, standing there behind the curtains like a child, watching her. But she didn't turn. Headlights moved across the top of Bob Hadley's cotton in the distance, but she couldn't hear the sound because the breeze was stronger now. Leaves rubbed together over the yard like dark hands. And then the screen opened and her suitcase tumbled down the steps. It struck against her back.

"Shoot!" She jumped, then turned to grab the case. "You aint changed a bit."

"They teach you to talk like that down yonder?" His voice came from behind the screen.

She looked up the steps, trying to make out his figure behind the mesh of screen. All she could see was an occasional swish of white from his shirt as he shifted position on the porch.

"I meant what I said. Just get on away from here."

"Pop."

"I meant it."

She could hear his breath, raspy, sporadic.

"Pop, the money was in my suitcase. Did you see it in there?"

"I don't go opening other people's property."

"Well, it is." She placed the case on its side and began to open it. "I'll get it for you."

"I don't want it. I don't want it anymore. It's gone, finished."

She latched the case without even looking inside.

"I got no business with a child your age. It aint my place."

"Pop, I'm not a child anymore."

"Oh, yeah? What grade you startin'?"

"Sixth."

"Well, see there. You're a kid."

"Pop, I was getting married down there. In Fort Worth."

"I don't want to hear nothing about that. Lord, no telling what you was fixing to do down there. With her. Lord." He opened the screen, not caring that she could see the way he looked. "If nothing else, I can tell you're your mother's daughter," he said. "You're just like her."

Gemma stared up at him, able to see the lanky round-shouldered old man now, wisps of white hair hanging over his forehead. The bib of his overalls sagged in front. "She says I'm just like you."

He didn't say anything.

"Pop, I'm tired. I haven't slept much the last couple of nights. See, there was this accident at Aggie's shop, that's where my mama works, and—"

"Stop it." His eyes were huge. "Stop it. I don't want to hear none about it, about any of that." He was breathing hard, his mouth slack. His eyes trailed down the steps toward her feet. "That don't matter to me no more."

He glared at her for a moment before closing the screen and going back into the house. She followed, walking through darkened rooms and setting the suitcase down next to her bed. He cleared his throat in the kitchen. In the doorway, she saw him sitting at the table, his hands folded in front of him. He looked down, as though he were praying, but she could see his eyes were fixed on the table. She shifted in the doorway, causing the house to make a sound like cracking knuckles. He knew she was there, but he didn't look up.

"Pop."

She took a step into the room, to the table. She pulled out her chair but didn't sit. That was when she noticed he'd done the dishes. The table was cleared, and the sink was empty. Only a few suds clung to the mouth of the drain.

"Pop, let me fix us some suppers," she said, looking back at him. He still wouldn't look up. He seemed to be concentrating on his hands, on the way they were laced together by the fingers.

"Catch something out yonder? I could fix that."

"Couple perch," he mumbled, clearing his throat almost at once to cover the words.

"You want me to fix them?" She opened a cupboard, a drawer, taking silent stock of what was there. She went to the stove and lit a burner. "I'll fix us some coffee while you clean the fish. Or do you want me to clean 'em?"

"Suit yourself," he said. "I don't care." She knew he was staring at her back now. She didn't turn, but took longer at the stove, adjusting the flame, brushing crumbs from the top.

"I don't know why you let them do that to your hair."

"It's a permanent," she said, washing her hands at the sink. "I like it like this. I may get me another in a couple months when this one grows out."

She looked for her apron, opening cabinets and drawers, finally finding it wadded up under the sink.

Dillard sat slumped at the table, staring at something in the darkness of her room, or maybe the front room. "Well," he said after a moment, working his jaw, "I sure hope you're not expecting me to give you one of them things."

🐓 *Bad news comes too late.*

Days passed. Neither of them had much to say. Ornery, she thought, watching him traipse out to the chicken yard as she beat the rugs draped over the line with a broom. Behind the crape myrtles, she could hear him spit. He cussed at Handsome and Ulysses. Wings flapped. They made gurgling noises deep in their gullets, answering him, following him about the yard as he spread feed for them and the hens. Don't make no difference to me, she decided, turning to the wall of rugs in front of her, pushing the horn-rimmed glasses up on her nose. Least he aint griping.

Dillard stumbled around the chicken yard, kicking up dust, scaring the hens, muttering. When the hens began to screech, she could hear him chuckle.

And later, sitting in a straight-backed chair in his room, watching him recover, she would wonder how everything could have happened so quickly in the short time she'd been back. She would watch as he slept fitfully, watch his broken body strain against each breath and think: wake up, Pop. Wake up and talk to me now.

"Nope," he'd said the first morning she was back. "You aint going."

"Why not?"

"You just aint. Don't take that tone." He'd stood at the screen, adjusting his straw hat before going out into the mid-morning heat.

Gemma stood at the kitchen window, watching him hobble down the road with his fishing tackle. He didn't look back. She watched until he was out of sight, shaking her head, wondering how long he intended to keep up that treatment. "I aint that hardheaded." Dillard kicked at stones in the road. His knees ached; every step hurt. But I'm going out yonder on my own, he said to himself. She aint takin' that away.

That first day, she'd stripped the beds, dusted, swept, washed clothes, and scrubbed the floors. He'd let dust settle in drifts in the corners. She found a pile of dirty socks under his bed. The freezer compartment hadn't been defrosted in months; the door wouldn't close. He'd let a light bulb burn out in the front room, and he hadn't replaced it. Now what could he have been doing in here, she wondered, trailing a finger around the walls, checking for dust, her eyes settling on the opened Victrola. A stack of mail had been crammed into the cookie jar. She found unpaid bills, circulars, and a blue envelope postmarked Baton Rouge. Dillard's name was written across the front in a broad, old-fashioned script. She laid the mail on the kitchen table, then put a pan of hot water into the freezer. Can't do nothing for hisself, she thought, wiping sweat from her face, looking inside the freezer at the cakes of frost.

That evening when he came in, she was at the sink, peeling potatoes. He shuffled into the kitchen, holding his side. He looked haggard as he pulled out a chair and sat down.

"I found that mail in the cookie jar," she said, drying her hands on her apron.

"That's where I put it." He stared straight ahead, breathing strangely, holding one hand to his chest.

"Well, that's not where it goes. They're gonna turn off the electricity if you don't pay your bill."

He mumbled something and scowled.

"I found a letter in there you aint even opened."

"It aint nothing."

"It's addressed to you: Homer Dillard," she said.

"I know what it is," he said, taking a deep breath, "and it aint nothing."

She came to the table. "Pop, you hurtin'?"

Dillard swallowed and closed his eyes. He took a handkerchief from his back pocket and blew his nose. Pecking at me, he thought, she's pecking at me.

"Pop?"

"I'm old!" he shouted all at once. She stepped back. "Aint you noticed that?"

"Course I noticed."

"Well, then why are you asking me stupid questions?"

He pounded a fist on the table and moved the mail away.

"Aren't you gonna open that letter?"

"I told you, I'm not." He'd gotten up from the table and gone to the back porch. She could see him standing out there, not doing anything, just standing, staring at the floor in front of the slop bucket.

After that he let her drive him to the lake every day.

"Might as well make yourself useful as long as you're here." He'd slapped the car keys on the table the following morning. Gemma had driven him out to Twilight Lake, over the backroads which zigzagged through the flat, low countryside from the farm. She could hardly keep from talking as they arrived and started up the steel-drum barge. The lake glistened. The smell of water and burning engine oil made her want to talk. But he kept to himself.

"I'm carrying you back to the car if you don't keep quiet," he said after she'd baited his hook. "You're gonna scare the fish."

All right, she nodded, sitting on the deck, her back against the encased motor. She watched him hover over the water, concentrating on the red and white bobber floating just off the barge. When it went under, she shrieked. Dillard almost toppled over the side.

"Keep quiet," he said, pulling the fish onto the deck. He

worked the hook from its mouth while she watched. "They's others down there too, you know." He tossed the fish into a bucket of water, then reached into the mason jar for another grasshopper. "Here," he said, trying to do it once himself. "Bait this dang thing."

Aint nothing changed, she thought, doing as he said. She watched him toss the speared grasshopper out over the surface. The sinker pulled it under. Heat from the deck began to blister through the seat of her overalls. She stared at his rounded back, at the way he became absorbed with his task. He didn't seem to know she was there. She shifted one leg under her, and instantly it began to bake on the tin deck. It felt good.

They would sit on the barge in the days to come for hours at a time without speaking. After a while, she didn't particularly mind that he wouldn't talk. It was enough for her to be there, reading sometimes, helping him bait hooks, dreaming, starting the motor when he was ready to come in for the day.

Dillard would stare across the fuzzy plane of water at the opposite shore, not able to see it clearly, but looking anyway, trying to recollect the twists and turns it took. It was straight along the southern shore, almost as though it had been manmade. Then it curled into tiny secluded inlets farther east. He never turned to look at her, though he knew she was staring at him, waiting for him to show something. Aint nothing to show her, he said to himself. Been so long, there aint nothing in my memory left of that woman, that Cora. Nothing about what she woulda been. Old. His sight could more readily conjure up the shoreline on the other side of the lake.

And Gemma, out with him every day on Twilight Lake, would wonder what he was thinking. I never knew her, did I? she wanted to ask. Did I? Did that round-faced, smiling woman she'd seen in high-collared white blouses in the photo albums even know about her? Gemma would gaze over the water at the other boats bobbing in the distance. Suddenly she would start, recall something—a voice, something brushing against her cheek—and she would know she'd been dreaming about her mother.

Gemma had been the one to finally open the blue envelope.

"Go on," he'd told her one afternoon late as he cleaned fish on the back porch. "Go on and do it so you'll stop pestering me about it."

"But it's addressed to you," she said, sitting down at the table, looking back toward the darkening porch where he sat gutting fish, cutting off their heads.

"So's them bills there," he said. "You can open all them too if you want. Pay 'em too."

She turned back to the table and ripped open the envelope.

"Who's Lottie?"

"Lottie?"

"It's from somebody called Lottie—that's what it says down at the end of it."

"Lottie?" She could hear the knife scrape across scales. His breath.

Gemma straightened her glasses and unfolded the thin sheet of blue paper.

"It says: 'Dear Homer, I hope this finds . . .'"

"Can't you read to yourself?" he called, his voice brighter than usual. "No, course you can't. I forgot."

She began reading it to herself, whispering the words out loud at first, then silently. Her eyes followed the swirls of black ink down the page, and slowly she understood. She dropped it to her lap.

"Pop, come here."

He didn't answer. The scraping noises stopped after a moment.

"Pop, you oughta come read this."

"I'm getting these fish dressed."

"Pop, it's news."

"I don't want to read it." His voice came from the darkness of the porch.

"You're gonna have to," she said. She got up from the table and moved to the doorway. She could see him sitting in the shadows by the cistern, frozen, hunched over the bucket between his legs.

"Pop, it's bad news."

And he was staring through the busted-out screen on the doorframe, thinking: I know what it says; I already know.

"It's about Grandma."

The shadow on the porch didn't move.

"Pop, who is that Lottie?"

"Down in Baton Rouge." His voice broke. "Cora's sister."

Gemma took a step onto the porch, but his voice stopped her. "I know what it's about," he said. "But it's too late."

"You have to read it," she said.

"Don't be tellin' me what I have to do."

"It's dated June twenty-seventh."

"It don't matter. It don't matter what date it's got on it. It's still too late."

He got up and moved past her into the kitchen. She could see him standing at the sink, looking out into the coming darkness. She put a hand on his shoulder.

"It says she went peaceful." She held out the blue sheet of paper. Dillard wadded it into a ball. She could see the whites around his eyes. His lips were pressed firmly together as though he were holding something in his mouth.

"It's too late," he said again, the wadded paper in his fist. He picked the envelope up from the table.

"Aren't you even gonna read it?"

He glanced at her, then threw the letter and envelope into the trash. She watched his body sway against the door as he left the kitchen. The back screen slammed. She followed, but he'd disappeared. His footsteps sounded in the darkness, dead grass crunching between the crape myrtles. In a moment she heard the gate to the chicken yard.

Gemma stood at the opened screen for a moment, waiting for him to come back. And then she returned to the kitchen and began to dry the dishes from dinner. In the morning, when she carried the trash out to the barrel they usually burned it in, the wadded blue letter was gone.

On a clear, unusually still afternoon, Gemma and Dillard steered the barge into the center of Twilight Lake. The air was heavy. She sat with her back against the motor, watching him as usual. Her mind wandered and she was hardly aware of thunder sounding in the distance. When Dillard turned once to look at her, he saw that she was crying. But he didn't say anything. And Gemma was thinking: did she even know about me? Does she think about me now? When she closed her eyes, she could see her mother's face, laughing, pointing a finger and laughing.

Dillard turned away from her toward the water again, his eyes clinging to the sight of the bobber. And out there, on the fuzzy surface, he could see her, Cora, her round face smiling up at him, curtsying then, and dancing, her long skirt billowing away from her body, dancing around and around.

🐓 *Fish surface just before a storm.*

"Pop." Something was wrong. She rolled to her feet, wiping her eyes. He sat at the other end of the barge, upright, staring across the lake. Then she saw him tug on the pole and bring in a fish. She stepped back as he made a streaking arc with it through the air and brought it down flopping on the deck. She heard it now, the thunder. "Pop, it's getting darker."

Dillard waved her away and squatted over the fish. Its gills opened and closed. He put a hand around it and wrenched the hook from its mouth. Gemma watched him drop it into the bucket and wipe his hand on his overalls.

A rumble came from the opposite shore. The sky was changing, becoming more overcast by the minute.

"I think we better be getting back," she said. He tottered to his feet and held out the hook for her to bait.

"It aint even three yet."

"But it's clouding up," she said. "I heard thunder."

"Aww."

"Didn't you hear it?"

He gripped the hook close to her face and after a moment she stabbed it through a grasshopper's back. The air had become thick, still. He hurried back to his seat, making clucking noises in his throat.

"Come here, Gemma," he said, his voice high. It made her move toward him. "Looky here. They's all coming up."

And over the side of the barge she could see the fish, surfacing, then disappearing, surfacing again in another spot. Bubbles formed and exploded on the water. Dillard's bobber went under.

"They're biting faster'n I can pull 'em in," he said, grinning, yanking on his line.

"We oughta start on back," she said, noticing that the sky had changed color. The blue had bled to a pale gray. A front of low-hanging clouds had begun to come toward them from across the lake, rolling like a huge gray quilt over the sky.

"Come bait this thing," he called.

"Just give me time," she said, looking upward, then going to the mason jar of grasshoppers. He was almost jumping up and down on the deck, keeping his gaze trained on the water, on the tiny bubbles forming around them. Gemma saw that the lake had changed color too; it was almost black.

"There's a storm fixing to come," she said, standing behind him, looking over his shoulder. He didn't say anything, but lopped the line over the water, almost giggling now at the gracefully swimming forms that surfaced so near.

"I think we oughta start up and go back in."

"I aint leaving while they're biting like this."

"I don't wanna get caught out here," she said, stamping a foot, then moving back across the barge. "You know I aint ever driven in the rain."

"It'll pass over."

"I don't think so," she said, staring at his back.

Dillard looked up quickly, then shot back at her: "It'll pass over, I'm telling you. Now keep quiet; you'll scare 'em off."

Clouds started to churn over their heads in a mass of grays and moss green. On the bank, trees had begun to weave. Leaves swished together so that it sounded as if rain was already pelting down against the earth. Thunder sounded again, and a wind rolled across the lake all at once, causing the barge to heave. Gemma steadied herself on the railing around the motor. The old man didn't seem to notice how low the sky was becoming. Suddenly huge drops splattered against the tin deck. And then a white finger of lightning touched the opposite shore and the earth trembled.

"I aint staying here another minute," she said, wrapping the cord around the motor. Dillard was pulling in another fish, laughing, holding his straw hat in place as he swung it around.

"Can't you see there's a storm?"

"I see it," he said, looking again into the murky lake, standing so close to the edge that he almost fell overboard as the barge lurched forward.

"What the heck you think you're doing?"

"We're heading back," she said, steering the barge toward shore.

"No, we aint." He held to his chair for balance. "We aint going in till I'm ready for us to."

But she drove them through the churning surfaces, above and below, toward the Chevrolet parked under the trees. Dillard squatted on the deck and rode with the bucket of fish between his knees, still holding the wiggling fish on the line with one hand.

"You better hope this don't stop soon's we get back," he shouted back at her.

Gemma pressed her lips together, glaring into the wind. Their car lit up suddenly in a flash of light. It had not yet begun to pour when she reached the pier and tied up the barge. He was behind her, mumbling, struggling to his feet, holding the line with the fish on the end.

"Throw that thing back," she said.

"I will not." He ripped the hook from its mouth and threw it into the bucket.

She moved up the bank of grass, trudging against the wind. When she reached the car, she rolled up all the windows.

"Come on here," she called. The barge was out of sight now, hidden by waving branches. She ran back, hearing his voice first, before finally meeting him halfway on the bank.

"It's a tornado," she said, taking the bucket from him and

turning back for the car. He scowled and followed, cursing under his breath.

"Too early for tornadoes," he said stubbornly, pouting, letting her take the pole and tackle from him. Finally he got into the car and stared through the windshield. Heavy branches dipped low in front of them. Down at the pier, the barge rose and slammed into the wooden pilings like a toy.

"Well, that's what it is," she said, raising her voice to be heard above the wind. She secured the pole in back, then got into the car.

"How do you know?"

Not answering, she started the car and backed away from the lake with such a lunge that he was knocked off balance.

"Take it easy," he said, holding to the dashboard. "You're gonna wreck us."

"I wanna get home before this hits." She stretched her neck forward, gripped the steering wheel, and drove slowly through the trees. Branches scraped the hood of the car. The air was tinted green, and the dirt road was barely visible. Debris blew across their path. The car bounced when they drove over dead branches. Suddenly the sky lit up again and thunder ripped through the woods.

"Now that struck something," he said, his face against his window.

She could not turn away from the windshield. Rain had started to splatter against it, and though the windshield wipers were on, she was only able to see a few feet in front of the car.

"Take it slower!" His face and hands were against the window.

"I am."

"Can you see where the heck we're headin'?"

"No," she said, her face straining forward. It was as though she felt her way along by memory, turning the wheel now and then to dodge trees that bent dangerously in their way. Drops of water seeped through the roof; her arms were splattered and her forehead became damp.

"If you can't see, then stop this car," he said, glancing over at her, rising in his seat. "Just stop it right now."

"I aint stopping out here," she said. "If a tree don't fall on us, we'd probably blow away."

He sat quietly beside her now, the bucket in his lap, and he stared through the windshield too. All he was able to see was a rush of wind and water swirling around, pounding down on them. Sometimes, out of the murkiness, a leaf would slap against the windshield and he would stare at it, a blackened silhouette against the storm before it was swept away. He thought: it's blowing away; the whole world's blowing away.

As she drove the car down the road leading to the house, Gemma could hear water rushing by on either side of them, flash-flooding in the culverts.

"I don't think we're gonna get over the bridge," she called. The wind was so high now they could barely hear each other.

"What?" He was against the windshield too, straining for some familiar sight, anything. "Then stop it. Don't try it."

"I told you I aint stopping this car!" she shouted. The car rocked on its axis, dipping forward and back in the blast of wind around them. She inched them forward until the car shed appeared immediately to the right. "We're here!" He didn't seem to hear. His hands pressed against the glass as though he were trying to keep the storm from caving in on them. "Pop, we're here!"

"Don't try it!"

She turned the wheels and crept the car slowly over the wood-planked bridge. Currents of leaves and debris swept along underneath them. Dillard sat with his eyes pressed tightly together, his head ducked almost to the rim of the bucket.

"My Lord!" She could hear his voice resound in the bucket. It was high-pitched, hollow, almost as though it were coming from under water.

She stopped the car. "Leave all this stuff in here," she called to him, turning off the ignition. She was sweating; it mixed with the moisture leaking through on them. "We can get it later."

"It aint gonna hurt them fish to get a little wet," he called. "Leave 'em!"

He tried to open his door, but it was instantly blown shut. He turned to her then, stricken, his face drawn. Gemma tried to wipe off her glasses, but they were only smeared more. He shoved on the door once again and was able to hold it open enough to get a leg out. The air was a putrid green, and a steady roar churned up leaves and grass. The house was not visible, though she knew it was there; it had to be there. As she squeezed herself from the car, a roll of baling wire skimmed across the ground. She heard a slam on the other side; he was outside too. She began to run through the storm, skidding against the ground, slipping on the paving stones. She dashed to the front screen and pulled it. It was latched. She turned to let him know, but he wasn't behind her. At once, she leapt from the steps and landed in the black muddy ooze of the flower bed. Stems of naked flowers still clung to the muck by their roots. She managed to pull herself up by gripping onto them.

"The front's locked!" It was no good; the wind swallowed her words. She could barely see the ground in front of her. The wind plastered her hair back on her head. She stumbled around the house, fingers clutching at the sides for support. Steadily, she made her way toward the back, bursting into the porch, panting, dripping into the puddles already formed on the floor. The walls of the screened-in porch glistened. She went into the kitchen, her feet clumsily plopping through water. A howl swept through the house. She climbed onto the counter, into the sink, and closed the window. The inside was soaked. Water formed in uneven puddles over the kitchen floor.

"Pop!" She heard a whimper coming from her room. Max was huddled in a wet furry clump on her bed. She wrapped the spread around him and came back into the kitchen. "Pop!"

He wasn't inside. She went to the porch, her feet making

sucking noises against the floor. Her clothes hung heavily on her limbs. Rain came through the wire mesh, soaking her face. She tried calling again, though she could hardly hear her own voice through the constant wail around the house. Opening the screen, moving down the steps, she thought: he's turned back; he's back in the car. She held a hand over her glasses as though it might help her see better. But the rain seemed to be coming from every direction. Her body was slanted almost to the ground as she moved forward. And then she saw it, the bucket, rolling along the ground on its side. Farther along, she saw where the fish lay scattered in a broken line, some of their mouths still working, their eyes huge, their gills flexed open. On her knees, her face close to them, she thought: they're dying, they're suffocating. "Pop!"

She set the bucket upright and scooped them inside. It blew over again at once. She looked up at the house, breathing quickly, wondering. And then she knew. He'd gone through the pecan trees and crape myrtles. The old cedar poles suspended in air by the clothesline swung crazily as she trudged past toward the chicken yard.

She opened the gate and ran toward the henhouse. Her feet squished in mud to her ankles. Already the yard was under water in places, and straw and feed swirled in hundreds of tiny funnels. She called for him again, though her voice was lost. She could feel the wind pushing her toward the low wooden structure. It was shoving too hard, though, knocking her into the swirls of muck washing over the ground. She reached the henhouse and fell against it, her knees butting into the mud. She tried the door, but it was locked. When she beat on the door and called to him, she knew it was no use. The wind was more powerful; it battered against the house with more force.

She heard the tin roof give first. It creaked and seemed to pry itself away from the structure of its own accord, slowly at first, then it was off—a wall of tin rattling through the wind like thunder. It flew through midair, hurling into the mud, then up again, smacking against the barbed-wire fence. With her hands over her head, she could hear the house moan as wood began to tear and bend at the joints. It was as though the winds had gathered themselves inside the roofless building, bursting it at the seams. She stepped backward, falling. The henhouse rattled; it seemed to pulse. Above her, she could hear it split at one corner. The other walls gave way and collapsed one after the other. As they crumpled into the mud, the force inside scattered hay and scraps of wood. From where she curled herself into the mud, she could see the sides give and fold. Wind carried nests through the air, eggs hurling in their own orbits. The nests kept their form, then suddenly exploded into thousands of particles of hay as they splattered against the tin roof wedged into mud. She tried to stand, but boards ricocheted over her head. One of the hens was drunkenly trying to burrow itself into the mud, only to be buried suddenly by falling timber. Another was swept along the ground like a tumbleweed, endlessly head over tail, a soggy mass of red feathers. Some of them hung lifeless, impaled on the ends of stubborn boards wedged in the ground. And then she saw Ulysses, the old rooster, his wings hanging limply. He was picked up by a gust of wind and flown through the air, two hens behind him in a sloppy formation. They were thrown across the yard until they splattered with dead thuds against the wide tin roof.

Gemma fought to stand. She called for him, her voice piercing now above the wind and the sounds of ripping lumber. She stumbled forward to the rubble, crying out when she stepped on a dead hen. She fell into the heap of splintered wood and mud, her face sinking in next to one of the chickens. She shoved it away and crawled forward, pulling away boards, the feed trough. She pulled two lifeless hens from the heap and saw him, his leg, through an opening in the wreckage. Standing, tugging at the boards, she only caused more of the heap to cave in on the old man. She knew it then; she thought: I killed him; he's dead. And then something hit her across the head.

When she awoke, she was clutching one of the boards to

her body. The wind had died, but rain continued steadily. She tried to sit. Her glasses had been knocked from her face. There was blood on her fingers when she touched her forehead. She moved off the rubble, chilled, disoriented. Her glasses were sticking out of the mud. She reached over to pick them up, though there was nothing to clean them with. Over the yard, she could see countless dead chickens, small mounds of dark red feathers. They stuck up from the water as though they were sprouting.

She remembered.

"Pop."

Behind her, she began again to pull away timber, tossing wood and debris to the side. She could see his leg again. It was bent oddly to one side. She ran a muddy hand over her face, blinking. Then she tugged at boards and dug until she could see an arm, his back, the side of his face. One of the hens was against his chest, as though he'd been holding it when the walls caved in. Gemma climbed over the mound. One shoulder was pinned under a beam. And when she was able to move it, she took the chicken from his arms and tried to lift his head. It fell limply against her chest.

The side of his face had been slashed by a nail and blood smeared against her shirt in a pink smudge. She tried to lift him, to put one hand underneath his body. But he was dead weight. She held him closely then, one hand shielding his face from the rain. She felt him stir.

"It's me," she said. "I got you now."

He lay motionless, his eyes fluttering. She could see him swallow, then his mouth move. It was as though the rest of his body was unconnected. She hugged him closer.

"What is it?" she pleaded. "It's Gemma."

Even though his eyes had not opened, she could see that he knew her, or seemed to. He ran his tongue over his lips and tried to say something.

"Can you move?"

But Dillard didn't seem to hear. His brow narrowed. He

said something, though there was no sound. Gemma held him in her arms, watching him repeat the same movements—the chin drop, his lips quiver into an oval.

"Pop? What? What are you saying?"

As the fine drizzle brought on darkness, she held him until she could barely see his face. He never spoke the word, though after a time she thought she could hear it: the name.

🐓 *Broken bones mend quickly during a full moon.*

His hospital room was at the end of the hall, facing the back, facing an abandoned barnlike structure. It had been the dairy. Had he told her that he once worked there? Did she know about that? He couldn't remember. It had been so long ago that he could hardly recall being there, or what he'd done. Juanelle had been a child. She had come to work with him sometimes. He could remember how she sat there watching him work, tinker with machinery, the cooler. She hardly took her eyes from him.

Now all in white, both arms encased in hard plaster and one leg as well, he lay in the end room. His cast was raised so that his leg appeared to be pointing at the window, indicating the dairy to anyone who happened to walk in. What had he done there? What was it? That girl, that tiny girl with long legs, watched every move he made, taking it all in as though she thought he might ask her to take over any moment.

And this one, Gemma, was sitting beside his bed. They had given him something to make him sleep. He knew he'd been out for some time; he still felt woozy. He couldn't move. Dull pains drove through his body, so many that he could hardly separate one from the other. Gemma sat next to him in a straight-backed chair, just sat there watching.

"How long I been here?"

"Two days."

He followed the line of his white cast, trying to see past it, past the window to that dilapidated barn out back. But his eyes were too weak. He couldn't put it together. Had he done the milking? That girl had made him so nervous. He could still see her, those big eyes bearing down on everything he did.

"My mouth's dry."

He tried to turn his head to watch her leave the room, but a jagged pain made him wince. And then he dozed. She was pointing, even though her mother had told her time and again not to, saying: "What's that? What's that thing there?" "That holds the cow in place when we milk her." She ran around the dairy, her voice echoing in the vaulted ceiling. "What's this? What's this?"

"Here, Pop."

Gemma held a glass of water. She tilted the curved straw to his mouth and held it while he sipped.

"We brought you to the hospital in Greenville."

He dropped his head back on the pillow. What was it? What was I doing there all that time? He heard her set the glass on the table beside his bed and sit again. Every breath made him ache. Was it in the barns? Cleaning up? That girl stood on a milk stool and watched him tinker with fan belts and cogwheels. He could remember saying: "Now stand back." And she had stepped off the stool and backed it several feet before climbing up again to watch him so carefully. "Are you having a big time with Pop today? Are you?" She grinned and nodded. One of her front teeth was missing.

Dillard could feel himself slipping back into darkness. He forced his eyes open once more. Gemma sat there rigidly, watching. She said again: "We brought you over to Greenville."

Well, that's mighty fine, 'cause Pop's havin' a big time too.

🐓 *A story before bed helps a child sleep easy.*

Gemma shook out a pair of long underwear and pinned it over the line. It was Sunday, not the usual day for wash, but she was getting it done early because school was to begin the next day. She moved the pin along the line so that the overalls had more room to ˉdry. Sunday. Not a day for washing. But with taking care of him, she knew she'd have to do it whenever she had the chance.

It worried her, taking care of him, now that he was home. How could she manage to tend to things and be at school too? "We'll look in on him," Doreen Hadley had told her. "We'll make sure he's got everything he needs till you get in from school."

Gemma didn't know about that. As a rule, the last thing Dillard would ever have wanted was to have Doreen or Bob or anyone fussing around his bed there in the back room. She had been surprised at how cooperative he'd been the past few days. Usually he'd pout and lock his bedroom door whenever he was laid up with a cold. This time had been different. He'd let her help him into the house when they'd come home Friday. He'd let her feed him his meals and smooth his bed. She'd even helped change his pajamas. Only once, when she'd tried to sponge him off, had he balked. "I can clean my own self," he'd muttered, grabbing the washrag from her. And somehow that had eased her mind, made her feel as though he was getting better.

Max stood at her feet, guarding the washtub of wrung-out clothes. She didn't have too many this week. He'd just been home three days, and the only overalls were hers. She reached down for them now, a clothespin in her mouth.

"You shoulda seen my dress with the pinafore," she said to the cat. He swatted at her hand. "I looked like something out of a magazine." She pinned up the overalls, feeling sad suddenly, feeling that tightness in her throat that she always felt whenever she thought about Fort Worth. Max sat with his feet together, looking up at her. "I wish I'd a brought it back so you coulda seen it."

The morning heat made her glasses slip down on her nose, and when she pushed them up, she noticed how burned out the field next to the house looked. Even with the rains a few weeks ago, everything still looked dry. She sighed, thinking how the dust blew in gusts along the highway in front of the gas station; she remembered it all at once. Draping a sheet over the line, pinning it in three places, she thought: are any of them missing me? Rory? Max rolled on his back in the grass.

And then she heard footsteps on the other side of the wet clothes, footsteps shuffling through dead grass. For a moment, she thought he'd gotten out of bed, but she knew that was impossible. Both arms were still in casts, and his leg was encased in plaster up to the hip. She heard Dillard cough then; it came from the opened window of his room. The footsteps stopped as though the visitor heard too. Gemma listened without moving a muscle, and they started again. Her heart began to pound. Something buzzed in her head. Max was crouched next to the washtub, ready to pounce. Gemma stood frozen in place, quietly hoping the feet would turn away before they reached her. Dillard coughed again behind the white, dead-still window shade.

She was afraid she would collapse into the empty washtub, and even reeled a bit when she saw the scuffed and muddied shoes stop behind the sheet. Maybe they'll leave, she thought, feeling her eyes tear as she stared at the shoes. A hand poked the wall of clothing, and then the feet turned, hobbling parallel along the line of wash toward the end. Fingers gripped the cedar pole, and then Beecham's head came around the corner.

"How do."

She couldn't speak. She stared at the withered black face. It wrinkled into a grin. He slunk around the hanging clothes and stood before her, more stooped now than she'd remembered. The top of his head looked polished in the sunlight. He shifted his weight; standing in one position more than a few moments seemed painful. Gemma couldn't manage to make a sound.

"They tell me Homer's back."

He shuffled from foot to foot, looking her over. He'd gotten much thinner; she could see the veins along his temple.

"That right? Homer come back?"

Gemma swallowed; her mouth was dry. "He came back from Greenville a couple days ago. Friday."

"Well, that's fine. I know he's glad to be home." He shook his head back and forth, grinning as though he suddenly remembered something. "Homer always liked his home."

"Beecham," she said, her voice raspy. She felt herself sway forward before finally crumpling against the washtub. Max scampered for the back door. "Beecham."

"Yes, ma'am. Aint you even gonna say 'how do'?"

She could feel her eyes fill, though she was laughing. Beecham limped over the ground in front of her, bending sometimes to peer into the washtub and touch the metal sides as though from some habit he'd developed roaming the hills of trash in the Twilight dump. Gemma got to her feet and put both arms around him.

"I thought you were dead," she whispered. "I thought all that garbage had covered you up."

"Well, I 'spect you was right. It did."

"But you're here." She felt his bones give. He seemed so brittle, fragile now, just like Dillard. "I thought I wasn't ever gonna see you again."

"Well, I'm here," he cackled, rubbing his nose. "I thought I never would be seeing you, either. But the good Lord, I reckon he was willing for me to come back for a time."

She held him before her, staring at him.

"Yeah, well, they tell me half a the places 'tween here'n Commerce got blowed away in the tornado. I guess y'all was lucky the house wasn't hit too bad. Some folks, the Turners over by the creek, well, they got their whole place washed away."

"That's what Doreen says."

"Yeah, I reckon Homer was lucky."

She turned suddenly toward the house. "I have to tell him you're all right."

"Homer? Why, he know it. Homer was the one that had 'em dig me out."

Gemma stood back, watching him nod and run his tongue over his gums.

"Yes, ma'am, I mean to tell you I was gettin' mighty worried down there. Saving up my breaths and talking to the good Lord 'cause I know it was my time and I wanted Him to know I was ready for it if that's what he wanted."

"You mean Pop got you out?"

"Yes, ma'am, that's what I'm tellin' you 'bout now. Well, I hear 'em up there talkin' and draggin' stuff offa me. First I thought maybe I was in heaven and it was angels. And I was talkin' to the Lord, singin' his praise in my heart, a-listening to those angels up there bringing me home. Then all at once, I heard Homer's voice and I knowed I wasn't dead at all, or leastways I thought I wasn't. My thinking was a mite scrambled, but I didn't think Homer'd passed over or nothing. But directly, I could see all them staring down at me, Homer in the big middle of 'em. They was staring at me for a long time before they realized they'd got to me. I was a mess. And the next thing I knowed, I was in a ammulance goin' to the hospital. I 'spect I was there 'bout two months. Doctors say my ribs is healing jus' fine."

"You look just the same."

"Well, I guess I do," he said, patting her arm. His grin was toothless. "Though I mean to tell you, I was banged up."

Gemma felt feverish. "Nobody told me you were all right. Why didn't he tell me?"

"Well, they all knowed it. I even got my picture in the papers." He pulled a damp, ragged clipping from his back pocket. It had been folded and refolded so many times that it had torn along the creases. The print had smeared, but when he held it out for her to read, she could see that it was him in the picture, Beecham, sitting up in a hospital bed with a bandage around his head. He pointed at the faded print. "It say here: 'Twilight man in satisfactory condition after being buried fifteen hours.'" He nodded. "I reckon I am. Satisfactory."

"Why didn't they tell me?"

"Well, where you been?"

"Pop never said a word."

Beecham stared down into the empty washtub. "They tell me it was him that made them come back for me. Preacher tell me they was there before, but everyone give up. Homer called 'em all back. I aint never thanked him yet."

The clothes hung heavily in the heat. Gemma could see the cat standing at the back door.

"I jus' come by to see him now. I'm stayin' up to Preacher Dixon's place 'cause my place it was blowed away in that storm." He tried to whistle.

"He'll be glad of the company."

Suddenly she remembered something. She told him to wait while she dashed to the house, almost tripping over Max. In her room, she pulled the suitcase from underneath her bed. It was still there, Beecham's oil-stained hat. She brushed it off and tried to put it back into shape as she rushed through the kitchen. Standing at the door to Dillard's bedroom, she said: "Pop, Beecham's come to see you."

Dillard lay flat on his back, his eyes closed. His brow was tensed, and the scar along his cheek was red. He had opened his mouth, and now he breathed heavily. Gemma knew he wasn't asleep. The white plaster around his limbs seemed to anchor him to the bed. He looked so small. Gemma stood watching him for a moment before she went outside to give Beecham his hat.

"He's sleeping now," she said, the hat behind her back. "But you wait for him."

"Well, Preacher's stopping round for me in a bit. He's back over yonder doin' some visitin'."

The old man's face lit up when he saw her take the hat from behind her. He put it on over the few worn-down nubs of hair he had left and said: "I jus' been itchin' to get better 'nough so I could hunt through that dump for my hat."

Later, though she brought it up herself while Beecham sat on the back steps, drinking iced tea, she got the feeling it had been Dillard's idea all along too. Beecham could sleep in the front room, at least for a while, she told him, straightening his pillow. And when Dillard was up and around, they could decide where to put the old man.

"Well, he aint takin' my room," Dillard said, his mouth clamped.

"I aint saying he should. I could give him my room. We could close in the porch or something. I don't know. But he oughta stay with us now. He'd be good company for you."

"I don't need no company. What I want with company?"

"Pop, I hate having to leave you while I'm at school."

He made a sound with his lips.

"What if you need something? What if the house catches on fire or something?"

"I hope you aint expecting that fool nigger to carry me outta here, or put out a fire."

"You know what I mean."

He didn't say anything.

"He can take care of you," she said, tucking in his sheet. "Y'all can take care of each other."

Dillard lifted his head from the pillow and gazed out the

window as though he might try to dive through it. Then he slammed his head down again.

"He's got the nastiest habits," he said.

"What kind of nasty habits you mean?"

"Heck, I don't know. Nasty. He's been living off yonder in that shack and messin' round that dump for so long, there's no tellin' what he does, what kinda filth he's picked up."

"Pop, he's been staying at Preacher Dixon's house. He's been in the hospital for two months. You know how clean they are there."

"It just don't seem right."

"It seems exactly right," she said flatly. "He should be living here with us. He used to live on this place, didn't he?"

"That was different. He was one of the field hands, him and the rest of his family. They lived out back there in the shack. It won't do for us to have a nigger moving into the house."

"It'll do fine. Nobody'll think any different. Beecham belongs here with you and me."

"I don't know." He stared at the ceiling. "I wonder if I could fix up that henhouse for him."

"You aint seen it, Pop. Not since the tornado. There aint a whole lot to fix up."

"Well, I bet I can fix it up. Heck, I built that thing in the first place."

She took a glass of buttermilk from the table next to his bed and held it to his lips.

"You gotta take it easy from now on," she said, watching him drink from the glass. "I 'spect you both gonna have to."

"I built that barge too," he said, dropping his head to the pillow.

"We'll see," she said.

"Besides, I'm gonna have to fix up something for my hens."

Gemma set the glass back on the table. "Even if you got the henhouse fixed up, you couldn't put Beecham out there too," she said. "We'll think of something."

At the door, she turned, to see him gazing out the window.

"Pop, am I right? About Beecham?"

He chewed his bottom lip. "I reckon. We'll set up something."

She saw his eyes close.

That afternoon, Gemma went with Beecham and Reverend Dixon to pick up his things. She was able to carry everything he owned herself. While she set up his cot in the front room, she told him how to play the Victrola.

"Gemma! What is that racket?" Dillard called through the house. And Gemma closed the door to her room while they played music. Dillard called her name again.

Later, in days to come, Dillard would spend most of his time staring out the window while she was at school. Gemma would come home to find him looking out at the burned-up landscape, and she would think: I wish there was something out there for him to see. In those weeks that would follow, he'd hardly ask for a thing. And Gemma would hope each day would be different, that he might ask to have his back rubbed, to eat, to get out of bed. But it would seem that whenever she was ready to tend to him, he was ready. He would lie awake nights. Sometimes Gemma would slip out of bed to check on him, and know he was awake though he would pretend to be asleep. Neither of them would say anything, though she would stay with him for a time before returning to her own bed.

And later, Gemma would miss Beecham now and again, only to find him weeding the flower bed, mowing, cleaning around the house. "Jus' like to keep busy," he'd tell her. He and Dillard would hardly speak, and when they did, it would usually be to pass along matter-of-fact information.

"I picked them tomatoes," Beecham would say to him sometime later, standing in the doorway, holding his hat in front of him.

"What tomatoes?" Dillard spoke to the ceiling.

"From them vines that wasn't blowed away."

Or: "Supposed to get up to a hundred today."

"Gonna rain. My joints is aching."

Beecham would stand in the doorway, nodding for a moment, then turn away. And Dillard would follow the outline of the water spot on the ceiling, follow it down the wall to where it disappeared at the foot of his bed, and think: Yes, you remember that summer we had back after the war when fires'd start right up out in the fields 'cause it was so hot? And we'd get up in the middle of the night and do our work by the lantern, so's not to have to swelter in the heat. You out there in front, holding the light for me to plow the garden under. It was so burnt up we thought it might catch fire too. Nothing was saved. No water then, 'cept in the tanks, and they was low. Remember? Paddling out yonder, water moccasins sunning in the mud. Floating out yonder, looking up at the sky.

That Sunday night, that night when Beecham appeared, Gemma washed the supper dishes and Beecham dried them. When they'd finished, he walked out onto the back porch, humming something. The screen opened and closed. The house grew quiet. She could see Beecham, his hands shoved into his pockets, kicking at dirt clods around by the butane tank, humming, trying to sing now and then. She dried her hands on a dish towel and stared out at the trees lit brilliantly by the sun on the horizon.

"Gemma?"

At first she didn't hear him call, but when he said her name again, she came to his door. Max was sitting on the bed, his paws resting on Dillard's cast. Dillard and the cat stared at her.

"You need something?"

After a moment, he shook his head. He still watched her. She came to the bed and threw Max to the floor. He followed her into the kitchen and she fed him the leftovers from supper. She'd just seated herself in the rocker and opened her Bible when she heard his voice again.

"I figgered you'd gone outside." He was staring at the failing light on the crape myrtle. Gemma stood in the doorway, the Bible to her chest.

"No, that was Beecham."

Dillard didn't say anything. The dry, turned-up ends of the bush outside had become a cool blue.

"You want me to sit with you?"

He sniffled and scratched his nose with the cast on his arm. He tried to say something, but the words fell against one another in his throat. Gemma sat in the cane-backed chair next to his bed.

"I can read to you. You want me to do that?"

He nodded. The light was so dim that he was a composite of shadows in white on his bed. She saw his mouth open, then close, as she flipped through her Bible.

"I 'spect I better turn on the light," she said.

"It hurts my eyes."

She pushed up her glasses in the middle with her finger and looked down at the page of fine print. She could see his head shift on the pillow as though he were uncomfortable. When she stood and moved toward him, he said: "I'm okay. Read." Through the dim blue light she could see his face. His eyes seemed to catch a reflection from outside. The wrinkles in his brow deepened, and his lips pressed together, once and then again.

Gemma stepped back from him, then turned to leave the room.

"Girl?"

She turned at the door. His head was lifted from the pillow, his eyes wide, startled.

"I'm coming back," she said.

And when he saw her again, she carried a magazine. She sat in the chair next to him.

"If you want to read your Bible, I reckon I don't mind," he said.

"I'll just read this magazine," she said, watching him. "It's a *Life*."

Dillard stared at the ceiling as she began to flip pages. She skimmed through, looking for something he might want to hear. Finally she chose something toward the back. She held the page close to her face.

"Now I don't know if this is all right," she began.

"It's all right," he said hoarsely. "Fine."

"This here's a story called: 'A New Life Begins for Janet Leigh.'"

"Who's that?"

"A movie star. She was in that Lassie movie, and that *Little Women*."

"Oh. Yeah."

"She's real good."

"I don't think I ever saw her."

"Well, she's a big movie star," Gemma said. She got up to turn on a light on the porch. A shaft of light came into his room, spilling across the floor. She held the magazine to one side so that the light caught it. Then she began to read, her voice uncertain at first.

"'A New Life for Janet Leigh. Janet Leigh has had a pretty successful career as a young (aged twenty-three) movie star. But no one could say that the career was very spectacular. Janet's wide, clear eyes and clean, pert all-American face has led M-G-M and RKO, the two studios who have divided her services, to cast her in a series of soft, silly, sentimental roles.

"'This month at last things began to look up for Janet. Her second marriage was front-page news when she sneaked off to Greenwich, Connecticut (explaining that it's such a romantic spot), to exchange rings and vows with twenty-six-year-old Tony Curtis, the smooth-faced, wavy-haired young movie star who is the current idol of the younger set. The wedding went smoothly enough although the best man, Jerry Lewis, arrived an hour late.'"

"I thought it was supposed to be the groom that was late." Dillard chuckled.

"Well, it was Jerry Lewis, the best man," Gemma said. A cricket began to chirp somewhere underneath the house. She could hear Beecham's voice every time it was quiet. He was sitting on the back steps, singing.

"Did this fella forget the ring or something?"

"I don't know," she said. "It don't say here. He was just late. That's the way those movie stars do sometimes."

"I'd a horsewhipped him if I was that groom."

"Well, it was okay, I guess," she said. "It says here: 'He more than made up for that by his chivalrous attentions to the bride (above).' It shows Jerry Lewis kissing Janet Leigh." Dillard made a sound with his lips. "'And back in Hollywood, Janet's employers decided that it was time to present her in roles which emphasized a quality of hers hitherto overlooked: sex appeal.'"

"Lord."

She looked up from the magazine. "You want me to stop reading?"

"Naw. Naw. Let's see what kind of carryings-on those folks are up to."

Dillard stared up into the shadows over his bed, listening to her voice begin again. And outside, Beecham's voice scratched over some tune, some hymn that Dillard couldn't name, though he knew it, had heard it a long time ago, standing up in that church.

"'The process of getting Janet out of the stays and shawls which she wore in such old-style pictures as *That Forsythe Woman* began two years ago when Howard Hughes, the boss of RKO, decided it was time for her to show off more of her charms.'"

Beecham's voice seemed to mix now with the crickets. Gemma could hardly tell one from the other. Only the palest light remained in the room where she read. And in the kitchen, where her voice was syncopated by the dripping faucet, the chickens on the wall almost became invisible.

"'Marge and Gower Champion, currently the top young dance team in Hollywood, were brought in to give her an exhaustive six-month, six-day-a-week training for dance routines in which her legs could be thoroughly appreciated.'"

"Heck," Dillard muttered, his raspy voice carrying through the house, through the kitchen and Gemma's room to the front room, where the cot was set up next to the opened Victrola. "She could shape up them legs workin' round here a bit."

And outside, through the opened windows, Gemma's voice could be heard again: "'Her new roles called for her to dress in bathing suits and long woolen underwear.'"

Dillard laughed out loud; he could be heard past the pecan trees, past the back steps, where Beecham sat.

What a friend we have in Jesus, all our sins and griefs to bear! What a privilege to carry everything to God in prayer!

"'As a result, there is little or nothing left of the old, demure Janet. . . .'"

"Well, I reckon that's it. That's a new life for Janet, all right," Dillard said.

"Oh, what peace we often forfeit . . ."

Beecham tapped his foot on the bottom step, keeping time. Night insects began to sing across the yard, in the trees. *"Oh, what needless pain we bear."*

"And see this ad here," Gemma said.

"It's too dark."

"Well, it's a permanent, like what I got. A Lilt."

"I know it; I know it."

"My hair was so pretty. I wonder if I'll get me another."

"Maybe Doreen'll—talk to Doreen 'bout that."

Beecham's voice gave then, the high baritone scraping, shattering. He began to cough, doubling over on the step.

"You know I didn't wear these glasses when I was in Fort Worth."

"Why not?"

"I didn't need 'em."

"Well, how'd you see anything?"

"Sometimes I didn't. One time when me and Mama and

Frank went to the drive-in, I sat through the whole picture and didn't even know that Donna Reed was in it."

"That a movie star too?"

"Yep."

"Well."

Beecham's throat was burning, and when he was finally able to get his breath, he sat back against the steps and wiped the sweat from his brow. He took his harmonica from his pocket and put it to his lips.

"Did I tell you 'bout the traffic they got there?" Her voice filled the night all at once, catching Beecham off guard. He stopped running up and down the harmonica and listened for a moment.

"No, you didn't."

"Well, it goes any time of day or night you can imagine. Even after midnight."

"Where they going then?"

"I don't know, but every time you look out the window there, well, cars are passing by. They're going somewheres, I reckon."

"I never heard a such."

"Well, it's true. All times of night."

And Beecham sat back against the steps, burrowing in, letting his feet flop and slide over the ground as he played.

"They sell everything in those stores."

Beecham plugged his tongue in the openings, inhaling, blowing, finding the tune.

"I don't guess I told you what I was going to be."

Dillard mumbled something.

"Well, I thought I might want to be a beauty operator."

Her voice could still be heard clearly in the night when Beecham had finished and his feet were still. He slapped spit from his harmonica into the palm of his hand and wiped it on his trousers. He leaned back, listening, both elbows wedged on the step above. The voices swam around him.